Also by Sarah Kuhn

HEROINE COMPLEX
HEROINE WORSHIP

HEROINE WORSHIP

SARAH KUHN

BOOK TWO OF HEROINE COMPLEX

DAW BOOKS, INC.
DONALD A. WOLLHEIM, FOUNDER
375 Hudson Street, New York, NY 10014

ELIZABETH R. WOLLHEIM
SHEILA E. GILBERT
PUBLISHERS
www.dawbooks.com

First Printing, July 2017
1   2   3   4   5   6   7   8   9

For Jenn Fujikawa, my twin sister who looks nothing like me—except on the inside, where we're exactly the same.

CHAPTER ONE

I LOVE BEING a superhero.

I love that sense of purpose, welling in my chest. That pride that comes with knowing I'm doing good in this world, protecting those who can't protect themselves. That satisfying sensation of my fist connecting with some demon asshole's face.

I love doing what I do *best*. Because if you can't be the best at something, what's the point?

"Help us, Aveda Jupiter!"

The voice rang out through the crisp morning air as I sprinted down the long slope of one of San Francisco's impossibly steep hills, catapulting myself toward the Mission's latest hipster brunch spot, Egg (because all hipster brunch spots need names that are minimalist yet also completely on the nose). A crowd of innocent citizens cowered near the doorway, menaced by a gigantic monster made out of cereal. I squinted at the thing. It was actually a collection of tiny cereal demons who appeared to have imprinted on a bowl of Grape-Nuts. Somehow, they'd figured out how to assemble themselves into a towering, vaguely human-shaped thing that looked like a swarm of crunchy beige flies and snapped, crackled, and popped with every move. Like Voltron, only part of your balanced breakfast.

"RAAAAWRRRR!" Cereal Monster bellowed, swinging a crumbly fist at a woman in a bright blue dress. She stumbled out of the way in the nick of time, her face twisted with fear.

"We need you, Aveda Jupiter!" she screamed.

"Thank god you're here!" added a man in a ratty flannel shirt.

"What would the city do without you?!" chimed in a teenage girl wearing clunky glasses and an oversized t-shirt with my face on it. "Also, I love your outfit!"

I was clad in a silver tank top bedazzled with about a thousand sequins, snug leather pants, and over-the-knee boots that were ready to kick some serious breakfast-time ass. The outfit was practical enough to allow for a wide range of movement, but sleek enough to show off the toned physique I'd spent hours perfecting at the gym. And my long black hair was of course pulled into its signature power ponytail, which whipped majestically in the wind as I motored through the last few steps down the hill.

"Love the hair, too!" Clunky Glasses yelped.

I narrowed my eyes at the Cereal Monster, taking stock of the scene. The thing's movements were labored and lumbering, but it had still managed to thoroughly destroy Egg's whimsical oval doorway and was stomping toward the screaming people on the street, swinging its massive paws.

"Hey, you!" I yelled, skidding to a stop in front of it. Adrenaline hummed through my veins, the heady anticipation of battle heightening my senses and making me feel so present and alive and *needed*.

"Rawr?" Cereal Monster turned to face me, its unwieldy body rustling in a way I might have been unsettled by if I hadn't faced countless demon threats way more terrifying.

I'd take this one down like I'd taken all of them down— with badass confidence, my fabulous outfit, and a series of powerful roundhouse kicks. It was the Aveda Jupiter Way.

I straightened my spine, my joints cracking and popping, sweat beading on my shoulder blades, my field of vision narrowing until it was just me and my nutritious nemesis.

"Prepare to be destroyed, you Frosted *Fakes*!" I growled.

"Whoa, excellent one-liner!" yelled Blue Dress Lady.

"You tell 'em, Aveda!" added Flannel Shirt.

"We love you so much!" wailed Clunky Glasses, practically in tears. "And your mother's wrong, those pants are *totally* flattering."

I launched myself into the air, my muscles humming with pleasure, my chest swelling with heroic pride, my—

"Annie?"

I was jerked out of my daydream by the sound of my given name. My *real* name, according to some, though I still secretly disputed that. I'd christened myself Aveda Jupiter when I was eighteen, and I'd never looked back.

I couldn't help but deflate as the action-packed scenario I'd been imagining melted away, morphing into the much more mundane existence that was my current reality. Where I was sitting at a boring breakfast table, eating Grape-Nuts that weren't even a little bit demonic, and wearing sweatpants.

Sweat. *Pants.*

Sigh.

Evie Tanaka, my best friend, current co-superheroine and former personal assistant, studied me from the other side of the breakfast table. Along with the other members of our strange little household/superteam, we were sitting in the cluttered kitchen of the lower Haight Victorian we called home. When there was superheroing to do, it also served as our HQ.

But right now there was no superheroing to do. There was, in fact, *nothing* to do. And as San Francisco's leading— well, co-leading—superheroine, I need things to do. Which is why I'd given in to a perfectly good daydream.

In reality, the only Cereal Monster I was fighting these days was a stray Grape-Nut I'd been chasing around my cereal bowl with my spoon. I'd nudge the Grape-Nut, it would bounce forward. My spoon, refusing to be deterred, would follow. I was basically simulating an extremely dull miniature car chase.

Watch out, Grape-Nuts! Aveda Jupiter has a spoon. And she's not afraid to use it.

"Annie?" Evie repeated. "Do you want another bowl of that?" She gestured to my Grape-Nut car chase arena. "Second cereal course?"

I did not want second cereal course, which came between first cereal course and chocolate pudding course. Evie had invented the breakfast course order a few weeks ago. It was quirky, adorable, and a little messy—just like her.

The truth was, I didn't want breakfast to drag on for another two hours, which was typical of breakfasts during our current state of Nothing To Do. Three months earlier, Evie and I had prevented the apocalypse. We'd destroyed a power-hungry demon princess bent on taking over the city, shut down all portals to the evil dimension known as the Otherworld, and turned San Francisco into a demon-free haven for the first time in eight years. It was a beautiful moment, and I'd felt hope and pride and love surging through me, a potent brew that powered me through the first month of absolutely nothing happening.

The second month, I'd started feeling twitchy.

The third month, I'd declared myself officially bored.

Now we were creeping into month four, and I was ready to start climbing the walls—literally.

"Of course," I said, forcing a smile. "Who doesn't love second cereal course?"

(Me. I don't.)

"Nate!" Evie called out to her hulking half-demon of a boyfriend. "While you're up, get Annie some of that saw-dust cereal she likes!" Nate, who was standing at the kitchen counter, surveying the cereal selection, turned and gave her an indulgent smile.

"Anything for you," he said, his deep rumble of a voice contrasting with the cozy atmosphere of the kitchen.

Thanks to his six-foot-four stature, harsh features, and shock of unruly dark hair, Nate—who served as our physician and demonology expert—had been described by some as "tall, dark, and glower-y." But when he looked at Evie, his eyes softened and the darkness receded. It was sweet, but it also made me feel like I was witnessing something intensely private and should avert my eyes. They'd been together since the events of three months ago and were as disgustingly mushy as two people in the throes of new love could be.

"Darling, you know I'm pleased as punch about your coupled-off bliss," said Lucy Valdez, our weapons expert and personal trainer, as Nate made his way back to the table. "But the goo-goo eyes quotient has been off the charts this week." She gave an exaggerated pout that would have melted the hearts of people who didn't know her as well as we did. Lucy was deceptively delicate-looking, tiny and elfish with a penchant for prim, girly outfits. But underneath that innocent surface lurked a powerful fighter with an extensive knife collection. "It's a bit rough on those of us who are tragically single," she continued, drawing out the pout.

"And that's everyone else at this table," piped up Evie's seventeen-year-old sister Bea. She shook her head, her cap of purple-streaked hair bobbing back and forth, and waved her bedazzled phone at Evie disapprovingly. "Tragically single people are the total majority."

"I'm sorry," Evie said, as Nate set Grape-Nuts in front of me and Lucky Charms in front of her. He settled into the chair next to her and ran an affectionate hand through her tangle of dark brown curls. She twisted sideways in her seat, draping her legs over his lap. "What would be an acceptable level of goo-goo eyes? Should we avoid looking at each other entirely?"

"Maybe take it down to one 'goo,'" said Scott Cameron, our resident mage. He gave her a teasing smile and a playful nudge. "Like, the singular goo."

"The singular goo!" Lucy chimed in. "I like it."

"The Singular Goo sounds like a comic book villain," Evie countered. "And a really shitty one at that."

"Speaking of comic books," I said, perking up. "I was thinking, we should reach out to the local comic book shops about doing personal appearances, see if any of them would

be interested in an official endorsement from San Francisco's most beloved superheroines. Endorsements represent
a significant portion of our income, and given that San
Francisco doesn't require much superheroing right now . . ."

*. . . this would be a fine way to ensure that we're still earn-
ing money, that we're making ourselves useful in some way,
and that we're doing something other than sitting on our
asses, eating endless bowls of cereal and chasing permanent
unemployment and oh, god, I can't take it anymore.*

I. Just. Can't.

That was the rest of what I'd started to say, unfurling in
my head, punctuated by a hint of maniacal laughter. But
the words died in my throat as I realized everyone was
looking at me like I'd grown a second head.

"We're totally fine on money for a while," Evie said, giving me an amused smile. "All those endorsement deals
you've done over the years—and the managing of our in-
vestments I've done over the years—have given us an excellent nest egg. Just don't go buying thousand-dollar boots
by the truckful, and we should be okay."

"Indeed," Lucy chimed in. "Now is the time to relax, take
a breath, and enjoy life."

"'Cause you never know when another demon portal's
gonna open up and send the city back into supernatural
chaos," Bea said, stabbing her phone in the air for emphasis.

"But . . ." I frowned at my bowl of Grape-Nuts, biting
back the rest of my retort.

But what if another portal never opens up?

What if no one needs a superhero anymore?

*What if that's the only thing I'm good at, the thing I've
trained my whole life to be—all twenty-seven years of it—
and suddenly I'm just . . . useless?*

I couldn't help but flash back to something I'd said to
Evie during a heart-to-heart we'd had in the aftermath of
world-saving.

If I'm not Aveda Jupiter, who am I? No one. Not really.

She, of course, had told me I'd always be someone to her.

But given that she was finally growing into her own super-heroine identity as a fire-wielding badass, given that no one *in the entire city* seemed to need Aveda Jupiter at the moment, how could that be true?

I shoved down the panic rising in my chest and looked up from my bowl.

"I did put up a tweet or two that you guys were looking to do more personal appearances, Aveda," Bea said absently. She set aside her phone and tapped away on her laptop, pausing occasionally to leaf through a big sheaf of papers she'd brought with her to the breakfast table, making notations in sparkly green gel pen. "People love seeing Evie's fire power in action. And, uh, your stuff, too."

"Don't you have enough keeping you busy?" Evie said to me. "What with organizing all your superheroine outfits into different closets, and adding a few hours a day to your already incredibly intense workouts and—"

"And even in this state of non-apocalypse, she finds a way to be an overachiever," Lucy said, arching a playful brow.

Everyone laughed and I attempted to force another smile. It was a warm laugh, an affectionate laugh—a familial laugh. Evie claimed our little crew was like a family, but I always felt a wall between me and everyone else, a wall that had originally been mostly of my own making since the team had been my staff, before Evie and I became superheroine partners. Even now, when that warm laugh was directed my way, I felt outside of it. Like I was watching a TV show about an intriguing alien species I could never hope to understand.

My gaze landed on the only other person at the table who wasn't laughing: Scott. I didn't know *why* he wasn't laughing, since he usually loved nothing more than teasing, making a joke out of everything. Though lately he hadn't been doing much of that with me.

Of course my gaze lingered, reminding me that even though I'd tried to deny it over the course of the fifteen years we'd known each other, he was ridiculously hot in a way that I still found distracting.

My gaze was kind of an asshole.

He didn't meet my eyes, as he was concentrating very hard on the orange he was peeling. As usual, he looked gorgeous in the morning: mussed golden hair falling over his forehead, blue eyes hazy with sleep, tanned surfer's biceps contrasting perfectly with the rumpled white t-shirt he wore to bed.

Not that I actually knew what he wore to bed. I was just guessing.

He smelled good, too. Like fresh-cut grass and sunscreen and the ocean. I watched as he bit into an orange slice, the juice dribbling out of the side of his mouth. His tongue flicked out to lick it off and—

No. Nope. Stop staring. You're about to look like a drooling moron. And that sort of behavior might be fine for Annie Chang, the ordinary girl I'd left behind so many years ago, the girl with no superpowers, the girl who was more than capable of having her heart broken.

But it was definitely *not fine* for Aveda Jupiter.

I turned away from Scott and his stupid, sexy orange and lamented for the millionth time that it really wasn't fair that he looked and smelled this good right after rolling out of bed, since I usually had to spend at least two hours conditioning, moisturizing, and twisting my body into just the right outfit in order to appear halfway presentable.

"Aw, you didn't pick out the purple horseshoes for me—maybe I should reduce that to The Singular Goo after all," Evie said, nudging Nate with her foot. She'd apparently moved on from teasing me and was picking through her second bowl of Lucky Charms.

"You're a superheroine, more than capable," he countered, his mouth quirking into an amused smile. "Why not just burn them out?"

"I try to keep mundane power usage to a minimum," Evie replied, fishing around for the purple marshmallow bits. They all tasted the same to me—pure sugar—but she claimed not to like the purple ones.

Nate watched her, still wearing that affectionate look. But I noticed something else lurked underneath, a flicker of feeling that seemed unsure.

"What's all this, Bea?" Evie asked, gesturing to her sister's laptop and stack of papers. "Are you making spreadsheets at the breakfast table again?" She threw Nate—who was known for his love of cataloging data and had been mentoring Bea in various scientific research methods—a mock-disapproving look.

Yes, heaven forbid that anyone try to do anything resembling *work* during one of these leisurely breakfasts.

"I've been studying all civilian-submitted reports on supernatural activity that Rose's Demon Unit has received over the years, trying to put them in some kind of order—and digitizing the shit out of them while doing so," Bea said, her voice taking on what she probably imagined to be a professional cadence. "They really are a mess."

"Mmm, data organization for fun," Evie said, giving Nate another look. "You are a terrible influence."

He gave her a small smile, but with that flicker of uncertainty again. He almost looked . . . nervous. Was something going on with them? Were three months of peaceful bliss wearing on him, too? Or was *their* peaceful bliss not as peaceful as I imagined?

So this was what passed for excitement now: cereal car chases and attempts to ferret out my best friend's relationship issues.

"It *is* fun, Big Sis," Bea countered, sticking out her tongue. "And anyway, I have to find *something* to do around here since our current state of low demon activity doesn't call for much of my social media manager prowess, and I'm not all superpowered like you guys." She waved a hand at Evie and me.

I shot Evie a meaningful look. *Now. Tell her now.*

But Evie just made a face at me and went back to

picking through her Lucky Charms. I squelched another wave of frustration. The amount of *not doing things* around here was spiraling to epic levels.

"That is so interesting that you would say that, Bea," I said, as casually as possible. I nudged Evie under the table with my foot. She defiantly moved her foot out of my reach. "So very, very interesting. Don't you think, Evie?"

Now everyone was giving me that "did you just grow another head?" look again, but I didn't care. I was tired of sitting here, dammit, and I was going to *make* something happen, something that should have happened months ago anyway—

"Annie!" Evie's strained voice cut into my thoughts. "Can you help me with a thing in the foyer?"

I huffed up from my seat and followed her. As soon as we were out of earshot of the others, she stopped, planted her hands on her hips, and glared at me.

"What are you doing?" she hissed.

"Trying to get you to do what you *should* be doing," I hissed back, crossing my arms over my chest. "Which is tell Bea about her superpower! She deserves to know. Hell, if we find ourselves attacked by anything even vaguely supernatural again, she *needs* to know."

"And I'll tell her," Evie said. "In my own timeframe."

"Your timeframe is taking *forever*—"

I was interrupted by a sharp knock at the door, three staccato raps that shut up both of us. Nobody had knocked on the door in weeks. Months. Nobody in San Francisco needed any superheroing, so who *would* knock?

A wisp of feeling sparked in my chest, something bright and sure and just a little bit manic.

Something's happening, I thought wildly. *It has to be something happening.*

"I'll get it!" I exclaimed, my voice way too loud.

I lunged the few steps through the foyer to the front door. Maybe someone needed help. Maybe someone needed saving. Maybe someone needed *me*.

It could be something simple, like a cat stuck in a tree. I could most definitely save a cat stuck in a tree. I could make that my new specialty or something. I'd be the best cat-in-a-tree saver San Francisco had ever fucking seen.

I flung the door open, my heart bounding through my chest, beating so loud I could feel the blood pulse in my ears. A mighty grin of anticipation stretched across my face and my thoughts pinballed through my head much too fast to make coherent sense. *This is it, this is it, I don't know what, but at least it's something, something to do . . .*

My smile disappeared as soon as I saw who was on the other side of the door.

"Well, hello there, Aveda Jupiter!" Maisy Kane—reformed half-demon princess, twee lingerie shop owner, annoying blogger—beamed at me.

She was wearing one of her usual fussy outfits, a red polka dot dress with a matching hair bow and shiny black wedges. When coupled with her demon hybrid appearance—flaky gray skin, crooked mouth, ghoulish glowing eyes—this should have given her the thoroughly bizarre appearance of Minnie Mouse as played by one of the Walking Dead. Instead she somehow pulled it off.

"Maisy!" Evie shuffled up behind me, eyeing our visitor suspiciously. "What are you doing here?"

"Isn't it obvious?" Maisy threw her arms wide, her crooked grin widening. "I have a very big problem. Humongous. Gargantuan."

She lowered her voice theatrically, eyes darting from side to side, as if making sure no one else was around to hear whatever shocking revelation was about to come out of her mouth.

"I need you to come down to my shop and investigate," she said. "It's such a big problem—and only San Francisco's two most glamorous superheroines can fix it!"

DIARY OF A REFORMED HALF-DEMON PRINCESS: PART 34

By Maisy Kane, Half-Demon Princess Editrix

Bonjour, my dear 'Friscans! Apologies for the lack of bloggy updates 'round these parts—your pal Maisy has a metric ton o' stuff going on!

First off, everyone keeps asking me about my transition to demon hybrid-dom. Dear readers, all I can say is, it's the absolute tops! My new appearance is quite the conversation-starter and you all know I love nothing more than making friends. Plus, my skin flakes off so much, I never have to exfoliate!

I've made all kinds of upgrades to your favorite quirky neighborhood lingerie emporium, Pussy Queen! Well, maybe it wasn't your favorite before, but trust me, it will be. In addition to ordering colorful new stock (is it just me, or did Shasta have completely pedestrian taste? Especially for an aspiring demon queen! So much beige, y'all), I've asked one of Bay Area fashion's leading lights, Shruti Dhaliwal, to open a wee pop-up boutique version of her fabulous vintage shop on the premises. Soon, you'll be able to pair your La Perla with a perfectly preserved frock!

I've also contracted barista Dave—of the dearly departed Sunny Side Café, RIP bestest brunch mimosas—to sling champagne and fancy coffee drinks for all our wonderful customers. There's no reason to get dehydrated while trying on dainties—and you can quote me on that!

And yes, the portal that opened up after the Ultimate Battle for San Francisco's Soul is still very much a presence in the shop. Please feel free to come by and take all the photos you like, no extra charge! Just make sure to tag #pussyqueen on Twitter, Snapchat, and Insta (and maybe even your pal Maisy—@halfdemonprincess—if you're feeling generous). I recommend keeping a safe distance, though, gentle readers. While said portal still appears to be fairly benign, it does present random bits of odd activity on occasion. And when it comes to the demon Otherworld, one just never knows, does one? Luckily, I've got my dear friends Aveda Jupiter and Evie Tanaka on speed dial and I'm extremely diligent about reporting every bit of activity. Girlfriends, thank you for always being there for me! #blessed

Power Watch: Readers, I'm still getting reports from those of you who noticed power level-ups after that little ol' earthquake during the Karaoke Battle That Will Live in Infamy! (Howzabout a rematch, Super Evie? Kidding! I could never out-Beyoncé you!) This week, Clarissa Davenport—greeting card designer extraordinaire behind Clarissa's Creations—wrote in to tell me that her ability to detect a lemon tree anywhere within a one hundred mile radius now extends to all kinds of citrus-growing plants! Wowza! (Who knows what the demons used that power for, but I'm betting it was super-evil.) Interestingly, there are those among you who are still not seeing an upgrade. Some of you report that you continue to be stuck with the same tame abilities you had before. All I can say is, have patience! When I agreed to minion for an aspiring demon queen, I never thought it would lead to being a successful businesswoman who hangs out with superheroine besties on the regular. Just goes to show that you can accomplish anything if you set your mind to it. Or even if you don't set your mind to it!

Superheroine Empowerment Corner: This week, A. Jupes and Evie were spotted doing a rare public demonstration for a tour group of underprivileged children. Evie graced the group with a truly jaw-dropping fire show while Aveda perfected her superheroine wave from the sidelines. Nice to see those two keeping busy in our currently evil-free city!

CHAPTER TWO

IN THE END, I begged Evie to go. I realize begging looks very unbecoming on a superheroine, but boredom had clearly made me desperate.

"You know it's going to be nothing," she muttered as we dutifully followed Maisy up the long blocks that led to Pussy Queen. "Just like all the other times."

"But isn't that part of our job?" I countered. "To investigate every cry of distress, no matter how small?"

"Not when they're all coming from the same person," Evie said, sending a pointed look toward Maisy's back. Nate had decided to join our little expedition, and Maisy, who had always nursed a bit of a crush, was dragging him along in front of us, trying to talk about their "shared experiences as fellow half-demons"—though their origin stories were different enough that she had that ghoulish gray-skinned appearance while he looked like "your basic human mad-scientist broody thug hottie," as Lucy was so fond of putting it.

Evie's eyes narrowed further as Maisy inclined her head toward Nate in a way that might be interpreted as flirty. "And not when that portal has done nothing but sit there for the last three months."

"Maisy usually calls or texts, though," I persisted, a thread of whine creeping into my voice. I was becoming less heroic-sounding by the second. "She showed up in person this time, so maybe she really is worried?"

"The only thing Maisy's worried about is keeping her

blog traffic up," Evie retorted. "And what better way to do that than a totally contrived in-store appearance by San Francisco's favorite heroines?" She sighed, softening her words with a smile. "But if you want to check it out, I'm game." She reached over and squeezed my hand. "And about the stuff with Bea earlier: you're right. I should tell her, I just . . ." She trailed off, gnawing at her lower lip.

"We'll figure it out together." I tried to make my voice reassuring. Emotional support wasn't usually my forte. "Just like always."

Her mouth quirked into a half-smile, and she winked at me. "Like the Heroic Trio: except there's only two of us."

Warmth surged in my chest. *The Heroic Trio* was an old Hong Kong action movie about a kickass triumvirate of Asian superheroines. Watching it together as kids and seeing superheroines who looked like us had inspired me and Evie in different ways, and the movie remained an essential touchstone of our friendship. That one little phrase reminded me that we were still *us*, the best version of us—that our recent defeat of an evil demon princess had coincided with Evie and me finally working through some very important friendship issues. Really, that climactic battle had been the culmination of several weeks of drama, which had kicked off when I'd sprained my ankle during a particularly strenuous workout and persuaded Evie to pose as me. Of course her long suppressed fire power decided to make itself known at an extremely inopportune moment and everyone believed Aveda Jupiter was the one with fire all up inside her.

The weeks I'd been laid up with that sprained ankle had driven me crazy. As I'd watched Evie successfully take on the Aveda Jupiter mantle, as I'd watched the entire city fall in love with her, I'd felt the role I'd painstakingly constructed for myself slipping away—and with it, any sense of identity I'd ever had. I'd felt what it was to not be needed. And I hadn't liked it one bit.

It had caused me to act like . . . well, "total raging bitch" was being generous. But it had also forced me to realize I'd been a bad friend to Evie for a good long while, so wrapped up in my quest for perfection and general superheroine badassery that I couldn't see our bond had become co-dependent and fractured and that I had a tendency to lay all my diva baggage directly at her feet. Or maybe "dump it on her head" was more fitting.

I wasn't exactly known for being subtle.

In the end, we'd finally repaired things. Evie had grown a backbone and become the superheroine she was meant to be, and I'd realized how badly I'd taken her for granted and made a vow to work on my friend skills. I was determined to be Aveda Jupiter 2.0: Awesome Superheroine Who Is Also the Most Awesome Friend. Evie—who'd been there for me through thick and thin, who was the closest thing I had to a sister—deserved nothing less. And when Aveda Jupiter sets her mind to something, that something is as good as *done.*

But in addition to not giving me the opportunity to be a superheroine, our current state of not doing things wasn't giving me much of a chance to prove my friend skills, either. I'd tried to make small gestures, like going along with her whole breakfast course order thing even though I secretly couldn't stand it, but I wanted something bigger. Grander. Something more *Aveda Jupiter.*

At least Evie had moved beyond being a personal assistant and come into her own as a superheroine. Now we were true partners, ready to fight evil and confide in each other and watch old Hong Kong action movies on an endless loop. The very thought made me smile, and I felt myself standing up a little straighter as we made our way to Pussy Queen.

"You know," I said to her, "I was thinking a screening of *The Heroic Trio* would actually be perfect fodder for a personal appearance. We could do a Q&A afterward, talk about how our first time seeing Asian women be superheroes onscreen inspired us to be superheroes in real life—"

"Or," Evie interrupted, giving me an amused look. "We could watch it together at home on the iPad. Which doesn't require getting out of our pajamas." She gave my arm a playful nudge. "Clearly the superior option."

Sigh. Clearly.

I kept trying to build our personal appearance empire— in addition to giving us something useful to do, it seemed like a good way of keeping ourselves relevant in a city that didn't currently need saving from demons. We were like Olympic athletes, I reasoned, and this is what we did between Olympics. But Evie almost never wanted to do the appearances. And no one ever requested me by myself, even though my telekinesis had gotten so much cooler after my earthquake-induced power level-up. I knew it wasn't as showy as actual fire, but it was still pretty freakin' cool.

I would just have to work harder to convince her that these appearances were necessary to our continued existence as superheroines. Especially if the Olympics never came around again.

The door chimes meowed as we entered the store. Ever since Maisy had taken over for Shasta, the place had quadrupled its quirk level. Shasta was the demon princess and aspiring queen responsible for the almost-apocalypse that had nearly destroyed San Francisco three months ago. She was also Nate's mom, which should have caused some post-battle awkwardness, but didn't seem to be a problem thus far. Everyone at HQ understood complicated parental issues.

I know I certainly did.

Shasta had set up a cover as a very human lingerie shop owner and sidekick to high-profile blogger Maisy. She'd actually been trying to take over the city for years, having staked out Earth as a truly fabulous realm, ripe for invasion. She'd tried a number of plans, including opening the very first Otherworld portal in San Francisco eight years ago. Her raiding party of humanoid demons had come through that one, set on invasion. But things didn't work out that way. Shasta's portal was so shitty and unstable it snapped shut immediately, killing her invasion team and sending their special demon superpowers into various San Franciscan bodies—like mine and Evie's.

After that, she'd been trapped here with no meaningful way of communicating with the Otherworld. She'd figured out how to open smaller, less powerful portals all over the city, but none of her grand plans had really worked until earlier this year, when she'd learned that turning a certain number of humans into human-demon hybrids would allow her to open a permanent conduit to the Otherworld. Maisy and a few other San Franciscans had fallen victim to this plan.

Maisy seemed to be taking her new hybrid status in stride, though, and I couldn't help but admire her business sense. Shasta had basically no imagination, so she'd kept everything pretty basic and boring, just a few sad racks of muted pastels, all cotton. Maisy had added a cavalcade of colors, prints, and textures, and organized them in a manner that was inventive and inviting. A table at the entrance featured a display of colorful panties, fanned out to look like a rainbow. A headless mannequin sported a peek-a-boo lace bra, matching thigh-high stockings, and a silky robe falling off its shoulders. Yet another display spotlighted underwear with animal prints, scattered artfully on top of a bearskin rug. And in opposite back corners were Maisy's latest additions: the small coffee and champagne bar manned by Dave, and Shruti's pop-up shop featuring vintage clothing and accessories. A light jasmine scent wafted through the air, bringing the whole room together.

The only off-note—and okay, it was kind of a big one—was the dormant portal smack-dab in the center of the room. It was an angry black slash on the floor, a stark reminder that Pussy Queen had played host to one of the most vicious demon battles in recent history. This black slash was all that remained of Shasta's attempt to open a permanent portal to the Otherworld. Most of the portals we'd encountered previously had been cute, glittery, golden

things on the ceilings of various San Francisco establish-
ments. This portal, however, was different—a pit of darkness on the floor. Evie had shoved Shasta's ass into the
portal and almost been killed in the process. I was nearly
passed out for most of the battle but had managed to use
my telekinesis to get her out of the way of the scary-looking
bolt of energy that shot out of the portal and smacked her
in the chest.

The portal had been dormant since then, though. Like
the rest of us, it hadn't done anything for months.

A flowery cursive sign warning patrons "DO NOT
TOUCH" hung from the silk ropes Maisy used to cordon
off the area. The portal glinted in the soft lighting of the
shop. Its insides had started as an unpleasant black sludge
and eventually hardened into something that resembled
crystal. Nate took samples on a regular basis, but the con-
sistency hadn't changed in the past couple months.

"Okay, Maisy, so what exactly is the portal doing?" Evie
asked. I could tell she was resisting the urge to roll her eyes.
"How is this time different from all those other times you
called us?"

"It's making gurgly sounds," Maisy said.

"Which is what it was doing before," Evie said.

My heart sank. This was probably yet another false
alarm. I eyed the portal, almost willing it to do something.
Give me something to fight.

"And earlier today, little sparks were shooting out,"
Maisy continued.

"Little sparks?" Evie echoed.

"Medium-sized sparks!" Maisy amended. "Bigger than
average, even."

Nate moved closer to the portal, brow furrowed, and
leaned in, trying to get a better look.

"I do not believe there is any significant change from the
last time we checked on this," he said.

"So it is, for all intents and purposes, still a big, dead
thing," Evie concluded. She shook her head, irritated. "If

we hurry, we can get back to HQ before our chocolate pudding course gets cold. Or I guess that would be warm? Before it becomes not pudding anymore, is what I'm saying."

"Wait!" I said. I was mortified to hear that thread of whine creeping into my voice again. "Since we're here . . . I mean, we should at least take a closer look, right? If we wait a few more minutes, maybe we'll see those medium-sized sparks Maisy was talking about."

God. Was I really begging them to stand around in a lingerie shop and stare at a freaking portal with me? The Aveda Jupiter of old would have scorned the very idea. But these days, my lack of being able to *do* things made me feel more like Annie Chang: a mundane who was still perfecting her superheroine bravado and getting it wrong at least half of the time, my boring Clark Kent alter ego who bumbled around hiding my fabulousness. And Annie Chang was currently having trouble articulating anything that didn't sound stuttering and unsure. But my desperation was flaring, stoked by the promise of having something to do, the promise of being able to *be Aveda Jupiter.*

I just couldn't sit through another chocolate pudding course.

"That's not a bad idea," Nate said, his voice turning thoughtful. "I'll take some new samples. Our most current batch is at least three weeks old and it's important to track even the smallest of changes." He reached into his pocket and pulled out a plastic baggie, a delicate tool that resembled a pair of tweezers, and latex gloves.

"You just carry all that around with you? A whole, like, portal sample-taking kit?" Evie gaped at him. "What am I saying? Of course you do."

Nate grinned at her, snapped on the gloves, and moved one of the ropes to the side. He hunkered down next to the portal, using the tweezers to carefully scrape bits of the glittery black stuff into the baggie.

"Aw, look at my boyfriend," Evie cooed. "He's so cute when he sciences."

I smiled, disarmed by the way her hazel eyes brightened as she watched Nate's brow furrow in concentration. It was nice to see her so happy, so at ease with herself. Before she embraced her fire power, Evie had often seemed like a skittery little mouse. She'd put on a front that was calm and collected and perfect for her role as personal assistant. But behind all that beat the constant pulse of fear that she was about to burn her entire life down. I hadn't really noticed at the time, because, let's face it, I hadn't been very good at noticing anything outside of myself. But it was easy to see the difference when you contrasted the Evie of then with the Evie of now. She still had the same unfortunate fashion sense—for this excursion, she'd thrown a hoodie and flip-flops over her pajamas and called it a day. But now she had a confident glow about her that came from knowing exactly who she was.

I envied that.

If you'd asked me who I was a few months ago, I could have answered confidently: professional superheroine and city-saver with an aptitude for powerful roundhouse kicks and excellent outfits.

Now I'd be more likely to say: professional identity-crisis-haver adrift in a city that doesn't currently need superheroes—and maybe never will again.

I just couldn't seem to locate the Aveda Jupiter mojo that had been so crucial to all my superheroing success. Annie Chang was threatening to take over for good.

I could *not* let that happen.

At least my outfits were still reasonably excellent, once I changed out of the breakfast sweatpants. For this excursion I'd made an attempt at classic Aveda Jupiter fashion— I was wearing a sleek black tank top with artfully placed sequins and matching spandex workout pants. I'd also dusted on silver eye shadow that contrasted dramatically with my dark eyes and done some careful makeup contouring to highlight my angular features. As a finishing touch, I'd pulled my hair into its power ponytail. But now, seeing

what a non-event the portal action was, I felt silly. Overdressed.

"Thanks for the extra care, Nathaniel," Maisy purred,
giving him an appreciative look as he bent over, glutes flexing underneath his jeans. She plopped herself on a brocade
chair in front of the dressing rooms. "I'll just be over here.
Watching you work."

"She's watching something," muttered Evie. "Not that I
can really blame her."

"Champagne while you wait, ladies?" Shruti strolled up
to us, toting flutes of bubbly gold liquid. She wore what was
surely one of her fabulous vintage finds, a bright pink cocktail frock with a sweetheart neckline ringed by tiny black
bows. The vivid shade looks gorgeous against her golden
brown skin.

"Love today's 'do," Evie said, gesturing to Shruti's
swingy, tousled bob, which was adorably accentuated with
a pair of sparkly bobby pins. "Noticed any power change
with the hair since the earthquake?"

"That's right, you can make your hair grow at will," I
blurted out, then felt immediately awkward. Of course
Evie, ever thoughtful, actually remembered what various
San Franciscans' powers were.

"Nothing yet," Shruti trilled. "But hope springs eternal."

Dave shuffled up behind Shruti, brandishing coffee mugs
with the old Sunny Side logo. He fixed us with an unnerving
stare.

"Patience is easy to wish for," he said solemnly. "But difficult to achieve."

We stared back for a moment, unsure how to respond.
Dave looked about as out of place as the portal. Though he
was in his forties, he still projected the aura of a slacker
college student: wrinkled tee, cargo pants, and plaid button-
down, topped off with an ancient-looking baseball cap. His
hair was long and unkempt, he sported a permanent five-o-
clock shadow, and he was pretty much always stoned out of
his mind. The Sunny Side Café, a longtime old-school break-

fast spot owned by Dave, had closed its doors recently, pushed out by the swank foodie brunch places popping up all over the Mission.

"Dave!" Shruti gave him a gently admonishing look. "What have we talked about when it comes to approaching customers? For now, leave it to me."

He turned his stare on her, then nodded and headed back to his perch behind the coffee bar.

"He's not great with the public," Shruti said as we watched him shuffle off. "And he's taking the closing of the Sunny Side really hard. So I tend to do double duty as frock seller and booze slinger."

"I'm surprised Maisy wants him around," I said. "Doesn't seem very on-brand for her."

"I think she feels a connection with him. In a way, they're both trying to reinvent themselves," Shruti said. "Plus he keeps the temperature pleasant. Notice how you don't even need a cardigan."

"Truly a mammoth accomplishment," I said. "No power level-up for him either?"

"I don't believe so," Shruti said, with an elegant shrug. "But we're not especially close, so I'm not sure he'd tell me." She waved the champagne at us again. "Soooooo . . . ?"

"No, thank you," I said. "I try not to drink during the day."

I'd actually taken up a bit of a day-drinking habit when I'd been injured, but now I was back to my old, disciplined ways. And right now I needed to stay sharp. Even if it was only to stare at that stupid portal for another few minutes. I would stare like nobody's freaking business.

"Let me know if you change your mind," Shruti said with a wink, strolling back to the coffee bar.

I continued staring at the portal.

"You okay?" Evie nudged me. "You seem almost disappointed that thing isn't about to explode San Francisco."

I leaned back against the table with the panty rainbow and crossed my arms over my chest, allowing my eyes to wander to the ceiling. "I thought maybe this time, it would actually be something. Second cereal course is great. But I don't feel very useful."

Evie studied me, and I detected a hint of amusement flitting through her eyes.

"I know you're used to being the life of the party—well, when the metaphorical party is some kind of demon attack," she said. "But—"

"But I should be taking this moment to relax and enjoy life. I know."

"You say that like it's a bad thing," Evie said, nudging me again.

"Aren't you even a little bit bored?" I blurted out. "You've finally embraced your awesome superpower and dedicated yourself to using it for good and you're not getting any opportunities to show it off. How can you be happy just . . . just *sitting* there, doing nothing and eating endless cereal courses?"

She cocked her head at me, her expression turning thoughtful. "Well. I guess I've never really been able to do nothing," she said slowly. "Not for a long time, anyway. After everything that happened with our parents, I had to take care of Bea, and then I had to deal with being all freaked out about my power twenty-four seven and learning how to suppress it, and then . . ." She shrugged, but I could hear the end of that sentence.

And then I had to spend what little emotional energy I had left putting up with you and your endless demands and diva tantrums.

"Anyway," she continued. "I've also never had what I have now. An awesome boyfriend. A supportive circle of friends who are like my family. An actually mostly pleasant relationship with my baby sister. A lack of that sense of impending dread about burning everything down around me. And time to enjoy it." Her mouth quirked into a slight smile. "I just kinda want to enjoy it, you know?"

"Of course," I said, feeling like the most massive of tools. Once again, I'd been so wrapped up in my own head, I hadn't noticed what was going on—what was *really* going on—with her. I still couldn't seem to figure this good friend thing out. How I could be there for her and show her what she meant to me.

"And if some kind of demon danger rears its incredibly ugly head, I'll step up and make with the superheroing," Evie said, flashing an exaggerated rakish grin and flexing a bicep. "I'm ready for that, Annie, I promise. I just don't see any need to—"

"To actively *wish* for some kind of demon danger to rear its incredibly ugly head thereby putting us and everybody we love in danger?" I finished, forcing a smile. "Right. That makes total sense."

And it did. Her wanting to relax made way more sense than me wanting major evilness to go down just so I'd have something to fight. But honestly, if I had to drag my spoon through that cereal bowl one more time while they all giggled about something I didn't get, and Scott sat next to me like a beautiful golden statue and I started to wonder if it was possible to feel jealous of an orange, I was going to—

GURGLE. GURGLE. GLUUUUUUUUUUUUUHH-HHHHHHHH.

We both jumped. My body responded instantly to the unexpected noise, my limbs snapping into a fighting stance, my eyes going to the portal. It had just emitted a sound like someone's stomach rumbling. Very loudly. After shotgunning a vat of cayenne pepper.

"Good gosh-dang!" Maisy exclaimed, leaping from her seat. "I told you guys it was acting up!"

GURRRRRGLE.

This time, the noise was so loud, the entire store seemed to shake. A handful of sparks shot out of the portal, then evaporated into the air.

"Indeed," Nate said, frowning at the portal. "Fascinating. Perhaps it is responding to my sample-taking by—"

"Nate!" Evie cried. "Get away from that, it might—"

GURRRRGLE . . . SLIIIIIIIIIIITTTTTTTH!

As if in response to her, a jagged bolt shot out of the portal and wrapped itself around Nate's arm. It looked like an extension of the portal itself, a massive, glittering snake made of black crystal.

"Holy shit!" Evie gasped.

"I've got him," I said, a bright thread of purpose flowing through my veins. I homed in on Nate, concentrating with all my might, every single one of my synapses firing. I felt like extra air was being pumped into my lungs, like my vision had suddenly gotten sharper and clearer.

I was suddenly ridiculously happy I'd worn my power ponytail.

I reached out with my mind, activating my telekinesis. When I'd first gotten my power, it had been fairly weak—I'd made up for that with strength and athleticism. But ever since my power level-up, it finally felt like something worthy of Aveda Jupiter, superhero: like long, invisible feathers unfurling from the center of my brain to wrap around whatever I was trying to move. I loved feeling like I had an extra limb, an extra sense. The only issue I'd had thus far was I had to be looking directly at whatever I was trying to move. I'd attempted to do things like use telekinesis to shut a door behind me as I was leaving a room, just because I thought the effect would be cool. But it never seemed to work. And as someone who liked to maximize her abilities, this was insanely frustrating.

I was confident that with enough time and effort, I'd be able to figure it out, but for now, I made do with what I was already good at. I stared at Nate, focusing hard, then wrapped my mental feathers around him and pulled, trying to get him free. The bolt-snake thing gripped hard, twisting Nate's shoulder into an exaggerated angle, as if to pop his arm from its socket. He cried out.

"Stop!" Evie gasped. Her face was pinched, terrified. "That thing's grip on him is . . . If you pull him away, you might sever his arm. Or split him in two or . . . or . . ."

"Dammit," I growled, loosening my hold.

The bolt wrapped more tightly around Nate's arm and slithered down his torso. His face twisted in pain.

"Evie," he gasped. "I—"

But she was already there, running to his side, right hand raised in the air so the fire could form.

"Annie!" she bellowed, and I understood what she wanted without her having to say anything more. I darted to the other side of the portal, adrenaline coursing through my veins like blood, like life. I was suddenly hyper-aware of everything around me, as if the volume on all of my senses had been turned way, way up. The light jasmine scent in the air mingled with undertones of Dave's coffee—a mix that probably would've been soothing under other circumstances, but now it seemed bitter and acrid, in line with that angry maw of dark energy at the center of the room. The bolt made ugly sucking sounds as it slithered down Nate's body. Out of the corner of my eye, I could see Shruti, Dave, and Maisy cowering behind the coffee counter. A shiver ran through me, and I realized the room was suddenly freezing cold.

The fireball formed in Evie's hand and she flung it with all her might at the bolt-snake thing—carefully aiming for a piece of the slithering mass that wasn't currently locked around Nate's body.

"Get away from my boyfriend, you portal snake asshole . . . *thing*!" she screamed.

Her fire hit the bolt and its grip slackened, letting out an ominous-sounding *HISSSSSSSSSSSS*. I breathed deeply, focused on Nate, and channeled everything I had into my invisible feathers. They flowed from my mind, wrapping around his body. I gave them a harsh mental yank and sent him flying across the room so hard, he smacked into the rainbow panty table. The panties flew everywhere, wispy snowflakes floating through the jasmine-scented air.

"Sorry," I muttered. I still didn't quite know my own post-level-up strength.

HISSSSSSSSSSSSSSSS.

The bolt recovered, flailing outward, expanding in size, trying to grab on to something, anything. Trying to suck something of this world inside the portal. Evie flung herself out of the way, and I jumped back farther. The bolt crashed into a rack of bras and sent them flying and now it was just a full-on blizzard of underwear swirling through Maisy's twee little shop.

I took a deep breath and reached out with my mind. The invisible feathers unfurled and wrapped around the bolt, encasing it firmly. I concentrated hard and pushed it to the ground, pinning it there. I could feel it resisting me, pushing against my hold. I concentrated harder, determined to keep the thing immobile.

"Now, Evie!" I cried.

She flung her fire at it. It arced from her hand, a blaze of light spinning through the air.

GLUUUUHHH . . . HISSSSSSSSS.

The fire hit the bolt and it dissolved into slime, an oily black blob that oozed its way back into the portal and winked out of sight.

And then there was silence as underwear swirled around us and Evie and I just stared at each other.

What in the world . . .

"Wowie!" Maisy squealed, shattering the quiet. She was still perched behind the coffee counter with Dave and Shruti, but now she was holding her phone up, filming us, her face lit with glee.

"That is the most action we've seen in months!" she crowed. "Finally, a full taste of what San Francisco's dynamic duo can do. The city better recognize!"

I knew this was Maisy talking, going on one of her usual hyperbole-laced bouts of speechifying, but damn. It felt good. Every word made the smile on my face stretch wider, made the rush of energy course through my veins faster. Because *this* was what my mind and body and soul had been craving all these months. I was invigorated. Alive.

I was Aveda Fucking Jupiter. The party was back. And I was the *life*.

I turned to Evie. We were both still breathing hard, faces flushed. I felt my grin widen and she smiled back and it was one of those moments where we didn't have to say anything, because we could practically read each other's brains.

The dynamic duo.

We were amazing *together.*

I know, right?!

Maisy gave us an expectant look, as if prompting us to make with the pithy superheroine catchphrases, already. I met Maisy's eyes and opened my mouth, hoping to verbalize everything I was feeling. But then I noticed she had moved her camera to focus on something off to the side.

Hmm, maybe Evie was going to start us off? I turned back to her. But she wasn't making with the catchphrases, either. Instead she was completely focused on the thing Maisy had adjusted her phone-camera to capture.

Nathaniel Jones. Big, scary half-demon. On bended knee. Presenting the love of his life with a gigantic diamond ring.

"Evie," he intoned, his deep voice low and serious. "Sorry, Evelyn. I should say Evelyn, right?"

"You can say whatever you want," she murmured. She sounded in a complete daze. I couldn't blame her.

"Evelyn," he continued, his mouth tipping into a gentle half-smile. "I meant to do this at breakfast, but—"

"The Lucky Charms," Evie squeaked out, putting it together. "The ring was in the Lucky Charms. That's why you didn't pick out the purple ones for me."

His smile widened. "Yes. I managed to rescue the ring from your bowl before we left HQ, just in case Beatrice decided to put everything in the dishwasher."

Oh. So that's why he'd looked nervous.

"Soooooo romantic," Maisy hissed in my ear. She'd moved in closer so she was standing right next to me, still filming.

"In any case," Nate continued. "I was going to try again

at tomorrow's breakfast, but this incident made me realize once again how short our lives are. How potentially fragile. How—"

"How easy it is in our line of work to get sucked into a big-ass portal and die an untimely and terribly undignified death?" Evie finished. Her words were teasing, but her voice was tremulous, full of tears.

"Yes—wait," Nate said, his brow furrowing. "I should have checked you and Aveda—and actually myself—for injuries or even simple wounds before I initiated this proposal. Perhaps I should do that now—"

"Don't you freaking dare!" Evie yelped. "I mean. Please. Just . . . continue."

"Very well." Nate smiled again. "Before I met you, I didn't know what it meant to love someone. I didn't know I *could* love someone. But you—and your ridiculous cartoon duck t-shirt—changed everything." He held out the ring. "So will you—"

"Yes!" she shrieked. "Oh my god, yes!"

"Awww," Maisy drawled as Evie tackled Nate and pulled him into a kiss worthy of a Hollywood end credits sequence. "The battle was an exciting appetizer. But this proposal video, my dears, *this* is the main course. Just beautiful."

It *was* beautiful. So why did I feel so deflated?

DEMON ENCOUNTER REPORT

Submitted to: Sergeant Rose Rorick (Demon Unit, SFPD Emergency Service Division), Dr. Nathaniel Jones (Aveda Jupiter, Inc.)

Submitted by: Beatrice Constance Tanaka (Super Awesome Note Taker/Researcher/Mentee who really deserves to be promoted to an official non-Mentee position at AJI, don't you think?)

Short Summary: Nate almost got killed, but then he didn't! Yay! *(Note from NJ: Please revise so this is less colloquial.)*

Long Summary: Analysis of all collected data (detailed below) on Otherworld Specimen #4595 is inconclusive, but seems to indicate it should now be classified as either **deceased** or **sent back to the freakin' Otherworld, YASSS!!** *(Note from NJ: This is not an official classification).* Specimen presented as a solid "energy bolt" that appeared to be of the same substance that makes up the Pussy Queen Portal (also known as the "dark portal" or PQP) and was definitely aggressive in nature, attacking N. Jones and threatening other individuals on the scene. Samples taken from PQP after the attack matched samples taken three weeks ago, but we are still upgrading the status of the portal from **dormant** to **suspicious activity/pending investigation.** Working theory is that a new specimen from the Otherworld was attempting to use PQP to come through to our realm—and probably not for anything fun, like roller-disco bootie cosplay mash-up night at the Palladium on Saturday! *(Note from NJ: I don't know what these words mean, but I believe this is editorializing.)* In any case, it did not leave anything behind and further gathering, testing, and analysis of PQP samples is recommended as is a thorough supernatural scan of the premises. Specimen was defeated through joint efforts from Evelyn Tanaka and Aveda Jupiter.

Addendum: Report Writer would like to issue a big SHOUT-OUT to N. Jones for popping the question in totally baller fashion and giving this particular demon encounter one of the best resolutions in recent history! I mean, I guess there's also the resolution where none of us are dead and that's good, too. But for serious, WAY 2 GO, future bro-in-law!!!

(Note from NJ: This addendum is unnecessary, colloquial, and contains too many exclamation points . . . but I will leave it as is.)

CHAPTER THREE

I SPENT MOST of the night lying awake, staring at the ceiling, trying to puzzle out my deflated reaction to Nate's proposal. I knew it wasn't about the proposal itself; anything that made Evie that deliriously happy made me happy, too.

I stared harder at the ceiling, trying to call up the exact sensation I'd felt watching Maisy coo over the newly engaged couple. The closest thing I could liken it to was the feeling that had developed the longer Evie posed as me: a toxic, queasy little knot at the bottom of my stomach, a snarky voice in my ear telling me I wasn't needed, I wasn't even wanted, look how well everyone got on without me. At times during the Evie-as-Aveda charade, it had almost seemed like Team Aveda Jupiter functioned better . . . without Aveda Jupiter. And now, when Evie and I seemed poised to finally emerge as a dynamic duo of evil-fighters, things were apparently more exciting when I was off-screen, cropped just out of frame.

Maisy's voice echoed through my head: This *is the main course.*

Was I really *that* much of a diva, incapable of sharing the spotlight with anyone else? Was that the real reason I couldn't figure out how to be a good friend? I thought I'd nipped my attention-craving insecurities in the bud. But perhaps I still had a long way to go.

These were the kinds of thoughts I couldn't share with anyone—not even Evie. I was more open with her than I'd ever been with anyone, but there was still a part of me I always kept hidden away, just for myself. One of the reasons she seemed to like me right off was that I never displayed any weakness. So at some point, I had unconsciously decided I couldn't.

I had to be Aveda Jupiter: her protector, her unofficial big sister, the one who took down the bitchy white girls who bullied us at recess. Sure, that meant stuffing down any fear or vulnerability of my own, but when she'd given me one of her big, grateful smiles and looked at me with something resembling awe, it had been worth it. That tiny, locked-away part of myself was like the truest version of Annie Chang: the soft, vulnerable piece I could never let anyone else see. The Clark Kentiest version of myself.

So, as I finally drifted into fitful sleep, I resolved: I would just have to try harder. Do better. Be the best superheroine and friend I knew I could be. That was the Aveda Jupiter Way. Identify the problem, then identify the *solution* and work hard and be awesome and through sheer force of will, fix it.

Hell, don't just fix it. Kick its ass.

When I was younger, one of my role models was Battle Angel Alita, the star of a long-running manga series. Alita was a beautiful young woman who also happened to be the toughest cyborg ever, a steely-eyed fighter who never settled for less than absolute excellence. (And despite what modern Hollywood adaptations might have you believe, she was *definitely* Asian.) In one of her most iconic panels, Alita stares into the distance, eyes narrowed, lips pursed, everything about her radiating total determination.

"I do my best in a fight—always!" she says. "It's that simple!"

And that, I decided at a young age, would be my credo. I do my best in *anything*—always. But in my current state of identity crisis-ing, my usual Aveda Jupiter mojo kept eluding me.

I supposed I'd have to try harder to locate that as well.

The next day, Evie and I decided to return to Pussy Queen and do a thorough search for any possible signs of lingering supernatural activity. Nate had tested the multiple samples he'd taken (and really, his dedication to science was extra impressive considering that he and Evie mostly wanted to sex each other's brains out after the big engagement) and there didn't appear to be any change in the makeup of the portal. I couldn't help but feel like it was mocking me.

Still, even though the portal refused to give us any clues, *something* had happened in those few thrilling moments, and nobody wanted another wannabe demon queen coming through, so a fact-finding expedition was in order.

Wow, leaving the house two whole days in a row. I tried not to get too excited.

Before we could head out, though, I had business to attend to. And not the kind of business I enjoyed—you know, the demon-fighting kind.

I tapped the recent contacts area on my phone, hit the appropriate number, and steeled myself. I had to psych myself up for this call every week, making my breathing even, making my voice neutral, and mentally going over every single one of my accomplishments since grade school as I waited for someone to answer. Sometimes I also lit the therapeutic candle Evie had given me that was supposed to smell like "peace of mindfulness," but it never seemed to perform its promised function.

Therapeutic candles are no match for the unstoppable force known as the Asian Mom.

"Anne?" the familiar, clipped voice finally said on the other end of the line.

"Hi, Mom," I said, wondering how she always managed to sound disappointed before I'd uttered so much as a word.

"You are early this week," she said, the disapproval ratcheting up a hair.

Who gets disappointed in someone for being *early*?

My mother, that's who.

Mom and I had a regular phone call every Tuesday at five p.m. It was part of the good Chinese American daughter code of duty, and since I was a bad Chinese American daughter in pretty much every other way—too loud, too temperamental, bad at math—I tried to adhere to it. But every once in a while, superheroing messed with the schedule.

"Evie and I have to go investigate some things," I said, cringing at the way my voice tipped up, automatically taking on the cadence of a small child trying to make herself sound important. Even after all these years, I was constantly questing for that unattainable treasure: the approval of my parents. "Possibly evil things."

"Mmm," my mother said, which was her usual response to anything involving my superheroing career. She always managed to inject that single syllable with a whole orchestra of disapproval. "How is Evie? Still seeing that boy who wears all the black?"

"Yes, Mom. In fact, they just got—" By the time I realized my mistake it was too late to change what I was saying. So I tamped down on what I knew was about to be a tidal wave of frustration and finished my sentence: "—engaged."

"Engaged!" my mother exclaimed. Well, not so much "exclaimed" as made her voice a tiny bit louder. My mother was not big on overblown displays of emotion. "Isn't that something? Maybe she can help you find someone."

"I don't want someone, Mom," I said through gritted teeth. "I'm doing perfectly well with a fulfilling career that allows me to save people's lives on a regular basis."

"Mmmmm," she said again, stretching it out a bit. "Yes. Well."

And then we lapsed into the awkward silence that had become a hallmark of our phone calls. When I'd first started superheroing, it had been a revelation. Finally, something that combined everything I was good at: athletics and fashion and protecting the downtrodden. And foolishly, I'd believed it would finally make my parents proud of me. But superheroing wasn't the life they'd had in mind for their daughter. It was flashy, glory-seeking. They wanted me to be more like my model minority cousin Sophie, who had been on the doctor track since the age of five. When I'd started out as Aveda Jupiter, I'd sent my parents news clippings about my exploits and all the people I was saving. They'd come back with: "That's nice. Did you hear about Sophie? She's a doctor. Also, she's getting married. To another doctor."

When it became clear they found my chosen occupation embarrassing, I'd concocted a cover story so they'd never have to be associated with it. Aveda Jupiter's parents were dead, killed in a tragic cable car accident before she'd been old enough to truly know them.

Annie Chang's parents, however, were alive and well and had plenty of time to tell her what a disappointment she was.

"Don't wear that greenish color you are so fond of to the wedding," my mother said, as if reading my thoughts. "It washes you out. Makes you look ill. Like you looked when you ate too much char siu at Sophie's valedictorian dinner and—"

"I got it, Mom. No green, no pork."

The awkward silence returned. And felt loud.

"Say hi to Dad for me," I finally said—my usual way of ending the call. My father preferred a silent mode of disapproval to my mother's more verbal methods and never talked on the phone.

"Please give our congratulations to Evie," Mom said. "I will send over some oranges."

"I'm sure she'll love that," I said, trying not to sound like I was wondering why my parents never sent *me* oranges. I liked oranges. (Almost as much as I liked watching Scott eat them, but that was a thought spiral for another time.)

I tapped "end call" on my phone and bounded downstairs, mentally cycling myself away from the tension my mother always instilled in me.

"There you are!" Evie said, as I reached the foyer.

"Here I am!" I agreed, trying to sound chipper. "So Rose is meeting us there. She'll bring one of those cool scanner things with her."

"Dang, the chosen scanner will be stoked," Evie said. "It probably hasn't seen any action in months."

"And neither have I," chirped Lucy, appearing by Evie's side. "So I'm coming, too."

Evie cocked an eyebrow and we exchanged a knowing look. Lucy had struck up a flirtation with Rose Rorick, the stoic head of the San Francisco police department's Demon Unit (a special squad in the Emergency Service division), a few months ago. It hadn't progressed any further, though—at least not yet.

"You two still haven't gone on an actual date?" I asked her.

"We haven't gone beyond a copious amount of texting," Lucy said, brushing her long, honey-colored locks off her face. "Last week, we graduated to the occasional use of emojis."

"Don't you usually move faster than that?" I asked.

"Yeah, you're like the Quicksilver of dating, only with way better hair," Evie chimed in.

"Oh, I am, darlings, I am," Lucy said. "But compared to my usual conquests, that Rose is a cool cucumber. I have to employ a more meticulous courting strategy."

"Oh, shit." Evie gawked at her. "Lucy. You *like* her."

"Pfft," Lucy said, suddenly in a huff. "Such language. Let's get going."

"Yes," I said, tightening my power ponytail. "Onward to Pussy Queen."

I pushed the door open, ready to begin our determined march and conduct whatever acts of superheroism the city might need.

Unfortunately, our determined march was cut short. Because the Victorian was surrounded.

Our HQ location was no secret; it was a regular stop for tourists and fans, and locals had mobbed the place right after Evie and I defeated Shasta, hoping to catch a glimpse of the heroines who saved the city. But the crowd had tapered off quite a bit recently and today wasn't quite at the mob level; there were maybe thirty people gathered and I recognized many of them as my—well, *our*—most dedicated fans. But they were still blocking our path, a loosely formed fence of humanity keeping us from continuing our journey to Pussy Queen.

We came to an abrupt stop on the porch, gazing out into the crowd, unsure of what to do. It was a situation we hadn't had to deal with for a while.

"Do you think they saw the video of us battling the energy bolt?" Evie whispered. "Maybe they're worried about the safety of the city or something?"

"Maybe," I said. "In which case, let's reassure them. It's what we do."

I faced the crowd and flashed them my megawatt grin, the one that had inspired more than a few loving photo collages on Tumblr. I felt out of practice. The act of stretching my face that much made my cheeks hurt.

"People of San Francisco," I said, making my voice as confident and declarative as possible, "I know the events that transpired at Pussy Queen yesterday must have appeared downright terrifying when viewed on video. And indeed, it was quite the epic battle. But rest assured that I, Aveda Jupiter, and my amazing co-heroine, Evie Tanaka, remain completely dedicated to your safety and well-being—"

"Evie!" A loud, braying voice from the crowd interrupted my speech. I scanned their faces, looking for the source, and found the towering mountain of a man Evie referred to as "Giant Dude." I think his real name was George. He had a wide, freckled face, a mop of sandy hair, and sported one of his usual threadbare "Over the Moon for Jupiter" t-shirts. Though he appeared quite genial, his enthusiasm for my various exploits tended to land on the wrong side of overpowering. I sensed Lucy tensing behind me, ready to take him down should he make any sudden moves.

"Evie!" he repeated. "Have you set a date yet?"

"What about a dress?" a girl in a tie-dyed smock dress piped up. "Are you going with a local designer?"

"Back up, first she needs a theme!" someone else cried, voice laced with disdain. "Everything—wardrobe, flowers, decorations—should revolve around that!"

"Tell us more about the engagement!" a girl near the back shouted. She clapped a hand over her chest and fluttered her eyelashes. "That video was *so* romantic!"

"Especially since Nate almost *died* before he got to propose!" Tie-Dye Dress yelped. "Thank god Evie was there to take down the enemy!"

I was there too, I thought, my inner voice small and plaintive.

Argh. My inner voice was sounding *way too much* like Annie Chang.

The crowd murmured in agreement, a chorus of adoring coos and "awwws" that swiftly devolved into more shouted questions about weddings, engagements, and if there were any plans for eventual superbabies.

Evie took a shaky step back, her eyes widening, overwhelmed by the attention.

"So this *is* about a video," Lucy hissed in my ear. "Just not the one we assumed."

No, it wasn't about that video. The one that featured actual world-saving. Maisy had been right: the proposal video was the main course.

"Come on, give us something!" Giant Dude bellowed. "This is basically as close as San Francisco's ever gonna get to a royal wedding!"

"Hells, yeah!" Tie-Dye Dress chimed in.

"Um . . ." Evie took another step back, her face going pale. She may have grown more confident since becoming a superheroine, but I got the sense that being the center of attention still wasn't really her thing. Especially when that attention focused on precious pieces of her life she'd rather keep private.

For a moment, I saw the unsure, pale-faced kindergartner I'd saved from humiliation years ago. We'd been the only two Asian American kids in class, and our parents sent in food for snack time that our peers deemed "weird." They'd teased me for trying to "burn their faces off" after scalding their over-eager mouths on my mom's homemade soup dumplings. (Really, it was their own fault for being so greedy and eating too fast. I'd held my head high and told myself their palates were simply not sophisticated enough for authentic Chinese cuisine.)

A week later, they'd dubbed Evie's spam musubi "human meat," bringing her to tears with their little kid cruelty. So I'd stepped in and taken the bullet. I'd crammed every single musubi down my throat, refocusing their attention on me. It had worked and suddenly everything had been all about crazy little Annie Chang. I'd decided back then that I was the stronger one, the one with guts made of steel. Seeing her face so terrified activated my protective streak — the piece of me that felt like it was my duty to save her. That it always would be.

I reached over and took her hand. It was cold and clammy. I gave her a reassuring squeeze and turned my smile wattage way up.

"Evie will answer all wedding-related questions in due time," I said, making my tone firm. "Official media inquiries should go through our press office. Now, Evie, why don't you hold up that door-knocker of a ring and everyone can take a picture. And then be on their way." I gave the crowd my best imperious look, indicating they shouldn't argue.

Evie gave me a grateful smile and flashed her left hand at the crowd, her ring sparkling in the hazy morning sun. The mob instantly snapped to attention, raising their phones in near unison to capture, tweet, and hashtag the moment.

"Let's get inside," I murmured to Evie and Lucy. "We'll

wait fifteen minutes for all this to disperse, then sneak out the back, just in case there are stragglers." Our determined march was delayed, but would not be halted entirely. I would make sure of that.

"Wait!" Evie grabbed my hand again and smiled at me. Her face had relaxed now that people weren't screaming questions at her. "There *is* one thing I want to announce."

An intrigued murmur shot through the crowd.

"Are you sure?" I whispered. "We've already given them something, now we can go back inside—"

"My maid of honor!" Evie cried, her voice becoming strong and sure. "My maid of honor is of course ... Aveda Jupiter!"

The crowd exploded in cheers. More camera-phones went off. And I just stared at her. I couldn't quite process what I was feeling, but it was a big mixed-up bag of emotions that took me off the sure path I'd been on, the path to getting us inside, back on our mission.

Did she really just say . . . ?

Evie turned to me, beaming, her eyes bright with tears.

"Annie," she whispered. "I know I haven't officially asked you yet, but you'll do it, right? I want you to be by my side on one of the most important days of my life. I want to be able to look over and catch your eye and giggle because we're both thinking of the same dopey *Heroic Trio* quote at the same time. I want ..." Her voice caught and I realized the tears in her eyes were mirrored in mine.

"What about Bea?" I murmured. It felt like the dumbest possible thing to say in that moment, but as my brain caught up to the feelings crashing through my heart, I realized I wasn't sure if this was an impulsive decision brought on by the presence of the crowd and if she was somehow forgetting her sister, who would undoubtedly be really pissed at me later.

"She's walking me down the aisle," Evie said. "You know, since our parents aren't around."

"And Lucy?"

"I'm officiating, love," Lucy said, flashing me a rakish grin. "I already have my outfit picked out."

"So . . ." The emotions that had been crashing through me came to an abrupt halt, and I felt myself deflating. I bit my tongue so I wouldn't say what I was actually thinking, which was that Evie had already talked to everyone else about their positions in the wedding. And I'd barely come in third.

"Of course I'll do it," I said, squashing my petty thoughts and forcing my megawatt smile to return. "Of course."

As she swept me into a hug and the camera-phones flashed more vigorously, warmth surged through my veins and my smile slowly turned genuine.

Because suddenly, I realized something.

This was it. This was what I'd been waiting for.

A mission.

This was going to give me the chance to fix *everything* I'd been struggling with recently. It would give me a new sense of purpose to latch on to. It would offer me the chance to prove that I could be a good friend. And it would help me reclaim the Aveda Jupiter mojo I seemed to have lost in the last few months—leaving Annie Chang behind for good.

Even if the Pussy Queen portal ended up being a big pit of nothing, and my attempts at building a personal appearance empire never took off and we were about to be resigned to another series of months of non-apocalypse and endless breakfasts, I would have *this*.

Because Evie needed me. Of course she did.

I felt the plan organizing itself into a neat list in my head, a column with efficient check marks next to each component.

Identify the solution to all my problems—*check!*

Work hard and be awesome—*check!*

And through sheer force of will, fix it—*check, check, check!*

Well. Check . . . pending.

Aveda Jupiter might be a diva. But she was also about to be the best fucking maid of honor this world had ever seen.

After we'd posed for another few rounds of pictures, I bounded back inside and set off for the narrow supply closet next to the downstairs bathroom. I required hairspray to refresh my power ponytail.

I felt rejuvenated. It was akin to the sensation I'd briefly experienced the day before, when Evie and I had vanquished the energy bolt. But this time, I was determined to make that feeling last. Okay, so maybe this wasn't *exactly* the type of heroic mission I'd imagined saving me from boredom. But being the best maid of honor ever—and ensuring that Evie had the best wedding ever—would help me reclaim myself. It would allow me to be the best Aveda Jupiter I knew I could be.

I seized on the feeling of purpose bubbling through me and practically skipped the remaining steps to the supply closet. Then I flung the door open and froze in place, halting in my steps when I saw who was inside.

"Oh. Hey," Scott said. He held up a roll of toilet paper. "I needed this."

"Right. Of course. That's a thing people need," I said.

God. What was wrong with us? We sounded like a pair of robots who were just discovering the miracle of human speech.

We hadn't really experienced any moments alone since . . . well, since right after Evie and I defeated Shasta. Evie had been badly injured during the battle and passed out for a full day. I'd waited by her bedside. Nate, Bea, and Lucy had all curled around her and fallen asleep, but I couldn't bring myself to close my eyes for even a second. I'd been told repeatedly she'd be okay, but a small thread of disbelief pulled at me. What if she never woke up? What if I lost the one person who'd always stood by me? What if I never got to tell her—

I hadn't been able to finish that thought.

So I'd just stayed there, awake and alert and shoving that bit of worry down as hard as I could. The only person who'd stayed awake with me was Scott.

Before I got injured and everything went down with Evie and Shasta and the demon hybrids, Scott and I hadn't spoken in years. We had a long, tortured history that involved me thinking he was in love with Evie all through high school, him kissing me in our early twenties, me shoving him away because I was convinced he was *still* in love with Evie, and us getting into a huge fight, which led to the whole not-speaking thing. We'd set aside our differences—sort of—when he'd joined the HQ fold earlier in the year. He'd come to work with us to help Evie. She'd desperately wanted to be free of her fire power and he'd been working on a spell that would pull it out of her and transfer it to me. Things hadn't quite worked out that way, but the level-up earthquake had given him a boost in his mage abilities. Suddenly he'd been able to heal my ankle on the spot.

He'd been passed out during our battle against Shasta, so as we sat by Evie's bedside, he'd asked me to recount it for him over and over again. At some point, I deduced that he actually had a pretty clear picture of what had gone down—he was just asking me so I'd keep talking. So I'd have something else to think about besides how fragile Evie looked, pale and unmoving in her big bed.

When I'd finally run out of steam, when I just couldn't repeat the story one more time and silence fell between us, he'd reached over, rested his hand on mine, and said, "She'll be okay, Annie. And so will you."

I'd wanted to luxuriate in the warmth of his fingers, in the way his eyes were open and gentle and looking at me with more affection than they had in years. But instead, I'd felt something shut down inside me. The way I was feeling—the way he seemed to make me feel whenever I let him get too close—took me back to that soft, vulnerable place I was always trying so hard to avoid. The Annie Chang place.

And I couldn't go there. Not when I was watching my best friend in the world hover near what looked very much like death's door. Not when so much of it had been my fault. I'd been the one who had wanted Evie to pose as me, I was the reason she'd been in the situation that had gotten her hurt.

So I just gave him a small smile and said, "I could use some coffee."

He'd squeezed my hand and left to get it.

Later, as we'd filed out of Evie's room, his fingertips had brushed against the small of my back. Or at least . . . I thought they had. I wasn't even sure anymore. But just in case, I'd rushed ahead of him once we made it out into the hall, putting a decent amount of physical distance between us. So he wouldn't get any ideas.

After that, I'd thought we were making some tentative steps toward friendship. Friendship with him would be okay. Friendship wouldn't make me feel so powerless. But instead, in the last month or so, he'd chilled toward me again. He was his warm, joking, laid back self with everyone else, but he responded to me in the stiff, formal way one might speak to their least favorite co-worker. He always seemed to go out of his way to avoid me, and we hadn't been truly alone together since that night at Evie's bedside.

Until now.

I stood frozen in place, lurking in the closet doorway for a few more seconds. It felt like years.

Enough of this, I told myself. *You just decided you're about to get your mojo back, you have a mission—and mooning over some guy to the point where you can't even enter a closet space without freaking out is definitely not in line with that. That's Annie Chang behavior and you are above it.*

Why was I here again? Oh, right—power ponytail. I straightened my spine and strode forward, keeping my eyes on the prize: in this case, a can of Aquanet gracing the middle shelf near the back. Unfortunately, the closet space was so narrow, it was hard to keep up my purposeful stride. And since he still wasn't moving, I had to contort my body to wriggle by him.

And goddammit, he still smelled amazing.

I twisted myself so I was facing him and attempted to shimmy past. But I was so focused on trying not to inhale his scent that I severely underestimated the amount of wriggle space I had, and bumped against his chest.

"Oops, sorry!" My face flushed, and I prayed the closet was dark enough that he couldn't tell. My hand shot out, as if to put space between us. Instead it landed on his chest. And stayed there.

All right, now my face was basically on fire. I probably looked like I did when I drank too much and got the classic Asian Flush. I felt like I was drugged, like being this close to him reduced me to some kind of feral animal, experiencing every sensation to its fullest, with no logical thought to get in the way.

I just couldn't seem to take my hand away. I felt the chest muscles I'd fantasized about all through high school, hard and unyielding underneath the frayed cotton of his t-shirt.

"Annie?"

I forced myself to meet his eyes. They were concerned, confused. For the first time in weeks, they held something other than cool distance.

"Are you okay?" he said.

I swallowed hard. My mouth was suddenly totally dry. This frightened little rabbit, this awkward girl who was felled so quickly by a rush of hormones . . . This wasn't me. *This wasn't me.*

And I was trying to be me again. I had a mission now and I couldn't get distracted.

"Of course," I said. I yanked my hand away as if I'd touched a stove and managed to wriggle my way over to the hairspray.

I expected him to take this as a sign that we were done with our conversation and he should move along, but instead he just kept standing there. I felt his eyes boring into my back as I reached for the can.

"So," I said briskly, racking my brain for clever things to say that would somehow dissipate the awkwardness of the moment. "I'm the maid of honor. For Evie and Nate's wedding."

"Oh." His tone was conversational, but strangely flat, as if he didn't quite know what the correct emotional response was. "That's great. I'm the best man."

"Really?" The word shot out of my mouth before I could hide my disbelief.

He laughed, and I was dismayed at the rush of warmth I felt in my chest. "Yes. Nate and I have, you know, bonded. I think I finally convinced him I'm not trying to get in Evie's pants."

"Not anymore, anyway." It spilled out of my mouth before I could stop it. It was a defense, a reaction—a way of making sure he didn't get under my skin and stay there and turn me into Annie Chang, Hormonal Rabbit. But it sounded snarky and barbed, like I'd been saving up that retort just for him.

He didn't respond, and I felt a sudden chill in the air. I tightened my grip on the hairspray, schooled my features into a look of business-like cool, and turned to face him. "I guess we'll be working together closely on this, then," I said.

"I guess so." His tone was just flat now. No conversational vibe, no unexpected laughter. And his expression matched that.

"We should throw them an engagement party," I barreled on. "Let me know what your initial thoughts are, but please remember, my standards are very high, so it may take us some time to work out the absolute best plan."

I gave him a brisk nod, then breezed out of the closet, hairspray in hand, head held high. He hadn't gotten to me and he wasn't going to. I could handle him.

Aveda Jupiter could handle anything.

CHAPTER FOUR

"WHAT DOES THIS button do?"

"Can I hold it?"

"Ugh, be careful—Rose is letting us handle very delicate equipment!"

Lucy burst into giggles after that unintentionally innuendo-laced sentence fell out of my mouth. She cast a sly look at Rose.

"Oh, I'm sure Ms. Rorick here is accustomed to handling delicate equipment," she said with a wink.

Rose actually looked borderline flustered, which was refreshing. Usually, she was the epitome of stoic, buttoned-up law enforcement—though we had gotten a glimpse of the real Rose when she indulged in a few drinks with us after Evie's big karaoke battle against Maisy. The real Rose cracked the occasional lazy smile, didn't shy away from dirty jokes, and possessed actual human emotions underneath her poker-faced exterior.

I hid a smile at Lucy's flirting and flicked my gaze around the shop, as if looking away might give her and Rose a moment of privacy. Maisy was actually leaving us alone for once, fussing with a mannequin near the back, attempting to lace its torso into a complicated-looking corset. Shruti was nowhere to be seen, but I knew she still had the main branch of her shop to manage and probably wasn't able to mind the pop-up version constantly. Dave was perched on his stool, leaning back against the wall behind the coffee bar, stoned as usual and practically asleep. When we'd arrived, he'd muttered something about how "there are no shortcuts to any place worth going" and that had been it as far as human interaction was concerned. Despite Shruti's best efforts, it didn't seem like his social skills were improving. I also couldn't help but wonder if he was just reciting bad fortune cookie messages to us, which seemed possibly kind of racist.

Rose, Lucy, Evie, Bea, and I were gathered around the portal. Bea had insisted on coming along after hearing Rose was going to be there, but her reasons were far less lusty than Lucy's. In addition to dedicating herself to learning more about the science of the Otherworld under Nate's tutelage, Bea had also developed a fascination with the bits of tech Rose's Demon Unit had used to scan the areas affected by portals when portals were still opening up on a regular basis. She'd spent a lot of time recently begging and wheedling Rose to let her "borrow" one of the scanners for experimentation purposes—or at the very least, to take it apart. Rose had thus far managed to put her off by claiming they were police property and had to be under her custodianship whenever they left the precinct, but I had a feeling it was just a matter of time before Bea got her to relent.

"Ahem." Rose cleared her throat and shook her head, as if attempting to shoo her flustered feelings away. She brandished the scanner at us: a clunky gray bar that looked kind of like the hand-held metal detectors TSA officials wielded with enthusiasm at airports. Only this one was designed to detect supernatural energies. The scanner was part of an array of tech that had been developed back when the demons came through the first big Otherworld portal. (And yes, the scientists who designed it had been deeply influenced by *Ghostbusters*. When the previously impossible suddenly becomes real, it's only natural to draw from established sources, even if they are fictional and kind of ridiculous.)

The hope was the scanners would be able to detect and predict portals before they opened. In reality, all they seemed capable of was sensing lingering supernatural energy and telling us the portals were closed and staying that way. When we'd scanned the Pussy Queen portal right after it had opened and closed the first time, the results had been inconclusive. But given that it had just done that all over again, it seemed best to give it another look.

"I'm going to scan the portal," Rose continued. "The read-out area—" She tapped a small black screen at the top of the bar. "—will flash red if there's any lingering supernatural energy to be found. Then—"

"Then it does a quickie analysis on elements that might make up that energy, and if further breakdown of those elements is required, you have to take the results to a lab and have someone look at them more closely," Bea piped up. "Right?"

"Right," Rose said, giving her an approving nod.

"Just thought I might need to translate for the jocks over here," Bea said, waving a dismissive hand at Evie, Lucy, and me.

"We're the *jocks* now?" Evie said, cocking an eyebrow. "Really? Since when have I done anything remotely jock-like? I still can't even run up a flight of stairs without losing my breath."

"You guys are the *muscle*," Bea insisted. "Me, Nate, and Rose are the *brains*."

"What's Scott, then?" I couldn't help but ask.

"He's the mystical, magical force that binds us all together," Bea said, without missing a beat. "Like...the *feels*."

"Oh my god, enough," Evie said, laughing a little. "Rose, please continue."

"Right," Rose said, just as Lucy raised her hand. "Um, yes, Lucy?"

"Does the scanner make a special beeping sound when it detects supernatural energy?" Lucy asked. "Because I think that would be much more exciting than the red light by itself."

"Yes, actually," Rose said. One corner of her mouth quirked up. "And you can also set it so the beeping picks up in speed the closer you get to the affected area. I'll make sure that feature is switched on for you."

She tapped something on the scanner and then held it over the portal, waiting.

We all watched, holding our collective breath.

Nothing happened. No flash. No nothing.

We exhaled.

"That's been the result every time we've scanned this portal," Rose said. "But we haven't scanned the rest of the shop since the portal first opened. Perhaps it's time to do that again, just in case anything escaped during this latest incident."

"Tip-top idea," Lucy said, giving Rose a flirty smile. "I'll help."

"I think we should let them handle that on their own," Evie said, placing a hand on my arm as I moved to follow them.

"Agreed," Bea said, trotting off toward Dave's coffee bar. "Maybe Lucy will be able to soften Rose up enough to let me play with the scanner. In the meantime, I need a caffeine injection."

"So this is morphing from a mission to us chaperoning some weird non-date?" I said, turning back to Evie.

She rolled her eyes at me. "Always the mushy romantic. But yes, basically."

"All right, then let's talk about my other mission," I said, my brain making the switch with ease. "Which is to make sure you have the best wedding ever. Have you thought about a date yet? Next spring would be beautiful. Or with summer, you could probably play up some kind of fire power theme—you know, because of the heat. Or you could go full-on holiday, though I'm not really a fan of that whole fur-trimmed cape look—"

"Actually," Evie cut in, giving me an amused look, "we're thinking of doing it soon. Maybe in a month?"

"A *month*?" I squeaked out. "As in four weeks? As in that is barely enough time to design flower arrangements and pick out favors and do any custom tailoring you might need and—"

"And I don't need any of that. I just need him. As soon as he asked me, I knew I wanted to make it official as soon as possible."

"Okaaaay," I said, my brain whirring, trying to rearrange all the plans I had been making.

"We want to keep things simple," she continued. "Like, find a backyard or a community garden or something? He has a suit already. And I don't need anything super fancy, I could even just get something at the mall—"

"Stop right there!" I blurted out, holding a hand up. I grasped her by the shoulders and fixed her with my most intimidating stare. "You are not. Getting your wedding dress. At the *mall*!"

She cocked an amused eyebrow and extricated herself from my grasp.

"Annie," she said gently—and I immediately recognized the "you're being a diva right now and I'm going to talk you off the ledge" tone in her voice. "I really want you to be my maid of honor. Even though some people—" She cut herself off abruptly, but I knew the end of that sentence had to be a more diplomatic version of: "thought it was the worst idea in the history of ever."

But that's because they were thinking of Aveda Jupiter as she'd existed before Evie and I had our big talk. The diva who couldn't share the spotlight. Now that I was working on reclaiming my mojo and becoming the best Aveda Jupiter possible, that was all about to change. Aveda Jupiter 2.0 would be just as good at being a friend as she was at everything else.

"Anyway," Evie continued, gentle voice still in full effect.

"I'm so happy you accepted and that you're so enthusiastic about everything, but I really need you to—"

"To make sure I remember this is *your* wedding, and it's about what *you* want. Of course. Done."

But even as I said that, I knew one thing for certain. This wedding was *not* going to be some half-assed, sloppy, multi-cereal-course affair. Not if I had anything to do with it. Not if I was going to accomplish my mission, being the best maid of honor I could be. Evie might not think she'd regret a thrown-together day, but she would, eventually. She deserved to have something incredible. Something perfect. Something only I could give her. She needed me, just like she always did.

"So you might not want all the bells and whistles," I said, trying to think of how I could ease her into a less slapdash mindset. "But it's a special day and you definitely want a couple nice things. Your dress, for instance—"

"Ooh, and what you wear *under* the dress." Maisy, who'd apparently been eavesdropping until just the right moment, swooped in, clapping her flaky gray hands together. "Of course you'll come to Pussy Queen for all your bridal lingerie needs."

"But first, we have to take care of the dress," I said firmly, determined not to get sidetracked. "It's the most photographed piece of clothing you will ever wear. Particularly since you refuse to invest in any kind of iconic superhero costume."

I cocked an eyebrow at her usual jeans/t-shirt/Chucks combo. She grinned and stuck her tongue out at me.

"You want something that's timeless, but uniquely you," I continued, warming to my topic. "Something that captures your spirit. Something no one else will have."

I tapped my finger against my chin, my eyes scanning the shop, going into a fashion fugue state. Lucy and Rose were huddled near a corset-wearing mannequin with the scanner, but there didn't seem to be a lot of scanning going on. More like giggly whispering, at least on Lucy's end. My gaze finally landed on the collection of colorful racks in the corner. Shruti's pop-up shop.

"Something vintage," I said, my brain clicking the pieces into place. "Yes. That's perfect."

"I don't know," Evie said. "Those old dresses are so narrow, sometimes they don't fit me in the hips—"

"So we'll get it altered," I said, waving a hand. "It will be one-of-a-kind and effortlessly stylish. Maybe we can ask Shruti to consult on this. Where is Shruti, anyway?" I asked Maisy.

"Indie Fashion Market in Dolores Park," Maisy said. "She has a stand there, but I believe she's also scouting for new stock."

"Indie Fashion Market," I repeated. "I've heard of it. And they have a whole bridal area, do they not?"

"It's still too soon to be thinking about dresses, Annie," Evie said. "I really don't know if—"

"It's not too soon if your wedding is in a month," I said. "If we don't get on this now, you'll be walking down the aisle naked."

"But—"

"Ladies!" Lucy strolled up, waving the scanner around, with Rose trailing behind. "We're getting no red light action at all, so what say we pack up and—"

BEEP!

The sound rang out through the shop, sharp and shrill, a single insistent note. We fell silent, our eyes going to the scanner—which had just let out the loudest, most unexpected noise.

It flashed red.

"Goodness!" Lucy exclaimed. "Could that be a false alarm or—"

BEEEEEEP!

Maybe I imagined it, but the sound seemed even louder and more insistent this time. I reached over, grabbed the scanner from Lucy, and brought it close to my face. I studied it, as if to confirm what the sound had just told us.

The light still flashed red.

"Whoa!" Bea scurried over to us, coffee cup in hand, her eyes keen with interest. "I leave you guys alone for three seconds and things get exciting!"

My heart sped up, and I took a few deep breaths, trying to calm down. I didn't need to be getting all hot and bothered by yet another momentary bit of excitement that was just going to end up being nothing.

"Move the scanner around," Rose urged. "See if you can pinpoint the center of the energy."

I took a hesitant step to the left, my eyes glued to the scanner. The red light vanished.

I took a step to the right. The whole shop had fallen silent and I could feel everyone's eyes glued on me, waiting to see what I would discover. I took another step to the right.

BEEP! BEEEEEP!

My heart leapt and sweat beaded my brow. I swallowed hard and moved to the right again.

BEEPBEEPBEEP!

"Keep it up!" Rose cried. "You're finding it!"

I took three quick steps to the right.

BEEPBEEPBEEPBEEPBEEP! BEEEEEEEEEEP!

The red light flashed, its quickfire strobe matching the pulse pounding in my ears.

"That's it!" Rose crowed. "That has to be it!"

I'd never heard her sound so excited. I took one more step to the right.

BEEPBEEPBEEPBEEPBEEEEEEEEEEEP!

Now the scanner was non-stop, beeping its urgent distress call. A series of numbers flashed on the read-out.

"Rose!" I exclaimed. "It's trying to tell us something."

Rose moved next to me, her brow furrowed. She took the scanner from me and studied the read-out. Bea lurked over her shoulder.

"Huh," Rose said, cocking her head to the side. Bea mimicked the motion, which I might have found cute if I wasn't dying of anticipation. "This code," Rose continued, pointing to the jumble of numbers, "indicates that we're picking up the leftover trace of something specific: a puppy demon."

"A puppy demon?" I repeated, not quite believing I'd heard right. The "puppy demons"—so named because that's how Maisy referred to them, apparently kept as pets in the Otherworld—were the mindless, piranha-like pests that had poured out of Shasta's smaller portals. In the past, they'd imprinted on the first thing they'd seen upon arriving in our world, which meant I'd spent a lot of my super-heroing career fighting evil versions of things like cupcakes and shoes. But since Shasta had been vanquished and the smaller portals had stopped opening, we'd not seen hide nor hair of the puppy demons.

"Yes," said Rose. "But like I said, it's a trace. The demon isn't actually *here* anymore."

"So when was it here?" Evie chimed in. "Because we haven't seen one of those things in months."

"Let's get to the more important question," I said. "Where did it *go*?"

We all took a moment to ponder that.

"If there's only one," Rose said hesitantly, "that means it can't do much damage."

"Yeah, the direst of situations is when *two* escape, breed like bunny rabbits, and proceed to eat whatever's in front of them," Bea said. "That's a potential city destroyer right there."

"I think we need to analyze these results further," Rose said. "See if we can get any clues that will answer these questions."

"All right," I said briskly, my brain snapping into battle mode. "Rose, you and Bea take this data back to HQ, confer with Nate, and see what you can find." It seemed we had a task. A potential *danger*, even. I was practically giddy at the prospect. But that didn't mean I was about to forget my other mission.

Aveda Jupiter could multitask like a motherfucker.

"In the meantime," I continued, "Evie and I have other important work to do."

"We do?" Evie said uncertainly.

"Yes. We're going to go to that Indie Fashion Market." I planted my hands on my hips, straightened my spine, and made my voice as authoritative as possible. "We're going to find you a wedding dress."

CHAPTER FIVE

I LOVE CLOTHES.

I know saying that is supposed to be a mark of the super-ficial, an indicator that you are perhaps less of a "real woman" than some of your more sloppily dressed cohorts — the whole "she wears short shorts, I wear t-shirts" thing. With all due respect to the great poet Taylor Swift (who I believe is fully committing to the character she created for that song), I think that's bullshit. I derive true inner strength from my best outfits, and nothing's more real than that.

When I was a kid, I would coordinate my sock color with my ponytail holder. Even though Evie teased me for my matchy-matchy tendencies, it always made me feel that much more pulled together, which gave me the extra shot of confidence I needed to be her playground protector. I also harbored hope that my parents would see this as indis-putable proof of my quest for perfection, even though I could only manage a B in algebra.

When Evie and I saw *The Heroic Trio*, I of course re-sponded to the fact that the three Asian women in the movie totally kicked ass. But I also *loved* their outfits, which ran the gamut from skin-tight red leather jumpsuits to pre-steampunk goggles and motorcycle boots. They looked fab-ulous. More importantly, they looked like they *felt* fabulous. To me, that kind of attitude was necessary if you planned on spending your days throwing yourself between packs of bloodthirsty demons and helpless human civilians. So when I became a superheroine in my own right, I knew fabulous costumes would be a cornerstone of my persona. I still had an instinctive lustful response—a sharp intake of breath, a sudden warmth in my chest—whenever I saw beautiful clothes laid out before me, waiting for me to touch, stroke, and covet.

The Indie Fashion Market provided that experience for miles. It was an outdoor extravaganza that took over the sprawling grassy expanse of Dolores Park every third Tuesday of the month. The park was stretched over a hill, a charming oval of space that made for fantastic views if you hiked up to the highest point. Of course, right now, the most fantastic views consisted of the racks and racks of fashion blanketing the hill. Wild splashes of color dotted the whole area, like a Jackson Pollock painting come to life. I took a deep breath, inhaling the scent of grass and trees and perfectly preserved Diane Von Furstenberg wrap dresses.

"Are you about to have an orgasm?" Evie teased, nudging me in the ribs, as we wended our way through the racks.

"This is an exciting situation for me," I said, my eyes darting around the feast of clothes on display. "And it will be for you, too, once we get down to the very serious business of wedding dress shopping."

"I told you, I don't want that to be serious business," Evie said, nudging me a little harder. "Let's just find something nice, simple, and not too binding."

I resisted the urge to roll my eyes. This was her *wedding dress* we were talking about. It required more thought than, say, a run-of-the-mill pajamas purchase. Though Evie probably would get married in her pajamas if she could. Which would happen over my dead body.

"Speaking of business that *is* serious, though," I said. "Another important part of getting married is resolving any outstanding emotional business you have with family. And in that vein, don't you think you should talk to Bea about her power—"

"Since when is divesting of family baggage an actual

wedding tradition?" Evie said. She kept her tone light, but I could tell I'd hit a nerve. "Especially among Asians. Aren't we supposed to stuff all those pesky feelings down and never speak of them again?"

"Not *these* Asians," I said, gesturing to us. "I believe you've actually benefitted from finally letting all those damn emotions out—I think Nate would agree with me. And don't use unfortunate stereotypes to justify your unwillingness to deal with this."

She laughed a little, her shoulders relaxing. "I know, I know. You're right. But the whole telling-Bea thing still has to be on my timeframe."

I stuck my tongue out at her, trying to give my words a playful cast. "Honestly. So many of your problems come from various flavors of avoidance and denial."

"And so many of yours come from barreling headfirst into things without listening or thinking about the consequences," she said, giving me an affectionate smile.

"And that's why we make a great team."

"We do," she agreed. "All right, all right—I'll think more seriously about telling Bea. I just . . . for so long, my power seemed like such a burden, and she's still so young and let's face it, not great with the impulse control, and I want to make sure I bring it up in the exact right way, and I can't seem to figure out what that is. It's a parenting discussion I'm one hundred percent not prepared for. I don't even know where to begin. Talking to her about sex was way easier, and I'm sure you can imagine how awkward that was."

I squeezed her shoulder. Evie's mom had died of cancer when Bea was only twelve and their dad had abandoned them for an ill-defined "vision quest" not long after. She'd been doing her best to raise her sister ever since. And in my opinion, she'd kicked major ass at a task that shouldn't have been hers in the first place.

"I know you'll figure it out. In the meantime, let's go wedding dress shopping!" I said, trying to sound extra cheerful.

"Ughhhhhhhh." Evie made her body slump over in an exaggerated way, like a cat who didn't want to be picked up.

"It's exciting! Be excited!" I said, jabbing her in the arm with my index finger.

"I am excited!" She straightened up and gave me an earnest grin. "But seriously. I am excited to get married. And to have you and our whole weird little found family involved in such an important event in my life."

We came to a stop in front of Shruti's booth, which featured a few racks of dresses and a table covered in festive brocade scarves and glittering brooches. Shruti was positioned between a dealer who seemed to specialize in gigantic hats and a vendor who only carried old school Gunne Sax. This abundance of prairie chic reminded me of Lucy, who, sensing the opportunity for more flirty Rose time, had decided to accompany Rose and Bea back to HQ.

When I'd first hired Lucy, I'd assumed she and I would bond over our obvious shared love of fashion. But our tastes didn't quite match up—she preferred way more lace and ruffles than I did—and she'd gravitated toward Evie instead. I'd pretended not to mind—but of course I had. Here I was, giving it my all to be awesome and charming, and Evie attracted the first cool girl with friend potential to enter our orbit in ages. And she accomplished that by doing absolutely nothing.

I supposed that, upon reflection, I could understand. Evie was approachable and friendly. I . . . had many good qualities, but those were not among them. Well, no matter. Now I was hard at work on Aveda Jupiter 2.0: Excellent Friend Edition.

We filled Shruti in on what had transpired at Pussy Queen as she sold a hair-clip festooned with tiny rhinestone flowers to a tall redhead outfitted in a simple t-shirt dress accented with a fluffy pink petticoat underneath. I took a moment to admire her intriguing contrast of modern and vintage.

"So you don't know where this puppy demon ended

up?" Shruti asked. "Or where it came from, even?" She was outfitted in another choice piece from her stock, a violet fit-and-flair number from the fifties, and her hair was long today, styled in an elaborate braided formation that wrapped around her head like sculpture.

The redhead fastened the clip in her hair and hurried off, giving Shruti a little wave.

"Thank you," the redhead called out, beaming. "I'll be in next week to check out your new stock!"

"Of course, always a pleasure!" Shruti said, waving back. "I should have a whole slew of lovely frock babies coming in." She turned back to us. "Sorry. About the puppy . . . ?"

"I'm guessing it came from the portal," I said. "But it's odd that we're finding a trace of only one puppy demon. Usually, they come through in hordes."

"Hopefully the tests Nate and Bea are running will tell us more," Evie said. "We're heading back to HQ in a bit, but in the meantime, Annie thought we should come . . . here." She self-consciously rubbed her thumb over her engagement ring.

"It's for your own good," I said. I turned to Shruti, going into all-business maid-of-honor mode. "Where's the wedding wear at this thing? My adorable bride bestie here wants to get married in a month, so it's crucial that we find her dress ASAP."

"Ah!" Shruti's eyes lit up. "You need the bridal tent. All brides need the bridal tent," she said, as one might say, "All humans need oxygen."

Shruti pointed to something behind us and we both swiveled to look. The bridal tent was easy to miss at first. A swath of white tenting perched on the far right side of the park, it wasn't as flashy as some of the more colorful displays. There was something pristine about that pure blanket of white—almost peaceful. But closer inspection revealed the long line of women snaking around the entirety of the tent. Clearly the stuff inside was a hot commodity.

"It houses the most unique collection of wedding gowns

you'll find in the city," Shruti said. Her voice had taken on a hushed, reverent quality. "Nothing mass produced and no super high-end designers. It's all vintage and local indies and everything's one-of-a-kind."

"That sounds perfect," I said. "Let's go."

"Um, I'm not sure—" Evie began.

"One does not simply *walk* into the bridal tent!" Shruti interrupted. "There are *rules*."

I cocked a skeptical eyebrow. "Like?"

"Like you need to get in line to sign up for a spot right when the Market opens," Shruti said.

"So we'll get in that line," I said, nodding toward the tent.

"That's the line for everyone who already signed up for a spot—and it's capped," Shruti said, shaking her head at my ignorance. "It's too late. All those spots were snatched up when the Market opened this morning. My last customer was just telling me she got the final spot, and she basically camped out the night before." Shruti nodded in the direction of the line. The redhead who'd just purchased the sparkly hair clip was scurrying over to plant herself at the very end. "You also have to prove you're engaged, no vendors or eBayers allowed," Shruti continued. "Which counts me out."

"And I bet you'd love to get inside," I said. "To score choice pieces for your stock."

"Well, yeah," she said. "I wouldn't even mark them way up or anything; I'd sell them only for a small profit. I only care about matching beautiful pieces of clothing with their rightful owners. I explained that to the Market powers that be, but still—nothing. I even tried to fake an engagement once. There's no way in. It's hopeless."

I studied the bridal tent, my eyes narrowing. I didn't believe in hopeless. And I was unaccustomed to taking "no" for an answer. In fact, that kind of obstacle only stoked my desire to attain whatever I was after.

The harder the challenge, the sweeter the reward.

I suppose this was yet another example of, as Evie had put it, me barreling headfirst into things. My parents used to refer to me as "xiao ju feng"—little hurricane. Hurricane Annie. But this was an important step in my maid-of-honor mission.

"We're getting in," I said firmly, flipping my power ponytail over my shoulder. I narrowed my eyes at the bridal tent and the huge line, a battle plan clicking together in my head: get in, find the perfect dress, be the perfect maid of honor. No matter what.

"Shruti, you're coming with us," I said. "We'll need your eye for style in there. Both of you empty your pockets and leave your bags behind so we're not weighed down by anything unnecessary. Bring all your cash with you, 'cause I'm assuming they don't accept credit cards."

"Annie," Evie said, "we don't have to get all crazy over—"

"We're not being crazy," I said. "We're being *determined*. Now. Follow me. I have a plan."

As soon as we reached the long, meandering line, I strode to the front and planted myself there, hands on my hips, and raised my voice.

"Citizens!" I bellowed. "Do you not recognize the glamorous celebrity bride in your midst? It's Evie freaking Tanaka!"

"Annie!" Evie shrieked in protest.

But she was drowned out by the "oohs" and "aahs" of the line. She tried to cower behind me, but I stepped to the side and put my arm around her shoulders, holding her in place. Finally, we were going to get something worthwhile out of that viral proposal video.

"We weren't able to sign up for one of those tickets to stand in line," I said, gesturing to the brightly colored slips of paper all the women in line were clutching as if they were made of gold. "But I'm sure none of you will block Evie and her entourage—" I gestured to myself and Shruti. Shruti, getting into my plan, waved enthusiastically to the line. "—from entering. After all, we want this darling daughter of San Francisco to have the perfect special day, do we not? And that starts with the perfect special dress."

The line cheered in agreement. Evie gave them a weak smile.

"We also have to get by the guard," Shruti hissed in my ear.

I turned to see a stern-looking woman wearing a blue security guard's uniform and about a million different lanyards bearing official Indie Fashion Market documentation.

"And you won't try to block us either, will you?" I said, giving her my best authoritative look. "Because I bet that would get caught on video." I inclined my head meaningfully toward the line. Many of the women already had their phones in hand, documenting the moment. "And we know how videos featuring Evie tend to go viral. I'm thinking your bosses really wouldn't appreciate it if they knew you tried to keep Evie Tanaka from her dream dress."

"I won't, I won't," the guard sputtered. "Really." Her stern face cracked into a smile and she nodded at Evie. "I'm a big fan."

"Good," I said. I drew myself up tall and stood at the front of the line with as much authority as possible. I turned to Evie to flash her a triumphant grin, but she was staring into space, like she wished she could disappear on the spot. She looked mortified.

Well. I was sure once we had her dream dress in hand, she'd thank me.

"It's noon," someone whined. "Let us in!"

"Yeah," the woman right next to us chimed in. "Our tickets say we will be allowed to shop from exactly noon until exactly two, and every second of that time is precious."

More voices joined in, a cacophony that morphed into a chant: "Let us in! Let us in!"

A weird thread of desperation laced itself through the air, and I felt myself picking up on it, my heart beating faster, sweat prickling the back of my neck. The tension of the line was rising by the second. I could practically feel Evie shrinking into my side. I laid a comforting hand on her arm and tried to make my smile reassuring: *We got this.*

The guard made a big show of checking her watch, then finally nodded and drew back the curtain to the tent. I expected the line to give us—the celebrity bride and her entourage—a respectful moment to enter.

That's the opposite of what happened.

Instead I felt a sharp poke in my back—an elbow? A finger? A fist?—followed by a voice hissing "*go*" and that was it. We were caught up in a stampede, a heaving mass of stomping sneakers, swinging purses, and sweat.

"Whoa!" I yelped, throwing a protective arm in front of Evie and Shruti. "I know this is an important purchase, but what the hell?"

"Like I said, everything's one-of-a-kind," Shruti said, ducking to avoid being hit by a woman who was flailing her arms out in all directions, as if trying to swim through the crowd. "There's only one dress in each size. So you've got to claim what you want fast."

I surveyed the scene. Racks and racks of white, cream, and ivory in every possible fabric formation were jammed together with what appeared to be no rhyme or reason. After the initial stampede, the brides had settled a bit, and were furiously pawing through the racks. Some had giant binders or meticulous spreadsheets they kept consulting.

"What's with the documentation?" I asked Shruti. I grabbed Evie's arm and yanked her out of the path of a woman who was charging forward with her eyes glued to her spreadsheet, not watching where she was going.

"One of the big bridal websites leaked what they claim is the layout of this place—a map of where each gown is," Shruti said. "So if you're looking for a specific dress, you can track it down before anyone else lays eyes on it."

I shook my head in wonder. There was obviously a lot of bridal bullshit I needed to catch up on. But I was more than up to the task. These other brides might have months of planning and strategizing and spreadsheets on their side, but Evie had something better. Evie had *me*.

"Out of my way!" a petite blonde shrieked, barreling past us. She had pulled a strapless, feathered creation over her clothes and was charging through the racks like a mini-Godzilla.

Or, I guess—a literal Bridezilla.

"I found mine!" she bellowed. *"I found it."*

The other brides were too caught up in their own scavenger hunts to pay her any attention.

"Let's split up," I said, my eyes darting around the room. I could practically feel the tension in the air, coating the claustrophobic interior of the tent with a palpable cloud of bridal angst. "Shruti, you start on the left side, we'll take the right. We're looking for something sweet, pretty, and above all, unique. A cut that will accentuate her curves. Possibly mermaid. No gigantic ballgowns and nothing that looks too much like a tutu. And not too much bling—that's more my speed." I gave Evie a smile I hoped was reassuring. She smiled back uncertainly, but her eyes looked terrified.

"Got it," Shruti said. "May the Force be with you! Or some other rallying cry that's way more appropriate for this situation." She plunged into the mass of gowns and brides, a blotch of violet darting through the sea of white.

I grabbed Evie's hand and pulled her along behind me, guiding her over to the last rack on the right side of the tent, making my movements sure and confident. Daring anyone to push or elbow or Bridezilla me.

"Dammit," a woman next to us hissed as she savagely pawed through the same series of five dresses over and over again. I glanced her way and realized it was Shruti's redhead customer, her hair clip glittering as she shook her head furiously at the dress selection. "I knew that asshole Caitlin would take the last size four Minji Chen empire cut with double-faced sateen train!"

Okay. I do love clothes, but I had no idea what she was talking about.

"Maybe you can find something else you like just as much," Evie suggested, helpful as always. "What about this one?" She pulled out a lace gown with delicate cap sleeves. "It's totally cute—"

"Hands off!" the woman growled. "I was already looking at that."

To prove her point, she snatched the gown out of Evie's hands and stomped off.

"Jeez," Evie muttered. "Who knew wedding dress shopping was akin to global warfare?"

"And she seemed so pleasant and cheery at Shruti's booth," I muttered. "I guess brides snap into battle mode in an instant."

Evie ducked as a blob of white organza flew over her head—a dress lobbed by someone apparently trying to keep a would-be bride from yet another coveted dress.

"Get away from that rack!" the dress thrower shrieked behind us. "If you so much as look at the Ambra Originals duchess gown, I will cut you!"

"Annie." Evie's hand clamped on my shoulder like a claw. "This is actually scary now, can we please—"

I didn't hear the rest of what she was saying. Because at that moment, after pawing my way through several dozen dresses and rejecting them immediately—too puffy, too cleavage-y, too weird—I found the perfect thing. It was made out of layers of soft chiffon, the delicate material contrasting perfectly with that sharp mermaid cut I knew would highlight Evie's curves. Strapless, sweetheart neckline. And best of all was the tiny bit of decoration: a series of bright scarlet silk flowers that crept up the bodice and swirled over one side of the neckline. Like a little trail of flames.

I could practically hear the choir of angels singing as I pulled it free from the rack. I didn't see a label, so maybe it was vintage? But I knew by eyeballing it that it was about her size.

"Here, try this on," I said, pushing the dress at her.

"I . . ." Her eyes darted around the room, searching for a place to change. But the bridal tent was definitely not home to anything so civilized as a fitting room. Women were dropping everything and yanking off their clothes, or pulling the dresses on over whatever they were already wearing.

"I'll stand in front of you," I said. "Don't worry, no one's looking. They're all too wrapped up in their own thing."

I gestured to the chaos, which seemed to have reached a fever pitch. Tension hummed through the air. Women were practically snarling at each other, trying to protect their bounty. I looked for Shruti, but couldn't locate her amidst the mass of tulle, sweat, and rage.

"You probably won't be able to get the whole thing on yourself," I called over my shoulder. "Let me know when you need help."

She was quiet for so long, I thought maybe she'd managed to sneak off and escape the tent entirely. After what seemed like an eternity, I finally heard her voice, small and uncertain: "Okay."

I turned to face her and my jaw dropped. She had managed to push past her embarrassment and get out of her clothes and mostly into the dress and she looked stunning. The soft fabric made her appear ethereal and timeless, while the cut kept it modern and even a little bit sexy. Her skin seemed to glow next to the cream of the chiffon, her freckles standing out adorably. And that little trail of scarlet flowers—wow. It just popped.

"Evie," I gasped. My eyes filled with unexpected tears. "You look like a bride."

"I do?" she said, smoothing the material over her hips and shifting awkwardly from foot to foot. "There are no mirrors in here, so I can't see . . ."

I whipped my phone out and snapped a quick picture.

"No pictures allowed!" someone screamed. "They should be kicked out!"

"Jesus," I muttered. I ignored them and showed Evie the

picture. As she studied it, a surprised smile spread over her face.

"Wow," she said. "I *totally* look like a bride."

"Okay," I said, "so we're buying this." A rush of pride surged through me. I'd completed a major step in my maid-of-honor mission! *Check!*

"Wait, though," she said. "Yes, it looks nice, but I feel kind of . . ." She picked at the bodice of the dress. "Constrained. And it's much fancier than what I'm used to."

"Exactly," I said. "It should be. It's your *wedding dress*."

My happiness was interrupted by a shriek behind us, which started as an animal-like yelp of fury, then morphed into actual words: "Oh my fucking god!"

I whipped around to see one of the Bridezillas from before — Shruti's redhead customer who had been so upset over her stolen Minji Chen whatsis whatever — stomping toward us, fists balled at her side. She'd pulled the lacy dress Evie had suggested over her clothes and it looked like it would be gorgeous on her once it was fitted properly. But right now, she clearly didn't care about that. Right now, all she cared about was rage. And it was aimed directly at us. The sparkly clip in her hair was coming loose, banging against her head in a way that could not have been pleasant.

"Listen, ho-bag," she screamed at Evie, "you need to keep your grimy mitts off my dresses!"

"But I'm not . . ." Evie shook her head in confusion and took a step back. "You're wearing your dress now. And I'm not touching it."

Bridezilla came to a stop in front of Evie and jabbed a finger in her face. "Not this one," Bridezilla growled. She gestured to Evie's chiffon number. "*That* one."

Evie frowned and a hint of anger sparked in her eyes. "This one's mine."

"No, it's not," Bridezilla said, leaning in even closer. Spittle flew out of her mouth and pelted Evie in the eye. "Take it off."

"Excuse me?!" Evie said. The spark in her eyes flared. "I don't think so."

"Let's calm down," I said, attempting to step between them. I addressed Bridezilla. "Look. You seem to have found a lovely dress for yourself, and I'm guessing you only need one, so—"

"You have no idea what I need!" Bridezilla shrieked. Her arm swept to the side and hit me square in the chest. I wasn't expecting that and it sent me tumbling backward onto my ass, the wind momentarily knocked out of me.

"How dare you!" Evie cried. "That's my maid of honor!"

I saw her hand raise, saw the very beginnings of a flame. *What the hell?*

What was she doing? Yes, Bridezilla was a jerk, but surely she didn't deserve to be burned for it? I scrambled to my feet and tried to hustle back to Evie's side. But a crowd was forming around the potential catfight. I found myself being pushed farther back as the mob of brides—formerly dispersed, now coming together to form one amoeba-like ball of rubbernecking—closed in, trying to get a good view.

"Evie!" I called out, but she couldn't hear me over the din of titillated murmurs.

"You need to learn some manners," Evie hissed, her angry gaze locked on Bridezilla. Bridezilla, apparently unafraid of the flame that was about to be all up in her face, grabbed the top of Evie's dress and yanked. I heard the *riipppppp* and the "Oh, no, you did *not*" and then I saw fire arcing through the air and all I could do in the moment was reach out instinctively with my telekinesis, my invisible mental feathers sweeping Bridezilla to the side before she went up in flames.

"Annie!" shrieked Evie. "I know that was you! What are you doing, we can't let this asshole bride get away with this!"

Evie's flame careened through the air and landed on a rack of dresses off to the side—and luckily, out of the way of any actual humans. I reached out with my telekinesis to grab a dress that had landed on the floor and tossed it over the blaze, extinguishing it. Then I turned back to the fight. The crowd had really closed in on them now and I could barely see what was going on. And if I couldn't see it, I couldn't move it.

Okay, fine. If I couldn't push my way through physically, I'd have to resort to something else. I reached out with my mental feathers and started moving people in my sight line to the side, creating a path to Evie and Bridezilla. A murmur ran through the crowd as they were unceremoniously moved. I couldn't move them all at once, unfortunately—a task of that size was outside the scope of my abilities, although I was determined to master it once I figured out the whole moving-objects-I-couldn't-see thing. But at least I'd be able to get eyes on Evie.

Bridezilla, undeterred by, well, anything—the fire or Evie's anger or the fact that I'd swept her out of the way just moments earlier—was on her feet and lunging for Evie again. I hustled down the path I'd created, reaching out with my telekinesis to move Evie or Bridezilla or both or maybe just to tell them to calm down and stop acting like unruly children, when all of a sudden, a long, dark shape flung itself through the crowd and wrapped itself around Bridezilla's neck.

"Shit!" I yelped, jumping out of the way.

I squinted at the shape. It looked like . . . a braid? Made of hair?

"Can't . . . breathe . . ." gasped Bridezilla. The braid pulled tighter and her face turned blue.

Evie didn't make any moves toward her and neither did anyone else—they all appeared to be frozen in place, totally confused.

That was fine. Aveda Jupiter was here and Aveda Jupiter would take care of this shit.

I flung my mental feathers at Bridezilla, locked them around the braid, and pulled hard. It loosened slightly. But not before Bridezilla let out a last, strangled gasp and crumpled to the ground.

The braid fell to the floor, and I whipped around, trying to find its source. It had snaked its way around the racks and through the chaos of the entire bridal tent. My eyes followed it to a lone figure standing on the opposite side of the tent, away from the gathered crowd.

It was Shruti. And the braid was attached to her head.

Her *hair* had nearly choked the life out of someone.

CHAPTER SIX

"SO ARE YOU evil now or what?" Bea gave Shruti a suspicious once-over. "Because it would be a total shame if I had to add someone with such on-point outfits to the Bad Guy List."

"I'm not!" Shruti insisted, as she had for the last three hours. "And, uh, thank you."

Bea gave her a solemn nod. Shruti probably had no idea that Bea actually did have a Bad Guy List, currently contained in a shiny silver notebook and rendered in a rainbow of sparkly gel pen colors. It was meticulously organized, down to Bea's hand-drawn grid that sorted various nemeses into specific categories like, "Actually Evil Down to Her Very Soul," "Marginally Annoying in Group Situations, Okay One-on-One," and "Cut in Front of Me at Starbucks, Jury's Still Out."

The aftermath of the bridal tent incident had been a confusing affair. I'd had to muster every ounce of that mojo I was working so hard to reclaim and project some serious authority in order to maintain a semblance of civilized behavior amongst the bridal mob. I was pleased, though, to have happened upon a situation where both my telekinesis and my top-notch maid-of-honor skills proved to be essential.

The redhead Bridezilla nearly strangled by Shruti's hair had been taken to the hospital, but was ultimately fine, save for some neck bruising. She and Evie had exchanged faint, hazy-eyed apologies as she'd been taken away—like they both had only a vague recollection of what had gone down.

I'd managed to get the rest of the brides to disperse and I'd also made sure we hadn't forgotten Evie's wedding gown in the process. It was torn down the side seam where Bridezilla had ripped it, but I was confident a good seamstress could take care of that. I'd even snagged a proper garment bag from behind the counter of the bridal tent before Evie simply wadded it up under her arm and dragged it back to HQ.

Sure, we'd just been attacked by a rogue Bridezilla, who in turn had been attacked by a rogue hair braid. But at least we'd gotten Evie's dream dress out of it.

It's important to acknowledge every victory, no matter how small.

Right after the incident, Shruti had appeared dazed. No, she couldn't explain what had just happened, and no, despite her ability to grow her hair at will, it had never acted in such an energetic, powerful fashion before. She'd thought Evie was in serious danger, had wanted to defend Evie from Bridezilla—had felt that want deep in her bones—and then suddenly, her braid was expanding and flying through the air.

Shruti had willingly returned to HQ with us and submitted to a multitude of medical and magical tests. Now we were all gathered in the cold gray basement lair that also served as Nate's laboratory, waiting for more information—about Shruti's braid and what had caused Evie and Bridezilla to wig out so badly in the first place.

"None of our testing indicates that Shruti is, as Beatrice puts it, 'evil,'" Nate said. He and Bea were standing in front of a giant white board at the front of the lab, facing me, Evie, and Scott. Rose, Lucy, and Shruti were leaning against a counter off to the side. "That is to say—uh, Bea, what are you doing?"

Bea looked up from the white board, where she was using her extensive palette of markers to scribble a diagram. Right now, it consisted of a stick figure in a violet dress with a happy face. "I'm illustrating your report for those of us who process info in a more visual way." She gestured to the stick figure. "See, that's Shruti with a smiley face. 'Cause she's not a bad guy."

"Got it," Nate said, without missing a beat. "In any case, our combined tests actually show that Shruti has attained . . ." He paused and turned to Shruti. "Do you want to tell them?"

"It's my power level-up," she said, giving us a small smile. "I guess it decided to finally take hold. In addition to being able to grow my hair, I can control it now—make it move around and stuff."

"Whoa, that has definite kickass superhero potential!" Bea yelped, drawing a long, undulating braid on the Shruti figure's head. "How cool!"

"What's not so cool is I apparently don't know my own strength yet," Shruti said, wincing. "Which is how I almost strangled that lady. It was like I reacted from pure instinct. I thought she was hurting Evie, and I desperately wanted to protect my friend."

"I had some weird instinct-type reaction back there, too," Evie said, frowning. She leaned forward and drummed her fingers on the countertop. "The way that bride came at me, the way she pushed Annie—it flipped some kind of rage switch in my brain. I normally wouldn't even think of using fire against non-powered humans, especially in such a mundane situation. And Bea, that looks nothing like me."

Bea was scribbling a stick-figure Evie, complete with bridal veil, fireball in hand, and exaggerated angry expression. "It's shorthand," Bea said, waving her marker dismissively.

"It does actually look a little like you," Lucy said. "Bea, draw me."

"But you weren't there," Bea said.

"Artistic license," Lucy said.

"Artistic license belongs to the *artist*," Bea said, pointing to herself with the marker. "And while we're at it, can we talk about the fact that I wasn't there, either? During kind of an important moment?"

"You wanted to witness a Bridezilla attack?" I asked.

"No," Bea said, whipping around and brandishing the marker at me in an accusatory fashion. "I wanted to be there when my sister picked out her wedding dress. And I'm guessing that as one of her closest friends, Lucy would have liked that, too."

"Well . . ." Lucy examined her nails and gave an elaborate shrug. "It might have been nice."

I felt a little wave of discomfort and realized it was Bea's anger, pulsing through the air. Her power was something Evie referred to as "reverse empathy": basically, she could project her own mood to influence yours. Now that I was aware of it, I could feel it manifesting from time to time, pressing gently against my own emotions, causing them to rearrange into a formation that was some weird amalgam of what I was actually feeling and how Bea was making me feel. It was disconcerting, to say the least.

"But you knew we were going to the Market to look at dresses," I said, my brow crinkling. "Both of you could have come along, but—"

But one of you was all hot to analyze puppy demon data and the other was all hot to analyze Rose's ass. I was the only one actually thinking of Evie.

I bit my tongue. That was the kind of blunt, authoritative statement I could have tossed off when we were still thinking of this operation as Aveda Jupiter, Inc. and my word was always the final word. But that wasn't the case anymore. Now Evie and I were equal superheroines and the group was more collaborative, with everyone welcome to chime in with ideas and strategy. I knew I was supposed to *like* the fact that the former Aveda Jupiter, Inc. was more of a team effort now, but there were certain elements I disliked heavily.

"We didn't think you were actually going to buy anything," Bea continued, her voice taking on a petulant teenage whine. "You were just supposed to *look*."

"And the point of looking is to *buy*," I snapped, unable to hold it in any longer.

Honestly. When Aveda Jupiter sets her mind to a task, she means to accomplish it. Otherwise, what's the point?

"Evie didn't seem ready to buy," Bea insisted. "She got engaged barely twenty-four hours ago!"

"And she's getting married in a month," I retorted. "Time is of the essence, and as maid of honor, I have to step it up in order to ensure—"

"Okay, okay," Evie said, stepping forward and holding her hands up. "Clearly a lot of shit went down in the bridal tent. Why don't you all come with me when we get the dress fitted? That's when the whole bride thing becomes real anyway, right? That's when the tears and drama and moments of ultimate bridal epiphany occur? Has no one else here watched *Say Yes to the Dress?*"

"Well." Bea fiddled with her marker, twisting the cap on and off. But she looked mollified. "I guess that would be okay."

"Sounds lovely," Lucy said.

Evie smiled at them, then gave me a wink. The peacemaker, as usual. I did my best to smile back, feeling slighted. I thought the dress had been a victory.

No matter what I did, the rest of the team still saw me as Aveda Jupiter, Diva Bully who pressures her friend into doing her bidding. Even though Evie and I had worked things out. Even though I was focusing my Hurricane Annie essence in the right direction, trying to accomplish my mission and help my friend step into the spotlight with grace and dignity—instead of claiming said spotlight for myself.

Well . . . it made sense. They were used to the dynamic between Evie and me being a certain way, they were used to *me* being a certain way. They couldn't see that I was becoming Aveda Jupiter 2.0: Still Awesome, But Now A Way Better Friend.

Or maybe they just don't like you—never have and never will, a little voice piped up in the back of my head. *They had to be nice to you when you were their boss, but now?*

Once again, the image is better with you cropped out of it. That's what everyone thinks. Even Evie probably thinks that.

I shook off the voice, willing it to shut up. That was the kind of voice Annie Chang would listen to. Not Aveda Jupiter.

I was struck again by the realization that I would probably never be a true part of the team "family" Evie was so fond of talking about. But at least I could get them to see that I'd changed. I would just have to work harder to make them see it. That was my way, after all. That's what I *do*.

"If we could get back to the matter at hand," Nate said. "Evie had just started to address the other side of the puzzling equation this incident presents."

"You mean that, beyond the Shruti of it all, she and our redhead Bridezilla nearly came to blows over a dress?" I said, relieved to be back on an apparently less controversial subject.

"People do get all kinds of out-of-control over fashion," Shruti said, toying with her braid. "Especially brides."

"The air in the tent did seemed charged," I said. "Emotional. But that near-brawl was a special level of extreme crazy, was it not? And highly uncharacteristic of our Evie."

"Right," Evie said. "As I was saying, I'm not really in the habit of using fire against non-powered humans. There was something disconnected about the anger I was feeling. I was sort of detached from it. And once it left . . ." She shook her head, as if trying to put her thoughts together. "It was totally gone. And I felt so confused."

"Which seems to match how Bridezilla felt," I said.

"Wait!" Bea, whipped around, hands gesticulating, and nearly dropped her marker. I was relieved to see that she seemed to have snapped out of her sulky state. Though her emotions were always extreme, she tended to bounce back quickly. Or maybe, as Evie was fond of hypothesizing, she just had a really short attention span. "This is making me think of something," she continued. "Hold on a sec."

Bea trotted over to a towering, overstuffed shelf of

books and papers in the corner—where she and Nate kept their various research—and pulled a massive folder free.

"Okay," she said, rifling through the folder as she crossed back to the white board. "So to preface what I'm about to info-dump on y'all, when we took a closer look at the scanner data from earlier, it didn't tell us much. Except for one data point, which I may have just found a connection for."

Oh, right. The puppy demon excitement from earlier. In the madness of the bridal tent, I'd forgotten all about it.

"Rose?" Bea said. "Want to share what we learned when we analyzed the scanner data?"

"Well . . . sure," Rose said, looking puzzled. "The data indicated our rogue puppy demon appeared in that area sometime in the last six months. The new data point Bea refers to is this: it seems this particular puppy demon never took corporeal form."

I frowned, my brain buzzing. "So it didn't imprint on anything? It just stayed floating in the air in some kind of shapeless, invisible state? Has that happened before?"

"Very rarely—at least as far as we can tell," Rose said. "This type of reading has only shown up a handful of times on our scans over the years, and we've always followed up by monitoring the area where we detected an incorporeal puppy demon particularly closely after an attack. But usually the reading would disappear once we eradicated whatever demons were left over."

"So they literally disappeared into thin air," Lucy murmured.

"That's always been our working theory," Rose confirmed. "That they simply evaporated once we took care of their corporeal puppy brethren."

"It's less of a theory and more of an unverifiable assumption," Nate interjected. "These cases—as few of them as there were—have always been documented, but nothing happened after to indicate that the incorporeal puppy was still among us."

"Hence the assumption," Rose agreed, giving Nate a nod.

"We monitored these things as best we could, but these incidents were so few, well . . ." She shrugged. "We just don't have much data, unfortunately."

"As you guys know, I've been studying all civilian-submitted reports Rose's department has received over the years on demon appearances, trying to catalog them and put them in some kind of order," Bea said, studying a crumpled piece of paper she'd pulled free from her folder. "Most of 'em are just cray-cray. People exaggerating what they saw or even making shit up entirely. Like, I don't think this Roger guy actually witnessed a bunch of high heel puppy demons doing a choreographed routine to 'Bad Romance' at that drag bar on Turk, but—"

"But—get to the point," Evie said, with a slight smile.

"But!" Bea said, stabbing an index finger in the air, "there are two instances of small groups of people sending in reports where—when they were on the scene of an attack—they suddenly felt super aggro. Just out of nowhere. They remembered feeling afraid of being eaten by demons, and then suddenly that turned on a dime and they felt *pissed*. And they couldn't really say why. In both cases, they chalked it up to heightened emotions from being in the midst of an attack. Basically, they decided they got their feelings wires crossed. In their brains or whatever."

"And let me guess," I said slowly. "Both of these attacks—"

"Both of these attacks were also cases where Rose's team picked up traces of incorporeal puppy demons!" Bea crowed, pulling another crumpled paper free from the folder. She waved it triumphantly in the air, then dumped the folder on the countertop and grabbed her marker.

"So your theory is that these incorporeal puppy demons affect human brains?" Nate said.

"Ding, ding, ding!" Bea sang out, scribbling a puppy with fangs and angry slashes for eyes over the Evie stick figure's head. "Maybe when they fail to imprint like their puppy pals, they get mad and look for something else to latch on to."

"Hmm," Lucy said. "That is most intriguing, but the puppy demon trace we found was at Pussy Queen, not the bridal tent. How did it get from one place to the next?"

"Corporeal puppy demons have been known to travel," Nate said. "They're not bound to their portal location. Who's to say the incorporeal version would be any different?"

"Great," I said, groaning. "So are we saying there's an incorporeal puppy demon on the loose? A *stray*? Just floating around in the air?" Frustration welled in my chest. I prided myself on my ability to punch, kick, and/or telekinesis any kind of demon monster into submission. But something that was invisible and had no form for me to actually punch? I had no idea how to fight that. I brought my hand to my lips, then hastily lowered it. I bit my nails when I was stressed. Raggedy-ass fingernails would not be a good look for a maid of honor, especially one who was in the process of reclaiming her superheroine mojo.

"What happened to the people who reported those ragey feelings?" I asked Bea. "Is it possible the puppy demon kept following them around?"

"Apparently, they went back to normal," Bea said, with a shrug. "Like Evie and Bridezilla. But there were a handful of people who reported these feelings at each attack and not all of them reported back in later. So it's sort of impossible to know unless one of them also had a supernatural incident afterward."

"But it appears none of them did, correct?" Lucy said. "Or surely we would have heard about it."

"Maybe," Bea said. "But like Rose said, there's so little data. And we're not sure if the scanners always picked the incorporeal puppies up. So there's no way of tracking that." She lifted her shoulders in a helpless sort of shrug.

"In other words, this area of study on the puppy demons contains a lot of unsupported suppositions and half-theories," Nate said, his brows drawing together. "Which I really do not like."

"All right," I said, blowing out a long breath and resisting the urge to cram my nails in my mouth. "What we need is a plan that attempts to connect some of these dots. To make the half-theories full."

"We could start with the scanners," Lucy said, turning to Rose. "True, we have no way of knowing where the puppy went after the bridal tent, but maybe we could start with the surrounding area and go from there?"

"I can organize my people," Rose said, nodding. "Get them to canvas with the scanners."

"We should probably scan Pussy Queen again, too," I said. "Just to be sure."

I looked over at Evie, expecting her to pick up the thread. Ever since she'd come into her own, she was usually the one to rally us, to bring us together and set us on the path of a plan. But she'd gone quiet during the last part of our discussion, and I noticed she looked a little pale. Something was obviously bothering her and I didn't think it was the fact that she had almost forgotten to use a garment bag to transport her dress. I nudged her in the ribs.

"We can set up a special inbox for people to send us tips about anything they might witness that's out of the ordinary," she said, snapping to attention. Her voice was faint. "Keep an eye out for it that way."

"Hello?" Bea said, waving her marker around. "We're totes forgetting the most important part."

"Which is?" Nate prompted.

"How do we catch this thing once we find it?" Bea said, drawing a little net over her cartoon puppy demon. "I mean, if we're picking it up on the scanner, but we can't see it, if it doesn't have an actual *form*—"

"Good point," Evie murmured, going even more pale. Seriously, what was wrong with her?

"Did the techies who developed the scanners ever come up with anything that might be useful in that regard?" Lucy asked Rose.

Rose looked thoughtful. "We have these trap . . . things," she said slowly. "The ones we used to contain the leftover corporeal puppy demons. If the portal was still open, we'd catch them and dump them back inside. If not, once they were in the trap for a while, they'd sort of disintegrate."

"Ooh!" Bea whirled back around, her eyes dancing. I felt that little wave of her emotions again, a brief rush of giddiness that was akin to a drip of morphine. "Maybe we can see about recalibrating them for the incorporeal puppies? Can I play with—I mean, *work on* one of the traps? I have some ideas based off the scanner tech that I—"

"Yes, okay." Rose smiled at her. "But only in a supervised environment."

"What about getting them into the trap?" I said. "Once again, we have the whole 'they're invisible and don't have bodies' problem."

"I might have an idea for that," Scott said.

I twisted to look at him, surprised. He'd been so silent this whole time, I'd forgotten he was there. He stared back at me with that strange, blank affect he seemed to have lately. Well, at least when it came to interacting with me.

"I've been working on a spell I think I can modify— something that separates different supernatural elements present in the atmosphere," he said slowly. "If I can adjust it just right—once the scanners sense the puppy presence, I might be able to find it, grab hold of it, and guide it."

"Guide it right into the trap!" Bea crowed.

"Aw, look at all of us, using our different skills," Lucy said, clapping her hands together. "It's like we're the X-Men. Only with less clones and intergenerational family drama."

I glanced over at Evie again, but even Lucy's joke didn't seem to be enough to draw her out of whatever funk she'd plunged into.

"Let's get to it, then," I said.

The room dissolved into random bits of conversation as we began to disperse. I moved closer to Evie.

"Hey," I said. "What's wrong? You went all quiet."

"Huh? Oh." She studied her hand, opening and closing

it into a fist. "I guess I hadn't really thought about . . . what I did back there. At the bridal tent. I've gotten so much better at controlling my power, it's easy to forget . . ." She swallowed and closed her hand again, leaving the rest unsaid. But I knew what she was thinking.

How destructive it is. How I could have hurt someone. Or worse.

I laid a comforting hand on her arm. "You have gotten great at controlling it," I said. "But it sounds like our friend the invisible puppy demon might have been controlling *you*."

"And we have no concrete way of finding it," she said, her frustration spilling over. "So what's to stop it from making me . . . from making any of us . . . "

"Don't go down that path," I said quickly, squeezing her arm. "We *will* find it. And we'll take care of it."

Even as I said this, a tremor of uncertainty ran through me. We couldn't see it, and that meant I couldn't punch it. And that was a problem. But I couldn't let Evie sense my worry. Especially not with her big day coming up. A stressed-out bride would definitely not make for a perfect wedding, one of the crucial end points to my maid-of-honor mission.

I schooled my features into what I hoped was a soothing look. It was a mirror of the one she'd been prone to giving me when she was my personal assistant and I was in a good diva rage about something.

"Why don't you go lie down?" I said. "Get some rest. Or get Nate to lie down with you. And *don't* get some rest."

She managed a little giggle. "Okay. Thank you." Her giggle sounded forced, but she gave me a small smile and squeezed my arm before wandering off.

It was enough to make me feel a small surge of triumph. Enough to make me feel like I'd come back from the dress faux pas. Enough to make me feel like I was on enough of a mojo-reclaiming roll to take on the last obstacle in the room.

I marched over to Scott and tapped him on the shoulder.

He was standing next to a small desk he'd set up in the corner of Nate's lab, to work on spells and other bits of magical research. And he appeared to be rearranging a stack of papers that looked like forms. Hmm. Forms for what? Was he getting into Nate's whole spreadsheet thing?

He turned and gave me yet another blank look. "Yes?"

"We have to plan that engagement party," I said, making it a command rather than a request.

"Okay." Still blank. Still detached. Still acting like I was some kind of nobody—a pesky, inconsequential gnat that could be easily swatted away.

Well, you know what? Aveda Jupiter was no fucking gnat.

He made a move like he was about to walk away. I stepped in front of him and put my hands on my hips.

"Stop it," I said.

"Stop what?" He raised an eyebrow.

"You know what!" I yelped, dismayed to hear that rising note of frustration in my voice.

No. Nope. *I* was in charge, here: Aveda Jupiter. Get out of here, Annie Chang. I threaded that steel back into my voice. "You've been acting like a freaking robot toward me for months! Ever since—"

Ever since you held my hand that night when everyone else was asleep. Ever since you told me everything was going to be okay. Ever since I thought you might take it further than that and—

I brushed the thought away. This was not about getting soft and mushy over him again. This was about working together on the wedding. For Evie. "—ever since . . . a long time," I finished, holding my head high. "I know you were mad at me for being a bad friend to Evie. But you and I were also actual friends at some point. And I thought we'd been making progress recently as far as getting back to that. Weren't we?" I tried to make that last bit sound like a stern "so straighten up" directive rather than a pathetic plea.

"Yes," he said slowly, like he wasn't entirely sure of the correct answer. His face remained maddeningly blank. I stifled my inner scream.

"Then why are you acting like this?" I growled.

He stared back at me, silent. And I couldn't squelch my frustration anymore. I was doing everything *right*. I was being a good friend, I was working efficiently on all of my missions, and I was reclaiming my mojo. I was being as honest as I possibly could be with him and he couldn't even give me the courtesy of a slightly varied facial expression?

I was suddenly transported back to one of the many days we'd all been sitting together in the junior high cafeteria: me, him, Evie. I was working diligently on my sixth grade presidential campaign while the two of them goofed around. The campaign had been incredibly important to me. Not only would a win secure me a modicum of power in all of the important student decisions affecting our school, but it would also show my parents that I was way better than Cousin Sophie, who'd only managed class secretary. I figured Scott and Evie knew I was working, so they'd keep talking amongst themselves and leave me alone. But Scott could never seem to rest until he'd annoyed me to the point of yelling at him. That day, he'd discovered a new trick wherein he stuffed as many grapes in his mouth as possible and talked through them, rendering his voice cartoonishly marble-mouthed. He kept trying to talk to me, kept leaning in closer and closer with his dumb mouth stuffed full of grapes, until finally, he spit out a little of the juice. Right on the pristine mock-up of my campaign flyer. I'd felt my simmering irritation finally boil over. But I didn't yell at him.

Instead I impulsively did the same thing I did now. I reached over and flicked his arm.

"Ow!" he yelped, just as loudly as he had back in sixth grade. "Did you just *flick* me?"

I crossed my arms over my chest and shrugged, trying to look superior. I couldn't believe he had reduced me to something so childish, but I would still own it. He stared at me in disbelief and shook his head. He shook his head for a long time, as if trying to shake something loose. And slowly, the disbelief turned into something I hadn't seen forever from him: an actual smile.

"You flicked me," he said, as if this was the punchline to a joke I didn't know. "Just like in sixth grade."

"Well, did it snap you out of it?"

He met my eyes. The blankness was gone. In its place was ... well, it wasn't quite the warmth and teasing I thought of as his usual expression. It was something else, something I couldn't quite get a read on.

"You're right," he finally said. "We were working on being friends. And we do need to plan an engagement party together. So let's try to do both of those things."

I gave him a brisk, business-like nod. "Excellent."

He nodded back, flashed me a half-smile—there was that thing in his eyes I couldn't quite read again—and left the room.

I leaned back against the counter and looked around. I was alone. Everyone else had cleared out. I'd been too wrapped up in my exchange with Scott to notice. I'd accomplished a lot, though.

Give best friend a much-needed pep talk—*check!*

Confront team member and maybe-friend who's been treating you like a robot—*check!*

Keep everything running smoothly re: planning the wedding of the year while also figuring out how to track down the rogue puppy demon—*check, check, check!*

And once I tracked it down, I'd figure out a way to punch it.

I knew I would.

DIARY OF A REFORMED HALF-DEMON PRINCESS: PART 37

By Maisy Kane, Half-Demon Princess Editrix

Morning, my dear flowers of 'Frisco! I'd like to take this opportunity to thank everyone who commented and/or wrote in to compliment me on the glorious Pussy Queen proposal video that will surely be looked back on as the first chapter in our city's greatest romance to ever unfold! Of course, the credit isn't all mine to take. I was merely lucky enough to have my little ol' shop chosen as the site of this historic moment and most credit should go to my dear friends Evie Tanaka and Nate Jones for deciding there was no better place! #natevie4evah!

And yes, to answer one of the biggest FAQs coming my way: *of course* you can count on me to provide the latest and greatest updates about what is sure to be the wedding of the century! As you all know by now, our darling bride-to-be was spotted shopping for a gown at Indie Fashion Market (which she heard about thanks to a tip from yours truly!) and the situation got a little out of control. Ladies, I know a wedding is a big deal, but it sounds like some of you in the bridal population of San Francisco are taking things to extreme levels! Let's learn a lesson from Evie and harness that power for good! She's always so wonderfully down to earth, with the Chucks and the messy hair and, well . . . it's refreshing to see that in both a bride and a superheroine! Take note: you don't have to be an over-the-top, glitter-encrusted diva to be beloved by an entire city! Better to be your most relatable, likable self!

You can catch video of the entire bridal tent incident on our Pussy Queen YouTube channel! Watch and thrill as Evie finds her dream dress, only to have it nearly ripped away from her! Aveda Jupiter, Evie's newly minted maid of honor was also on the scene, using her trademark intimidation tactics to try to get the crowd under control. Constructive criticism, A. Jupes: you catch more flies with honey! Evie would be the first to tell you that.

COMMENTS

HaightHoney2000: I saw this on YouTube! That one bride was all up in Evie's biz-nass over a dress and then that other lady's amazing hair power took over?! Luckily it all seemed to be a misunderstanding and Evie is way too gracious to get in a true brawl with anyone—even if it is over a to-die-for dress!

IWantToElope: Was that a Marcus Wong our adorbs Miss Tanaka was wearing? The shape looked like one of his!

QuirkyBride: Don't think so—I've practically memorized his catalog from this season in anticipation of my appt at his salon next week!!!

IWantToElope: Ooooooh, luuuuuuuuucky!

HaightHoney2000: I love that Evie seems so sweet and *normal*.

QuirkyBride: She needs to give her maid of honor a few tips in that area. I heard from fellow brides on the scene that Aveda totally cut the line—flounced up to the front like she owned the place and started doling out orders to everyone! Bullied a security guard, even! Poor Evie must've been soooo embarrassed!

IWantToElope: Maybe that's why she got upset. Aveda put way too much pressure on her and stressed her out! Who wouldn't have a bit of a meltdown?!

HaightHoney2000: Ugh, that's the last thing anyone needs, a pushy maid of honor who wants to steal your glory! Aveda needs to learn that there's only room for one diva per wedding and that diva is THE BRIDE.

CHAPTER SEVEN

I MAY HAVE checked off a bunch of important tasks on my mental list, but there were certain things a list just couldn't account for. Like my mother, who decided to show up on our doorstep the next day.

"Oh . . . uh . . . Mom," I said. It wasn't much of a greeting, but she'd taken me by surprise. She stared back at me, unblinking and still. Even her tight formation of black curls, the success perm so many Asian moms adopt in later middle age (Evie and I referred to it as Asian Old Lady Helmet Hair and had made a pact that we would never let each other succumb to it) remained unmoved by the San Francisco breeze. For a moment, I had the wild thought that she was a statue rather than my actual mother. But then she looked me up and down, and I came to my senses. No statue could possibly summon a look that disapproving.

"Anne," she said, brandishing a small, carefully wrapped package, "I have brought Evie an engagement present."

"Another one?" I stepped to the side so she could bustle her way into the Victorian. "She got the oranges you sent over yesterday. We've barely made a dent in them."

I was already scanning my brain, trying to think of how I could get her in and out in the most efficient manner. I had about a million maid-of-honor tasks to get through, including figuring out catering for the engagement party, and Rose was supposed to come by at some point to discuss further steps in incorporeal puppy demon hunting, and then there was my mid-afternoon workout, which I had envisioned being half an hour longer than usual to account for—

"Anne," my mother said, cutting into my runaway train of thought. "What happened yesterday? At the bridal tent?"

"What?" I said, wondering if I'd heard right. "How do you know about that?"

"I read about it on the internet," she sniffed, frowning at me. "And watched the video. I really don't understand why you always feel the need to be so *aggressive*."

"E-excuse me?" I sputtered, trying to calm the sea of frustration rising in my gut. Of course her interpretation of what happened in the bridal tent was going to cast me in the most unfavorable light possible. Even though, it could be argued, I'd saved the day.

"Being a good maid of honor means everything is in service of the bride," my mother continued. "Why didn't you ask Evie how she felt rather than giving in to your temper and moving people out of the way?"

"I'm sorry," I said, as frustration continued to surge through me like a particularly insidious poison, "but I was kind of busy trying to save my best friend from setting everything on fire—no time to stop and have an in-depth conversation about feelings."

"Always so dramatic," my mother *tsk*-ed, shaking her head. "That temper of yours has never done you any favors. And it especially won't do you any favors when you're in a dangerous situation—"

"I'm in dangerous situations every day of my life," I blurted out, finally letting my frustration boil over. Despite my parents' best efforts, I'd never quite mastered the stereotypical Asian repression of feelings. My stew of emotions was like . . . well, a hurricane. I could never seem to tame it, shove it down, or keep it from completely destroying the emotional landscape around me. "And I was taking Evie's feelings into consideration because I'm pretty sure she was having the feeling of wanting to not be assaulted by an out-of-control Bridezilla!"

My mother pressed her lips into a thin line. "This is a very important position Evie has entrusted you with. You would do well to—"

"To control myself and not go all hurricane on her, I know," I said, trying to keep the growl out of my voice. I started stomping toward the kitchen, motioning for my mother to follow. "Come on, Mom. Let's go give Evie your present so you can be on your way. I'm sure you have lots of other important things to do today."

I burst into the kitchen to find Evie and Bea facing off against each other, bodies rigid with tension.

Apparently it was Bring Your Family Issues to Work Day at HQ.

"But why can't I perform my karaoke medley of riot gr-rrl classics at your wedding?" Bea said, her voice twisting into a whine. "I've been preparing for weeks—"

"You can't have been preparing for weeks," Evie said through gritted teeth. I could tell she was trying desperately to keep her cool. I guess that was better than her being all freaked-out about the bridal tent and her fire power. Sort of. "I only got engaged a couple days ago."

"And I've been preparing for that moment for weeks," Bea countered. "Because I knew Nate was going to propose. I knew I had to be *ready*."

"So perform it for me in private," Evie said. "If it's really just for me—"

"It's meant to be sung to a crowd," Bea said firmly, crossing her arms over her chest. I felt a sudden wave of irritation coursing through me—Bea's power at work again—and noticed Evie go a little pale. "And I don't understand why you're being so weird about it."

"I'm not being weird. I just—"

"Oh, for fuck's sake," I blurted out. "You so are."

Both sisters swiveled to look at me. I realized they'd been so locked in their argument, they hadn't heard us come in. Behind me, my mother cleared her throat, and I could practically hear what was going through her mind.

Always so dramatic.

Don't be aggressive.

I felt the frustration and emotional stew surging through me again, and I couldn't stop myself from striding over and planting myself between Evie and Bea. I couldn't seem to figure out how to communicate effectively with my mother, but I could so clearly see what was going wrong between them, and dammit, I wouldn't be doing my good maid-of-honor duty if I stood by and watched it happen. And anyway, Evie's outright avoidance of this particular issue really, really needed to be dealt with before the wedding.

I turned to Evie, giving her my best imperious look. "Tell her."

She paled further. "Wh-what?"

"Yeah, what?" Bea chimed in. "Tell me *what*?"

"Anne," my mother admonished, stepping into the kitchen. "Really. Must you cause drama—"

"I'm not *causing* anything," I exclaimed, my frustration bubbling over yet again. "Evie. You've avoided this for long enough. And it's going to get worse the longer you avoid it and you know that. So. Tell. Her."

Evie gnawed furiously at her lower lip, her expression slowly slackening. "Okay, okay. Bea. You . . . kind of have a superpower."

Bea's eyes looked like they were about to pop out of her head. "I have *what*?"

"There's no 'kind of' about it," I said, impatience getting the better of me. "You have an actual superpower. We've been calling it reverse empathy. Basically, you can project your emotional state onto other people. And you apparently got a level-up when that last portal opened, because you're the one who shattered Shasta's force field when you screamed during the Pussy Queen battle, leading us to believe that if you vocalize your emotional state in a certain way . . . well, you can do even bigger things. Which is why Evie doesn't want you to karaoke a fifteen-minute set of pure rage at all her closest friends and family. Which makes sense."

I stopped to take a breath, nearly slumping over from the verbal vomit I'd let loose with. I could practically feel my mother's disapproving gaze boring into the back of my head. I didn't know what I'd done wrong this time, but I was pretty sure she'd find *something*.

Bea was speechless, looking from me to Evie and back again. "Is that . . . is that true?" She squeaked. Her voice was tremulous and her bottom lip quivered, like she couldn't figure out if she was supposed to cry or laugh or both.

"It is true," Evie said, low and measured. She glanced at me with an expression I couldn't quite read. "I didn't figure it out until the final battle with Shasta. And then I was waiting for the right moment to tell you." She twisted her hands together, nervousness surfacing in her eyes. "I know that with my power, it was such a burden for so long, and I didn't want to put all of that on you. You've been through so much—"

"And that means . . ." Bea interrupted, cocking her head to the side in wonder, "that means I saved the day? With Shasta? I mean, kind of. Or I at least helped?"

A surprised smile overtook Evie's face. "Well, yeah. You totally helped save the day."

"Holy shit." Bea grinned. "Holy. Shit. I'm gonna be a totes amazeballs *superhero*. Just like my sister!"

She lunged forward, all gangly teenage limbs, and I hastily ducked out of the way to allow her a clear path to Evie.

"Come on, Mom," I said, inching out of the room as Bea engulfed Evie in a hug. "Let's give them a moment to be all sisterly."

"But my gift," my mother said, waving her package insistently.

"I'll be sure to pass it on to her," I said, taking the package from her.

"Oh, wait, Aveda!" Bea exclaimed, wriggling free from Evie's embrace. "I meant to tell you, someone sent in an appearance inquiry!"

"Really?" I said, surprised. All of the business with the wedding and the puppy demon had distracted me from my burgeoning personal appearance empire. Not that it was much of an empire yet.

"Yeah," Bea said, her eyes rolling skyward as she tried to recall the details. "Um. You know what, I think it was Cake My Day. Can't remember the exact occasion, but I'm sure it's something fabulous. I'll forward you the specifics."

"Excellent," I said briskly. "Evie, perhaps we can discuss our strategy for the appearance later this afternoon."

"I do remember the email suggested that maybe Evie could use her fire power for a live flambé demonstration," Bea said.

"Oooh, I love that," I said. "Did they have any suggestions for me?"

"Um . . ." Bea's eyes darted back and forth. "I don't remember the whole request, so. I'll have to check?"

That told me everything I needed to know. I tried not to visibly deflate, even as I felt my mother's eyes boring into my back.

"You know what, guys, I'm really not up to doing the whole personal appearance thing right now," Evie piped up. And I noticed she'd gone a little pale again. "After the bridal tent, I'm not sure . . ." She trailed off and I realized she was worried, once again, about an unseen force taking hold and making her lose control of the fire power. Which, come to think of it, maybe wasn't the worst thing to be worried about, considering there was a rogue puppy demon on the loose.

But how could I restore her confidence? How could I get her to let go of the fear and claim her rightful place as both an awesome superheroine and a badass bride?

My eyes flicked from her to Bea and back again and then suddenly, I had it. An idea.

When she was my personal assistant, Evie had hated my Idea Face. My Idea Face, she claimed, never led anywhere good. In fact, it usually led to her being covered in demon slime or me throwing a fit about something or both of us in ridiculous outfits. But this time would be different. This time, my Idea Face was absolutely going to make her life better.

"Of course," I said to her. "I can handle this one on my own. But we should still get together later to discuss the engagement party. There are so many details to go over."

"Sure, Annie, sounds good," she said, giving me a half-smile. But her eyes were hooded and I couldn't quite get a read on what she was really thinking. Maybe she was still dwelling on the bridal tent incident. Or maybe she was irritated I'd just accelerated the "timeline" she kept referring to when it came to talking to Bea. It was for the best, though. She'd see that once she had time to process everything.

"I really want to keep it simple, though," she said. "Just like the wedding. Nothing too complicated. Nothing too fancy."

"Of course," I responded. But I was already thinking of flower arrangements and catering and decorations and ... okay, so my vision might not exactly be "simple," but I was pretty sure this would be like Evie's gorgeous wedding gown. She hadn't known she'd wanted it until she'd witnessed the full glory of how it looked on her body. She couldn't buy into the fabulousness until she actually saw it. And I'd make sure she saw it.

My mother, apparently bored with our talk of personal appearances, engagement parties, and superpowers, cleared her throat.

"Sorry, Mrs. Chang, didn't mean to ignore you," Evie said, smiling at her. "Bea and I had some things to work out. Did I hear you say you brought a gift?"

"Yes," my mother said eagerly, snatching the gift out of my hands. "Getting engaged is such a big milestone in a young woman's life, I thought you deserved an extra present."

"How nice," Evie said, taking the package from her. "Why don't I open it while I walk you to the door? I know you must have a busy day ahead and we've already kept you here long enough."

She winked at me as she took my mother's arm and steered her toward the door. I felt a momentary rush of warmth as our near-telepathy snapped into place, that bond that always seemed to make itself known when one of us needed it most. That feeling was swiftly replaced by annoyance as my mother murmured "so thoughtful" under her breath and cast a disdainful gaze my way. The message was clear: *Unlike you, Anne.*

If there was one person who consistently brought Annie Chang to the surface, it was my mother. It was like every bit of training, every safeguard I'd put in place, every painstaking second I'd spent making myself into an awesome superheroine evaporated on the spot.

Annoyance melted into something else entirely as Evie led my mom out of the kitchen, arms linked, heads bent together. They looked so close. Like a perfect mother-daughter duo. If I'd snapped a photo, it would have been worthy of a greeting card.

I'd been cropped out again, and the photo was better for it.

I suppose it was no surprise that my mom might prefer a daughter like Evie, someone who was kind and thoughtful instead of loud and hurricane-like. I shook off my sudden stew of feelings and turned to Bea. I couldn't get distracted. It was time to put my latest idea/mission in motion.

"So. Bea," I said. "Now that you know about your reverse empathy, I think you should get some practice actually using it."

Her brow crinkled. "Practice? I mean, I'm not even one hundred percent sure how it works."

"This is the perfect way of figuring that out," I barreled on. "It's just a little thing, a way of getting your feet wet. When Evie's in the room, see if you can project a general feeling of calm. See if you can project it out enough to soothe her."

Bea's brow crinkled further. "Without telling her? 'Cause that has definite sisterly piss-off potential."

"That's why you keep it subtle," I said. "So she won't even be able to tell you're doing it. She's about to be a bride and we have to work as a team to make sure she maintains emotional balance. Especially in the face of an invisible puppy demon. It's for her own good."

"Well . . ." Bea hesitated, her eyes conflicted as her desire to maintain honest sisterly relations warred with her scientist's desire to experiment with her new talent. "I guess I can do that. Like you said, I'll keep it subtle."

"Perfect." I nodded, triumphant. Once again, I had managed to accomplish a lot in a fairly short timespan.

Line up more personal appearances to ensure continued validity as a superheroine—*check!*

Figure out a way to keep best friend calm and bridal ready—*check!*

Maintain emotional equilibrium in the face of an unexpected and extremely aggravating visit from my mother—

Hmm. That one was still *check pending.* Maybe it always would be.

Chapter eight

FOR THE NEXT few days, I kept myself on high alert, just in case the unseen puppy demon decided to rear its incorporeal head. The rest of the team, meanwhile, threw themselves into heavy info-gathering mode. But nothing showed up on the scans from Rose's team, and our inbox stayed empty. We talked to the redhead bride again, but she had no new feelings of unbridled rage to report. Meanwhile, Bea took it upon herself to track down and interview the various citizens who'd reported their own feelings of rage during demon attacks in the past. But they, too, had nothing new to offer.

The threat hung in the air, persistent, menacing, uncertain. I kept steady watch for it, but I was also determined to stay on task with my maid-of-honor duties. I made feverish lists, appointments, and spreadsheets of things that needed to be done. Or, more accurately, I enlisted Bea's help in making said lists, since I was unaccustomed to performing such assistant-like tasks. That had been Evie's job.

Still, I was confident in my ability to make the most fabulous choices in all facets of wedding planning. In addition to telekinesis, I prided myself on possessing the superpower of impeccable taste.

I hadn't been able to talk much to Evie herself, though. Every time I tried to approach her about the wedding, her bedroom door was shut or she slipped away before I could show her one of my many spreadsheets or she just straight up didn't answer my texts. I assumed she was processing everything: being engaged, the bridal tent incident, finally telling Bea about her superpower. It was a lot, and the good friend I was set on becoming knew it was probably best to give her space.

Three days after our apparent truce, Scott and I were about to go through our first major test as co-engagement party planners: cake tasting. We were crowded around one of the white marble tables at Cake My Day with a bounty of sugary treats spread out in front of us.

After Bea forwarded me the details of the personal appearance request at Cake My Day (which were quite scant—just the time of the event and the suggestion for Evie's flambé demonstration), I'd had a brainstorm. According to Evie, we were still set for money for a while. So instead of having Bea bill for my usual appearance fee, I'd requested the bakery provide desserts for the engagement party and wedding. They'd get excellent product placement at the parties of the year, and we'd get the city's most elegant desserts for these sure-to-be-epic events. Win-win.

Letta Wilcox, the bakery's ever-mopey owner, agreed to the idea immediately and even conveniently scheduled things so we could come by for the tasting right before my fabulous appearance.

"So you've got red velvet with cream cheese frosting, vanilla with buttercream, and my personal favorite, double dark chocolate with mascarpone whipped cream," Letta was saying. She pointed to each cake sample in turn, her monotone delivery at odds with the sweet swirls of pastry in front of us. I tried not to stare too longingly at the pillowy cakes topped off with the bakery's signature sparkle-infused frosting. I'd fallen off my usual superheroine diet plan while I'd been injured, but I'd managed to get back on the mostly carb-less horse recently, even with all the multi-course breakfasts. Much as the public adored me, they also had a tendency to take notice whenever one of my costumes started looking even a tiny bit snug. Although maybe they wouldn't notice as much these days since they were so captivated by Evie's impending nuptials and badass fire power.

Still. It would do me no good to slack. Excellent discipline was a hallmark of my superheroine success, and I would do well to remember that. Even if I did have the occasional craving for sugar and starch, for chocolate and French fries, for my mom's fried rice and xiaolongbao.

"Thank you, Letta," I said. "And really, excellent job with the remodel."

Cake My Day had been home to a vicious demonic cupcake attack right before I'd hurt my ankle. The cupcakes had trashed the place, but now it seemed restored to its former glory, gleaming white surfaces with gold accents and sparkly pastries everywhere. Even a few of Letta's beloved porcelain unicorns had made a triumphant return. Not all the clientele was back, however—other than me and Scott, the only two people in the place were a pair of ladies huddled around a table near the back. Like us, they were sampling a variety of cakes. I took note of their stylish dresses, red and white numbers that appeared to be from the fifties, the skirts poufed out thanks to liberal use of petticoats. I admired people getting dressed up for seemingly mundane outings. Perhaps they would stick around for my appearance.

Letta responded to my compliment with one of her noncommittal shrugs. "It was all the construction guys. I didn't really do anything."

"Always a big bundle of joy, that one," I muttered as she shuffled off.

Scott chuckled and I tried not to let my surprise show. Even though I'd basically forced him out of his detached demeanor, I still wasn't used to getting more than a blank look.

He offered me a fork. "Ladies first?"

"No, you go." I waved a hand and picked up one of the spreadsheets Bea had made for me. "Let's see. For the engagement party, we still need to finalize flower arrangements, decorations, and make sure the invitations get sent out on time."

"So we need to do all the same stuff for the engagement party as we do for the actual wedding?" Scott forked up a huge bite of red velvet and cocked an eyebrow at me.

"The engagement party should be like a preview of the wedding, so yes," I said. "Maisy will surely write it up, as will other outlets. It must be perfectly executed."

"Hmm." Scott licked frosting off his fork, then pointed it at me. "And when you say invite list—I mean, we're really just inviting the people who live with us, right? Evie, Nate, Bea, Lucy? Can't we just tell them where to show up?"

"I thought I would include Rose as well. She and Lucy have a mutual attraction." I shrugged. "I think they could be a good match. They complement each other—that whole opposites attract thing."

Scott laughed, his eyes widening in disbelief. "Wait. You, Annie Chang, are playing cupid?"

My spine stiffened, and I gave him a cool look. "Why is that funny?"

He grinned at me, shook his head, and shoveled more cake into his mouth. "Because you've always been firmly anti-romance."

"I have not!"

"You were the only eighth grader in history who tried to stage a protest against 'any and all Valentine's celebrations' at our junior high."

"That's because those 'celebrations' were *unfair*," I sputtered. "The administration did away with the perfectly good rule they had going in elementary school, where if you were handing out Valentines, you had to give them to everybody."

"And what?" he snorted. "Nobody gave you any?"

"No," I shot back, my face getting hot. "Nobody gave *Evie* any."

His grin faltered.

"I mean, not nobody," I corrected. "We both got a few.

But she didn't get one from that idiot Jay Tran—you remember, she was desperately in love with him for years."

"I remember. I took her to prom when he somehow 'forgot' to ask her."

"Right." I felt my flush intensify, my cheeks burning up. I remembered because that prom date—and the fact that they'd ended it by losing their virginity to each other—had triggered years of jealousy in me. Even though Evie had told me over and over again that the sex between them had been dreadful, I couldn't quite shake the idea that she'd always been his first choice, and when he'd kissed me, it had been because she wasn't there.

"She was devastated," I said. "I couldn't just sit there and do *nothing*."

"I stand corrected. Your protest was actually very . . . nice."

"I am capable of being nice," I said, going back to my spreadsheet. "No need to sound so surprised. And don't talk with your mouth full—it's disgusting."

He gave me a big, cakey grin, teeth ringed with crumbs and frosting. "Yes, ma'am," he said. With his mouth full.

"You are a child," I said, suppressing my own smile. I paused and studied the grid Bea had made for me. "I was also thinking," I said hesitantly, "that I could invite my parents."

Scott nearly choked on his mouthful of cake.

"Your parents," he said, sounding out each syllable. "Don't they always make you feel bad about yourself?"

"Why are you complaining?" I said, keeping my tone light and shoving aside the memory of my mother getting under my skin just three days ago. "They love *you*."

It was true. I may have always disappointed them, but my parents had taken an instant liking to the scrawny little white boy Evie and I started bringing home with us in sixth grade. He charmed them like he did everyone, with an easy grin and those eyes that never stopped teasing. He was the only person in history who could get away with calling my mom "Mrs. C," like some kind of old-school sitcom reject.

"I can't fault them for their excellent taste in their daughter's white dude sidekicks," Scott said, flashing me that easy grin. "But you'll be stressed out from planning this whole event, and we still have that puppy demon floating around. I don't know if it's the best thing for you—"

"I know what's best for me," I said, in a tone that indicated the subject was closed. "Anyway. They care about Evie. She's the closest thing I have to a sister. And it might be nice for her to have some parental type figures around since hers . . . aren't."

I made a check mark next to my parents' names. It was what was best for Evie. For the event. And that's what was important. I felt Scott's eyes boring into my skull, so I made some other random marks on the spreadsheet, pretending to study it further.

"Annie—"

"I don't want to talk about it!" I snapped. "It will be fine."

"No, I just meant—will you put that thing down and look at me, please?"

I lowered my spreadsheet and looked at him warily. He held up a forkful of dark chocolate cake and smiled again, but his eyes were softer, less teasing.

"I was going to ask if you want to try some of this? You haven't had any." He waved the fork under my nose. "It's really good."

"I trust your judgment." I batted the fork away. "I don't need to taste it."

Undeterred, he offered the fork to me again. My eyes couldn't help but lock on the cake. It looked all moist and melty, with blobs of frosting oozing around it. The scent of chocolate wafted up, sweet and decadent. Dammit. Dark chocolate was my favorite: that undertone of bitterness, that hidden depth of rich flavor.

"Come on." He waved it closer to my face. "Just one bite."

"I have to fit into my bridesmaid dress," I protested.

He brought the fork closer. Now the scent of chocolate felt like it was shooting straight to my taste buds. I could practically feel the gooey cake/frosting combo on my tongue. My mouth watered.

"You work out like ninety hours a day," he said. "You'll be fine."

"There aren't ninety hours in a day, genius." I'd meant for that to sound cutting, but it came out breathy and hushed, almost like I was . . . turned on.

Which I most certainly wasn't. Not even a little bit.

He leaned in, and I was suddenly very aware of the fact that his chair had scootched up next to mine. How had that happened? I was sure we'd started off sitting on opposite sides of the table. Why was he so close? The scent of the cake mingled with what I knew was the scent of his skin. Chocolate, ocean, sunscreen, frosting. It was like summer and dessert and everything good, and I couldn't help it. I licked my lips.

"It's so good," he said. "It melts in your mouth."

He leaned in closer and I got that heady, drugged feeling, that same feeling I'd had in the closet. Like I was all nerve endings, incapable of processing logical thought. Why did I let myself get this way around him? Why did I let him get close to me at all?

"Just one bite," he repeated. His voice had gotten a little rough, a little husky. Or maybe that was my wild, fevered, all-nerve-endings imagination taking over.

I gave in. I parted my lips and let him slide the fork in my mouth and . . . *god*. Okay, yes. It was that good. It absolutely melted in my mouth. I savored the taste—every crumb, every bit of frosting, every note of dark sweetness. A tiny moan escaped my throat.

Scott slid the fork out and gave me a satisfied smile, but there wasn't a trace of smugness. No, it was earnest and open. The kind of smile I hadn't seen from him in a good, long while.

"Oh," he said. "You've got a little bit of frosting—here, I'll get it." He reached over and swiped his thumb over my lower lip. The warmth of his touch, the fact that he was touching me at all, the fact that I could still taste chocolate . . . everything intensified the sensations overwhelming me and I did the only thing that felt right in the moment.

I flicked my tongue over his thumb.

We both froze. I heard his breath catch a little.

"I was trying to get the frosting," I said.

My god. Was that the dumbest thing I could have said or what?

But I couldn't help it. He always made me feel like my brain was leaking out of my ears, like I didn't possess any superpowers at all. Like I was most definitely back in the Annie Chang place.

He ignored my dumb reply and locked his gaze with mine, his breathing going a little uneven. His eyes were suddenly very serious, at complete odds with how they usually looked—playful, teasing. Or how they had looked recently, when he'd given me the cold shoulder. No, I'd only seen him look this particular brand of serious one other time: the moment before he kissed me all those years ago. It was an irresistible flicker of intensity, a hint that underneath his easygoing exterior, he felt so much more.

I stared back at him. His thumb was still brushing against my lower lip, a touch that was feather light, but felt like the hottest brand ever.

Was he going to kiss me now?

Would he taste like chocolate?

Would I—

"Aveda?"

I nearly jumped out of my skin. Letta was standing over me, mopey stare in place. How long had she been there? How had she moved so soundlessly? Or had I tuned everything out while I was . . . what was I doing?

I blinked wordlessly at Letta, trying to gather my thoughts. Scott had removed his hand from my lips, so that helped.

"You asked me to tell you when we were fifteen minutes out from your appearance," Letta droned on. "And, well. We are."

"Of course!" I exclaimed, way too loudly. "I'm ready. Or I will be ready. In fifteen minutes."

I sat up straighter and smoothed my hair into its power ponytail. Shaking off those last remnants of unsure, unsuperpowered Annie Chang so I could give my adoring public what they wanted: Aveda Jupiter in all of her fabulousness.

My public was not as adoring as I'd expected.

They were also much louder, stickier, and a good two decades younger than I'd expected.

"THIS IS BORING!" one of them shrieked, smearing sparkly frosting all over her ruffly pink dress. "SUPER-HERO LADY IS BOOOOOOORIIIIING!"

That started up a chant of "BO-RING! BO-RING!" amongst the partygoers. Because, of course.

"Letta," I hissed, as I surveyed the unruly mob in front of me. "You didn't tell me this was a *children's birthday party*."

"You didn't ask." She gave me a mildly injured look. "The personal appearances form on your website doesn't have a place for that info. All it asks for is time, date, and if the facility in question has an adequate supply of fire extinguishers on hand."

"Ugh." I couldn't think of anything more eloquent to say. She was right. I'd have to get Bea to fix that.

In the meantime, I'd have to deal with . . . this.

I studied the mob again. It wasn't actually that much of a mob. There were only about fifteen of them. Fifteen sugared-up, hyper five-year-olds, who had probably been expecting . . . I don't know. What did five-year-olds like?

"Mommy, I thought we were getting Queen Elsa of Arendelle!" the birthday girl shrieked. She was the one who'd been smearing frosting all over her dress. She regarded me with narrowed eyes. "She is *not* Queen Elsa of Arendelle."

No, I was not. Though I was surprised these kids had apparently never heard of Aveda Jupiter. Maybe they weren't from San Francisco?

"Elsa is, uh, busy today, sweetie," the birthday girl's mother said in the weariest voice ever. "So we got you a real life superhero. Isn't that cool?" She turned to me, wild-eyed, like, *Back me up, here?*

Birthday Girl, refusing to be placated, crossed her arms over her chest and shook her head furiously. "I want a *cool* superhero. I want *Evie*. Not . . ." She eyed me up and down, disdain leaking from her every pore. " . . . her friend."

Oh. So she did know who I was. Sort of.

"Evie is busy today, too," I said, scouring my brain for something "cool" to say. Yes, that's right. Suddenly, my greatest wish was to appear cool—or at least not totally dorky—to small children. "She and Elsa are, um, hanging out. Doing cool things together."

I heard a snort of laughter and jerked my head up to cast a glare at its source: Scott, who, for whatever reason, had wanted to stay and watch, even though I'd told him repeatedly that he was free to head back to HQ. The two poufy dress-wearing women had also opted to stay, though they were still deeply involved in their cake tasting and weren't paying much attention to me trying valiantly to make the best of what was threatening to become a truly humiliating situation.

"Oh! Kay!" I said loudly, clapping my hands together and plastering a huge smile on my face. "So. Even though Evie's not here to set anything on fire, I have some pretty cool powers to show you."

"Like *what*?" Birthday Girl said, tapping her foot impatiently.

"Like this." I reached out with my mental feathers and grasped several packages from the teetering mountain of

Birthday Girl's gift pile. I concentrated hard and floated them through the air, making them dance in formation. I was gratified to hear a few "oohs" and "ahhs" from my kid audience. *Yes.* I could get through this.

"Excuse me, Miss!" One of the poufy-dress-wearing women at the other table called out to Letta, punctuating the enthralled silence that had fallen. "This red velvet doesn't taste very *red*, if you know what I mean. Can we get another serving?"

"Red velvet is actually buttermilk and cocoa powder with red food coloring," Letta said, in her usual monotone. "What really makes it is the cream cheese frosting."

"Yes, well, that's quite lacking as well," the woman sniffed. "And I must insist on nothing short of the best for my wedding."

Yeesh. Another Bridezilla?

I blocked her out and carefully lowered the presents back to the gift table. A smattering of semi-enthusiastic applause rippled through the kids, and I gave a little bow.

"That was fine," Birthday Girl—the only kid not clapping—said. She raised an unimpressed eyebrow. "Can you lift anything heavier? Can you lift a *person*?"

"Yes, of course," I said, trying like mad to excise the haughty tone that seemed to be creeping into my voice. "If you go to the Aveda Jupiter, Inc. YouTube page, there are multiple videos that show me in action, moving citizens out of danger and—"

"Whatever," Birthday Girl interrupted. She stomped forward, planting her hands on her hips. "Can you lift *me*?"

I hesitated, realizing I should have totally anticipated that question. I glanced at Birthday Girl's mom. Surely she'd shut the whole thing down? But she just shrugged.

"It's her birthday," she said. "She can have whatever she wants."

"Yeah!" Birthday Girl said, giving me a mean smile. "And I want to fly."

"Well . . . all right." I wasn't sure why I was so nervous.

I'd moved plenty of actual people before—but in those cases it had been instinctual, necessary for their safety, and hadn't come with such obvious liability issues. I reached out with my mental feathers and wrapped them around Birthday Girl, lifting her a little ways off the ground.

"YEAH!" she screamed. "Higher!"

I raised her a little bit higher.

"HIGHER!" She insisted. "I said I want to *fly*."

I tightened my hold, making sure it was secure, and lifted her up higher, higher, higher—until she was nearly touching the ceiling.

"Yessssssss!" she shrieked.

"I said I wanted another sample of red velvet, bitch!"

The words cracked through the air, disrupting my concentration. Bridezilla again. Or maybe Cakezilla? I tried to block her out. Birthday Girl was *finally* having a good time, and I didn't want to ruin it.

"Carol," I heard her companion say, "we can get more cake, we just have to—"

"No!" Carol growled. I heard a smacking sound and then glass shattering against the floor.

"Wheeeee!" screamed Birthday Girl as I moved her around a bit, trying to simulate an actual flying experience. "Best birthday ever!" I doubled down on my focus, blocking out everything except my mental feathers, my hold, and Birthday Girl floating through the air.

"Like I said, I'm happy to provide you with additional samples," Letta said to Cakezilla Carol. "But you really need to settle down."

"Settle. Down?!" Carol bellowed. "This is my wedding we're talking about. A once-in-a-lifetime event—"

"Um, this is actually your third wedding," her friend murmured.

I swooped Birthday Girl lower, close to the ground, trying to give her a bit of a ride. She giggled.

"—and I will not have my guests eating this *garbage*—"

I'd been concentrating so hard, I hadn't realized Cakezilla

Carol was on the move. But suddenly she was crashing into my field of vision, suddenly she was blocking Birthday Girl from my view, and suddenly I felt my mental feathers evaporate, unable to hold something I couldn't see.

"Ahhhhhhhhhh!!!" Birthday Girl let out a piercing scream and I heard an ugly-sounding *crunch* and oh no, no, *no* . . .

Chaos erupted immediately.

Usually I'm the first to act when chaos erupts. But this time, I was rooted to the spot, my vision clouding over, caught in some kind of frozen fugue state. I heard Birthday Girl's mom screaming, all the kids screaming, Birthday Girl's inconsolable wails, Cakezilla Carol stomping off, Cakezilla Carol's friend trying to placate her . . .

And all I could think was, *Goddammit, Aveda Jupiter. You really fucked up this time.*

I was finally snapped out of my fugue state by a familiar voice: gentle, mellow, soothing: "See, it's just a scratch—she'll be fine." Scott.

I shook my head, forcing the room to come back into focus around me. Scott was kneeling next to the sprawled out Birthday Girl, his hands cradling her elbow, and speaking very sincerely to her distraught mother as the other kids looked on.

"Scott . . ." I forced my legs to move, crossing the room to them. "I—I'm so sorry," I said to Birthday Girl's mother. "I lost my hold, I couldn't see her and—I'm sorry."

"It's all right, Annie." Scott again. Still with that soothing voice. "She wasn't too far off the ground—her elbow got knocked around, but I used a Level One healing spell and now she's just fine."

Birthday Girl beamed at him adoringly and who could blame her? He was easy to adore.

"To be safe, take it easy for a few days," Scott said to Birthday Girl, giving her his charming, lopsided grin. "Even Queen Elsa needs her rest. No more flying, okay?"

"No flying!" she agreed with a giggle.

"Now that that's taken care of, can we get back to what's important?!" a voice bellowed behind us, and I whipped around to see Cakezilla Carol advancing on Letta.

"I need more red velvet," she growled. *"Now."*

"Hey!" I darted over to them, planting myself between Letta and Carol. I may not have Scott's amazing soothing powers that worked on the brattiest of five-year-olds, but I could at least handle this. "This is no place for that kind of behavior," I said, giving Carol my best imperious look. "Why don't you cool off? Take a walk around the block." I inclined my head at Carol's friend, who scurried to her side and laid a hand on her arm.

"No." Carol shoved her friend so hard, she stumbled backward. "Get out of my way," she hissed at me.

I crossed my arms over my chest. "I don't think so."

"Raaaaaaaaaaaaahhhhhh!" Carol let out a cry of anger so raw, it sounded like an animal baying at the moon. I was so startled by the sound, I didn't react fast enough when she charged me with enough force to knock my body out of the way.

Then she went for Letta's throat.

CHAPTER NINE

"YOU CAN QUESTION them if you want." Rose gestured to the two disheveled women slumped behind one of Cake My Day's marble tables. The bakery wasn't quite the disaster area it'd been after weathering a demonic attack, but it was still a mess, cake and broken plate pieces all over the floor. Carol, the woman who'd gone after Letta, stared into space and toyed with the can of Sprite in front of her, as if tapping it in just the right way would unleash the secrets of the universe. Hard to believe that a mere thirty minutes ago, she'd been wreaking pastry-related havoc. Her friend, whose name was Gwen, rubbed her back in a soothing fashion.

I'd managed to jump up and get Carol in a chokehold before she reached Letta. As soon as I'd gotten an arm around her neck, she'd gone limp and then seemed confused. Just like Evie and the redhead Bridezilla in the tent.

We'd sent the birthday partiers home, and Scott had called Rose, who hustled over with several members of her team, as well as the scanners and one of the traps she and Bea had been working on—a small gray box that popped open and closed with the touch of a button. Like the scanners, it looked ridiculously old school (and ridiculously *Ghostbusters*-influenced), but I was hoping it would be effective. Rose had detained Carol for questioning and her team was scanning every inch of Cake My Day. So far, they hadn't turned up anything.

Where had our little stray puppy demon gone?

"Letta's not pressing charges," Rose said, nodding

toward the counter area. Letta was cowering behind a towering cookie display, looking like a moderately more alert version of her usual gloomy self.

"Really?" I said. "Cakezilla Carol almost ripped her throat out!"

"She said, and I quote, 'Everyone gets a little worked up over pastry sometimes.'" Rose shrugged in a "what can you do?" sort of way.

"It is sort of not her fault," Scott pointed out. "If we're going with the theory that this was our friend the lost puppy demon again."

"Where did that thing *go*?" I grumbled.

"We'll keep looking," Rose said, gesturing to her team, still hard at work scanning the bakery. "We can't hold her much longer, so if you want to ask her something, do it now. But honestly, she mostly just seems confused."

I frowned. "Then I doubt there's anything useful I'll turn up."

"You never know," Scott said. "You can be pretty intimidating."

I gave him a look. But I was suddenly suppressing a smile again, like when he'd given me that dumb cakey grin. And my heart was suddenly beating a little bit faster, like it had when I'd seen him tending so gently to Birthday Girl.

Oh, no. Nope. That definitely would *not* do. Especially not when there was evil to be vanquished, a rogue puppy demon to pursue, and maid-of-honoring to be accomplished in the midst of it all. No time for sappy, Annie Chang–style feelings.

"Let's take them somewhere quiet," I said briskly. "Like Letta's office in the back. I'll try asking them to go through the experience again. Maybe something in their responses will give us a clue. And Scott . . ." I paused, a wisp of an idea floating through my brain. "Why don't you move around the room with one of the scanners while I'm talking to them? Maybe the puppy demon will make a return appearance. We'll take the trap with us, too."

"Won't that look weird?" Scott said, as Rose passed him the scanner and trap. "Me pacing, waving that thing around?"

"So be stealthy," I said.

"Stealthy—got it." Scott took the scanner from Rose then flailed his arms around like an air traffic controller. "So like this?"

I put my hands on my hips. "No."

"How about this?" He did a few supremely dorky dance moves, dangling the scanner like a robot arm.

My lips twitched. "No."

"How about—"

"Stop trying to make me laugh!" I blurted out. "This is serious."

He grinned at me—and this time, it was definitely smug. The same grin he'd given me a million times throughout junior high and high school, whenever he'd gotten me to break or giggle or respond to him in a way that let him know he'd gotten under my skin.

"Hey, you wanted to be friends," he said, as if I should have known better.

Let's face it: I should have.

Rose cleared her throat. "So like I said," she began, "we can't hold Carol for much longer, and I really need to wrap things up here—"

"Right," I said. "Sorry. Some people on my team are incapable of behaving in a mature fashion."

I turned away from Scott before he could respond and stalked over to Cakezilla Carol and Gwen.

"Ladies," I said, projecting Aveda Jupiter authority, "if you'll follow me, I'd like us to have a little chat in Letta's office." Cakezilla Carol's eyes widened and she seemed about to protest—but then she gave a meek nod, stood, and shuffled behind Scott and me as we headed into the back area of the bakery. Gwen followed her.

Letta's office was roomy, but dimly lit. A single rickety lamp cast a soft glow over the *Hoarders*-level clutter and the remainder of Letta's porcelain unicorn collection, which was positioned haphazardly all over the room. Unicorns seemed to be shoved into every available corner and shelf, their tiny eyes boring into us from all sides, their rainbow manes flickering in the hazy light in a way that almost seemed eerie. I suppressed a shudder—really, who wanted to conduct an interview surrounded by miniature unicorns?—and gestured for Carol and Gwen to sit in the two chairs in front of the messy desk. I took the seat behind the desk. It just seemed right. Scott positioned himself in the far left corner of the room, cocked an eyebrow at me, then very solemnly patted one of the unicorns on the head. I frowned at him: *Cut it out.* Unfortunately I didn't have quite the level of near-telepathy with him that I had with Evie.

Cakezilla Carol was still clutching the Sprite can in a death grip. The index finger of her other hand started tap-tap-tapping the lid. Gwen kept patting her on the back, trying to soothe her.

"So. Carol," I began.

She reluctantly met my eyes, and I realized that she didn't just look confused—she looked scared. Hmm. I hadn't thought much about how I was going to go about talking to this woman. If she was scared, my trademark Aveda Jupiter Intimidation Tactics probably weren't going to work on her; she'd only retreat further into her shell. She didn't seem to be a fan, so I couldn't use that to my advantage. And I didn't exude a friendly, comforting vibe that would make her feel instantly at home, like we were just a couple of gals chatting in a totally non-threatening manner.

I suddenly wished Evie was there. Because that's exactly what she would do. But everything had happened so fast, and now there was no time to call her, and my unfriendly uncomforting vibe would just have to do.

"So," I said again. "About what happened earlier—"

"I'm sorry!" Carol interrupted. Her finger tap-tap-tapping on the Sprite can picked up in speed. *Taptaptaptap.* "Like I told Sergeant Rorick, I don't know what came over me. One minute, I'm here with my maid of honor, stuffing my face with delightful red velvet. The next, I can't stop focusing on why the red velvet doesn't taste exactly right and how I need it to be exactly right, exactly *perfect* for my big day and . . . and . . ." Her lower lip trembled.

"It's okay, Care," Gwen said. "It's your wedding. Every bride gets a little crazy over her wedding."

I glanced over at Scott. He had moved a fraction to the right and was scanning the area inch by inch, his brow furrowed in concentration. But nothing yet. No light, no beep.

"Have you had any feelings of rage recently?" I asked. "In that out-of-control way?"

Carol shook her head slowly, her Sprite can tapping ceasing for a moment. "Just the usual things," she said. "Like, my future mother-in-law wanted to add seven hundred of her closest friends to the guest list, but I doubled up on yoga classes and felt totally better. Or, you know, the printer I wanted to use for my invitations went out of business and the replacement I found doesn't carry extra thick rose-tinted cream card stock—"

"I told you, the ivory will be great," Gwen said. She was obviously repeating something she'd already had to say a million times.

Something flashed in Carol's eyes. The briefest hint of a feeling that looked a whole lot like anger. It was there and gone in a split second, but I still saw it. I looked over at Scott again. Still scanning. Still nothing. No puppy demons among us. Cakezilla Carol's simmering discontent seemed to belong only to her.

"The ivory will be *acceptable*," Carol corrected, her teeth gritted. Her index finger resumed tapping on the Sprite can. "And barely so. The lower end of acceptable, one might say."

Her voice had taken on a new cast, a different cadence. There was an edge to it that hadn't been there before. It wasn't quite rage, but it was teetering toward something on that spectrum.

Interesting. Could the puppy be here, and we just weren't picking it up on the scanner? And was it about to make Carol go full Cakezilla? I decided to push her a little bit more.

Aveda Jupiter might not be a comforting presence. But she sure as shit knows how to push people's buttons.

"That sounds terrible," I said. "You've probably been dreaming of that rose-tinted cream since you were a little girl—"

"Or since her last wedding," Gwen muttered under her breath.

"—and now you have to settle. Who wants to do that on the most important day of her life?"

Carol nodded, that spark flashing in her eyes again. "Tell me about it. I'm going to have to look at that half-assed ivory all the time in my memory scrapbook."

I leaned forward, trying to match her vehemence. "And every time, you'll be reminded of—"

"Of what a fucking failure my entire stationery strategy was," Carol hissed. "The rose tint was so different, so unique, so *Carol*, and now it's just . . . just . . ."

"Ordinary," I said.

"Ordinary," she spat out, as if it were the worst curse on the planet. "Fucking ordinary."

I sneaked a surreptitious look at Scott. He'd sidled up behind Carol and Gwen and was scanning the area right next to their heads. Carol was too wrapped up in her rant to notice and Gwen was too busy trying to comfort her. Scott met my eyes and gave a small head-shake. Nothing yet. But Carol's rage was definitely festering. There was *something* going on there. Come on, puppy. Show yourself.

"Ordinary," I repeated. "That's almost worse than having an awful, Pinterest-fail wedding, isn't it? Having one that's just—" I made an exaggerated snooze face, as if I was about to fall asleep. "—boring."

"That's totally worse!" shrieked Carol, the spark in her eyes flaring into complete anger. She smacked the Sprite can, sending it flying across the room. Gwen ducked out of the way, and the can smashed into the wall, narrowly missing a few unicorns and sending an eruption of soda fizz everywhere.

"Annie," Scott said. His voice held a note of warning.

I ignored him. I was on the brink of something, I could feel it.

"Calm down, Care," Gwen said, her eyes pleading. "At least you found a dress you really love—"

"Don't get me started on the dress!" Carol screamed.

She leapt to her feet, the flash of anger in her eyes flaring. She slammed both hands on the desk and glared at me, as if it was all my fault.

"You love the dress!" Gwen protested weakly.

Carol's head swiveled to look at her, like something out of *The Exorcist*.

"But ... I ... need ... undergarments!" she bellowed.

I jumped to my feet, slammed my hands on the desk, and matched Carol's wild-eyed glare.

"Look at me, Carol!" I demanded. "Look at me and tell me what you mean by ..."

Had she really just said *undergarments*?

Carol's head swiveled back to me. The rage was practically rolling off of her now, fanning out in a pissed-off aura. I jerked my head frantically at Scott, who'd moved to a different area of the room. He was staring at Carol with a strange, blank expression on his face, as if she had just shared something particularly captivating.

"Scott!" I barked.

He snapped to attention, his eyes clearing, and rushed toward us with the scanner.

"The dress," Carol huffed out, her breath wheezing fast and furious little gasps between each word. "The dress won't fucking hang right unless I have the right *undergarments*!"

BEEP BEEP BEEP! screamed the scanner. Fucking finally. I was so engrossed in my questioning of Carol, the sound startled me and I jumped.

And that's when Carol threw herself over the desk and directly at my face.

I jumped out of the way and she crashed on top of the desk, unseating a whole file cabinet's worth of papers, her arms flailing.

"Annie!" Scott yelled.

"Get back!" I barked at him. "And get Gwen—"

But he was already on it, hauling a screaming Gwen out of Carol's way. Carol recovered and scrambled over the desk, but now I was ready for her. I dodged left, dodged right as she lunged for me, her movements clumsy, her breathing labored. She clearly didn't have any experience fighting, so what was she doing?

Or what was the puppy demon *making* her do?

"Mass-produced underwear is a scourge!" she screamed. "The correct wedding look starts with the foundation and that means *custom fucking lingerie!*"

I dodged her again, then slipped under her flailing arm to position myself behind her.

"You can find plenty of that in San Francisco," I said firmly, slipping one arm around her shoulder and the other under her armpit. "So what's the problem?"

"It's not right!" she screamed. I felt spittle splatter onto my arm as I subdued her, forcing her arms into an upright position so she couldn't get at me. "It's not right!" she repeated. "It's new. It's new and IT'S! NOT! RIGHT!"

I positioned a knee against Carol's back and—with a little help from my telekinesis—slowly lowered her to the ground. She twisted in my grasp, attempting to get free, but it was no use—I'd practiced this hold hundreds of times during self-defense training with Lucy. And my telekinesis only sweetened the pot.

"Gaaaaahhh!" Carol screamed in frustration, thrashing around in my grasp.

"You calm down!" I growled. "We'll find you some damn custom-made underwear. Just calm . . . *down.*"

And just like that—she did. Her body slackened like a

puppet whose strings had been cut and she went limp against me.

What in the world?

I checked her pulse. It was slow and steady. She was unconscious, but still very much alive. Rose chose that moment to burst into the room.

"Aveda . . ." she said. She looked around, taking stock of everything. Me cradling unconscious Carol on the floor. Scott consoling the now sobbing Gwen in the corner. Sprite dripping down the wall in sticky rivulets. And the unicorn mob, still staring at us with beady, painted-on eyes. "We heard screaming," Rose continued. "What happened?"

"I'm not sure," I said. I frowned at Carol's inert form, willing it to tell me something. Anything. She remained stubbornly unconscious.

Only one thing to do, then. Because Carol actually had done what I'd hoped she would: she'd given me a clue. Or at least part of a clue. And it was up to Aveda Jupiter to make it into a whole fucking clue.

I squared my shoulders and spat out a completely improbable phrase. "I think I have to go talk to Maisy about custom underwear."

CHAPTER TEN

I'M NOT SURE what I expected out of yet another visit to Pussy Queen, but it definitely wasn't the sight that greeted me when I flung the doors open and stalked in.

Maisy had dismantled all of her displays and created one massive new monstrosity next to the dressing room area, just a few feet away from the portal. Three mannequins were grouped together and sported various white lacy lingerie concoctions and veils on their heads. The one in the middle had a hand raised, an artful crumple of orange and red tissue paper resting on her palm. Like a flame.

"Is that supposed to be me?" Evie gasped, trailing in behind me.

"I think my white board version was better," Bea said.

"It was really artistic, Bug," Scott said.

I'd called HQ on our way to Pussy Queen and asked Evie to join me on my fact-finding expedition. Bea had tagged along—I'd suggested she start following Evie around and monitoring her every mood. Just to ensure Evie stayed relaxed. Meanwhile, Nate had gone to the hospital to check on Cakezilla Carol, who had drifted back into consciousness right before being taken to the ER. She was undergoing a series of tests to make sure nothing was seriously wrong. We'd scanned the bakery again, but the puppy was nowhere to be found.

"Isn't it gorgeous?" Maisy trilled, sashaying up to us and gesturing to her display. "I've had so many brides-to-be

coming in the past few days, most of them newly engaged."
She beamed at Evie. "You've really started a trend."

Evie blushed and shrugged, fiddling with her engagement ring. Hmm. We needed to get her proper media training. If she was going to be the star of the wedding of the
year, she had to learn how to work that shit.

"New libation," Dave said, shuffling up behind us. He
held out an old, chipped Sunny Side mug filled to the brim
with murky-looking liquid. "Wisdom can only be attained
when the glass is full."

"I'll leave it full, then," I said, holding up a hand. "No
thank you."

"Dave!" Shruti rushed over to us and rested a hand on
his shoulder. "It's great that you're being proactive, but
we've talked about using the nice glasses for drinks—
remember?"

He frowned at her as if he wasn't quite processing her
words through his stoned haze.

"I am alone on the path once again," he said, his face
morose.

"You're not alone, I swear," Shruti told him. "I know you
miss the Sunny Side regulars, but Maisy said she's going to
do a special promotion featuring your brunch mimosas—
maybe some of your old customers will stop by."

"I am no longer what I once was," he responded.

She sighed and patted his shoulder. "I know adjusting to
new things is hard. But you're doing fine. Why don't you go
test out some recipes?"

"Is he getting better or worse?" I asked, cocking an eyebrow as Dave shuffled off. "Or is he just always stoned?"

"Hard to tell," Shruti said, with an elegant shrug. Today
her hair was shoulder-length and wavy with glamorous
side-swept bangs. "I think he really misses the Sunny Side,
you know? He's feeling a little lost in life, and getting used
to his gig here is an ongoing process."

"He's trying to reinvent himself," Maisy mused. "I can
relate."

"Maisy," I said, trying to get us back on track, "your new display actually relates to what we need to talk to you about."

"We know you stock bridal lingerie—" Evie began.

"An extensive collection," she chirped.

"—but do you ever do anything custom?" I asked.

"Hmm." She tapped a flaky gray finger to her chin, her glowing eyes narrowing. "I of course do alterations so everything fits the body perfectly, but custom from scratch? I haven't delved into that particular arena. I'm not sure my sewing and design skills are up to par yet. Though that is certainly something I've considered using to expand my business: sexy, one-of-a-kind pieces for the unique bride." She grinned at Evie. "Maybe you'd want to model a sample look? We could Snapchat the shit out of that."

"Um, no, thank you," Evie said. She looked a little nervous. I gave Bea a subtle nod. She nodded back and focused on Evie, her eyes practically boring holes in the back of her sister's head. Evie's shoulders relaxed.

"Have you sold anything to a bride-to-be named Carol—Carol Kepler?" I asked.

"That name doesn't ring a bell, and I'm usually quite good at remembering the specificities of my clientele, but I can check my sales records," Maisy said, bustling over to the register.

I watched as she shuffled through some papers, studying them carefully, and replayed the scene from earlier in my mind. The way the rage had sparked in Carol's eyes, then flared as Scott approached with the scanner.

"Did you try that guiding spell you've been working on?" I asked him, remembering the strange, blank expression that had overtaken his face for a moment. "Were you able to grab on to the puppy in the air or . . . ?"

"Not exactly." He frowned, looking contemplative. "I was getting ready to put the spell in motion when Carol started to freak out, but then . . . something weird happened in there. It was a split second thing, and I've been trying to figure out what it means. I can't remember it exactly because everything happened so fast, but..." He paused, his eyes wandering to the ceiling, trying to call up the memory. "Right before the scanner beeped, I swear there was this moment where I felt connected to the supernatural energy in the room."

"Like you mind-melded with the puppy?" I said.

"Sort of." He paused again. "When I'm prepping to do a spell, I start by reaching out with my mind to access those Otherworld magics—and yes, Bea, you've told me before that that sounds like 'some totes mumbo-jumbo-laden pseudo-mysticism.'" He gave her an indulgent grin.

"Well, it does, though," Bea muttered.

"Anyway, as I was reaching out this time, something brushed up against my mind. It was fast, but I'm pretty sure it was whatever was affecting Carol, which we're hypothesizing is the puppy—and in that split second, I could sense what it was feeling, what it was thinking."

"It was *thinking*?" Bea said, quirking a skeptical eyebrow. "Because when we were dealing with puppy demons on the regular, they never seemed smart enough to come up with a plan beyond 'I want to shove everything in the immediate vicinity into my piehole.'"

"That's the thing—that's what I've been trying to figure out," he said. "This puppy seems to have thought patterns that are more complex than usual. I mean, the fact that it has thought patterns at all—"

"Would you say it's, like, sentient, even?" Bea said. "Because a sentient puppy demon has the potential to be frakballs terrifying."

"Tentatively, I guess I would," he said, giving her a wry smile. "Which I know is never good enough for your and Nate's classification system, but it was definitely in distress and it definitely wanted something. It was thinking about how it could get it, how it could—"

"What did it want?" I interrupted. "Undergarments?"

"Maybe," he said, shaking his head in frustration. "Like I said, it was so fast."

"Well, what do we *think* it wants?" Evie said. "What's the endgame of making people pissed off at totally weird moments?"

"Maybe it's just flitting around *wanting* random shit," Bea said with a shrug.

"And yet . . ." I squeezed my balled fists tighter, willing myself not to cram my nails in my mouth. "There is something about what this puppy demon's been doing that doesn't seem completely haphazard."

"How do you mean?" Evie asked.

I chewed on my lip, nearly drawing blood. Argh. My fidget impulse was trying to swap gnawing my lip in for biting my fingernails. I wasn't a dog; I should be disciplined enough to not chew on *anything*.

"In the past," I said, thinking it over, "when an incorporeal puppy demon has presumably been on the scene, several people from that incident have reported ragey feelings. Which also seemed to be what happened in the bridal tent with Evie and the redhead Bridezilla. But in Cake My Day, it only targeted one person. Carol. And—"

"—and it targeted her repeatedly," Scott said, finishing my thought for me.

"And all three people who have experienced puppy demon rage recently have something in common," I continued.

"They're all brides!" shrieked Bea. "Well. Brides-to-be." Her brow furrowed. "But if it is targeting a specific kind of person on purpose, then back to Evie's question: What's the plan? *Why?* What does a lost puppy demon want with a bunch of human women who are obsessed with table settings and flower arrangements?"

"Hey!" Evie protested. She poked Bea in the arm. I was pleased to see that the tension seemed to have left her body entirely. "Kind of a sweeping stereotype right there."

"Sorry, hashtag 'not all brides,'" Bea said. "And anyway, the blame really should be put on the wedding industry and, like, society for stressing ladies out and giving them a bridal complex, all in the name of attaining some imaginary ideal of perfection."

"You may not have a bridal complex, but you are still a bride, Evie," I said. "The most high-profile bride in the city, in fact." I studied her, the wheels in my brain turning. She shifted uncomfortably. I probably had my Idea Face on again. "What if we use this knowledge and try to draw the puppy out?" I continued. "I mean, we could try to stalk every bride-to-be in the city and see where it turns up next—"

"But like Maisy said, there are a lot of brides-to-be right now," Shruti piped up. "I'm booked solid with vintage dress consultations for the next three weeks, and Maisy can barely keep that bridal lingerie she's pushing in stock. You'd need an army to keep track of all of 'em."

"And if we draw it to us and isolate it, maybe we can take it down entirely," I said.

"Or at least find out what it wants—what it ultimately wants, beyond dresses and underwear and such," Bea said.

"Yes," Scott said. "And when we get back to HQ, I'm going to see if I can work a component into the guiding spell that might allow me to connect with the puppy more properly. To actually mind-meld with it in a way, see if I can sense what it's feeling."

"You're both very concerned with the wants and needs and feelings of a faceless energy force that keeps trying to kick our asses," I said.

Bea shrugged. "We're the givers on this team."

"But hold on," Scott said, giving me a skeptical look. "Are we talking about using *Evie* to draw it out, making her a target for this thing?"

"I'll be by her side to protect her," I said, waving a hand. "This isn't like when we sent her off on all those missions as me on her own."

When you *sent her off on those missions, you mean*, I

chastised myself. *Without thinking twice about her safety or well-being.*

I brushed the thought aside before it reared up and sent me into a guilt spiral. Things were different now. I would *make* them different. "I'm back at full strength," I said. "I'll die before I let anything happen to her. *Anything.*" I gave him a challenging look. I wasn't sure why I needed him to know how important this was to me, but I did.

"Plus we've got all our X-Men talents to contribute this time," Bea piped up. "I've been working on the traps with Rose and Nate and they should be ready to contain even the most incorporeal of demon asses."

"You don't have to convince me, guys," Evie said, reaching over to take my hand. "I think we should give our puppy the biggest, shiniest, bride-iest target in the city. So it can't resist." She gave me a game smile. I sensed uncertainty underneath, like she was trying to put on her best brave superheroine face, but couldn't quite mask the doubts she was struggling with. I squeezed her hand.

"I have an idea!" Maisy shrieked, suddenly back at our sides. We all jumped. "Oh, and I have no records of a Carol Kepler buying anything here."

"Is teleporting part of your new demon hybrid skills?" I asked.

"No," Maisy said, waving a desiccated hand. "But y'all are really bad at paying attention to your surroundings when you're deep in battle-planning mode. Shasta and I used to talk about it all the time."

"Touching," I muttered. Evie giggled. "So what's your plan?"

Maisy threw her arms wide and gestured to the mannequin in the center of her display—the one with the crumpled paper flame ball.

"Perhaps you aren't ready to model custom lingerie, Evie," she said, making her voice extra dramatic. "But what about modeling your bridal finery for all the world to see? I bet that would be a real event."

"And I'm guessing you're about to suggest a perfect location for such an event," I said.

Maisy batted her eyelashes. "I have great lighting in here. Just saying."

"Maisy's shop totally has cool cachet, especially after the proposal video," Bea said. Her eyes drifted to the ceiling and I could practically see her social media manager wheels turning. "A dress reveal—a proper one—would be a big deal. True, phone camera footage from the bridal tent was posted on YouTube, but it was shaky, not that great. You couldn't really see all the details, and the dress was sort of being ripped off of Evie's body at the time anyway. Meanwhile, no one's seen your maid-of-honor dress at all, Aveda—that could be a real selling point."

"I don't have a dress yet," I said, even though I'd already decided on the perfect gown, a dramatic scarlet silk sheath to match the flowers on Evie's bridal wear.

"I can help with that," Shruti said. "Whatever you're envisioning, I can either find in my existing stock or special order for you. I've got good relationships with a lot of the bridal vendors and boutiques in town, and at least one of them totally owes me a favor."

"Close up the shop and do it as a photo shoot," Bea said, warming to the topic. "Only staff and Team Evie/Aveda allowed, and we'll release the photos exclusively on Maisy's blog afterward. That way, we know Evie will be the only bride present. The only thing for the puppy to affect."

"And it will ensure no civilians are around to get hurt whenever this thing shows up," Evie said, nudging Bea in the ribs.

"Oh, right. That too," Bea said.

"So it's settled!" Maisy exclaimed, clapping her hands together. Little bits of gray skin flaked off and fell to the floor. "Pussy Queen presents: the grand reveal of Evie Tanaka's wedding gown and Aveda Jupiter's maid-of-honor frock!"

"This actually sounds like a plan," I said. I planted my hands on my hips, straightened my spine, and narrowed my eyes at the mannequins, as if they were an army I was about to command. "All right, troops," I said, "prepare to deploy the motherfreakin' fashion show."

CHAPTER ELEVEN

THE MORNING OF the big Pussy Queen photo shoot, I rose at six a.m., went on a run through the swooping hills of Buena Vista Park, then returned home to do a two-hour kickboxing workout in the gym. Though we had new weapons in our arsenal—the traps, Scott's spell—I was still determined to fight this thing the old-fashioned way: I would figure out how to kick the puppy demon's ass. Even if it didn't currently have a corporeal ass for me to kick. And that meant being as fit and ready and as *Aveda fucking Jupiter* as possible.

I was so focused on planning my workout, going over each move in my head, I nearly ran into Scott, who also appeared to be heading for the gym.

"Oh, sorry," I said, stepping back before I had an unfortunate collision with his chest.

Or maybe it wouldn't be *that* unfortunate.

Stop thinking like that, Annie.

I'd been distracted enough by Carol's antics and our Pussy Queen plan that I'd managed to put the sexy cake incident out of my mind almost entirely. Now it threatened to rear right back up and dominate my brain as my eyes wandered over that chest I'd nearly bumped into. And the arms. The arms were nice, too.

Stop. It.

"Are you going to the gym?" I said, forcing words to form on my tongue. "Is that a thing you do?"

I knew Scott worked out, I'd just assumed he did it elsewhere.

"I stretch in there sometimes after surfing," he said, giving me his easy smile. I tried to ignore the glow that bloomed in my chest and finally noticed the telltale signs that he'd just come back from the beach: his hair was wet and his t-shirt was sticking to his torso in damp patches that defined the muscles underneath extra well. Which must be why I'd noticed them. Honestly, you couldn't really blame me, given the way they were just out there like that.

"But I try to do it when no one else is around," he added.

"You don't want anyone seeing your extra dorky yoga-esque moves?" I asked, arching an eyebrow.

"Eh," he said. "I gave up trying to look cool years ago."

"You do, though. Sometimes," I blurted out. I could practically feel the Aveda Jupiter side of me pinching my inner Annie Chang—who seemed determined to rise up and make herself known at the most inconvenient of moments. "Like at the bakery the other day, with the little birthday girl. She *definitely* thought you were cool."

I expected another easy smile, but instead his expression dimmed, his eyes becoming hooded. "I was . . . that was . . . nothing," he said quickly, waving a hand.

"It wasn't nothing," I said, since I could never seem to let anything go, even when someone was giving me all the necessary signals to do so. Bratty Birthday Girl was right about one thing: Queen Elsa of Arendelle I was not. "It wasn't nothing," I repeated for good measure. "Your healing spells are really something. Or they've become something. You called the one you used on the birthday girl a 'Level One'— I didn't know you had that kind of classification system for them?"

He shrugged and rocked back and forth on his heels. "That's something I've been working on with Nate and Bea. Down in the basement lair." This time he did smile, but something about it seemed forced. I cocked my head, studying him more intently. What was going on with him?

"Anyway," he said abruptly, nodding toward the gym. "I use the gym when no one else is around. Because I don't want to bother people when *they're* using the gym."

I felt my cheeks warm. I was the only one who used the gym. Well, sometimes Lucy, but that was usually during one of our training sessions.

"I've heard . . . people like peace and quiet during their workouts," he added.

"People do. But they won't mind if you're just stretching in the corner. Quietly."

He nodded and his smile turned genuine. "Noted."

Maybe we were doing okay at the whole "being friends" thing.

We filed in and he retreated to a back corner of the room, settled himself on a mat, and folded his torso over his legs, touching his toes. Which he *should have* looked completely dorky doing, but of course he didn't. I'd always admired the way he managed to make moves like that appear effortless and even a bit graceful during the horrors of the stretching section in sixth grade gym class—before he'd filled out, when he was still all scrawny limbs and that ever-present grin, the goofy kid who cracked me and Evie up with endless inappropriate comments during sex ed.

When he'd first attached himself to us, it had never occurred to me how weird it was that this random little white boy wanted to be best pals with two semi-outcasts who didn't have any friends other than each other. It was only later, far into adulthood, that the pieces started coming together. He was an outcast too, bullied by all the other boys in our grade for having the nerve to be a runty daydreamer who tended to wear clothes that were always a little threadbare and sometimes verging on being a size too small.

Things had only gotten worse when those boys found out that the nice, frazzled, exhausted lady who worked the counter weeknights at the 7-Eleven was none other than

Scott's mom, Lynne, who took on a variety of crap-paying jobs to put herself through law school while keeping herself and her son fed, clothed, and alive.

Everything came to a head one day when the other kids took it upon themselves to come up with "hilarious" nicknames for her and pelted Scott with them mercilessly, chasing him down the hall and chanting like misguided members of a disturbingly pre-pubescent cult. All the nicknames they came up with were unimaginative, terrible, and not particularly true, like "Lazy Lunch-Lady Lynne" (working multiple jobs is the *opposite* of lazy; she wasn't serving *lunch*, she was making change for Slurpees; and she'd ended up becoming a badass in the world of family law, making more of herself than any of those little assholes. But what are twelve-year-olds if not kind of dumb and endlessly cruel?) Eventually, they'd taken to lobbing each syllable at Scott like tiny verbal bullets from a machine gun: "La! Zy! Lunch! Lay! Dy! Lynne!" screamed the chorus, over and over again, until little Scotty Cameron decided he'd had enough. He'd whirled around and screamed that he would fight anyone *"to the death"* who dared say another word about his mom.

It was quite a sight: a too-thin little boy in too-small clothes, non-existent chest puffed out, red-faced with righteous fury.

He had, of course, gotten his ass beat.

But I remembered thinking in that moment that he was a superhero in the purest form of the word—someone who stands up for others. And since I could never simply stand by and watch something like that happen, I'd shoved my way through the crowd, ignoring the protests of Evie (who was already crying), and planted myself between Scott and the other boys before they could give him yet another black eye.

"You want to talk about lazy?" I'd spat out. "Let's talk about your stupid insults, which don't make *any freaking sense.*"

None of them had wanted to fight a girl, so they'd all backed off. The next day, Scott sat next to me and Evie in Biology. And after that, he was always there.

Sometime around sophomore year, muscle had rippled its way onto his rangy frame. At the time, I'd thought it was just, I don't know, a natural step in his Hot Guy Evolution, but later I'd realized it was something he'd worked hard at, taking up surfing, lifting weights, working out on the regular. Even though he'd found friend solace with Evie and me, he'd been determined to make sure those kids couldn't hurt him again—with their words or their fists. As someone who had spent years crafting her own brand of armor—and who felt like she still had to work at it every single day—I could relate.

Thanks to the muscles, his goofy grin had suddenly seemed downright rakish and plenty of our fellow hormonal teenagers had taken notice.

But I had noticed him before that.

What was I doing again?

Oh, right. I turned away from him, closed the distance between me and the boxing bag, and snagged a pair of hand wraps from the windowsill. I liked the precise, methodical process of wrapping my hands with the long strips of cotton. Three times around the wrist, three times around the knuckles, repeat. Loop each finger. Go back to the wrist. These simple motions put me in a focused, zen state, ready to take on my opponent. I slipped on my boxing gloves and stared down the bag: a long, black column of vinyl, stoic and unmoving. Blank and non-judgmental. I got into my stance and let my mind zero in on the movements, nothing else.

Jab, cross, hook.

Jab, block, spin, backhand.

Spin, backhand, kick! Kick! Kick!

Roundhouse kicks were my favorite. The bag made the most satisfying *thwack* sound, my leg connecting and sinking in, pure motion and force, and it was just me and the bag, me and the bag, me and—

"Annie?"

I fell out of my stance and made an unflattering "eep!" sound.

"Scott!" I whirled around and frowned at him. "I thought we talked about the whole peace and quiet thing?"

"I know," he said, guilt flashing over his face. He was still on the mat and pretzeled into a new stretch, one leg drawn to his chest, his torso rotated halfway around. He should have looked ridiculous, but no. Still hot.

"Sorry," he added. "I just remembered something, and I realized it might be important since you might've made further plans since the last time we talked about this, although I know you've been busy preparing for the event today and—"

"Spit out, Cameron!" I sputtered, still flustered from being interrupted mid-kick.

He untangled his limbs and studied me. "Evie wants to have the engagement party at The Gutter."

I shook my head at him, certain I had misheard. "What?"

"That place is special to her and Nate for a lot of reasons. And she doesn't want anything fancy."

I was still shaking my head. The Gutter was a dank, grimy hole of a karaoke bar beloved by Evie, Lucy, and a fine array of senior citizens and seedy characters. It was also the site of one of Evie's greatest triumphs—defeating Maisy at a supernaturally enhanced karaoke contest—but other than that, I could not fathom what she saw in it. And it was definitely no place for a proper engagement party.

I had envisioned something sumptuous and beautiful, a tea room overflowing with flowers or a sweet garden setting with whimsically mismatched china. Champagne and tiny sandwiches and that dark chocolate cake from Letta's bakery. (Okay, maybe the red velvet since I clearly couldn't be trusted around anything involving dark chocolate.)

Instead, Evie apparently wanted beer and nachos and a bunch of randos caterwauling their way through auto-tuned pop songs. And even worse, she hadn't trusted me with this information. She'd relayed it through a third party.

"I'm sure she was going to get around to mentioning it to you," Scott said, as if reading my thoughts. "It's something she tossed off to me in passing when we were cleaning up the breakfast dishes the other day and I thought—"

"That you should let me know as soon as possible. Of course," I said, forcing a smile. "Thank you."

I turned back to my bag, ending the conversation.

Jab, cross.

I focused on the opponent in front me, trying to get back to the moves, trying to make the fight fill my brain so I wouldn't think about anything else. But I couldn't deny the swell of frustration in my chest.

Jab, cross, hook, cross.

As maid of honor—hell, as Evie's best and oldest friend—I was the one she should have gone to first with all things wedding-related.

Hook, cross, spin, kick. Kick!

And anyway, we'd worked through our issues and now I was kicking ass as maid of honor. There was no denying that.

Kick! Kick! Kick!

So why did she feel the need to confide in someone else? Why was I getting cropped out of the picture *again*?

Kick kick kick kick kick!

Why—

"Annie?"

I whirled around, breathing hard.

"What?!"

Scott held up his hands in surrender. He was standing now and had moved closer to me. But not too close, I noticed.

"I lied," he said. "Just now, I totally lied. She did ask me to talk to you about it. She said she was pretty sure you had a whole elaborate vision in your head of what the party should be and she was afraid to bring up anything different and apparently this thing happened with Bea—"

"Right," I interrupted. "That."

My shoulders slumped. I remembered how she'd shut down and avoided me after I'd barged in and forced her to tell Bea about her power. Well ... really, *I'd* ended up telling Bea. I'd hurricaned all over the place. But hadn't the outcome been good? Maybe it didn't matter.

She didn't need Hurricane Annie fucking up her special day.

I cocked my head at him. "Why are you confessing mere minutes after lying to my face?"

He shrugged. "I think you deserve for people to be honest with you. I tried to tell her that."

That frustration welled in my chest again, pushed itself up into my throat, forced the beginnings of tears to prick at my eyes. I shook my head, willing them to retreat. I needed to be at full Aveda Jupiter strength today, and getting lost in this weird maze of emotions was definitely not helping. Get out of here, Annie Chang.

"Thank you," I said briskly. "Now if you'll excuse me, I really need to finish my workout."

I turned back to the bag, expecting that to be the end of it.

Instead, I felt his hand rest on my shoulder.

"Annie ..."

"God." I whirled back around and glowered at him. "Why won't you stop ... bothering ... me?" I growled.

He studied me for a moment, his face unreadable. Then he nodded at the bag.

"You want a real sparring partner?"

"You kickbox?" I snorted in disbelief. Scott might work out and he might have bulked up enough to scare off his grade-school bullies, but he was definitely *not* a kickboxer. That required specific technique, which I'd spent years perfecting.

"I know a few things," he said. "I can pick the rest up. Come on."

He got into a stance that was all wrong. He didn't know a thing. He was trying to distract me from my spiral of bad feelings again. Just like he had the night Evie had been injured and he made me tell him the same story over and over again. For some reason, that only stoked my stubbornness, only made me want to dig in and simmer in my bad feelings. Or at the very least, to call his bluff.

"Fine," I said. I shucked off my gloves and got into my (correct) stance. "Soft punches and kicks. Taps, no power."

He threw a clumsy fist at the space next to my left ear. I dodged easily and shuffled to the side. Kickboxing is like ballroom dancing—someone always leads. That person is dominant, the one controlling the fight. You can run the whole thing without throwing a single blow. I forced him to follow my lead for a few more shuffles, hands up, protecting my face. His hands were all over the place, hovering near his neck, his chin, nearly falling to his sides. I could have decked him if I'd wanted to.

Instead, I locked him into my rhythm, my pace, my movements. He was just mirroring whatever I did—and not very well. We did that for a few moments more, neither of us attempting to land a single blow. Sweat beaded the back of my neck as I concentrated on controlling the dance. I found myself lasering in on that idea, that control, and my focus took over. The bad feelings started to melt away, as if I was sweating them out of my body.

Finally, Scott's left leg swung out for a kick, but at that point, I'd already mastered the dance and had him right where I wanted him. I reacted instantly, a combination of technique and instinct, and swept my arm under to grab his leg, throwing him off balance. Then I pulled hard on his leg and pushed all of my weight against him.

"Wha?" Confusion flashed over his face—confusion so pure, it was almost comical. He stumbled backward and landed hard on his back and I threw myself on top of him, straddling him at the waist, making myself as heavy as possible. I planted my hands on his biceps, pinning him in place, and gave him one of my imperious looks.

"You do *not* kickbox," I said. "Admit it, you were trying to distract me."

"I . . . no, of course not, I . . . *ow*!" he yelped as I pressed myself more firmly against him, throwing my weight on top of his solar plexus. "Why are you pressing so hard? Are you using telekinesis?"

"I don't need to," I said. "I'm just that strong."

"Okay, okay! Yes!" he gasped out. "I hate seeing you go into that spiral of feeling bad about yourself. You used to do it all the time with your parents and now you do it with Evie—"

"I thought you *wanted* me to feel bad about Evie!" I eased up on him so he could breathe a little easier. "I thought you wanted me to feel bad about everything! Isn't that why you were so pissed off at me for so long? Why you avoided me? Why even when we started talking again, it was like you could barely stand me, like you'd rather be *anywhere* than trapped in a room . . . with me . . ." I trailed off as the words clogged in my throat again, threatening to turn into tears. I swallowed hard and let go of his arms, sitting up straight. Still straddling him, but no longer putting all my weight into it. Tears filled my eyes, and I wobbled. Fuck. Why was I letting myself get so upset?

His hands went to my hips and steadied me, saving me from toppling over. He met my eyes and there was something soft and sad there, something I couldn't quite define. A hint of that intensity I'd seen at the bakery, rising to the surface.

I realized that we were locked in an extremely intimate position, that my hands had somehow come to rest on his chest, that I could feel muscle and heat and his ragged breathing. And I could feel all of these things *everywhere*. In my palms pressed against his chest. On my hips, cradled by his hands. And especially at the point where I was straddling him.

Yes, I definitely felt it there.

My own breathing turned ragged.

That haze of sensations descended on me again, and I couldn't process a single thought beyond what I was feeling in that moment. Nothing beyond *him*.

I've always had a certain stance on sex. Chiefly, that it seemed messy and awkward and not worth the hassle. My first excruciating, fumbling encounter was back in high school, right after Evie and Scott had done the deed. I was annoyed that 1) Evie had punched the V-Card first and 2) it had been with Scott. I decided I'd better get to it quickly. I went on a date with some loser Sophie set me up with, and we got semi-amorous in his childhood treehouse, which was crawling with all kinds of disgusting vermin. He knew what went where, but that was about it. In preparation for the experience, I'd studied up on female sexual response, so I tried to instruct him on the finer points of what a curious teenage girl might prefer. He did not take that well and kicked me out before I'd even reached the plateau phase of arousal. I had to make a slow, perilous walk of shame down the rickety treehouse steps: devirginized, but completely unsatisfied.

I'd had a few interludes after, but they'd all gone about the same, and when I'd made the commitment to being Aveda Jupiter, I simply didn't have time to pursue such things further. I got myself a vibrator, learned all the best techniques for making use of it, and relied on that to relieve all urges and unwanted tension. After all, who knew what I liked better than me? Bringing another person into the equation seemed like an unnecessarily complicated proposition. Since getting together with Nate, Evie had tried to tell me what it was like to lose yourself in someone, how much better sex could be if you let go of your inhibitions and got wrapped up in the moment (and also managed to find a partner who actually knew what they were doing), but I couldn't see what all the fuss was about.

Until now. With Scott all hot and hard beneath me. Now I could *definitely* see it.

Even when he'd kissed me all those years ago, it hadn't felt like this. It had been soft, sweet, romantic. A teenage fantasy made real. This was nothing like that. This was urgent. Wild and necessary.

Our gazes locked. Neither of us could look anywhere else. It was like we were sparring again, caught in the kick-boxing dance. But this time, I had no idea who was leading. My ponytail had come undone when I knocked him to the floor and my hair fell around my face, making me feel caged in. The flush warming my cheeks deepened.

His hands moved over my hips and up my back, coaxing yet firm. He pressed his fingertips against my back, urging me to fold toward him, and suddenly I was basically lying on top of him: chest to chest, my hands trapped between us, every part of us touching. I could feel his breath, warm on my face. His eyes searched mine, stripped of anything teasing or gentle or silly. They were raw with want, with need.

That's how I felt, too. Like every cell in my body needed to be closer to him, even though we were currently positioned as close as two people could be. The sensations washing over me intensified and my nipples tightened against the hard muscles of his chest and I was all nerve endings again and oh my god—

He kissed me.

It was not soft. It was not sweet. It was all fire, all demand. His tongue sliding against mine, his hands tangling in my hair. He flipped me onto my back and now there was no question of who was leading. It was him. And goddammit, I'd follow him anywhere.

His hand gripped my hip and pulled me tighter against him so I could feel . . . oh, god. Yes. *That*. That long, hard length pressed right between my legs. I moaned against his mouth, and he let out something that was half gasp and half growl, a groan that seemed to come from somewhere deep inside of him, and I was so overwhelmed—

"Knock, knock!" Lucy's voice rang out through the gym. We both froze, all tangled up in each other. Then instinct kicked in; I managed to push off from his chest and we sort of rolled away from each other.

Lucy bounced in, grinning away, then stopped and cocked an eyebrow at us. We may have been untangled and apart, but we were still sprawled in completely awkward positions on the floor, skin slick with sweat, breathing hard.

"Well," Lucy said. "I'm sorry to interrupt the extreme physical fitness that's obviously taking place here. But the time has come and we must depart for Maisy's boutique."

Right. I took a few deep inhalations, centering myself, trying to breathe out the sensations that had overtaken me.

Time to kick some invisible puppy demon ass.

CHAPTER TWELVE

I COULDN'T BREATHE. Fear gripped my heart like an icy hand, each cold finger wrapping around my most vital organ until my entire chest felt frozen. I opened my mouth, dying to scream, but no sound came out beyond a pathetic little "eep." I willed myself not to faint on the spot.

Aveda Jupiter does not faint. Even in the face of horrors untold. Even when confronted with the most horrifying thing of all time, more terrible than fanged cupcakes, megalomaniacal demon princesses, and stray puppy demons combined.

I forced my breath out so I could keep myself upright. So I could face it. So I could take down this awful monster, this *thing* they kept saying was—

"Your bridesmaid dress!" shrieked Evie. "Do you love it?"

It was the worst thing I'd ever seen.

It had a high neckline, a scratchy-looking lace bodice, and a drop waist festooned with a big-ass bow. You would think it couldn't get any worse after the drop waist, but you would be wrong. That atrocity flowed into a tiered— *tiered*—satin skirt and was topped off with puffy sleeves so enormous they looked like shoulder pads that had gained sentience and were trying to eat the rest of the dress. And the whole thing was done up in that special color that only existed on the bridal spectrum of the eighties: seafoam green.

I opened my mouth again and only managed a croak. We were huddled in one of the Pussy Queen dressing rooms with Shruti, waiting for the photo shoot to begin. Maisy had drafted Dave to film the proceedings—even if we didn't attract the puppy demon, she'd have another viral video on her hands. As usual, I couldn't help but admire her ingenuity while also being slightly appalled.

I'd go first in this monstrosity, then Evie would reveal her glorious bridal wear. I stared at the dress, wondering if Scott had a spell that would change it into something else entirely.

Okay, time to remember: this event was primarily for supernatural evil-fighting purposes.

But what would my adoring fans think when they saw me in *this*? Well . . . maybe they wouldn't care. They seemed a lot less adoring these days.

"You chose this, Evie?" I said, just to make sure I had the sequence of events right.

"Evie and I wanted to surprise you!" Shruti crowed.

"Did it work?" Evie asked, clapping her hands together.

"Oh, definitely," I murmured. "I'm definitely surprised."

As my assistant, Evie had chosen clothes for me before, particularly when superheroing became so overwhelming I needed her to take on more of my day-to-day tasks. She'd most famously chosen a dress for me to wear to a benefit that was sparkly and gorgeous, but also kind of see-through. Evie had ended up wearing it while she was posing as me, and Maisy had taken notice and posted a rather catty write-up.

But Evie had never selected anything this flat-out dreadful before.

"It's a little old school," Shruti said, fingering the satin. The material was so shiny, light reflected off of it in a way that felt almost violent. Like it was stabbing me in the eye. "I found this stash of eighties pieces at one of those clothes-by-the-pound places last month and thought I could put them out around Halloween time. But Evie was adamant that you would want something super unique."

"It's *very* unique," I said, trying to sound as if this was a positive attribute. "But I'm a little concerned it will clash with the red in Evie's gown." I gestured to Evie, who was already wearing her show-stopping mermaid number with the little scarlet flowers.

"Not to worry, everything goes with that lovely bit of bridal finery," Shruti said, beaming at Evie.

Evie's smile wavered and she tugged at the bodice. "Everything except my desire to eat ice cream," she said. "It's kind of tight. And scratchy."

Really, scratchy? Compared to what she wanted *me* to wear?

"The shape is so dramatic," Shruti continued. "Very reminiscent of a Marcus Wong. But it isn't, right?"

"It doesn't have a tag, so I'm not sure who designed it," I said. "But as I was saying, I wouldn't want to do anything that draws attention away from the bride."

"Oh, Annie." Evie took my hand. "You know I don't care about stuff like that. I want you to have something dramatic, flamboyant—the type of thing you love! And I thought it would be fun to go *really* vintage with it."

"How . . . nice," I said, giving her a weak smile. The Aveda of old would have definitely thrown the hissyfit of all hissyfits over this.

"What about the dress I asked you to order, Shruti?" I said, trying to keep my tone neutral as I pictured my gorgeous scarlet sheath floating into the ether.

"Not to worry, I never placed the order," Shruti said with a grin. "That confirmation number I gave you was totally fake. All part of maintaining the ruse!" She nudged Evie and they giggled conspiratorially.

"Mmm," I said, not trusting myself to say more. *You are no longer the hissyfit-throwing type*, I reminded myself sternly.

Especially given that I really didn't want to do anything that would make Evie distrust me further. She already felt she couldn't confide in me about where she wanted the engagement party, and anyway, we had more important things to worry about right now. Like drawing out the puppy demon and kicking its incorporeal ass before it could wreak any more havoc on innocent brides-to-be.

"I love it—of course I love it," I said, making my smile more convincing.

Dave popped his head in and surveyed the scene, his face bearing its usual dazed look.

"Fortune favors the bold," he said, handing Shruti a pair of champagne cocktails. They were golden with a small burst of orange in the middle.

"Ah," Shruti said, taking the glasses from him. "I think that means it's just about showtime, girls."

"A small frog knows when to leap," Dave said, nodding, then ducked back out.

"This is Dave's special cocktail for today," Shruti said, passing us the drinks. "It actually looks pretty good—especially served in the correct glass instead of one of his old mugs. I believe we're calling it the Firestarter, in honor of Evie, the bride. Oh, but Aveda, I know you don't like to drink during the day."

"I'll make an exception for such a special occasion," I said, downing a big gulp of the thing. I eyed the bridesmaid dress again. And took another gulp. Shruti gave us an encouraging nod and exited.

"All right," I said, throwing one last side-eye at the green monstrosity in front of me. "Let's do this thing."

I straightened my power ponytail and wriggled out of my clothes and into the dress, trying not to grimace as the cheap lace bodice rubbed against my skin.

"Attention! Attention, please, y'all!" We heard Maisy trill.

Wait. "Y'all?" Who was she talking to? Our little crew? I knew they were positioned around the store: Lucy with the scanner, Nate and Bea with the trap, Scott prepping his spell. I peered through the cracked dressing room door. The store was closed for the event, but a small crowd had formed outside and was trying to get a glimpse through the front door. Which Maisy had cordoned off with a bit of fancy gold rope, but otherwise left open.

"Maisy!" I hissed.

"Excuse me!" she said to the crowd, then hustled over to the dressing room door.

"What's going on?" I demanded. "No one else was supposed to be here! We purposely didn't release the time or date of the shoot! We're supposed to be keeping civilians out of the line of fire, remember?"

"Oh. Well. Yes." Her glowing eyes darted back and forth. "I *might* have tweeted that we'd be closed during the hours of twelve and four today and I guess people picked up on the hint!"

I narrowed my eyes. "That's all you said?"

Her eyes were shifting around so fast now, they were basically a blur. "I . . . might have . . . used a hashtag."

"Which was?"

She muttered something.

"Speak up!" I growled.

"#specialsecretsuperherobrideevent," she whispered.

I rolled my eyes. Great. Now we had the extra complication of trying to protect innocent San Franciscans from whatever chaos the puppy demon might cause. "Tell Lucy to guard the door. No one gets in."

Maisy nodded and skittered off. The buzz of the crowd picked up as she whispered to Lucy, who took up her post by the door. I leaned forward, trying to catch snippets of what people were saying. Maybe that would at least tell me if our nefarious stray puppy demon was making itself known.

". . . I heard she had something custom-made . . ."

". . . not a traditional bride—and that's why we love her . . ."

". . . do you think she'll wear a veil . . ."

Hmm. Nothing about that sounded particularly evil.

"Oh! Should I wear a veil?" Evie squeaked into my ear. She'd sidled up next to me and was also trying to listen to the crowd.

"I actually thought of something else." I grabbed my bag from the brocade-covered dressing room stool and found the small box I'd picked up from the florist earlier that day. I handed it to her and she popped it open, her eyes widening in delight.

"Little red flowers!" she exclaimed. "Like the ones on the dress!"

"Yes," I said, plucking the flowers from the box. "I thought we could pin them in your hair?"

"Aw, check it out," she said. "We both surprised each other with something awesome!"

"Uh, yes," I said, grabbing a handful of bobby pins from my bag. I started to artfully pin the flowers in her hair, so they looked like they were gracefully cascading through her tangle of curls. I bit my tongue so I wouldn't mention that the bride wasn't really supposed to surprise the maid of honor—especially with such a hideous piece of non-couture.

"—and we are just ever so gosh-dang delighted that Evie Tanaka has chosen this shop as the place to reveal her glorious bridal look." Maisy's voice wafted in from the other room. "Especially given her checkered history with the place."

The crowd tittered and I peeked through the doorway just in time to see Maisy gesturing expansively at the portal. Dave stood in front of her, filming with a phone-camera.

"My god, just get to it," I muttered, pinning the last flower in Evie's hair. "It doesn't have to be a Broadway-level production."

Evie giggled. "Really? Aveda Jupiter is against someone being all theatrical?" She turned to me and pulled a mock surprised expression, bugging her eyes out and dropping her jaw. I couldn't help but giggle, too.

"All right, all right," I said. "So 'Broadway-level production' is kind of my jam. But she's milking it and we've got an invisible puppy to catch."

Evie grinned at me and reached over to squeeze my hand. "We got this," she said. "The dynamic duo is on top of this shit."

I smiled back and felt that warmth surge between us—that indescribable bond we'd lost for so many years and rebuilt stronger than ever.

Or so I'd thought.

"Evie," I said impulsively. "You can tell me what you want when it comes to wedding stuff. Even if you think it runs counter to what I'm envisioning. It's your day, and I just want to help make it everything you've ever dreamed of."

Her smile faltered. "Scott told you about The Gutter."

"Yes. And I think we can have a perfectly lovely engagement party there." Well, maybe not exactly "lovely." But I could make it work. I knew I could. "And I'm sorry about what happened with Bea the other day," I continued. "I was just trying to—"

"Help. I know." Maybe it was my imagination, but her smile seemed to fade, and she pulled at the bodice of her dress again. "I know that's what you're always trying to do."

"But it's what you want for your party that's important," I said. *Even though you might not know* exactly *what you want until I show it to you.*

"I want to keep the engagement party easy, casual," she said. "Karaoke and garbage food and fun with friends."

"All right," I said, my brain already cycling through all the ways I could execute that and still keep things as tasteful and fabulous as she deserved. "You don't have to worry. I'll take care of it."

Her smile widened again and she squeezed my hand.

And then, finally, we heard Maisy say the magic words we'd been waiting for: "And now, Pussy Queen is proud to present Aveda Jupiter in her fabulous, never-before-seen maid-of-honor dress!"

I swept out of the dressing room and camera flashes went off. Shruti was taking the official photos, but thanks to Maisy, we had dozens of phone-cameras to contend with as well. I gave it my all, waving to the crowd, megawatt smile in place. The dress might be awful, but I knew how to work it.

The buzz from the crowd grew loud again.

"...interesting choice..."

"...is it a theme wedding..."

"...is the theme 'prom nightmare'...?"

I groaned inwardly, but didn't let it show. No, I kept that smile plastered on as I ascended the platform Maisy had erected especially for the shoot, right next to the portal. It was like a mini fashion runway with just enough room for Evie and I to stand and wave. Maisy stood in front of the platform and gestured expansively as I struck my first pose. I smiled at the crowd—pushing and shoving at each other, trying to see through the doorway. Lucy stood firm, sending them a warning look. I deployed one of my patented Aveda Jupiter Tricks of Crafting a Perfect Superheroine Image to make them feel more at home, attempting to make direct eye contact with each and every person there. It made my fans feel like they had a special connection with me. In this case, it also gave me an opportunity to survey the scene, to see if anything was amiss.

My gaze shifted to the right and landed on Scott, who was standing near the back of the store. He gave me an incredulous look, gestured up and down his body, and mouthed, "WHAT?"

So he also thought this dress was hideous.

I gave him a subtle shrug, like, "I don't even know."

He pulled another goofy face and I couldn't help it: I giggled.

Then I quickly schooled my expression back to fabulous, imperious form. Aveda Jupiter might have a famed megawatt smile, but when faced with legions of adoring fans, she certainly did not *giggle*. That was reserved for private moments with Evie.

"Okay!" Maisy cried. "Now, are we ready for the main event?"

The crowd screamed in the affirmative.

"I said," Maisy chirped, milking it once again, "are we *ready*?"

The crowd turned up their scream so loud, the whole building seemed to shake. I kept my smile in place and inched to the side, so Evie would be positioned in the center, right where I could keep an eye on her when the puppy demon decided to attack.

My scratchy lace bodice chafed against my skin. I felt sweat bead underneath the high neckline and trickle down my back, into impossible to reach places. I tightened my smile.

I'd dealt with overwhelming crowds of adoring fans millions of times.

I'd kicked a variety of demon asses millions of times.

I'd maintained my tough, fabulous, charismatic persona while wearing extremely binding clothing *kazillions* of times.

I could certainly handle one hideous bridesmaid dress.

But my god, that itch was like nothing I'd ever felt. When we were through vanquishing evil, I was going to have to talk Evie into letting me wear *anything* but this.

"Here she is!" bellowed Maisy. "Our beautiful bride of San Francisco: Evie Tanaka!"

Evie sashayed out, waving to the cameras and the crowd. The gown hugged her body perfectly, the little red flowers rippling as she walked. And the flowers in her hair did indeed look like they'd just been scattered there, like she was an adorable wood sprite who'd run through the garden.

Applause crashed through the crowd, and I found myself joining in. Evie climbed up on the platform and struck a pose and the camera-phones went wild, desperate to capture her every bridal move.

"Speech!" someone screamed from outside. "Speech-speechspeech!!"

I homed in on where the words were coming from. It was Giant Dude, who had managed to push his way to the front and was now standing in the center of the doorway, being elbowed from all sides by other fans who didn't appreciate his aggressive tactics.

Hmm. A speech might be good, actually. Now that we were up on the platform, presenting ourselves, baiting the puppy demon with all our might, we needed to prolong the moment. Give it time to come out.

Evie turned to me with her deer-in-headlights look. We hadn't discussed anything past posing for the cameras—since, after all, this was only supposed to be a private photo shoot.

"Um, yes," I said, trying to sound encouraging. The neckline of the dress felt like it tightened further, as if attempting to stop me from speaking. And the itch . . . *fuck*. I was going to rip this thing off of my body at the earliest possible moment. "I am so proud to be standing up here as Evie's maid of honor—"

"Not you!" Giant Dude bellowed. "We want to hear from the bride!"

"—and I think this is a wonderful opportunity for her to tell you what your support means to her," I continued through gritted teeth. Sigh. Giant Dude used to hang on my every word. I guess times really had changed. "I can only imagine that having the whole city so invested in every single tiny detail of your special day feels very . . . well, special."

I cocked an eyebrow at Evie, urging her to pick up the thread.

"That's right," Evie said, but her voice sounded a bit robotic. She was reorienting herself, getting into Public Evie mode. Putting on her crowd-pleaser face. Silence hung in the air a little too long, so I gamely clapped my hands together.

"Yay!" I said, attempting to get the crowd to cheer her on. Which they did without too much encouragement.

"Yes," Evie said. Her voice still had that odd, robotic quality, but at least she was continuing to speak. "It is special. San Francisco is my duty, my love, my life—"

I frowned. That was a fine sentiment for the moment—but it was also one of *my* most famous catchphrases.

"I love San Francisco so much," she continued. "That

I—*ow*." She gasped, her hand going to her ribcage. "Oh . . . oh, dear. I think I'm having some indigestion, I—ow." She clapped her other hand to the other side of her ribcage.

Oh, shit. It was happening. It was totally happening. The puppy demon was doing something to her. But why was it affecting her in this way? It was supposed to make her angry, irrational. Not punch her insides.

"Owwwwwwwww!" Evie wailed, falling to her knees.

Well, whatever. Something was attacking my best friend and I had to act, even if it was a different evil than what we expected. Even if it was just some bad tuna she'd eaten for lunch.

I got my game face on and dashed to Evie's side, grabbing her shoulders.

The scanner chose that moment to start shrieking: *BEEP BEEP BEEP!*

"Yes, we know!" I yelled over my shoulder. "Some supernatural bullshit is definitely present! Scott, can you—"

But he was already on it, moving toward us, brow furrowed with concentration as he put his spell in motion. As planned, Maisy, Shruti, and Dave had booked it for the relative safety of the dressing rooms and were hiding out until we conquered this thing. I was dimly aware of the crowd still assembled right outside, now erupting into a confused murmur.

"Lucy!" I yelled.

"Okay, loves!" she shouted to the crowd. "I think we need to shut the door now!"

I heard the door slam, and the buzz of the crowd was suddenly muffled. Then Lucy, Nate, and Bea were all at my side, clustered around Evie. Nate held the trap, ready to open it on cue. Evie slumped to the side, her face contorted in pain.

"Evie!" I cried, my hands tightening around her shoulders, not sure what else to do. I'd had high hopes for figuring out how to kick this dumb incorporeal puppy, but now that I was staring it in the face, all I could do was scream ineffectually and wait for Scott's spell to take root. I scanned the air around us wildly, as if the puppy would suddenly appear because I'd willed it to. "Get away from her!" I cried, frustration spiraling through me. God, there was just . . . there was nothing I could *do*. I felt powerless. I felt Annie Chang rising up inside me, ready to crumple and burst into tears.

"We have to wait," Nate said, his voice tight with tension. "Until Scott finds it and guides it into the trap, we can't really—"

"So we just have to sit here and watch this?" Bea protested. "It's so . . . so . . ."

We were all helpless. It was the worst feeling in the world.

Evie's eyes started to roll back into her head and desperation clawed at my chest. This was different than before, different than the puppy just making her act, as Bea would say, "extra aggro." This time, it seemed like it was *attacking* her.

I hadn't considered how dangerous this actually was, hadn't thought about the fact that we were gambling with Evie's life by putting her out as bait. No, as usual, I'd simply thought I could handle anything and that would be enough.

What if it wasn't?

"You can't have her!" I shrieked, addressing the air above us. "You *can't*—"

Suddenly, Evie's head popped up, her eyes focusing on me with unnerving intensity.

"It's new," she intoned. "It's *all new*."

The voice coming out of her body was deep and watery, like her usual voice had been slowed way, way down.

"It can't beeeeee newwwwwwwww," she continued, her voice slowing even further.

What she was saying didn't make any sense, but it pinged something in my brain, something familiar. What was it?

"Can't be new!" she repeated insistently and then she started shaking her head back and forth furiously, as if trying to get free of something.

"Evie!" I cried. Desperate, ineffective. Impotent. I moved my hands to her waist, trying to anchor her to the ground. "Evie—oh, shit!"

My palms felt like they had been submerged in fire ants—prickling and burning up. I let go of her and jumped backward, shaking my palms, trying to get rid of the searing pain. She stood up and stared out into the shop, her eyes vacant.

"Scott!" I yelled. I whipped around to look at him, to see where he was at with the spell. He had stopped in the middle of the store and was frowning as his eyes scanned the air.

"I . . . something's not right . . ." he said. "Just give me a few more minutes . . ."

"We don't have a few more minutes," I snapped. "Why won't that damn thing show itself?"

A howl pierced the air: wild, savage, barely human. It sounded like an animal caught in a trap. I turned back to Evie, who was doubled over in pain again, screaming so loud, I thought she might shatter every bit of glass in the store.

What was this thing *doing* to her?

"Tooooo newwwwww," she wailed.

"I can't take this," Nate growled. "I can't just watch—"

"What else can we do?" The last word came out strangled, almost like a sob. I was saying it just as much to myself as I was to him. Desperation rose in my chest again, and I tried to shove it down. I felt so powerless, so helpless, so . . .

The neckline of my dress pricked at me again, constricting against my skin, and the itch flared back into being, that fucking itch. Haze coated my vision, and I just couldn't take it any longer. I reached up and yanked at the neck and heard that satisfying *rippppp* as the cheap lace and satin gave way in my hand. The dress fell away and I was standing there in nothing but my bra and underwear, and then I could breathe again and I wasn't itchy and I felt my vision clearing—

"AHHHHHHHHHHHH!" Evie shrieked, throwing her

hands in the air. She collapsed to the ground, shaking, clawing at her torso, as if she was trying to do what I had just done, as if—

Wait.

That was it. It was—

"The dress!" Scott called out. "It's not in the air, it's in the dress! I can feel it, but I can't seem to get a handle on it ... I ... fuck. It's like it's ... *trapped* in there."

What the hell? The fucking puppy demon had somehow gotten into the dress and was trying to fucking *kill her*. I reached out wildly with my mental feathers, trying to burrow into the dress, inside the fabric, trying to grab hold of the puppy. But it was no use. I couldn't *see* it. So I couldn't grab hold of it.

Fuck it. I was going to have to try a different tactic. "Open the trap," I hissed at Nate.

"What?" He stared at me. "But what are you ... we don't know what effect it will have on her if you try to ..."

"Maybe not," I said. "But like you said: we can't just fucking *watch* it take her."

He was frozen in place, gazing at me with a look full of panic and pain and terror.

"Please," I said. I touched his arm, hoping it would shock him out of whatever fugue state he was going into. "I love her too. I *need* her too."

He nodded, his features resolving into a look of grim determination, and he popped open the trap.

Evie screamed. I focused on her and that damn dress. I reached out with my mental feathers and clamped on hard to the dress, harder than I'd ever clamped on to anything before. Then I pulled, trying to get it off of her. She screamed louder and clapped her hands to her waist. Now it looked like she was trying to hold the dress to her. And I could feel the dress resisting me, pushing back at my mind.

So we were going to have to do this the hard way.

Keeping a firm telekinetic hold on the dress, I charged forward and planted one hand on Evie's hip, using my other hand to try to get at the zipper. She screamed again. The dress pushed back against my mental feathers and Evie batted at my hands, trying to get me away from her. Despite the haphazard way she was batting me, she managed to block me from the zipper, so I gave up on that strategy and focused on getting a firm grip on the skirt.

"Yes, I know," I said through gritted teeth. "I thought this was the perfect frock, too. But it's really . . . not . . . fitting . . . right." And with that I tightened both my mental and physical grips and pulled with all my might.

Ripppppppppppp!

I tore the dress from her body and suddenly it was burning my palms, giving them that fire-ant feeling again. I ran to the trap and stuffed the dress inside. Nate slammed the trap shut. And Evie passed out on the spot.

Nate rushed to her side, cradling her in his arms. "She's breathing," he gasped, his voice hoarse. His face sagged with relief, but he was shaking.

"Let's get her to the hospital," I said. I kicked the remnants of my awful bridesmaid dress out of the way. "And somebody throw this godforsaken thing in the trash."

DIARY OF A REFORMED HALF-DEMON PRINCESS: PART 42

By Maisy Kane, Half-Demon Princess Editrix

Dear 'Friscans, lend me your ears! I'm afraid your pal Maisy has to get all unfun for just a moment. To answer the questions pouring in, yes, there was a big bridal fashion photo shoot at Pussy Queen earlier today, and yes, there were some technical difficulties. I'm afraid said difficulties mean I will *not* be posting video from the event. Your pal Maisy usually believes in freedom of the press at all costs, but I have received a decree from the powers that be at Aveda Jupiter, Inc., stating that if I release said video, I will no longer be privy to any exclusives regarding the #natevie wedding—and I know my readers live for that, so I must comply!

Please don't blame Evie for this, I know it's not her choice. When I say the powers that be at Aveda Jupiter, Inc., I mean . . . well, just that. But don't worry, #natevie fans, I'll still be bringing you all the latest scoops—you can always count on your pal Maisy!

COMMENTS

MillsAlum97: Soooooo . . . no video, but did anyone actually go to Evie's big bridal fashion show?! I know they weren't letting anyone inside, but I heard she looked stunning!

HaightHoney2000: I was there and she so did, but in that classic Evie way, like she hadn't thought about it much. I don't think she even did her hair, it looked so gorgeous and natural and she had just sort of thrown these little flowers in it! I want to do that with mine!!!

EastBay4Evah: I was there too!! It ended . . . abruptly. Like, Aveda kind of ruined the moment by coming out wearing this BATSHIT INSANE MONSTROSITY . . .

HaightHoney2000: There was no "kind of," it totally stole attention from Evie! Typical Aveda Jupiter. Anyway, then Evie started giving a speech, but right in the middle of it, she seemed to be having some kind of, I don't know, nervous breakdown? A stress freak-out?

EastBay4Evah: Yes! And they shut the door and just, like, *ended* it. I'm betting Aveda was stressing Evie out again. Parading around in that awful dress, hogging the spotlight, trying to upstage Evie at her own bridal fashion show! She had to know that fugly dress is all we'd be talking about! She probably forced Evie to let her wear it!

HaightHoney2000: Or maybe Evie didn't even know that's what Aveda was going to be wearing?!?

EastBay4Evah: Word on the street is Aveda's the one who called for the video to be suppressed. She really can't stand anyone else getting attention, and Evie in that gorgeous dress was definitely going to get attention!

MillsAlum97: Damn. As a bride, I would not stand for that shit. I know we love Evie for being so grounded and normal, but I kinda hope she goes full Bridezilla on Aveda's ass.

CHAPTER THIRTEEN

"YOU KNOW, if either of us was going to literally die for fashion, I always thought it would be you." Evie grinned up at me from her bed, where she was currently ensconced in a mountain of pillows. I gave her a wan smile in return, but I knew my face was creased with worry. She had regained consciousness and been pronounced fine at the hospital, and now she appeared to be mostly back to her sweet self.

I, on the other hand, couldn't stop replaying the horrific scene that had unfolded before us: Evie nearly killed by an invisible force, me unable to do anything except freak out. Maisy had begged to post the video she'd gotten from the fashion show portion of the day, but I'd put the kibosh on that immediately—even the most careful editing wouldn't mask the truly bizarre turn events had taken, and I certainly didn't need that preserved forever on the internet.

Nate fluffed one of the pillows propping Evie up. She reached out and squeezed his hand.

"Stop," she said softly. "I'm fine."

"You could have not been fine, though," I blurted out, slumping next to her on the bed. "I don't know why I thought it was a good idea to risk you like that, why I ever let you—"

"Annie." She dropped Nate's hand and took mine. "I agreed to it, remember? You didn't 'let' me do anything. And like I keep saying . . ." She leaned forward and exaggerated each word. "I. Am. Fine."

I squeezed her hand and nodded briskly, blinking back

tears. *Go away, Annie Chang,* I thought fiercely. *Get your meek little Clark Kent ass outta here. Aveda Jupiter has to think.* I felt Scott watching me from the other side of the room and studiously avoided his gaze.

"Cheer up, oldsters!" Bea piped up from her perch on the rocking chair next to the bed. "Dang, it's like a mausoleum up in here. It's not like any of you never had a brush with death before."

"True," murmured Lucy. "Though this is perhaps not the best time to bring that up, Bea. As the kids say, 'too soon.'"

"I am one of the kids," Bea said, with an eye-roll. "Anyhow. I just meant we should move on to talking about what we've learned about our pal, the invisible puppy demon. Obvs, it used a dress to attack us this time. Oh, and sorry, Evie, your dress got pretty beat up. I don't think we can salvage it."

"Too bad," Evie said, her voice faint.

"It is too bad," I agreed. "It really was perfect. But don't worry, we'll find you something even better. Even more fabulous. More dazzling."

"Right. Dazzling," Evie said, giving me a look I couldn't quite decipher. "Anyway, yes, the two brushes I've had with the puppy felt different. In the bridal tent, it was a shift in mood, like I was suddenly filling with rage. Whereas this time . . ." She winced. "It was a physical thing, actually pushing against my skin. Stabbing me, basically."

"And it stabbed my hands when I tried to touch it," I said.

"As if it found a new, more effective way to attack," Nate said.

"So the puppy demon is *learning* things?" Lucy said. "Delightful."

"If it has a higher brain capacity, as we've theorized, that makes sense," Bea said. "But in order to do what? Once again, why? At Pussy Queen, it appeared to be attacking only Evie. As badass as you've become, Sis, what does attacking one person gain?"

"Scott," I said, "during the attack, you said you could feel the puppy even though you couldn't grab on to it—does that mean you were able to use your spell to connect with it?"

"Yes, that part of the spell was at least semi-successful," he said ruefully. "I couldn't hold the connection for very long, but I did get a sense of what it was thinking." He frowned, as if trying to put the pieces together. "This time, it was like I was overloaded with all of its emotions at once: anger, frustration, and . . . conflict. Huh. You know, I think there was conflict *within* its thought patterns."

"Like it's fighting with itself?" Lucy said, quirking an eyebrow.

"Like it's working with something else," Scott said. "Or fused with something else. It was like part of it wanted to do one thing, and part of it wanted to do another."

"So there's a whole other component we need to look for?" I pressed. "Something else that's helping power the puppy?"

"I'm not sure." Scott shook his head, frustrated. "I wish I'd been able to connect with it for longer, but at the time, the most important thing was . . ." He glanced at Evie.

"Getting that fucking dress off of Evie ASAP," I supplied.

"I'll test the dress we secured in the trap after we're done here, see if that produces any clues," Nate said, his demeanor becoming more even-keeled as his analytical brain latched on to what needed to be done. "I'll get to it as soon as I make sure . . ." His gaze slid to Evie again and she gave his arm an impatient poke.

"*Fine*," she repeated insistently, pointing to herself.

"Maybe we captured the puppy. Maybe it's, like, still inside the dress," Bea said. "That would mean, hey, ta-da, our work here is done!"

I nodded and resisted the urge to bite my nails. Somehow, I had a feeling it wasn't that simple. It never was.

"If it's still in there . . ." Scott frowned contemplatively. "I'm wondering if there's another component I can add to the guiding spell, something that will actually let me pull the puppy out of the dress. I think I can modify the spell I was working on to pull Evie's power out of her back when she was posing as Annie."

"That guiding spell just keeps getting add-ons," Bea said, arching an eyebrow. "Or is it up-sells? Like how I always end up getting candy at the movies on top of my extra-large popcorn. I like to mix them together—you know, sweet and salty—and—"

"Let's look at the other data this incident presented," Nate interrupted before Bea could get too far into her junk food tangent. "What about the words Evie was saying?"

Evie shuddered. "That part was extra freaky. I felt like I was trapped inside my body, I could hear my voice saying things, but it wasn't *me*. It was so . . ." She shook her head, worry creeping into her expression. "I *really* hate being out of control like that. I . . ." She trailed off, swallowing hard.

"You kept saying something about 'new,'" Lucy prompted. "I would say you were expressing general distaste for the concept."

New.

The word lodged in my brain. Simple, inane. Why had it pinged something for me back at the shop? Why was it pinging something for me *now*?

"Carol!" I exclaimed out loud. Everyone looked at me in confusion. "Carol also said something about 'new.' After she was done yelling about her custom lingerie."

"So the puppy demon is anti-newness," Lucy mused. "But what does that tell us?"

We fell silent for a moment, puzzling it out.

"Let's keep thinking on that one," Bea finally said. "Moving forward, if we don't find the puppy in the dress—"

"Then we need to figure out where it will strike next," Scott said.

I allowed myself to look at him. He met my eyes and gave me a tired smile that stabbed right at my heart. I hastily looked away.

"Seems like dresses are its new thing," Bea said, twisting a purple lock of hair around her finger.

"Wedding dresses," I said. "Or at least that wedding dress in particular. It may be our best lead. So in addition to testing what's left of the dress, we should try to figure out why the puppy chose this dress in particular. And where it might go next."

Bea nodded solemnly. "We follow the clothes."

I never expected those words to fill me with such dread.

"Shruti can probably help with that, maybe give us an idea of where to start," I said. "Since she seems to know the local fashion and bridal scenes so well. Evie, do you want to reach out to Shruti and see if she's willing to help? Are you feeling up to it?"

"Sure, but I think you should do it, Annie," Evie said. "She seems to really like you. She totally wants to be your friend."

"Me?" I said, my brow furrowing. "But you're—" I cut myself off before I completed that thought: *the one everyone likes better.* "The bride," I substituted. "That gives you more authority to—"

"—to ask for someone's help in a supernatural investigation that's only loosely connected to the wedding?" Evie gave me a puzzled look. "Not really."

"Oh. Well, then, of course I can do it," I said, feeling silly.

She gave me a tired grin and I felt my worry rising back up, threatening to smother me. I flashed back to the night after the battle with Shasta, Evie unconscious in that big bed, with me desperately needing her to be okay. And knowing it was all my fault if she wasn't.

She could have not been okay today, too, an irritating little voice in my head reminded me. *And it would have been all your fault. Again.*

"If that's all, then Evie needs to rest," Nate said. He kissed the top of Evie's head and stood. "And Bea and I should get to work running tests on the wedding dress." He turned to Scott. "Can you assist us with the magical component once we've done the initial run of tests? Say, in about an hour?"

"I'll be ready," Scott said.

As everyone filed out, I hung back, my eyes roaming over Evie and her giant mountain of pillows.

"Okay, this is getting ridiculous," she said. "I expect it from Nate; he's weirdly overprotective considering that I can burn almost any danger I might encounter to the ground. But you? Aveda Jupiter? You know what it takes to be a superheroine, how tough we have to be. Do I have to get 'I AM FINE' tattooed on my forehead?"

"That's one look I would not recommend for your wedding," I said, trying to give my voice that imperious cast.

She giggled and I couldn't take it anymore. I felt Aveda Jupiter crumbling around me and suddenly I was flinging myself on top of her, burying my face against her shoulder and trying to choke back the sobs that had gathered in my throat.

When Annie Chang comes out, she doesn't half-ass it. That's one thing she has in common with Aveda.

"We all felt so helpless," I said, my voice catching. I couldn't meet her eyes, so I kept talking to her shoulder. "*I* felt so helpless. I don't think I've ever thought about how . . . how you could just be taken from me in an instant. I mean, I guess I thought about it that night when you were passed out after the battle with Shasta, but this time . . ." I took in a deep, quavery breath. "It was happening right in front of me. And I couldn't do anything. I never thought about that when you were posing as me. When I *made* you pose as me. But oh god, Evie . . ."

I forced myself to look her in the eye. "I don't know what I'd do without you. Please don't . . . don't ever make me have to be without you."

She gave me a slight smile, and I realized her eyes were filled with tears. "Ditto," she said. "Ditto so hard."

I laughed a little, relief I couldn't quite quantify whooshing through me. She pulled me into a hug and I hugged

back hard. And just for a moment, I allowed myself to luxuriate in the soft swirl of emotions wrapping itself around
me. I let myself just be Annie Chang.

I didn't have the strength to be anything else.

After I left Evie to rest amidst her pillow mountain, I found
myself at loose ends. I worked out for a while, my muscles
knitting together, my Aveda Jupiter armor rebuilding itself
around me. I needed to talk to Shruti about following the
clothes, but first I wanted to see if Nate and Bea's testing
had led to any further information that might prove useful
on that particular mission. I waited an hour, two. As my
waiting bled into a third hour, I hovered around the basement entrance, hoping they would emerge. And somehow,
I found myself descending the steps. It couldn't hurt to
check in, right?

But Nate and Bea weren't in the lab. It was just Scott,
crouched behind his desk, sifting through a stack of papers.

"Where are they?" I said, looking around. "Are the tests
done?"

"Not quite." He gave me a tired smile. "Their analyses so
far are inconclusive and apparently require even more
analyses—like, analyses on top of analyses—so I suggested
they go consult with Rose, see if she has further insights to
offer."

I cocked an eyebrow. "They couldn't just call her?"

"I suggested they go talk to her in person so they could
have productive in-person work time. Also . . ." He hesitated. "I think they needed a break. They were both getting
intense, staring at everything in that wall-eyed way where
it's easy to miss things." He toyed with the papers in front
of him. "That's Evie's fiancé, Evie's sister. And they both
had to watch . . ."

Her almost die, my brain helpfully completed.

I nodded briskly. I had to build myself back up again,
emerge from my unfortunate lapse into Annie Chang–ness

at full strength. It wouldn't do the team—or our incorporeal puppy hunt—any favors if I was on the verge of falling
apart.

"How about you?" he said as I sat down across from him.
"Are you okay?"

"Why wouldn't I be?" I forced a grim smile. "The dress
didn't try to murder *me*."

"No." He reached over and took my hand. "But it hurt
your hands, didn't it? When you ripped it off of her?" He
examined my palm, stroking his thumb over the skin. A
flurry of tingles rushed down my spine, and I tried not to
flash immediately to us in the gym, kissing, his gorgeous
body pressed against mine. I shook my head and attempted
to squelch the blush rising in my cheeks. It had been a mistake. We probably didn't even need to talk about it since it
was so *obviously* a mistake. I pulled my hand away. And
changed the subject.

"What's this?" I said, gesturing to his stack of papers. "A
new spell?"

"No," he said, covering it with his arm. "It's . . . nothing."

I craned my neck so I could see the sections of the top
piece of paper that were still visible. It didn't look like a
spell. I nudged his arm to the side.

"Is that an application?" I scrutinized the grid-like formation asking for name, birth date, education, and so on.
"For San Francisco University? Thinking of Bea's future?"

"Thinking of mine." He tried to make it sound light, but
it came out weighted. Something flashed over his face, and
I couldn't quite put my finger on it—but it was akin to that
deep seriousness he'd had right before I thought he was
going to kiss me at the bakery, right before he kissed me in
the gym, that rare bit of intensity that told me there was
more going on underneath his mellow exterior than he
tended to let on.

"You went to college, though," I pressed, wiggling the
paper out from under his arm. I studied the application. It
was still blank, devoid of the information required by that

grid of tiny boxes. "And you don't seem to be thinking about it so much that you've actually filled any of this out."

"Annie . . ." He blew out a frustrated breath and took the paper from me, adding it to the stack and shoving the whole thing off to the side. He studied me for a moment, wheels turning, like he wasn't sure where to start. I stared back, defiant, like: *Well? Answers, please?*

Aveda Jupiter is accustomed to getting answers out of people.

I won the stare-off and he finally heaved an even bigger sigh and slumped back in his chair. "I was thinking of going back to get my master's. In social work."

I gaped it him. "But . . . why?"

He gave me an amused look. "Is it so unthinkable that I'd want to do something other than be at your and Evie's beck and call for the rest of my life?"

I shook my head, feeling stung. "That's not what I . . . I mean, that's not how I see it."

"Gah." He ran a hand over his face and leaned so far back in his chair he nearly tipped over. He looked exhausted. "I'm sorry. That came out mean. I guess, like everyone, I'm wrung out. After today." He studied me again and I felt myself wanting to squirm under the steadiness of his gaze. Now that intensity in his eyes wasn't a mere flash; it was right there on the surface, and it wasn't going away. It was disconcerting, but it also made my heart beat faster. It felt like I was getting a rare, private glimpse at the real Scott and that, like me, there was a part of himself he kept secret from everyone else, a hidden, deep down piece that only emerged when he was at his most vulnerable. It was like seeing someone totally naked. And I desperately wanted to see more of it, even though I knew that would likely bring Annie Chang rushing to the surface.

"Look," I finally said. "We said we were trying to be friends, right?" *Even though we've definitely been doing things that are perhaps . . . beyond the scope of that.* I brushed the thought aside. "And friends sometimes talk about things." At least, that's what I'd always heard. I really only talked about "things" with Evie. And even then, not everything.

"I guess before I joined the team earlier this year, we hadn't talked in a while," he said slowly. "Not since . . ."

Not since that night he kissed me. And I pushed him away.

"Anyway." He toyed with the edges of the papers. "Before that, I'd been volunteering at one of the foster care centers my mom works with—they have an afterschool program where the kids get to try out different activities, and I taught them a few surfing basics. I ended up sticking around for some of the other programs, helping them with their homework, stuff like that. And I really liked it. It made me feel like I was actually, I dunno, doing something. Something useful. Being my own kind of superhero."

I flashed back to that day in sixth grade: his chest puffed out, his face red. Ready to take down those jerky "Lazy Lunch-Lady Lynne" kids. Ready to protect those who couldn't protect themselves. Even though he couldn't really protect himself, either.

"Evie didn't tell me you were doing that," I said. "I had no idea."

He shrugged. "I didn't tell her. I didn't tell anyone."

"I'm surprised you didn't tell Evie, though. You two have always been so . . . close." Even though I hadn't been trying to, I automatically put a weird, suggestive emphasis on "close."

He gave me a look.

"I'm sorry," I said hastily. "I don't know why I do that. Well, I do . . . sort of. I have a hard time. Letting things go. Even though you guys hooking up on prom night isn't something for *me* to let go, it's not like I'm, I don't know, Nate, or . . . or . . ."

God. I sounded stuttery and unsure, flailing around for the right words like a drowning woman in search of a life preserver. I took a deep breath, composed myself, and told my Annie Chang side to shut up, please.

"I didn't tell anyone," he repeated. He gave me that unnervingly steady look again. "Sometimes you and Evie are so caught up in your own world, the world that's just the two of you and all your issues, there isn't a lot of room for anything else. Or anyone else."

I couldn't really argue with that.

"We're working on our co-dependency problems," I said, trying to make my tone light. "Anyway. You're thinking about going back to school. But it seems like instead of doing things to put that into motion, you're mostly staring really intensely at the application. What's the hold-up?"

"I'm not sure what I want anymore," he said, his eyes rolling upward to explore the ceiling. "When we all got our powers back in the day, I was like, this is it, we're finally gonna be superheroes. Invincible. Able to leap tall buildings in a single bound and defend the downtrodden. And some of us did. *You* did." He gave me a gentle smile and I tried to ignore the way my face heated, the flush creeping up the back of my neck. "But the spells I was able to do were so weak. Inconsequential. I don't know why I even thought I *could* be a superhero, the first time I realized I had any kind of power, I — "

He cut himself off, a faint blush suffusing his cheeks.

"What?" I said, unable to suppress my curiosity. "You know, I've never actually heard your origin story."

"I . . . it's not that interesting," he said, in that hasty way that indicated it was actually *totally* interesting. "One day, I was wondering what it would be like to look like someone else. What my life would be like, if . . . people would react differently to me."

I nodded, even as my brow crinkled in confusion. We'd gotten our powers when we were eighteen — he'd already gone through his pipsqueak-to-heartthrob makeover. Most people seemed to react to him just fine, to put it mildly.

"I was thinking really hard about this, apparently," he

said with a wry smile. "And I felt something brush against my mind. I realized later it was that Otherworld magic—that I was gaining access to it for the first time. And then I glanced in the mirror and I looked like someone else."

"Your first glamour!" I exclaimed. "Who did you look like?"

"It's not important—"

"It so is! This is a crucial part of your origin story! Who did Scott Cameron—bona fide high school hottie, excellent specimen of teenage malehood—want to be?"

"I looked like . . . the guy in that comic book you like. Figure Five or something?"

"Figure *Four*?" I squeaked. Figure Four was Battle Angel Alita's love interest, a square-jawed, kind-hearted hunk of a man whose image I'd tended to linger over even when I was flipping through pages I'd read a zillion times. Scott hadn't really been into the manga, though, so why had he—oh. *Oh*.

"Yeah," Scott said quickly. "After that, I realized I could access and manipulate those magics brushing against my mind to do small things. The glamours. The love tokens. It was cool at first, especially when I realized I could use these dopey little spells to make a living—Mom and I never had much, so it seemed impractical *not* to use my power for that. But I never felt like I was actually making a difference in the world."

I nodded—more just to show I was listening than in agreement. I knew Scott had made decent money for a while selling love tokens online. I'd thought it was a means to an end, a way to support himself while he indulged in the things he really enjoyed, like surfing and, uh . . . well. I wasn't sure what else he enjoyed, other than being a goofball, stretching in a distractingly sexy way, and standing up for people even when it wasn't necessarily in his best interest to do so.

It was odd that I'd known him for so long and apparently didn't know him well at all.

Except I felt like I did. Like I knew him better than I knew anyone—other than Evie, of course. I couldn't explain why. It had something to do with seeing him at what I knew were his truest moments—those rare flashes of intensity. The pure rage when the kids had made fun of his mom. The way he was looking at me now, exhausted and stripped of all barriers, unable to cover up with a joke.

"Then we got our power level-ups," he continued. "And now ..."

"Now you've got major magic," I said. "You can heal injuries and shit. Like my ankle. Or that little girl's arm at the bakery. You can help people in an even more concrete way than the master's in social work would allow."

"That's how I *should* feel." His eyes wandered to the blank application. "But instead I feel like some kind of choice has been taken away. I shouldn't want this anymore." He tapped the application. "But some part of me still does, even though it seems like a waste of this level-up gift I've been given. So. I don't know. Every time I start to think about it, I can't figure out what I actually want. I just feel confused all the time."

I gnawed on my lower lip and resisted the urge to blurt out that I felt exactly the same way. That ever since everything had changed—with my injury, with Evie, with the power level-up, with feeling useless and unneeded and cropped out of every single metaphorical photo, with the months of unwanted leisure and everything in between—I hadn't been able to figure *anything* out. Not one damn thing. And that every time I thought I'd set myself on the right path, the map changed.

"For most of my life, I feel like I've pinned my hopes on some dumb fantasy that could never be true," he said. "Like back in school, when I tried to take down those kids who were being little shits about my mom. I honestly thought the sheer force of my anger would allow me to totally kick their asses." He gave me a sheepish look. "Or when we got our powers, and I thought I was going to be a real superhero. Or . . ."

His gaze lingered on me and I felt my face flush again. I wondered if he was thinking of that time he'd kissed me and I'd dashed *that* fantasy.

He stared at the application again, as if willing it to divulge all the answers. "I don't know which is which. What's the fantasy? And what's real? I still want to help people, but I don't know the best way. I don't know if going after something I feel like I still want, but shouldn't, is selfish. And I feel like I really should have all this shit figured out by now." He met my eyes and his expression was so open and earnest, so shot through with that naked vulnerability, my breath caught. "Do you ever feel that way?"

So many responses were on the tip of my tongue.

Yes, of course.

Yes, all the time.

I mean . . . not so much in the past, but now? I don't know what I'm doing. I don't know what's real. Or who I am.

But I couldn't seem to let any of these words escape. They took me back to that stuttery, unsure place I loathed so much—the Annie Chang place. The place I was trying like hell to escape.

So instead I schooled my features into my best Aveda Jupiter look of detached sympathy and said: "No, not really. The power level-up has given me everything I've ever wanted."

His eyes clouded over, and I got the sense that, once again, I had somehow Hurricane Annie-ed all over the place. Perhaps there was nothing I could do about that. Perhaps that was a necessary step on my path to full mojo reclaiming. And hey, I'd actually managed to be in a room alone with him for more than five minutes without trying to kiss him, pounce on him, or inappropriately eat cake with him.

"Well!" I said, making my voice overly bright. "I guess

I'll go check on Evie. Let me know when Nate and Bea get back."

As I marched upstairs, I tried to congratulate myself on maintaining strength during what could have become a vulnerable moment. Instead of breaking down and crying all over him like I had with Evie, I'd kept my cool.

Resist temptation—*check!*

Make crucial progress on your mojo-reclaiming mission—*check!*

Avoid kissing someone you shouldn't be kissing—*check, check, check!*

I should have felt empowered. Instead I felt thoroughly, inexplicably miserable.

CHAPTER FOURTEEN

AFTER WE DECIDED to follow the clothes, the clothes decided to make things difficult.

Evie's dress was just a dress, no supernatural energy lurking in its delicate chiffon folds. We weren't sure when, exactly, the puppy had escaped, but Bea was hard at work on improving the trap, trying to add some kind of element that would keep it good and locked in next time. In the meantime, we destroyed what was left of Evie's dress—just in case.

I was still determined to follow *something*, so the next day I called Shruti and explained our theory about the puppy demon figuring out how to use Evie's wedding dress to attack her.

"Where do we go from here? What, in your expert opinion, is the most useful line of clothes-related investigation?" I asked. I was holed up in my bedroom, phone jammed against my ear.

"Hmm," Shruti said. "Well, even though we don't know where the puppy's gone, we can look into the origin of Evie's dress, see if that tells us anything."

"It didn't have a label." I allowed my eyes to wander to a small cobweb in the corner of the ceiling and resisted the urge to claw my way up the wall and untangle it. "I thought maybe it was vintage."

"All dresses originate somewhere," Shruti said. "But that one actually looked like a modern design to me. Remember how I said it resembled a Marcus Wong?"

"I assume Marcus Wong is a wedding wear designer I know nothing about?"

"A *San Francisco–based* wedding wear designer," Shruti crowed. "I think we should pay a visit to his show room. Like fashion detectives."

"Fashion detectives?" I couldn't help but laugh. "Imagine that on a business card."

"We should totally get those made," Shruti said.

"And even if he knows nothing about Evie's dress, at least we'll be in a place with a ton of wedding gowns and a ton of brides," I said, warming to the idea. "Maybe we'll get some clues as to where the puppy is likely to strike next."

"I'll text over the address," Shruti said. "Meet you there at two?"

"Affirmative, fashion detective," I said, and hung up.

🔥

I decided Shruti and I should undertake this particular mission ourselves. Evie was still resting after her ordeal, and if Marcus Wong and his dresses were connected to our puppy in any way, I didn't want to spook him by crashing his show room with a whole entourage of people.

Located on a tiny, crooked street in an up and coming neighborhood, Marcus's bridal show room was a fascinating mix of flash and class. It was also the only "fancy" business on the block, which was otherwise populated with crumbling empty storefronts and hole-in-the-wall liquor marts. Marcus's sign—giant red letters that screamed WONG in a style that resembled graffiti—made the whole enterprise stand out even more. His window display, meanwhile, depicted wedding dress–clad mannequins engaging in what appeared to be some kind of blood sport: they all wore elaborate antler headdresses and had slashes of red smeared across their faces and on their hands. And they were posed as if menacing each other. Like wild animals.

"What's the deal with this guy?" I asked Shruti, gesturing to the window. "I know the bridal tent was basically a war zone, but I thought the designer show rooms liked to keep the veneer of refinement going."

"Marcus prides himself on designing for the alternative bride," Shruti said. Today she was wearing her hair in Princess Leia–style buns and had donned a chic peachy-pink vintage trench coat in honor of our fashion detectiving. "He was a performance artist in his youth, and believes weddings are the purest form of performance, best expressed through the gown."

I studied the gowns in the window. Once you got past the rather alarming display, they were quite beautiful, and they did have that swooping, exaggerated mermaid shape that made Evie's dress stand out.

"All right, fashion detective," I said. "Let's move in."

We entered the shop, and I did a double take. The place was *packed*. It wasn't quite the savage chaos of the bridal tent, but there was a definite buzz in the air as brides-to-be pawed through the racks of dresses and inspected the various mannequins on display.

"Ladies, ladies!" A slender, pinched-looking Asian man clad in all black waved his hands in the air, looking fretful. His voice was soft and lilting and punctuated with a slight French accent. "Please. Stop touching everything! You must have an appointment to browse our stock and even then, it is only to be taken off the rack by a certified Marcus Wong consultant."

"Is that Marcus?" I asked Shruti.

"No," she said. "That's his assistant, Franz. Marcus only appears at the end of each consultation to give his blessing to the dress purchase. Or to *not* give it."

"Marcus can nix a potential buyer?" I shook my head. "If Evie's dress was his, how did it end up somewhere as accessible to the masses as the bridal tent?"

"An excellent question for the fashion detectives to ask," Shruti said. "Ah! There he is." She gestured toward the opposite side of the room, where a wizened elderly stump of a man in a schlubby gray t-shirt, sweats, and flip-flops had emerged from the back. He looked like he'd be more at home dropping acid and dispensing loopy wisdom on Berkeley's Telegraph Avenue than designing high-end wedding finery. Marcus studied a woman wearing one of his spectacular mermaid creations, his eyes narrowing in appraisal. She looked back at him anxiously, twisting her hands together, awaiting his approval.

"That's Marcus?" I said. "I was expecting someone more ..."

"Youthful? Hip?" Shruti said. "Appearances can be deceiving. Marcus is as avant-garde as it gets."

Marcus studied the blond, petite bride-to-be. I realized I recognized her as one of the brides from the Market tent. I guess she hadn't found anything there. Or if she had, she'd lost it in the puppy demon chaos. Finally, Marcus gave her a small, curt nod. She let out a scream of joy, clapped her hands together, and lunged at him, arms outstretched for a hug. Franz immediately stepped in front of Marcus and shook his head at her.

"Marcus does not allow touching, as outlined in the forty-page waiver you signed upon booking your appointment," he said. "Please step back and take joy in the knowledge that he has approved the dress to grace your body."

The bride nodded, cowed, and smiled gratefully at Marcus. I practically expected her to bow. Marcus, for his part, did not offer any further facial expression.

"All right, no touching," I muttered. "Let's go. Keep your eyes and ears open, straighten your spine, and put a bit of swagger into your step—like we're here on official business. Which we are."

"Girl, you are fearless!" Shruti said, beaming at me.

We made our way across the plush carpet—which was the same violent red as the graffiti sign outside—and through the bridal crowd, focused on Marcus. We were almost at his side, when a woman nearly crashed into me, as she attempted to race through the mass of bodies.

"Hey!" I said grabbing her by the arm. I was about to tell

her to slow down, watch where she was going, and not kill herself over a dress, when I realized I recognized her.

"Gwen?" I said, not quite believing it.

But it was. Cakezilla Carol's best friend and maid of honor. Gwen smoothed the skirt of her dress and gave me a haughty look that seemed completely at odds with the timid woman at Cake My Day.

"Aveda," I said. "Remember, I was there when ..." I trailed off, not sure how to complete that thought. *When your friend lost her shit and nearly killed people over red velvet cake and custom lingerie* sounded so awkward.

"I know who you are, Aveda Jupiter," Gwen said, giving me the stink-eye. "You ruined Carol's wedding!"

"Excuse me?" I wasn't even sure where to begin with that statement. Her friend had been affected by an evil puppy demon and tried to kill me. How was I responsible for ruining her wedding?

"And now!" Gwen continued, her voice rising. "Now you're trying to ruin Evie Tanaka's too!"

"What!" Shruti cried, stepping forward to stand next to me. "That is one hundred percent not true! Aveda is busting her butt to be the most perfect maid of honor ever!"

"That's not what I heard!" Gwen said, her eyes taking on a vengeful gleam. "I heard Aveda totally monopolized Evie's bridal coming-out by wearing a trashy, attention-getting dress! It's not even the wedding day and already she's upstaging the bride!"

"Up-upstaging?" I sputtered. "In that hideous dress? No offense," I added to Shruti.

"None taken," she said. "Evie and I wanted something dramatic to match your taste, but we may have gone a little *too* vintage with that one."

"I'm onto you, Aveda Jupiter," Gwen said with a sneer. "And me and all the other San Francisco brides-to-be will not allow you to—"

"Wait a minute," I interrupted. "Since when are *you* a bride-to-be?"

"Since Carol started having doubts about her wedding after her little encounter with you," Gwen sniffed. "I got engaged as a show of solidarity."

"That doesn't seem like the best reason to get engaged," I said. "Or the best way to be a friend to Carol."

"It's what she wanted," Gwen insisted. "And you're one to talk about being a best friend, stealing Evie's thunder like that!"

Before I could retort, she swept off in a tizzy. I shook my head in dismay. How was I getting a reputation for being a drama queen when I was actively trying not to be a drama queen?

"Let's talk to Marcus and get out of here," I said to Shruti. I suddenly felt as if all the brides in the store were glaring at us, as if they'd overheard that entire exchange and had joined Gwen in taking up the cause against me.

Shruti didn't respond. I turned to look at her. She was staring after Gwen, her brow furrowed.

"What is it?" I asked.

"Something's pinging for me," she said. "Something about that girl."

"Like your fashion detective sense is tingling?" I joked.

She gave me a half-smile. "Something like that. It will come to me, I'm sure."

We wended our way through the remainder of the bridal crowd and finally reached Marcus, who had just moved yet another bride to tears by issuing a decree that she was allowed to purchase one of his glorious creations.

"Excuse me," I said, reaching over to tap Marcus on the shoulder. Before my finger could connect, Franz darted between us and looked at me like I was a bit of garbage scraped off someone's shoe.

"You need an appointment," he snapped.

"Actually, I don't." I straightened my spine and gave him my best imperious look. "I'm not here to try on gowns. I'm here to ask questions in an investigation crucial to the safety of this city."

I tried to make eye contact with Marcus, but he was staring into space, as if transfixed by something just beyond my left ear. He mumbled something under his breath, a few words that I couldn't make out.

"Marcus says you may ask one question," Franz said.

I bristled, a retort springing to my tongue about how no one limited Aveda Jupiter to anything. Then I realized that wasn't the best way of getting answers. Playing this bizarre little man's game for a few minutes probably wasn't going to kill me.

Probably.

I pulled my phone out of my pocket and tapped on the picture I'd taken of Evie in the bridal tent.

"This dress," I said. "Is it one of yours?"

Marcus turned his unfocused gaze to the picture. Franz cocked an eyebrow. Shruti and I tilted forward as a weighted silence fell over us, waiting to see if he was going to give us something, anything. Marcus scrutinized the photo further, his brow furrowing slightly. The buzz from the crowd in the salon seemed to recede. I realized I was holding my breath.

Then Marcus muttered something unintelligible to Franz.

"It was his dress at one time," Franz said.

"'At one time,'" I repeated. "What does that mean?"

"That is more than one question—" Franz began, but Marcus muttered something else.

Franz pursed his lips, clearly displeased at the fact that his boss was allowing us to break an arbitrary rule. "He says it was an experiment gone wrong. An aberration. The red element was simply too vulgar."

"His sign is red!" blurted out Shruti. "As is the carpet in here!"

Marcus muttered something else.

"He says those are entirely different reds," Franz said. "They are in the crimson family, whereas the flowers creating the unfortunate menstrual-esque punctuation on that dress are on the scarlet spectrum. Marcus was trying something new, playing with repurposed vintage fabrics. It did not work and therefore the label was stripped and the dress was banished to the riff-raff of the Indie Fashion Market. And we do not speak of it."

Marcus lifted a finger to his lips. *Shhh.*

"I see," I said, trying to make sense of what he was—they were?—saying and how it fit in with everything else. "So have you noticed anything weird happening here at the shop? Brides behaving strangely when they put on certain dresses?"

Marcus shook his head and muttered something else.

"Marcus says all brides behave strangely," Franz said, his lips drawing into a thin frown. "Your time is up. You may leave now."

"But—" I said.

"Good-bye!" Franz said, making his voice loud and insistent. Marcus gave us a delicate finger wave. "If you need help seeing yourself out, Gregory will show you the way." He gestured toward another black-clad figure—a tall, broad man with a shock of silver hair who was apparently serving as Marcus's bouncer. Gregory gave us a muted sneer.

I blew out a long breath and, for the second time in the span of five minutes, reminded myself that blowing up and demanding answers probably wasn't going to get us anywhere. At least not right now.

Even though I totally could have kicked Gregory's ass if I'd wanted to.

Instead I simply gave a small nod and turned and marched out of the store, hoping Shruti was following me. I suddenly felt like all eyes were on me again, like the assembled brides-to-be were just waiting for me to do something particularly diva-esque so they could tweet about it. I wasn't about to give them the satisfaction.

Once we were back outside, I turned to Shruti. "What did all of that mean?" I sputtered. "Because from where

I'm standing, I don't think any of that was useful information."

My hands curled into fists at my sides and I ordered them to relax. I couldn't let the frustration take over. Shruti's face was thoughtful, and she tapped her index against her chin, as if trying to recall a memory that was just out of reach.

"What is it?" I asked.

"Maybe nothing," she said. "Maybe something." She met my eyes, her expression grim. "We need to go to Pussy Queen."

"Why won't you tell me what's going on?" I asked as Shruti rummaged through a stack of Polaroids. We were back at Pussy Queen, huddled in Shruti's pop-up shop area. Maisy had run out to do some errands, leaving Dave to mind the store. He was behind his counter, staring into a mug of some kind of beverage, as if it possessed a hypnotic quality. I felt a pang of sympathy for him; he really didn't seem to have anything to do except hang out here, smoke weed, make weird drinks, and dispense the occasional bits of fortune-cookie-style wisdom. I wondered if he felt like I did when we'd been in our non-apocalypse lull, suffering through an endless string of breakfast courses, feeling bored and useless and wondering if I'd ever get to do anything worthwhile again.

Dave looked up and met my eyes, as if sensing my thought tangent.

"If winter comes, can spring be far behind?" he said solemnly.

Or maybe not. Maybe, unlike me, he was content just sitting there. The room took on a sudden chill and I shivered.

"It's okay, Dave," Shruti said, her tone soothing, as she continued to rifle through the Polaroids. "Maisy tried doing that promotion where we offered his classic Sunny Side mimosas, and I was hoping some of his old customers from the café would show," she murmured to me under her breath. "But none of them did. I think he's feeling a bit stung. He's been having difficulty controlling the temperature in here as well as he usually does."

Dave went back to staring at his mug, a slight frown creasing his brow.

"Here it is," Shruti said, pulling a Polaroid free from the stack and passing it to me.

I studied it. The photo depicted a displeased-looking man with a shock of silver hair holding up a red silk dress. "It's Marcus's bouncer!" I said. "Gregory."

Shruti nodded. "I'm not good with faces, but I never forget a dress." She tapped the red dress in the photo. "And he bought this frock baby from my pop-up a few weeks ago. Remember how Franz said Evie's dress was a result of Marcus trying to use vintage fabrics? His minion must have been scouring different shops, looking for material for Marcus to repurpose. And then they used this one to make the red flower part." She frowned at the photo. "If only I had been here at the time, I would have stopped him. No one should be allowed to use beautifully preserved vintage as their personal scrap heap."

"So you weren't actually here when he bought this?" I scrutinized the photo, as if I could will it to reveal further information to me.

"No." She took the photo back and flipped it over to reveal a date from three weeks ago, rendered in Maisy's scrawly handwriting. "Maisy sells things for me when I have to be at my original shop or the booth at the Indie Fashion Market. All I ask is that she commemorate the moment with a Polaroid. I like to know where each of my babies has gone off to."

"So we know where Evie's dress originated: it's a mashup of Marcus Wong and bastardized vintage. But what does that mean?" Frustration mounted, and I grabbed the stack of Polaroids and started flipping through them myself.

"There didn't appear to be anything evil happening at Marcus's shop, and we still have no idea where our little puppy friend is going to strike next and—whoa." I stopped and made myself go back a couple Polaroids. I'd been flipping through them so fast, I'd almost missed it.

But there it was, clear as day—Cakezilla Carol and her best friend Gwen. Standing in Pussy Queen with their arms around each other, beaming at the camera and clad in what were presumably their newly purchased vintage dresses. They were different from the outfits they'd been wearing at Cake My Day, but just as stylish. "Is this why Gwen looked familiar to you?" I said. "She and Carol bought things from here?"

"It must be," Shruti said, taking the photo from me. Her brow crinkled. "At least I remember this photo, but I'm pretty sure . . ." She flipped the photo over. Maisy's scrawly handwriting again. "This is another one of Maisy's sales."

"But Maisy was adamant that Carol hadn't bought anything here before." The back of my neck prickled, like a trail of ants skittering up my spine, leaving a creepy itch I couldn't scratch. "Why would she lie?"

"Let's check her records for this date," Shruti said, tapping the numbers scribbled on the Polaroid. "She keeps them in a big binder behind the counter."

I nodded, my eyes sweeping over the store. It was abandoned, not a customer in sight. No one except Dave.

"Do we need to distract him?" I asked, inclining my head toward the ever sleepy barista. "Or is pawing through Maisy's sales records something you do all the time?"

"Not really," Shruti said. "But no, I don't think we need to run any major diversions Dave's way. I mean, look at him."

Dave was still staring into his cup of liquid, as if having a very serious telepathic conversation.

We sauntered across the shop—I was super aware of the fact that I was trying to saunter as casually as possible, even though Dave clearly gave less than a shit about whatever we were doing—and settled in behind the counter.

"Here," Shruti said, pulling a massive binder from a cubbyhole under the counter.

"Wow." I eyed the thing as Shruti flipped it open and began searching for the date in question, running a finger down a page that contained a messy grid featuring an array of names, dates, and numbers, scribbled in various colors of pen. "This seems very old school. Why doesn't Maisy keep her records on an electronic system?"

"Apparently that's what Shasta did," Shruti said. "Maisy is always trying to differentiate herself from her former bestie, and she says taking a 'lo-fi approach' is part of that."

"I respect the use of a traditional paper system," I said, thinking of Bea and Nate's numerous spreadsheets. "But this thing looks like the 'serial killer's notebook' prop on every crime procedural."

"Here it is." Shruti tapped the page with her index finger. "Carol Kepler and Gwen Martinez. They both bought dresses from my pop-up. That's odd, Maisy charged more than what I'd originally priced these frocks at. And . . . hmm."

"What 'hmm'?" I peered over her shoulder. Even then, I couldn't make sense of Maisy's scribblings.

"It looks like they also placed a special, custom order," Shruti said. "Which is odd, because I thought we weren't taking those yet. I mean, if Evie had actually agreed to model bridal lingerie, Maisy would've gotten right on that. But otherwise . . ." Shruti trailed off, her eyes narrowing at the page of records.

"Are there other custom orders noted in there?" I said, nodding at the binder.

"Let's see . . ." Shruti started flipping through the pages again. "Ah. Yes. There are two more on this page and . . . three more on this one!"

I frowned. "A customer's name slipping Maisy's mind wouldn't be weird. Maisy working on some special custom order project and not blabbing about it would be suspicious, since she likes to make sure everyone's clued in to her fabulousness, but still not *totally* weird. But Maisy outright lying about both things?"

"Weird," Shruti agreed. "Definitely weird."

"Weird like maybe she's hiding something." My neck prickled again. Maisy—former sidekick to an evil wannabe demon queen, let's not forget—was apparently hiding something that seemed to be connected to the puppy demon's recent victim and her newly engaged best friend. That was worth looking into, at the very least.

"How do we figure out what these custom orders are?" I said.

Shruti drummed her fingers against the countertop, considering. "Maisy keeps all of her projects in the alterations rooms in the back. Even though we haven't started taking custom orders yet—or so I thought—she's been working on her sewing and design skills. No one's allowed back there except her."

"Wait. Now you're telling me Maisy basically has her own Bluebeard's chamber? Because that should definitely also go in the weird and suspicious column."

"She says it's her sacred sanctum, the one place where she can truly engage with her creative spirit," Shruti said with a shrug. "Look, I know she puts on a relentlessly chipper front, but the whole Shasta thing messed her up. She's trying to figure out who she is now, and I try to give her space to do that, even when it involves bizarre requests."

I frowned, thinking it over. It could be that all of this was innocuous, a series of Maisy quirks coming together to spell out something that looked suspicious, but actually meant nothing. But when you considered the strange, winding path that had led us here, it didn't feel like nothing. It felt like a lead Aveda Jupiter should follow.

"So can we sneak back there?" I asked. "Is it locked with a thousand deadbolts or something?" Once again, I cursed my inability to telekinesis things I couldn't see. I didn't have

X-ray vision, so I couldn't see the inner workings of the lock—otherwise I probably could have used my brain to pick it.

"It *is* locked," Shruti said. "And Maisy keeps the key with her at all times, but . . ." A contemplative smile spread over her face. "I think I can open it." She took a deep breath and allowed her gaze to go unfocused. Her hair unknotted itself from the Leia buns, twitching outward and curling, latching on to the handle of a drawer under the counter and pulling it free.

"Oh!" I exclaimed, my eyes going wide. "You've been working on your power level-up!"

"I have," Shruti said, beaming. "And it's strange, but I'm starting to be able to feel things with my hair—it's as if the ends are additional fingertips. Or an additional sense."

"That's so cool!" I said.

"It *is* cool," she said, her smile turning thoughtful. "Or at least I hope it is. It's interesting—I've always felt a bit conflicted about my power—"

"Conflicted, really?" I interrupted. "But why? Even in its lesser state, it always seemed to enhance all that inherent personal style you've got going for you."

"Thank you," she said with a laugh. "I think it's because, I don't know, it had to do with my hair having some sort of supernatural quality? My parents are more traditional Sikhs than I am and they both have this amazing, super long, uncut hair. When I was younger, so many of the kids in my class used to tease me, ask if my dad's hair was a 'monster' or if it had 'evil powers' and was that why it was so long, why he wore a turban?"

"Ugh." I made a face. "Tiny racists can suck it. I remember mean little white kids asking me if my dad was a magic martial arts master—if he knew any 'ancient Chinese secrets.'"

"Lovely," Shruti said, with an eye-roll. "Anyway, the fact that my hair actually *does* have some kind of supernatural power has always been a bit . . . disconcerting. And when my level-up first manifested, and I didn't know how strong I was, when I reacted instinctively and nearly choked that lady who was hurting Evie . . ." She shook her head. "I don't know. It gave me an uncomfortable feeling. Like my hair suddenly *did* have evil potential."

"All powers have the potential for good or evil," I said. "And I know what you mean—we superheroines of color always have an extra layer of pressure to represent well. But it's the person attached to the power who determines what they use it for." I gave her what I hoped was an encouraging smile.

"Well, I *want* to use it to be a massively cool superheroine with a massively cool power," Shruti said, striking a pose. "And gloriously fashion forward ensembles."

"In that case, you have nothing to worry about," I said, my smile widening. "You're well on your way. Now. Would you like to demonstrate said cool power and pick the lock on Maisy's chamber of secrets?"

"Yes," Shruti said, beaming. "And thank you."

We cast another furtive eye at Dave, who was still staring into his cup, then walked over to the curtain that led to the back hallway of Pussy Queen. I'd never seen this part of the store, but witnessing it now, I was unimpressed. Boxes were piled against the walls in haphazard stacks, bits of ribbon and lace were scattered here and there, and everything was covered in a fine layer of dust. Maisy had done a stellar job revamping the front-facing part of the shop, but this area was clearly due for a makeover.

We reached a doorway at the end of the hall that had been painted a cheery shade of pink, but now the color had faded and the paint was patchy and chipped. It looked like a version of Barbie's Dream House that had gone into foreclosure.

Shruti breathed deeply, allowed her eyes to go unfocused again, and the ends of her hair twitched. They floated upward, the tendrils entwining themselves into the lock, twisting back and forth. I heard a *click*. And we were in.

If the outside of the door had given me a Barbie's Fore-closed Dream House vibe, the actual room took things in more of a Miss Havisham direction. There was a collection of ornate-looking chairs covered in what once must have been a sumptuous gold brocade. Now they were buried in dust and cobwebs, the gold devoid of any sheen. A battered desk was shoved into the corner and littered with papers that seemed to bear more of Maisy's messy grids. Bits of material—lace and satin and silk—were tossed here and there. And in the back . . . I squinted, trying to make out what appeared to be a collection of headless, armless dress forms.

I shivered. Even if Maisy wasn't up to anything weird, this room was definitely creepy.

"Found the light!" Shruti called out behind me. She flicked it on and the room was flooded by harsh fluorescent illumination, casting a sickly glow that only made it creepier.

I crossed the space to the dress forms, trying to get a better look. They were outfitted in concoctions of white lace lingerie, like the ones Maisy had put on the Evie man-nequins in her display. But something about these garments was different. They were more elaborate, the stitching more precise, the lace more delicate. And they all had a bit of colorful fabric sewn in around the bustline—a deep crim-son brocade on one, a vibrant emerald silk on another.

"Wait." Shruti's fingertips drifted to the crimson bro-cade. "I recognize this fabric. I need to double-check, but . . ." Her eyes scanned the dress forms, her brows knit-ting together. "And they all have some sort of label."

I lowered my gaze and saw what she was talking about: each dress form had a paper tag attached to the waist with a bit of twine. I lifted the tag on the center mannequin and read what was calligraphied on it: *Carol Kepler.*

The chill running up my spine increased in intensity. I lifted the tag on the dress form right next to it. *Gwen Mar-tinez.* Shit. What did it mean?

I reached over to lift the tag on the last dress form, but

before I could touch it a loud *BANG* rang out from the other side of the room. Shruti and I both jumped.

"Excuse me!" a voice rang out.

We both whipped around, but I already knew what we were going to see.

Maisy. Standing in the doorway, totally pissed off.

"Ladies," she said, planting her hands on her hips. "What the hell are you doing back here?"

CHAPTER FIFTEEN

"OUT, OUT, OUT!" Maisy ordered. She stomped across the room and planted herself between us and the dress forms. "Aveda, I know you're a celebrity, but even famous people need boundaries." She gave me a not-at-all-gentle shove toward the door. "And snooping around someone's private inspiration space is definitely violating boundaries."

"I'm sorry," I said, thinking fast. "But as I was telling Shruti here, I've been dying to find Evie a special engagement gift, and custom lingerie seems like just the thing."

"And, I, uh, thought you might have some samples back here I could show Aveda," Shruti improvised. "Even though you haven't officially delved into the custom-order business just yet."

Maisy kept shoving us toward the door, her movements so insistent, they kicked up the clouds of dust blanketing the ornate, Victorian-style chairs. I sneezed. I could have pushed back with my telekinesis, but now wasn't the time to get into a knock-down, drag-out fight with her. Not if I wanted more information on what she was doing.

Instead, I allowed Maisy to prod us out of the room and slam the door behind her. She turned to face us, her flaky gray face screwed into a look of suspicion. "As I've told Evie many times, I'm happy to design something for her," Maisy said. "But she has no interest, so I'm not sure what poking around in my private area accomplishes."

"Poking around in your what, now?" Shruti said, giggling. I gave her a look.

Now was the time to go on the offensive—at least a little bit. I didn't want to push Maisy physically, but I needed to flip this conversation around on her in order to take control. As in the kickboxing dance, I needed to make her follow *me*.

"I thought you weren't making custom bridal lingerie yet," I said, examining my nails and affecting as nonchalant a pose as possible. "I mean, you made a real point of saying that when it was brought up."

Maisy's eyes shifted back and forth. I'd thrown her off balance. Good. "Well. I, uh. . . ."

"And strange how you also claimed Carol hadn't shopped here before—how adamant you were about that—when there's a dress form in there with her name on it." I arched an eyebrow at her. "Care to explain?"

I stared her down, waiting for the moment when I could sweep her legs out from under her and knock her to the ground. Metaphorically speaking, that is. Maisy met my gaze and stared back, her eyes expressionless. Which was extra creepy, what with her glowing demon eyes and all. For a moment, we just stood there, caught in a stare-off, the tension mounting with every moment of loaded silence. Shruti looked from me to Maisy and back again, unsure of what to do.

Then Maisy's face broke into a wide smile, and she threw back her head and laughed.

"Oh, A. Jupes!" she said, her tone resetting to its usual saccharine-coated cadence. "I can never get anything by you, can I?" She leaned in close, as if about to reveal the biggest, juiciest secret of all time. "You got me. I am designing a bridal lingerie line and I've already lined up select clientele. But I have some nerves about showing off my designs before I've gotten them just right—and I've also been waiting for our wee li'l Evie to come around to the idea so I can make her the face of the campaign." Maisy held up her hands like a director framing a shot. "But I can't let her in on anything I'm doing until I have her explicit consent. You won't say anything, will you?"

Maisy smiled at me hopefully—but I couldn't help but feel something else was lurking underneath her cheery grin.

"How are you getting this select clientele to keep the secret as well?" I asked. "Do you have them sign some sort of NDA?"

"Well, basically," Maisy said, waving a desiccated hand. "One reason I haven't designed many sets yet."

"Why don't you let me take a closer look?" I said. "I know Evie's taste. Perhaps I can guide you toward a design that will make her come around."

Maisy's grin disappeared entirely. Her face went deathly sober, and her arm shot out to block the door.

"I'm afraid that isn't possible," she said, her tone firm. "I have a very strict policy about people seeing my designs before they're one hundred percent ready. They must be absolutely perfect—and these aren't even close. I'm sure you understand, Aveda. What with *your* constant quest for perfection."

She schooled her features once more, giving me a toothy grin. I gritted my teeth. Every muscle in my body was screaming at me to push past her, bust the door down, get a closer look at the dress forms. Declare some kind of supernatural state of emergency.

But there were still too many unknowns. If I alerted Maisy I was onto her, it would give her time to undo or hide whatever she was doing. I needed to draw her out in a more organic way, to force her to reveal whatever she was up to because she had no idea I suspected anything. Part of controlling the dance is knowing when to pull back.

I let out a deep breath and forced my face into a bland smile.

"Of course I understand," I said. "But . . ." I gave her a wistful look. "I know Evie would love your creations if she could just see them. Try them on, even. Really get a sense of how good she looks in them and how good they make her feel. What if you brought one to her engagement party as a surprise gift? She might even agree to do an impromptu photo shoot on the spot!"

"Really?" Maisy said, and now there was definitely another element creeping into her expression. It was the depraved spark of someone who sensed she could get some really good PR if she milked an opportunity just right. Or maybe it was the look of a supposedly reformed half-demon princess who'd secretly returned to her evil roots and saw an opportunity to attack the most high-profile bride in the city.

"I didn't know I was even invited to the engagement party," Maisy said. "I thought it was only for family and the closest of friends."

"And what do you think you are?" I countered, giving her a big, fake smile. "Please. Your invitation's in the mail." Or at least it would be once I got home and told Bea to go to the post office. "Bring the lingerie and I'll help with the surprise. I'll help with the whole thing."

Maisy's ghoulish grin stretched the entire length of her face.

🔥

"I wish I'd gotten a better look at that creepy lingerie," I muttered.

We were back in Shruti's pop-up area, where she was pretending to help me find something to wear to the engagement party. Maisy, for her part, didn't appear to be paying attention to us anyway. She was ensconced behind her counter, sketching new lingerie designs with gusto.

"Hmm," Shruti said, her expression going contemplative. "Remember how I said I recognized the fabric in the bustlines of those corsets?" She flipped through her Polaroids again and pulled out a series of shots of jewel-toned gowns. "The fabric came from these dresses, I'm sure of it." She frowned at the Polaroids. "This lot came in from an estate sale a few weeks ago. I let Maisy have first crack at these dresses because I figured she wanted some fabulous things to wear around the store. But it looks like she just cut them up and used them in her possibly evil custom lingerie project." She shook her head mournfully. "My poor babies."

"Maybe she's figured out how to control the puppy," I said. "Scott said the puppy might be connected to something else—maybe that something is her?" I studied the Polaroids. "So somehow Maisy or the puppy demon—or the Maisy/puppy demon team-up—have figured out how to, what? Use repurposed fabric from vintage dresses—like these and the dress Marcus's minion bought—to attack people?"

"I'm definitely not letting her near any more of my stock," Shruti said, eyes narrowing.

I blew out a long breath, trying to pull together all the disparate threads of what we knew so far. Had Maisy used Marcus's dress to attack Evie? And was she planning on using her custom lingerie to try again? But what did taking Evie out get her—other than getting rid of the city's most popular superheroine and bride-to-be, of course? There had to be a more nefarious plan underneath that, something that involved ruling the city the way Shasta had once dreamed of.

In any case, it looked like we were going to have to make Evie bait again. But this time would be different. This time, we had more information, a good idea of how the puppy was going to attack. My strategy for taking it down would be more meticulous, more brilliant. I'd do a better job of protecting her.

And somehow, I'd kick that damn puppy's ass.

I hustled back into HQ, full of purpose. I couldn't wait to tell Evie what Shruti and I had uncovered. With each step, I felt more revitalized, more sure of myself.

Between the two of us, Evie and I would devise the perfect trap for the puppy, using all the knowledge we'd gained through our various confrontations—*check!*

And we'd capture it before the engagement party really got going, thereby preserving the festive nature of the event—*check!*

With evil vanquished, it would clear the way for Evie to have the perfect wedding she deserved, with me working at my highest level of kickass maid-of-honor mode to ensure everything went off without a hitch. *Check, check, check!*

I was practically humming by the time I reached Evie's door. I stopped abruptly and knocked. Knocking prior to entering was something I'd recently added to my good-friend arsenal. Evie had gently reminded me quite a few times that knocking before making your presence known in someone else's space was the respectful thing to do, but it hadn't really sunk in until I'd barged in on her and Nate having intimate relations in the middle of the afternoon.

Now I always remembered.

"Come in," she called out.

I marched in, prepared to unleash my righteous speech of renewed purpose. But something stopped me.

Evie was lying in bed surrounded by her mountain of pillows. Her face was pale, drawn, making her freckles stand out more than usual. And she was staring up at the ceiling like she'd just seen a ghost. She didn't say so much as hello, didn't even acknowledge that there was someone else in the room with her. She looked like she wasn't even completely aware there *was* someone else in the room with her.

"Evie?" My brow knitted in concern, and I made my way over to the bed and sat next to her. "What's wrong?"

She turned to look at me, sitting up slowly.

"It's ... we ..." She shook her head, as if she couldn't quite get the words right. "Bea, Nate, Scott, and Rose worked together to run a bunch of tests on the trap while you were out. Even though the dress came back negative for supernatural energy, they thought there might still be *something* lurking in there."

"And was there?" I put a hand on her shoulder, trying to encourage her.

"Sort of." Her eyes went unfocused again. "It was another trace, like the one we found at Pussy Queen—a blip that indicated the puppy *was* there at some point."

"But we already knew that, right? Like, that's an educated guess we could have made, given the context clues? Of the dress trying to murder you?"

"Well, yeah," she conceded. "But further analysis of the trace indicated the puppy is definitely connected to something else—remember how Scott theorized that was a possibility?"

"Yes," I said, my brain whirring.

She twisted her hands together. "The tests show that something else is very likely . . . human."

That stopped my brain in its tracks for a moment.

"The data doesn't tell us much more than that," Evie barreled on, her words spilling out. "But somehow it's latched itself to a human. Whether the human is aware of this, we don't know. We're not sure what the nature of the connection is."

"I know who it is!" I blurted out. "Or at least, I think I do."

I proceeded to explain my theory about Maisy, the puppy, and custom bridal lingerie as weapon. She nodded, taking in my words. I thought the additional information I'd uncovered might make her feel better, but her face remained unsettlingly pale.

"Maisy is only part human now, though," I said, trying to work it out. "Does the data allow for hybrids?"

"It is, in Bea's words, 'way vague,'" Evie said. "So it's definitely possible."

"'Way vague' has got to be the most unhelpful classification ever," I muttered.

"Maybe it's someone else—a non-hybridized human?" Evie said. "What about Shruti? She's the one who was selling all these shady clothes in the first place and—with the exception of Cake My Day—she always seems to be around when the puppy's causing trouble."

"So maybe she led me down the Maisy path to cover her

own tracks?" I mused. "It's possible. But she's so ...." So ... what? Nice? Cool? And for whatever reason, so interested in being my friend, which I couldn't help but find flattering? But maybe that was part of the ruse. Maybe the only reason anyone would *ever* want to be my friend was because it was part of their totally evil plan to take over San Francisco.

"She seemed genuinely surprised," I finally said, "that Maisy and Marcus Wong had cut up some of her 'frock babies.' I mean, who knows, maybe she's an excellent actress. But she did lead me directly to the creepy lingerie, and if she's the one behind everything, wouldn't she want to keep that hidden?"

"Given Maisy's past, she does seem like a more likely candidate," Evie said. "Sure, she's been nicer to us in the wake of the big Shasta battle, but there's no denying that she's always out for herself."

I agreed. "Even when she's kissing our asses, her ultimate goal is still to contribute to the general fame and awesomeness of Maisy Kane, supposedly reformed half-demon princess. What if she's trying to accomplish what Shasta set out to do?"

"If so, attacking one bride at a time seems like a pretty shitty plan," Evie said.

"There must be an endgame we can't see," I said. "Or maybe the puppy is controlling *her* in some way, maybe she doesn't even know she's doing it."

"So she'll come to the engagement party like some kind of curse-wielding evil fairy godmother, and I'll put on the lingerie," Evie said. "Like I did with the gown, only this time—"

"This time we know going in that that is very likely how it will choose to attack, and we can prepare for it," I said firmly, my brain tracing the lines of the battle plan as I put it together. "I'll rip it off of you as soon as that thing starts to affect you, and we'll stuff it in the trap—which will be new and improved, thanks to Bea's work, so hopefully it will stay in there this time."

She nodded, but she had gone pale again, her face taking on that weird, pinched quality. "You promise you'll rip the lingerie off right away?" she said, her voice trembling a little. "So it doesn't make me do anything I might regret? Like, you know, kill everyone at my own engagement party?" She attempted a laugh, but it sounded hollow.

"I promise." I gave her my best look of solemn determination.

But even as she nodded back, I could tell my assurances weren't enough. I could pep talk her all I wanted, I could get Bea to reverse-empath soothe her all I wanted, but those were Band-Aid solutions. Temporary and unsatisfying.

Her face had gone from pale to an almost grayish cast and while she was obviously trying to rally, I knew her better than that. She was thinking back to the tent, back to the incident at Pussy Queen. Thinking about what would happen if she wasn't in control of the fire. She was still scared of what the puppy might do. Or what the Maisy-puppy combo might *make* her do.

"Hey," I said, trying to make my tone light. "You still got *The Heroic Trio* on there?" I nodded at the iPad lying next to her mountain of pillows.

"I do," she said, perking up slightly.

"Let's watch!" I grabbed the iPad and cued up the movie. "Oh, and . . . and let's have some sugar, too!" I snagged a bag of Kasugai lychee gummy candies from her nightstand. I felt like I was haphazardly throwing random happy-making things at her, hoping at least one of them would work. It was the only thing I could think of to do.

She leaned against my shoulder and I tilted my head so it rested on top of hers. We ate candy and watched the movie.

"Look at them," Evie murmured, running a finger over the figures on the iPad screen. "Now we really are like that. Except there's only two of us."

Warmth surged in my chest and just like that, we were twelve again, caught up in the costumes and theatrics and ass-kicking onscreen. The first time we'd seen it in the musty old Yamato theater, I'd reached across the seat and squeezed her hand so hard, she'd winced a little. But I couldn't help it. I needed to know that she saw what I saw, felt what I felt. That this was a key moment of connection in our mind-meld space of best friendship—that we could *be* that.

Regret stabbed at my heart, and I realized I'd missed the easy way we used to connect. That closeness we'd once shared had slipped away a little more each year as I'd got more wrapped up in my rising celebrity and she'd gotten wrapped up in suppressing her power. I'd put on a front of us still being as close as we ever were, but the truth was, the more co-dependent we became over the years, the more our actual friendship disintegrated.

But now we'd brought it back. And I was determined not to let it go.

As the movie continued to play, she seemed to relax a little, chewing on the candies and smiling affectionately at all of our favorite moments: Thief Catcher donning her signature goggles for the first time, Invisible Girl conversing with her hot, nerdy love interest about lilies.

Perversely, the more she seemed to relax, the more distracted and tense I became. The thoughts piled up in my head and made it impossible to concentrate on anything except how pale her face had been only moments before and that worried crinkle that kept appearing on her forehead.

The plan Shruti and I had discussed seemed obvious at the time, but now ... Now I realized there was no way I could put Evie in danger that way again. I'd done it when I'd made her pose as me, and I'd done it when I'd suggested we make her a target with the whole bridal fashion show idea. I couldn't ignore her burgeoning fear, her doubt in her ability to be a superhero, and I couldn't risk her life.

That wasn't being the Aveda Jupiter I knew I could be— the Aveda Jupiter who was reclaiming her mojo and emerging

more awesome than ever. It wasn't being the friend who'd
tried to protect her for so much of our shared childhood,
who'd saved her all those times before.

No, I would have to scrap the initial plan. I would have
to take this thing on myself. And I would have to win.

I just had to figure out how.

🔥

I left Evie's room an hour later with a renewed sense of
purpose. This time, I would approach our battle plan the
right way—I'd put myself smack-dab in the line of fire instead of offering Evie up like some kind of sacrificial lamb.
When we were kids, I'd never let on that sometimes the
bullies scared me, too. As little Kelly Graham stomped
over, each step of her tiny sneakers shaking the ground like
she was some kind of miniature Godzilla in pigtails, screaming taunts about our "weird eyes," I betrayed no flash of the
insidious curl of fear slithering through my stomach. No, I
just made myself stand up straighter and stepped in front
of Evie. She was already crying—and that meant I couldn't.

It was time for me to step in front of her again.

But I still couldn't get a handle on the how. I had to
transfer the target that was currently planted firmly on
Evie's bridal back to myself. I needed to figure out some
trick of "look over here!" misdirection. In the past, I'd had
no problem calling attention to myself, but the evil puppy
demon didn't seem interested in picking up what I was putting down. I mean, it had even bypassed my horrific bridesmaid's dress. So what else could I do?

How could I make myself more appealing to a force that
only seemed interested in women with one thing in common, women who were about to embark on a major life
step that I wasn't even close to, as I'm sure my mother
would be quick to remind me—

Wait.

"That's it!" I shrieked into the empty space of the hall,
then quickly clapped a hand over my mouth. No need to

broadcast my intentions to the whole household. For now, only one person needed to know about what I had planned.

I hustled downstairs to my bedroom and rummaged around in my assortment of old keepsake boxes until I found what I was looking for. I plucked it free, dashed back up the stairs, and knocked on Scott's bedroom door. I bounced on my toes, waiting for what seemed like an eternity as I listened to his footsteps padding toward the door.

"Hi," I said when he answered. I held out the keepsake I'd gone in search of: a cheap plastic ring with flaking-off gold paint and a giant fake ruby in the center. "I need you to propose to me."

CHAPTER SIXTEEN

FOR A MOMENT, Scott just stared at me. Then at the ring. Then back at me again. Finally, he ran a hand over his face and shook his head in confusion.

"What?" he said.

I jiggled the plastic ring at him. "Propose. Ask me to marry you. It doesn't have to be fancy, you don't even have to get down on one knee—"

"Annie!" He gave me a look of barely contained exasperation. "I . . . why don't you come in?"

He stepped back from the doorway to allow me through. I entered and he shut the door behind us. I looked around for a place to sit, but he didn't have much in the way of furniture, just a few of his beloved surfboards propped against the wall, and the bed, which was just a queen-sized mattress on the floor, no frame to speak of. I lowered myself to perch on the edge of it.

"This kind of looks like you're still in college—perfect if you end up going back to school," I said, gesturing to the room. My fingertips brushed his plain white comforter, and I was surprised at how soft it was, definitely a high thread-count. "Though *this* is very nice." I patted the comforter. "Silky. Luxurious, even." I was babbling to fill the space since he seemed determined not to say anything. I couldn't help it. I was giddy with the idea that I might be able to finally beat the thing that had been vexing us so much. He sat down next to me and didn't respond, just kept looking at me with that exasperated expression. "I've never been in here," I blurted out. "Why would I be, I guess."

"Why would you be?" he echoed. He scrubbed a hand over his face again and studied me. "So what's going on?"

"I . . ." Oh. I had Hurricane Annie-ed again. Just barged in and spat out a bunch of words without providing any context. And it probably seemed extra weird since the last time we'd talked one-on-one, that day in the lab, I had shut down our burgeoning intimacy and pulled away from him.

I knew it was for the greater good, all in the name of banishing Annie Chang so I could be Aveda Jupiter to the fullest—but he didn't know that. For him, my extreme fluctuating reactions were probably just confusing. Writhing around on the gym floor with him one minute, acting like it had never happened the next.

He was still studying me, and I saw that flash of seriousness again, that little window into what he was feeling beneath his easygoing exterior. And this time, he looked hurt.

I could handle him being angry, I could handle him being frustrated, but the hurt pierced straight to my heart and made me think of that scrawny, screaming, red-faced little boy he'd once been, his rage masking deep wounds he didn't want anyone to see. I turned away and studied his surfboards—pleasant hunks of plastic in gentle shades like aquamarine and pale pink. They had a soothing, almost meditative quality.

"I'm sorry," I said. "I . . . Things have been so chaotic lately and I didn't mean to crash in here and demand something of you without explaining. Let me back up. I need you to propose to me so I will officially be a bride-to-be and can draw our friend the evil puppy demon to me instead of Evie. It won't be real, of course, but the demon won't know that." I turned to face him and held out the plastic ring again. This time, he took it, holding it between his thumb and forefinger, studying it thoughtfully.

I wondered if he recognized it. But, no—he probably didn't remember. I should have grabbed something with less potential baggage attached, but I didn't actually own any other rings. Rings got in the way of punching things.

"Is this a ruse we have to maintain for anyone other than the puppy demon?" he asked. "What about our friends?"

"Oh, god, of course not," I said.

"Your parents?"

"Double of course not."

"And this fake engagement idea is occurring to you now because . . . ?"

"Right, I should probably back up even further." I filled him in on what Shruti and I had discovered and my theory about Maisy being connected to the puppy.

"So I'll let Evie think we're still going along with the 'Evie as bait' plan—but instead of putting her in the line of fire again, I'll greet Maisy when she arrives and intercept the lingerie," I said, working it out. "Evie will be distracted by all the other guests—and hopefully by the amazing time she's having. I'll steal away to the bathroom and try it on. It will attack me. If you can't pull it out with the spell you've been working on, do things the old fashioned-way. Rip it off me and stuff it in the trap, which Bea will have perfected by then. And . . . we win!"

I gave him what I hoped was an ingratiating smile and made jazz hands. He stared at me. But at least the hurt had mostly disappeared.

"Or maybe we don't totally *win*, but we'll have trapped it, and once the party's over, we'll figure out how to destroy it or send it back to the Otherworld," I said. "Maybe you'll be able to connect with it again, get more information. And Evie will have a great party without having to worry about any of this."

Scott frowned. "What about Maisy?"

"What about her?"

"We don't know what the nature of her connection to the puppy is," he said. "She could be the one controlling it, which means *she's* actually targeting brides-to-be. And she knows you're not a bride-to-be."

"Mmm, good point," I said. "I'll let it slip to her that I'm engaged, but it's absolutely top secret. Even Evie doesn't know and I'm . . . I'm giving her a huge scoop! But only if she keeps it to herself until after the party's over."

He kept frowning. "There are still so many unknowns about how this thing works. And do we need to worry about capturing and subduing Maisy as well?"

I thought about it. "If she is the one behind all this, it seems like she needs the puppy demon to do her evil bidding. Like, she can't do it herself—otherwise why would she use such an odd and not always terribly effective method? So once we neutralize her source of power, we can quietly take her into custody."

He studied the plastic ring, still looking doubtful.

"Think of it this way: if I'm a bride-to-be, it makes me a target for all future encounters," I said. "Meaning that no matter what happens, I can finally be in direct contact with this thing. And I can protect Evie."

He shook his head, as if trying to wrap his brain around everything. "So why not tell Evie—and the others—what you're doing?"

"Because it would make her feel like less of a hero," I said. "She's already doubting herself so much and it would look like I think she can't handle this—and I don't think that. I just can't put her in danger again. Only you and I need to know about this plan." I gave my most authoritative Aveda Jupiter nod.

He stared at me. He still didn't look convinced—but he appeared to be listening, taking in what I was saying.

"You and me," I said slowly. "I know we haven't always seen eye to eye—to put it mildly. But we've been making decent strides in our quest to be friends. And one thing we have always been able to come together on is protecting Evie. This *thing* is getting under her skin in a way that's threatening to undo all the progress she's made in her

life—the way she's become a hero and found love and is
about to be the most beautiful bride . . . and I can't let all of
that be undone. I just can't. No one deserves to be happy
more than she does." My voice quavered and I realized I
was on the dangerous verge of tears. "Please?"

He studied me for a long moment. I couldn't tell what he
was thinking and I was so sure he was going to hand back
my cheap piece of plastic and tell me to get lost.

Instead he met my eyes and held the ring up.

"Marry me."

I shook my head, sure I had misheard. "Wh-what?"

Amusement flickered through his eyes for the first time
since I'd entered the room, and I saw a flash of the Scott
that was so familiar, the Scott that was always trying to
make me laugh.

"I'm sorry," he said. "Was that not good enough?"

He lowered himself the short distance from mattress to
floor, affected an exaggerated deathly serious face, and
held out the ring as one might hand a sacred offering to a
priestess.

"Annie Chang," he said, making his voice as deep and
serious as one of those "in a world" movie announcers.
"Will you do me the supreme honor of—"

"All right, all right, very funny," I said, unable to suppress my smile. I held out my hand and waggled my fingers.
"Ring me."

He slid the cheap piece of plastic onto my finger, then
squeezed my hand and brushed a quick kiss against my
knuckles.

"Hey," I said, my cheeks warming. "I think we're going
to need to establish some ground rules for our fake engagement, since we're trying to be friends."

"Is that what we're trying to do?" he said, keeping his
tone light. "Because I don't think the way we used the gym
the other day was very . . . friend-like."

"And I think we can both agree that was a mistake," I
said firmly. "A momentary lapse in judgment." Now he was

looking at me in his usual teasing way, and I was looking at him in my usual imperious way. We were back to our usual selves, our dynamic restored. It should have made me feel more comfortable, but instead I suddenly felt twitchy, off-kilter. Like we'd flattened ourselves into two-dimensional versions, put on half-disguises that didn't quite fit.

"In any case," I barreled on. "Kissing any and all body parts is definitely not friend-like."

"You always have so many rules, future Mrs. Cameron." Scott grinned at me as he boosted himself back on the bed.

"That kind of banter is also not friend-like," I said, holding up a warning finger. "And for the record, I would keep my name. It's an important part of my identity as both an empowered superheroine and a proud Chinese American woman."

"Of course." His face sobered a bit. "So. We've made you a target. Are you ready for whatever that's going to bring your way?"

I stared at the fake ruby on my finger, its chipped red paint creating a speckled pattern that gave the illusion it was sparkling in the light. Almost like a real gemstone. I took in a deep inhale, trying to center myself. "I guess we're about to find out."

DIARY OF A REFORMED HALF-DEMON PRINCESS: PART 46

By Maisy Kane, Half-Demon Princess Editrix

Yes, 'Friscans, the rumors are true: Evie Tanaka is having the most fabulous engagement party tonight and yours truly is invited! Your pal Maisy will be sure to report back with all the deets!

In the meantime, many of you have written in to insist I embark on some investigative reportage of the recent exploits of ever-newsworthy maid of honor Aveda Jupiter. Dear readers, I'm afraid this one is a conflict of interest! Despite some recent questionable behavior, I still consider A. Jupes a very close friend. I know barging into Marcus Wong's bridal boutique and causing a scene doesn't sound like tip-top maid-of-honor behavior, but I'm sure we can trust our Evie to lead her down the right path—you know, the path *away* from being forever labeled an "attention-hog diva and raging bossypants bitch who can't stand to let anyone else have the spotlight," as one of my more colorful commenters put it!

COMMENTS

QuirkyBride: I think it's high time we staged a *bridal intervention*! I was actually at Marcus Wong's the day Aveda barged in! As usual, she acted like she owned the place, pushed her way over to the man himself, and started making all kinds of demands!

IWantToElope: #thatssoaveda

MillsAlum97: Soooo . . . do we think she's gone rogue in planning her maid of honor attire? Did the seafoam monstrosity not work out?

QuirkyBride: But MW doesn't sell any bridesmaid dresses, only wedding gowns—OH SHIT!

MillsAlum97: OH SHIT

QuirkyBride: I mean . . . she wouldn't, like . . . wear a *wedding dress* as her bridesmaid dress? Like . . . a *white wedding dress*? Would she?

IWantToElope: #thatssoaveda

Chapter seventeen

WHEN I LAY a trap, I do it beautifully.

Or at least that's what I used to think. But recently Evie had gently informed me that the Hurricane Annie nature of my personality meant my strength was really more along the lines of being a Forceful Bludgeon for Good rather than a meticulous strategist. I tended to barrel into situations like a bull in a china shop and rocket my way to the other side through sheer force of will. There was usually a positive result, but also a totally wrecked china shop to contend with.

This time I had to be more subtle or everything would be ruined. I wanted the engagement party to be beautiful, I wanted Evie to enjoy every minute, and I wanted to take down the nefarious puppy demon once and for all.

Needless to say, I had my work cut out for me. But Aveda Jupiter never shrank from a challenge.

"I can't believe what you've done with the place," Kevin, the owner of The Gutter, said. He gave me a massive eye-roll as he sized up his usually scummy karaoke bar. "I don't mean that in a nice way."

"Yes, I got that." I gave him a withering look. Kevin still held a grudge against Evie and me for disrupting his precious karaoke contest during her stint impersonating me. Not so much of a grudge that he hadn't jumped at the chance to get free publicity out of hosting the city's favorite superheroine for one of the most important parties of her life. But enough that he'd given me major attitude throughout the entire planning process.

I actually had done a nice job with the place, even if Kevin didn't appreciate it. I'd exchanged the worn, patchy red velvet tablecloths for elegant cream linens and tiny silver vases of fresh flowers. I'd also draped the scuffed, beer-stained karaoke stage in cream linen and rented a proper tux for Stu Singh, The Gutter's old codger of a piano player. Like Maisy, he'd been hybridized by Shasta, but was making a go of a semi-normal life and was at his station behind the piano every night. For this occasion, I'd instructed him to change up his usual bombastic repertoire of show tunes with soft, atmospheric music, the better to enhance the engagement party vibe. I'd tried to get Kevin to wear a tux as well, but he'd refused, opting to simply drape a blazer over one of his usual empowering message t-shirts. (This one said, "BLATASIAN 4 LYFE, SUCKA.")

As a finishing touch, I'd positioned and lit candles everywhere. I wanted the whole place to have a beautiful glow about it, to represent the glow of new love. Even if I was planning on using that soothing atmosphere to catch a demon hybrid lingerie vendor in an act of wrongdoing and take down a pesky stray puppy demon for good.

Evie would bask in the adoration of everyone gathered, and I'd tell her afterward that, "Oh, yeah, I also managed to take care of that other thing that's been bothering us so much lately, and now nothing can possibly interfere with you having the most perfect wedding day ever." My Aveda Jupiter mojo would finally be reclaimed and I'd have finally proved myself as both a superheroine and a friend.

"Are you sure this is what our little Tanaka girl wants for her big party?" Kevin asked, his eyes narrowing. He planted his hands on his hips and jutted his chest out, the material of his t-shirt flowing over his three-hundred-pound frame. Kevin managed to make even the most basic of movements look simultaneously graceful and sassy. "Her tastes tend to be a little simpler than yours."

"Trust me, I know what she wants way more than you do," I said, giving him an imperious look.

Okay, so the party wasn't *exactly* what Evie had described to me. But I knew once she saw it, she'd love it. It would be way more memorable than bad junk food and worse karaoke, and she'd be grateful to me for realizing how important it was to craft a beautiful party to commemorate such a momentous occasion.

"I think it looks great," Scott said, loping up behind us. He gave me his easy smile and touched my back in greeting. "And so do you."

My cheeks warmed, and I self-consciously smoothed the skirt of the scarlet sheath I'd originally wanted to wear as a bridesmaid dress. In the invite, I'd requested that everyone dress in semi-formal attire and even listed a few descriptive examples in case people were confused. Scott had exchanged his usual beach-friendly wear for a dark blue suit, a light blue button-up that brought out his eyes, and a tie with a nice pinstripe. He looked distractingly handsome. Of course.

But I couldn't get distracted tonight. Especially not by my fake fiancé. That was *not* part of the plan.

We'd actually worked well together throughout the week. I'd told him to let me handle all the details for the actual party since I knew how to make it perfect, but we'd met up to talk out the demon puppy–capturing plan. As long as I kept my mushy Annie Chang side at bay and he kept things light and even-keeled, our rapport was . . . well, actually friend-like.

I realized then that we'd been standing there for nearly a full minute of silence, him touching my back, me blushing like mad.

"Whoa," Kevin said. "Awkward silence alert. Are you guys doing it or what? Because Tanaka always said—"

"Why don't you go check on the food, Kevin?" I said, my teeth gritted. "Our guests should start arriving any minute."

Kevin gave me a glower, then flounced off, muttering something about "last time I host this entitled-celebrity BS" under his breath.

"That wasn't very friend-like," I said, stepping away from Scott and giving him a stern look.

"What, you ordering Kevin around like that?" he said, mock innocent. "I agree, it wasn't very friend-like at all."

"You know what I mean." I poked him in the chest. "Oh, your tie's crooked. Let me ..." I moved in closer and straightened it. Which was a mistake, because now I knew exactly how good he smelled. Even better than usual.

"You can't just tell me I look nice. You can't give me a compliment like that," I said, trying to focus.

"I'm not giving you a compliment. I'm stating the truth."

My cheeks flushed further. Maybe there were *too* many candles in here. That beautiful warm glow I'd wanted was starting to feel like standing in the middle of a bonfire.

"Annie." He gestured to my fingers, which were still fiddling with his tie. "This doesn't seem very friend-like, either."

"You're right." But before I could pull my hands away, he covered them with his own. My palms pressed against his chest, and I could feel his heartbeat. It brought me back to the moment in the gym, his fingertips against my back, me on top of him, feeling his heartbeat *everywhere.*

Yes, I was now convinced those candles were a completely terrible idea.

He released one of my hands, keeping hold of the one that was still wearing the plastic engagement ring. I'd flipped the fake ruby around so it faced my palm. The clear plastic band was fairly invisible otherwise, so no one at HQ had noticed and started asking awkward questions about it. And hopefully that would continue to hold true tonight.

"So you're all ready for puppy demon entrapment," he said, flipping the ruby so it perched on top of my hand.

"I am. Are you?"

"Yes. I've been working on my spell and Bea has reinforced the trap with some kind of new metal component that should contain the puppy better." He ran his thumb over the fake ruby. "I never knew you kept this. I don't think I've seen it since we won it from that bubblegum machine at the swimming pool."

My heart skipped a few beats. "Summer between sixth and seventh grades," I said, making my tone light. "We were trying to win Evie that little plastic hedgehog and kept getting crap like this instead. I didn't think you remembered." I tried to pull my hand away, but he held tight.

"How could I forget?" he said, running his thumb over my knuckles. "I proposed to you then, too."

"You did not *propose*," I retorted, giving him a withering look. "You told me that if no one was willing to marry my 'crazy butt' by the time we were thirty, you would 'take the hit' and I should hold on to the ring just in case."

"Wow." He laughed and squeezed my hand. "I was such a little asshole."

"*Was?*"

He laughed again and met my eyes. "And you kept it all this time. You probably thought I didn't recognize it."

I shrugged. "I thought I was the only one who remembered our *first* fake engagement."

His gaze turned from teasing to something soft and earnest.

"You're not," he said.

My heart caught in my throat. I opened my mouth to respond, but nothing came out.

"Anne."

I knew that voice. Low, measured, disapproving.

I whipped around to find my parents standing next to us, wearing matching expressions of disappointment. I wasn't sure how they could be disappointed in me before I'd even said anything, but these were my parents. They always found a way.

"Mom. Dad," I said, hastily flipping the ruby back around on my finger. I stepped in to hug them. Even that simple gesture made me feel like an overeager dog, wagging my tail and pissing on the furniture, hoping to get a reaction I was never going to get.

"Why are you so flushed and out of breath?" my mom said, her brow wrinkling suspiciously. "Are you doing those breathing exercises I sent you on the email?"

"I'm fine, Mom." My smile turned into a rictus. "It's just a little hot in here."

"Mmm." Her eyes swept over the room, taking it all in. And clearly finding it wanting. "Too many candles. Heightens the temperature in an unnatural way. You should drink more water so you stay hydrated and it doesn't catch you unaware."

"I'm *fine*," I said, my voice twisting into a whine. I took a deep breath and reminded myself of the goal of the night. It wasn't to please my mother, which would have been impossible anyway. It was to kick some supernatural ass and keep an evil demon hybrid from ruining my best friend's wedding. I'd let myself be momentarily distracted by Scott's stupid hotness, but my parents appearing was like a splash of cold water to my face, waking me up. Reminding me of my mission. It would be incredibly counterproductive to let them distract me as well.

"Mr. and Mrs. Chang," Scott said, giving them a deferential nod and a warm smile. "So nice of you to join us for the party. Annie really transformed this place. It's usually much more dank and grimy."

"Mmm," my mom said again, but this time it was accompanied by the half-smile that she only gave to people who weren't me. Well, really, only to Scott. "And you have transformed yourself nicely as well, Scott. There's nothing quite like a good suit."

"Wise words as always," Scott said, his smile widening. "Can I show you to your seats?" His fingertips brushed my lower back. He was trying to reassure me, to tell me not to get wound up in whatever perceived slights my mother might throw my way. My shoulders relaxed a tiny bit, and I felt like I could breathe normally again.

"Yes, Mom and Dad, go sit down," I said. "The food should be out soon."

"Hopefully nothing too fancy," my mom sniffed. "Those rich sauces don't sit well with my stomach."

And my shoulders were up around my ears again.

"Come with me," Scott said to my parents, pressing his fingertips against my back in a last, reassuring touch. "Let's leave Annie here to greet the bride—who I believe just walked in."

"We got this," he whispered in my ear. "Just keep smiling and keep an eye out for Maisy."

I mouthed "thank you" and told my heart to stop beating so fast as he guided my parents away.

"Annie!" Evie made a beeline for me, her curls bouncing around her shoulders. "Wow," she said, her eyes widening as she took in The Gutter. "The place looks so . . . different."

"Mmm, yes, love, not exactly what I was expecting," Lucy said, as she and Bea strolled up behind Evie. Lucy was toting a black plastic garbage bag so large and overstuffed, it looked like one wrong move would send her tiny frame toppling. Neither of them had paid attention to my note about attire. Evie was clad in her usual jeans-tee-Chucks combo and Lucy was wearing a ruffled cotton dress with a floral print and a vaguely nineties vibe. It was cute, but hardly semi-formal. Bea was wearing a short black dress— more fun party girl than semi-formal, but at least she'd tried.

"Uh, what have you got there, Lucy?" I asked, deciding to address the garbage bag issue first.

"Well. Yes. That's an interesting story," Lucy said, her gaze shifting back and forth. Evie caught her eye and burst into giggles.

"What?" I said, trepidation building in my gut.

"You see," Lucy said, "I thought the idea behind this party was a little . . . different than what it apparently is."

"She thought it was a *bachelorette* party," Evie blurted out, her eyes lit with glee.

Oh. Oh, no.

Lucy opened the bag so I could see. And the pile of

rainbow neon-colored condoms, dildos, and vibrators nearly exploded all over the Gutter floor.

"Lucy!" I gasped. "You have to . . . that's not . . . what this is about!"

"We know, we know," Evie said, though she couldn't seem to stop giggling. "Don't worry, we'll keep this stuff in the bag."

"Why don't you give me the bag?" I said, holding out a hand. My tone made it clear that this wasn't a request.

"I always thought you were the *fun* one, Aveda," Lucy said, arching an eyebrow as she passed me the bag. "And honestly, I thought we might be in need of a little extra fun after you and Evie trap the puppy demon."

"So let's come up with something that doesn't involve allowing bags full of sex toys within the sight line of my parents," I said.

Evie giggled again, then shook her head, looking confused. "Man," she said. "I don't know why I'm so giggly, given that we have to take care of the whole puppy demon thing before the party can really get going." She sobered, worry creeping into her expression.

I met Bea's eyes and she gave me a little nod. I'd asked her to focus extra hard on adjusting Evie's mood tonight, which must've been why Evie was all giggly over dildos in the first place. My hope was that Evie would end up having such a good time, she'd forget all about the mission — and by the time she remembered, I'd have taken care of it. Best maid of honor at work. I mentally patted myself on the back for managing to keep myself from spilling the beans to her about the change I'd made to the plan. Like I'd told Scott, I didn't want her to have any more doubts about her ability to be a hero. I would handle this. Just like I always did.

Bea focused on the back of Evie's head and Evie's shoulders relaxed, her smile returning.

"We'll be ready whenever Maisy gets here," I said, giving Evie's arm a reassuring squeeze. "Now why don't you go greet your other guests? Kevin will bring the food out shortly."

"Oooh!" Evie said, her eyes lighting up. "The unholy combo of spam musubi and nachos will soon be mine!"

"Er, not exactly," I said. "I asked him to make a few adjustments to his usual menu. To make it more engagement-party friendly."

"Like the adjustments you made to the décor?" Lucy said, her eyes flitting around disapprovingly.

"Yeah, they kind of make it more boring-people friendly," Bea chimed in. I gave her a look. She was supposed to be helping me. She shrugged as if to say, *Well, they do, though?*

"Hey!" Evie said, elbowing Bea in the ribs. She gave me one of her game smiles. "Annie's just being creative, playing up the contrast between the supposed classiness of all this bridal stuff and the trashiness of all the karaoke we're going to sing later."

"No karaoke," I said. "I think we all know how quickly that can devolve. You definitely do not want to hear Scott's take on the divas of yesteryear." I tried to crack a game smile of my own, but they all stared back at me, puzzled.

"So," Evie said slowly, "we're at The Gutter and we're not doing karaoke—"

"—or eating the delicious garbage food," Lucy chimed in. "In other words, we are in no way using this fine location for any of its true and intended purposes."

"We might as well go to some sterile downtown hotel ballroom with three-hundred-dollar steaks," Bea said. Then quickly added, "Sorry" when I gave her another look.

"I'm sure it will be great," Evie said, but her game smile was starting to waver. "Annie's obviously put a lot of work into—"

"Into completely ignoring what you actually wanted and would enjoy," Lucy muttered.

"Excuse me," I said, bristling. "But I don't recall her asking for a dildo sampler platter either."

"Okay, okay," Evie said, putting a hand on Lucy's arm. "Let's not turn this into some kind of roller derby girl brawl."

"*That* would actually be cool," Bea said.

I forced my shoulders to relax. "Why don't you all go find your seats?" I said. "And try the antelope skewers, they're delicious. I'll go put this"—I gestured to the dildo bag—"out of sight."

Evie nodded. "Come on," she said, steering Lucy and Bea toward the tables. I tried to smile at her, but she had already turned away.

Well. I couldn't worry about that right now. I had several missions to accomplish, and I had to keep multitasking like a mofo. And hopefully she'd warm up to the party once she realized how preferable a beautiful—and beautifully presented—meal was to fake cheese and drunken singing.

I could do this. I could do everything, dammit.

I hustled over to The Gutter's stage and dumped the dildo bag behind a speaker and underneath a particularly voluminous drape of linen. When I turned back around, I took a moment to survey the room. Guests were trickling in and mingling, but no one seemed interested in finding their assigned seats. Or eating the antelope skewers Kevin was grudgingly shuttling around on a silver platter. And it looked like only about half of them had paid attention to my semi-formal edict. Nate and Rose were standing off to one side, talking. Lucy and Bea were clustered around a table. Lucy plucked an antelope skewer off of Kevin's platter, took a bite, and turned a little green. She tried to set it down delicately, but the sauce smeared all over the cream linen of the tablecloth. Bea draped a napkin over it and they made a face at each other. Clearly, antelope was not to their taste. Scott was still valiantly entertaining my parents, paying rapt attention to something my mother was saying. And Evie . . .

I frowned, scanning the room again. Where was Evie?

I finally spotted her standing near the entrance, locked

in conversation. With Maisy. My stomach dropped. Argh. Evie wasn't even supposed to *see* Maisy. I should have kept an eagle eye on the door instead of dealing with those stupid dildos.

Okay. Fine. I could improvise. The night was still young, the party was still fresh, and there was still time to serve my beautiful meal, give some beautiful speeches, and capture the rogue puppy demon before it turned this whole evening into a big, fat, flaming disaster. I squared my shoulders and marched over to them.

"Maisy!" I exclaimed. "You're here!"

"She's here," Evie agreed, giving me a conspiratorial look and nodding subtly at the elaborately wrapped package tucked under Maisy's arm.

"Engagement party selfie!" shrieked Maisy. She whipped out her phone and held it up, leaning into us. "Ooh, so cute," she cried, looking at the screen, then thumb-typing on the keyboard to post it. "Totally uploading. Hashtag NATEVIE!"

"There's a hashtag for my wedding?" Evie said.

"Naturally," Maisy said, thumb-typing away. "Let's see what the fans are saying. Awww, they love your outfit of course—so unique, so you," she said gesturing to Evie's jeans. "They think Aveda's a little overdressed, though. It's cool, Aveda, I'm totally down with wearing a good ball-gown for any and all occasions."

"This isn't even a ballgown," I muttered.

"Some fans would dispute you on that," Maisy said, scrolling through her feed. "It does seem a bit odd that you're *so* dressed up. Way more than the actual bride. Like this is an occasion to celebrate *you* rather than—"

"What a lovely gift!" Evie said, a little too loudly. She gave me a meaningful look, trying to steer us back to the task at hand. "Maisy, let me take that to the gift pile in the back room—"

"No!" I blurted out. They both gave me a quizzical look.

"I mean, you shouldn't leave your own party. Not even for a second."

"I shouldn't?" Evie said, her brow knitting in confusion.

"I can take it back," I said, reaching for the package. "And then, uh, you can come meet me in a bit if you want to check out the whole pile of, uh, gifts, and . . ." I sounded ridiculous. Was one little hitch really enough to disrupt my entire freaking plan?

"No need to take anything back, ladies," Maisy trilled. "As you know, Aveda, this one is very special. And I'd really very much prefer if the bride opened it right now."

I'll bet you would, I thought grimly.

"It's not really about what you prefer, though, is it?" I said, holding out my hand insistently. "You can't force her to open it if she doesn't want to."

"Well, maybe she does want to," Maisy said, bristling a bit. "Maybe you should stop speaking for her and let her decide for herself."

"As maid of honor, part of my job is to—"

"—is to help the bride have the best experience for *her*. Not for you." Maisy narrowed her eyes at me and pulled the package further out of reach. "So why don't you stop trying to make this all about Aveda Jupiter and—"

"—and I really just want everyone to enjoy the party!" I said, plastering a big, fake smile on my face. I lunged and snatched the gift from Maisy. "Especially Evie. The gift opening should be a big production near the end of the night, don't you think? For maximum fabulousness?"

They both stared at me, confused. But for completely different reasons. I decided to keep barreling on.

"Evie," I said. "Why don't you go mingle? I need to talk to Maisy about something."

"Well . . . okay," she said. She was still staring at me, like, *what are you doing?*

I tried to make my features reassuring. *I've got it under control. Just trust me.*

"What was that all about, Aveda Jupiter?" Maisy said, planting her hands on her hips as Evie moved back to the crowd of party guests. "I know you are unaccustomed to playing sidekick, but really, this is getting to be a bit much—"

"I have an exclusive scoop for you," I blurted out. "I mean, if you can keep a lid on it until after the party."

That got her attention. Maisy pressed her flaky gray lips together and frowned at me. "I'm listening."

"I'm engaged." I twisted my plastic ring back around so the fake ruby was visible.

Maisy looked at me curiously, her eyes narrowing. Not quite the reaction I'd been hoping for. "You are? At the same time as Evie? And you're telling me at . . . Evie's engagement party?"

"I . . ." I realized then that I was basically playing into the spotlight-stealing narrative all the bride-to-be commenters were setting out for me. The one Maisy seemed to be buying into.

"I'm . . . keeping it a secret for now!" I improvised. "You know, so as not to take any attention away from Evie. You're the first person I'm telling. And if you can keep it quiet until after the party, I'll let you announce it on your blog. Exclusively."

"Hmm," she said, her ghoulish eyes glowing. "I suppose I can do that. For Evie."

"For Evie," I agreed. "Now let me put this with the other presents and—"

"—and she'll still model it for an exclusive photo shoot at the end of the night?" Maisy said.

"Of course. I didn't want her to do it now because, uh, not everyone's here yet. You should have the biggest audience possible for your custom lingerie debut."

"I suppose that's true," Maisy said, but she was still studying me with narrowed eyes, as if trying to work something out.

"Why don't you go find a seat? I'll take this back ..." I made vague motions toward The Gutter's back hallway.

As Maisy wandered off, I took care to saunter toward the back hallway that led to the bathroom. No sudden movements, and I didn't let the glee show in my face too much. But I held the package tightly as anticipation bubbled in my chest, my blood fizzing with the promise of battle.

This was it. I was about to capture that damn puppy once and for all.

I made it down the hall and eased open the door to The Gutter's tiny, single stall bathroom.

"You made it," Scott said, ushering me inside and locking the door behind us. He was holding the scanner and already had the trap set up, perched precariously on the toilet tank. There was nowhere else for it to perch. The bathroom was about the size of a somewhat generous closet and contained only the essentials: toilet, sink. The water-damaged walls looked like they were covered in some kind of intricate pattern—actually years of patrons carving their initials and messages of varying vulgarity into the wood until its original texture was completely changed. There was enough room for me, Scott, and the trap. But not much room for anything else.

I swallowed hard, trying to contain the nerves dancing double-time through my stomach. I suddenly realized my brilliant plan involved cramming both of us into a very tight space with me in nothing but my underwear. And then asking him to *rip off* my underwear.

Not very friend-like, for sure.

But this was important. This was part of my mission, my duty, my way of ultimately defeating evil. And it *had* to work. Surely I could handle a few minutes of an uncomfortable situation for the greater good.

"Set up the trap," I said, making my tone brisk and business-like. "With your back turned to me, so I can change."

He raised an eyebrow, but didn't argue. "Yes, ma'am."

I tore open the package and pulled the bundle of white lace free. It had the telltale crimson fabric sewn into the bust, I noted. I changed as efficiently as possible, shimmying out of my dress and underwear and hoping that Kevin wouldn't suddenly decide he needed to come back here to, say, flush those damn antelope skewers down the toilet. I rearranged all necessary body parts into the bra, panties, and garters.

"You can turn back around," I said.

He swiveled back to face me, then froze, his eyes going wide. I could tell he was trying to avoid looking anywhere below my neck. And failing miserably.

"I, um . . ." he stuttered.

"Keep it together, Cameron," I said, snapping my fingers at him. "Have you never seen a scantily clad woman before?"

"I-I have," he managed. "But not . . ." He forced his gaze upward, to the ceiling, and I tried not to let that sentence auto-complete in my head.

But not you.

"Is the trap ready?" I asked, hoping to get us back on track.

"It is," he said to the ceiling. "Locked and loaded. Are you feeling anything?"

I bit back all the extremely inappropriate thoughts dancing through my head and focused on the places where the lingerie was touching my skin. It just felt . . . nice. Light, soft, lacy. A bit on the flimsy side, even. No evil vibes, no stabbing sensation.

"Maybe we need to give it a few minutes," I said. "Evie was wearing her dress for a bit before it officially attacked."

"Do you need to do something to activate it?" he said.

"I don't know. What was Evie doing right before it attacked?" I called up the memory, trying to replay it step by step.

"Giving a speech, right? Of sorts."

"Oh, yes. She was so nervous. She started reciting my catchphrase. San Francisco is my duty, my love, and—"

"My life," Scott chorused with me. He finally met my eyes again and gave me a lopsided grin. "I always liked that one."

"Oh, really?" I arched an eyebrow. "I didn't think you liked *anything* about Aveda Jupiter."

"It's not that." He hesitated, his eyes roaming my face. The silence stretched between us and I squirmed uncomfortably. I suddenly wished he'd go back to ogling my breasts. "I liked—*like*—quite a bit," he said, his gaze earnest, unguarded. "How brave she is, how bold. How once she decides to do something, that motherfucker is as good as *done*. How willing and single-minded she is about throwing herself in the path of danger if it means saving others. Like that day back in sixth grade, when she threw herself in front of a certain wimpy little nerd with delusions of grandeur." He gave me a rueful grin.

"A wimpy little nerd trying to stick up for his mom who was raising a kid by herself and training to be a totally bad-ass lawyer," I corrected.

"Whatever the case, he was forever grateful. That was some bona fide superhero shit. And at such a young age."

I shrugged. "Even Annie Chang had her Aveda Jupiter moments back in the day."

He gave me an amused look. "Of course she did. They're the same person." Before I could correct him, he continued. "In any case. I think over the years, things got . . . tangled. I know there was some unhealthy co-dependence on both sides of the equation with her and Evie—yet I only seemed to blame her for that." He raked a hand through his hair, looked up at the ceiling again, then back at me. "And I think some of that came from the fact that I was upset she pushed me away that time we kissed," he finally said. "My fragile male ego took a definite beating over that. And that's not really fair, to hold a massive grudge against someone when all she did was . . . not feel a certain way. If she didn't feel the way I did . . . well, I can't change that. She has every right to feel—or not feel—the way she does."

My face was on fire. "She didn't have the right to say the awful things she said to you afterward, though," I said, my voice small. I was fully aware of how ridiculous we sounded, talking about me in the third person like I was some kind of fictional character we'd read about in a comic book. But it seemed to be the only way either of us *could* talk about this.

He gave me a weary smile, a look that seemed to contain every regret either of us had ever experienced. It made my heart ache. And it should have made me want to put up that wall between us again—the one that kept me from being Annie Chang and kept him from showing me all that buried intensity—to ensure that both of us were safe. But I suddenly, really, thoroughly did *not* want to. I wanted to hold on to this moment forever, this moment where it felt like we were both, for once, being fully ourselves. With all the weird angles and broken bits and little pieces we usually kept hidden.

"I said some things, too," he said. "And in the spirit of this friendship we're trying to build, I propose we start letting that shit go."

I matched his half-smile. "Proposal accepted. For real this time."

"The fake one doesn't seem to be getting us anywhere," he said, nodding at my plastic ring. "Are you feeling anything weird? From the lingerie?"

"No," I said, frustration nipping at me again. "I don't understand. I know Maisy was up to something with all this, I *know* it—"

"AVEDA JUPITER IS A MENACE."

The words cut through the air, blasting in from the main room. We'd been able to hear the general buzz of crowd noise and Stu's piano playing through the bathroom door. But this was loud, distinct. Like the person was bellowing into a megaphone. And with a sick, sinking feeling, I realized I recognized the voice doing the bellowing.

"*Shit,*" I growled, throwing the bathroom door open.

I sprinted down the hall toward the main room, my heart rate ratcheting up with every step.

"Wait . . . Annie!" Scott called out.

"Stay there!" I yelled back at him. "I'll handle this!"

I made it to the main room, already at least half-aware of what I was going to see. Still, the reality of it was a bit of a shock.

There, onstage, microphone clutched in hand, was Maisy Kane. Her glowing eyes looked especially malevolent as they landed on me and she raised a flaky gray finger to point in my direction.

"As a journalist," she spat out, "it is my duty to expose her!"

What the hell? Was she foregoing the lingerie attack plan to do something else evil?

"Maisy," Lucy growled, moving to the side of the stage, "you said you were going to make a toast. This hardly seems like—"

"I am making a toast! A toast to justice!" Maisy bellowed.

I had no idea what she was up to, but it didn't matter. She was about to put the entire party in danger and I had to stop her. I sprinted up to the stage and grabbed her arm, trying to wrest the microphone free.

"Come with me right now," I said, projecting my trademark authority. "I'll give you a chance to explain—"

"Oh, I don't think so, Aveda Jupiter!" Maisy shook free from my grasp, skittered away from me, and pointed that accusatory finger at me yet again. "Look at her!" she screeched. "My intrepid bridal commenters were right, she *is* trying to take all the wedding attention! Trying to take the spotlight from Evie!"

I whipped around to face the crowd, to calm them and

tell them not to be alarmed, I had this Maisy threat under control. But when I saw their faces, I realized I'd grossly miscalculated what the reaction would be.

No one was looking at Maisy. Everyone was looking at me. And they all looked varying degrees of confused.

I remembered then that I was wearing nothing but bridal lingerie. *Evie's* bridal lingerie.

"Stealing the gift I made especially for Evie for herself!" Maisy spat out. "I knew she was acting shady, so like the ace reporter that I am, I went and investigated the gift table and my contribution was nowhere to be found." Maisy pressed a fluttery hand against her chest, as if this was the most upsetting thing imaginable. "And that's not even the worst of it . . ." Maisy grabbed my hand sporting the plastic ruby and held it up. "She's *secretly engaged!*" I was too shell-shocked to pull away from her. The crowd remained silent, as if they couldn't even begin to comprehend the breadth of my self-aggrandizing nature.

"Annie . . . ?" Evie said uncertainly.

"And!" Maisy bellowed, her glowing eyes settling on something behind me. "She has *this* hidden up here on-stage!" She stepped around me and dragged the big trash bag from its cream linen hiding place. I noticed then that the linen had fallen away from it a bit and the bag was gaping open, exposing the brightly colored collection within. And Maisy must have spotted it.

. *Fuuuuuuuuuuuuuck.*

Without further ado, Maisy upended the bag, dumping a rainbow cornucopia of sex toys all over the stage.

Now the party guests weren't so silent. Scandalized murmurs rippled through the crowd. And though I couldn't make out the exact words, I was pretty sure none of them were complimentary toward me.

"I mean, what was she going to do with all this?" Maisy crowed, gesturing expansively to the sex toys and condoms. "Bring them out and embarrass poor Evie, I bet! Ruin the party, get all the attention for herself, and take Evie's place as San Francisco's favorite bride. Not that that's even possible."

"That's not what I'm doing!" I snapped. I moved toward Maisy, tripped over a stray vibrator, and hastily used my telekinesis to move it out of the way. "But as for whatever *you're* trying to do: it's over. We're onto you."

Maisy danced out of my way, then stopped and cocked her head to the side. "What?"

"Give up!" I said, trying to sound forceful as I attempted to maneuver my way around the minefield of sex toys. They just kept rolling into my path, forcing me to stumble around and hop over them like a hapless character in a videogame. I managed to grab on to a few of them with my mental feathers, but I still felt clumsy, awkward. "Hand over the puppy demon and let us take you into custody!"

Maisy's gray brow crinkled. "Puppy? Aveda Jupiter, you have really gone off the deep end this time."

I stopped trying to maneuver my way around the dildos and looked at her—*really* looked at her. And that's when I realized she had no fucking clue what I was talking about.

Unless she was a phenomenally good actress and an evil mastermind who had absolutely zero desire to gloat about her evil plan and take me down and all of that seemed . . . unlikely. I looked down at the lingerie. It wasn't doing anything. Except sitting on my body. It was just freaking lingerie.

Evie's lingerie.

Evie stepped onstage and planted herself in front of me, arms crossed over her chest, her face a mix of confusion and concern.

"Annie," she said slowly. "What's going on?"

"You . . . you heard what's going on," I said. "Apparently we were wrong about Maisy." I gestured toward Maisy, who was now off to the side of the stage and locked in furious conversation with Lucy, trying to make sense of everything. Unfortunately, no one else was doing the same. No, the rest of the party was still staring at me and Evie, facing off, surrounded by a cavalcade of sex toys.

"I got that," she said, "but I don't understand ..." She gestured up and down my body. "...this. Why are you wearing that? And what's this about you being engaged?"

"I can explain everything," I said, holding up my hands. "Just give me a chance—"

"I know people have been saying stuff about you online and I haven't believed any of it," she said, her voice going dangerously quiet. "But are you ..." She looked at the lingerie again. "... are you not getting enough recognition for your maid-of-honor duties? Because—"

"That is *not* it," I said firmly. "I was trying to take care of the puppy demon plan while you enjoyed the party—"

"That was not the plan," she said, shaking her head. "The plan was for us to take care of it together—"

"But you were so worried!" I protested. "You thought it was going to try to control you and—"

"And that doesn't mean I can't handle it," she said, drawing herself up tall. Anger sparked in her eyes. "I'm more than capable of overcoming my fear and dealing with whatever we're up against. I'm a superhero now—"

"*Now!* But that's a recent development and I know you've had some nerves about it. I have way more years on the job, more experience—"

"Which you never hesitate to remind me of—"

"And it's up to me to protect you!" I interrupted, determined to get her to see my point. That I'd done all of this because I cared about her. "I thought it would be best for you if—"

"Best for me?!" Evie looked at me incredulously. "You're not my *mother*, Aveda. And I think I've more than proven I don't need you to protect me." She glared at me. "If you wanted to change the plan, you could have *talked* to me— like a mature adult. Like you think *I'm* a mature adult. Instead of just *deciding* all of this by yourself. We're supposed to be equal partners in this whole superheroing endeavor. But ..." She studied me intently, her gaze like a laser cutting through my skin. I shifted uncomfortably. "... that's really not okay with you, is it? *Nothing's* okay with you unless you're the star and I'm the sidekick."

I shook my head, unable to think of how to respond. My gaze slid toward Bea and I gave her a little nod. Maybe we could get Evie to calm down and I could explain my position without her interrupting or getting upset or—

"Bea!" Evie shrieked. She whipped around and glared at her sister. "Stop it! I . . . I know that's you, trying to calm me down and I don't want to be calm right now, I don't want—"

"Sorry!" Bea cried. "Aveda and I were just trying to—"

"Aveda!" Evie turned back to me. "You're doing this, too? Getting my own sister to *control* me?"

"Not control," I said. "Soothe. You've been so stressed out about the wedding and the puppy demon and—"

"And this isn't the first time, is it?" Evie said, realization dawning in her eyes. "You've . . . you've been doing this for weeks now? That's why I was so weirdly giggly earlier. Why my moods have been swinging all over the place since I got engaged . . ." The anger seemed to drain from her in an instant, her shoulders slumping. And slowly, her burgeoning rage was replaced with something much worse.

Sadness. Disappointment. Defeat.

"You know," she said quietly. "Everyone said it was a mistake to make you my maid of honor. That you would try to make it all about you, that you would never be okay not being the center of attention, that you would try to pull some *stunt* . . ." She drifted off, shaking her head, then met my eyes. "I kept insisting that you wouldn't. That things were *different* now. That underneath all the drama, you're so loyal and generous and we've finally worked everything out between us and *you* were the one I wanted standing next to me . . ." Her voice caught and she pressed her lips together in a thin line, fighting back tears. I was too numb to cry.

"I think you should go," she finally said.

I didn't know what to do, what to say. My mind had gone

totally blank. Silence blanketed the air and everyone was still staring at me. I couldn't bear to look at my parents. At a loss for what else to do, I fell to my knees and started shoving sex toys back into the garbage bag. It was the only goal that seemed achievable at the moment. I was dimly aware of Scott sidling up to me, wrapping his jacket around my shoulders, and gently tugging me to my feet.

"Come on," he murmured.

I shuffled next to him, my mind still blank, tuning out the eyes that were still on me, the murmurs that started up as I headed for the exit, whispers about this complete fucking disaster of a party. When we finally got outside, the cold night air hit me in the face, waking me up a bit. Scott's jacket was still wrapped around me. And I was clutching the bag of sex toys in one hand like a talisman, gripping so hard, my knuckles turned white.

"So," I said. "I guess Maisy isn't evil. And the puppy demon isn't possessing my underwear. And maybe I fucked things up so badly, none of it matters, because nobody will ever talk to me again."

Scott rested his hands on my shoulders. "Why don't we go home?" he said.

I took a deep breath, trying to get my wits back about me. I focused only on the present, not allowing any thoughts about what had just happened into my brain.

"I'll go," I said. "You need to get back in there and see if there's any of the party that can be salvaged."

He frowned. "Maybe you should try to talk to Evie—"

"No." The word escaped my throat in a strangled sob. I shoved my tears down, determined not to cry. "No," I said more steadily. "I think that's a pretty terrible idea right now, and I'd rather not add on to the parade of terrible ideas already implemented tonight."

"You can't walk home like that," he said, motioning to my underwear/suit jacket combo.

"Go back inside and get me my dress. I'll wait out here."

He gave me a skeptical look.

"I'll telekinesis and/or beat up anyone who looks at me funny," I added.

He shook his head. "Annie . . ."

"Please." I pulled away from him and gathered the jacket more tightly around me. "I know you want to say something that will make it better, but there's nothing you *can* say. I had two missions tonight, I fucked both of them up, and I really, really need to be alone right now."

He looked like he wanted to say something else, but finally gave up, nodded, and went back inside.

And I was alone.

Chapter Eighteen

WHEN I'D DONE the walk of shame down those rickety treehouse steps so many years ago, I'd thought it was surely the most embarrassing version of such a thing I'd ever experience.

Now, as I tromped through San Francisco wearing my rumpled dress and carrying a giant garbage bag full of condoms and sex toys, I realized that was patently untrue. This was definitely the worst walk of shame ever. And I hadn't even had sex beforehand.

I couldn't believe that a night that was supposed to end in triumph had actually ended with me having a huge fight with my best friend on a grotty karaoke stage in my underwear and that my parents had witnessed the whole thing.

Forget being a Bad Chinese American Daughter. I was an Embarrassing, Exhibitionist, Totally Delusional Chinese American Daughter. That definitely wasn't making it into the Christmas newsletter.

I continued my death march toward HQ, my big bag o' dildos smacking against my hip as I walked, as if punctuating every step with a mocking chant.

Dumb. Dumb. Dumb.

I let the chant take over as I stomped. The chant drowned out any coherent thoughts threatening to worm their way into my brain. Why was I still holding on to this stupid bag of sex toys, anyway? I guess it had seemed like dumping them outside the bar for guests to eyeball on their way out would only add insult to the injury of an already terrible party. Also, my death grip on the bag gave me a tenuous hold on the real world. The grip, the bounce of the bag against my hip, the chant ... those were the only things keeping me tethered here instead of sinking into a never-ending spiral of guilt and regret.

Dumb. Dumb. Dumb.

I chanted for a few blocks, breathing out the word over and over again. It kept me focused.

Until I saw something that made me grind to a complete halt.

I only noticed it because of the light spilling out from the big front window, casting a golden glow onto the street. It was such a contrast to the other businesses on the block, which were all darkened and shuttered for the night.

I stopped abruptly and stared, homing in on the shop. It was Marcus Wong's boutique — and the window display had changed. The bloody warriors from before had been replaced by a solitary mannequin, positioned dead center. It stood there, facing front, arms resting at its sides. A lone figure against a simple background of pure white. It took me a moment to process what it was wearing. An ivory dress cut in that signature dramatic mermaid shape the designer favored. And peppered with tiny red flowers.

I blinked. I felt like cold water had been dumped over my head. It was just like Evie's dress, I was sure of it. But how had it gotten there? It had been destroyed, and Marcus was so adamant it was a failed experiment anyway and ... and ... and ...

My brain short-circuited, stuck on a single word again. Unable to process anything further. I had to get a closer look. This was too weird. Nothing made sense. And I felt the burning need to *make* it make sense. To somehow, against all odds, still have this night end in triumph. That need consumed me, overwhelmed everything else, blocked out all common sense and logic, and I found myself walking over to the door and turning the knob. Somehow this dress was the key to the puppy demon drama that had been vexing us—and I was going to prove it.

I don't know what my plan was if it had been locked or if an alarm sounded or if police had showed up right then and there to arrest the city's original (but currently very unpopular) superheroine. Luckily the door was unlocked, and I walked in with no trouble at all. I didn't even think about how odd this was, a fancy boutique that was clearly closed for the night being unlocked and unguarded. I was too focused on the *need* to make things right. To save the day. To be the heroine I kept claiming I was.

I dumped my dildos by the door and climbed into the window display, approaching the dress trepidatiously. It just sat there, icy and beautiful and still. I reached out a finger to touch it, then jumped back, as if it were about to bite me.

Nothing. It was doing nothing. It was just a dress.

But . . . no. It couldn't be just a dress. *How* could it be just a dress? Something weird was going on here and this dress was the key. And I had to prove it. I had to redeem myself. I had to show everyone that I was Aveda Jupiter, dammit, and I was going to solve this entire mystery and save the city.

I reached out with shaking hands and unzipped the back.

I at least had the wherewithal to move from the window area and into a section of the boutique floor hidden from outside view, so I wouldn't flash the entire city. I kicked off my heels, feeling the plush red carpet between my toes. There was a strange sense of reverence as I pulled the dress over Maisy's bridal lingerie. Maybe it was the eerie silence of the store, maybe it was the feel of the soft chiffon on my skin, maybe it was the idea that what I was doing was so momentous, it was going to solve our puppy demon dilemma once and for all. Whatever it was, it made time slow to a crawl, amplified the soft swooshing sounds as the material settled on my frame, caused the air to take on a sudden chill.

As I drew up the zipper, the long, drawn-out *shhhhhh*

sound seemed particularly ominous. I turned and faced myself in the mirror.

"Come on," I murmured to the dress. "Do your worst."

Then I waited.

And waited.

The silence seemed to thicken around me, pressing
against my skin, making the dress feel heavy and cumber-
some. But it wasn't *doing* anything. Just like the lingerie
hadn't done anything.

Fuck. Had I been wrong *again*? Was I really that far off
my superheroing game? At least this time there was no one
to witness it.

"Oh, Annie Chang," I said to my reflection. "What the
hell is wrong with you?"

I reached around for the zipper, ready to grab my stupid
bag of dildos and go the fuck home and never tell anyone
about this . . . when I felt it. The sharpest, most intense pain
I'd ever experienced. Stabbing directly into my side, as if
someone had appeared out of nowhere and knifed me with
an entire butcher block of sharp objects.

"Oh . . . *god* . . ." I screamed, falling to my knees. I
clutched my ribs. It was like a knife made of fire. And it was
expanding by the second, an incredibly painful fungus
overtaking my entire torso. I felt like I was about to go up
in flames on the spot.

"*Shit*," I wheezed. I grappled for the zipper of the dress,
clawing at it with both hands. The pain in my side morphed,
as if the knife made of fire was growing and twisting, and I
slumped to the floor entirely. Stars danced in front of my
eyes and I felt like I was going to pass out.

No, I thought. *Breathe through it, goddamit.*

"You're not going to get me, you stupid fucking *thing*," I
screamed. The pain twisted again, as if in response. Now it
felt like it was wrapped around my whole body, or worse,
like it had seeped through my skin and was twisting every
single one of my internal organs into the most unnatural
shape possible.

I reached out with my mind, trying to get at the zipper with my telekinesis. But it was no use. I couldn't see the zipper. I tried again and again, but to no avail. This stupid ... *limitation* on my power was going to kill me.

I tried twisting around to see if I could spot the zipper in the mirror, but a film descended over my vision, blurring everything, and I realized I was about to pass out or maybe die—really, either would be fine if it just stopped the horrible pain overwhelming all of my senses, making it impossible to think or breathe or even scream. I thought I heard my name being called, but I knew that must be an aural hallucination, some weird trick of the mind that happened right before someone succumbed to the arms of death.

It hit me suddenly that I'd never be able to talk to Evie or Scott again. Evie's last memory of us would involve me totally embarrassing her at her own party and Scott would never know ... never know ...

My eyes filled with tears, and I was overwhelmed with desperation, regret, and deep, piercing sadness. I always managed to pull away from him. Even in the Gutter closet, when we'd let our guards down, when he'd said I'd had every right to not feel the way he did back when he tried to kiss me ... I hadn't responded. I'd let him think I didn't feel anything. I'd pulled away from him *again*. This horrible, consuming pain was stripping me of all the rationalizations I had used—that keeping him at a distance was for the greater good, that I couldn't let Annie Chang take over and get soft about him. All I could think now was that I *needed* him to know how I really felt. How I'd wanted that moment when we were finally and fully ourselves with each other to last forever. How he made me feel *everything*.

And goddammit, I wanted to tell Evie I hadn't ruined her engagement party on purpose.

Fuck this.

Aveda Jupiter never went down without a fight.

I wasn't going down without a fight.

I threw my mental feathers out with renewed vigor, tried

to force them through the pain and the resistance I was getting from the dress, grappling around behind me, trying to get at the zipper—or any part of the dress, really—even though my vision was clouding over and I couldn't see *anything* . . .

And then suddenly, I heard a loud *ripppppp* and felt cold air hitting my bare skin and my vision started to focus again and I realized strong hands were gripping my shoulders and Scott's face was blurring in and out and he was screaming my name over and over and over again.

I blinked once, twice. Aware of the total absence of pain. It was like a balm all over my body. Maybe this was what death felt like?

As my vision cleared, I realized I wasn't dead or even unconscious. I was sprawled on the plush red floor of the boutique and Scott was actually there, and I wasn't wearing the dress anymore. In fact, I wasn't wearing much of anything. I looked down at my body. All I had on was Evie's lacy bridal lingerie, which now sported more than a few interestingly positioned holes. My brain seemed to light up, returning to full alertness.

"The dress," I croaked out. "Where's the dress?"

"It's in the trap," Scott said. "You had managed to get it partway off your body, and I got it the rest of the way and stuffed it in the trap . . ."

He trailed off, his breathing ragged. I took stock of his features. His eyes were wild, lit up by a combination of anger and confusion and naked terror.

"And the puppy," I managed. "Is it still . . ."

"The scanner's not picking anything up, and I'm not sensing anything, so it's not in the air," he said. "If it was in the dress, it should be trapped in there—luckily I still had the scanner and the trap with me when I used a tracking spell to find you. I never should have let you go off by yourself, I—"

"Good," I interrupted, my voice weak and thin. "That's good. Maybe we caught it this time."

"What the hell were you thinking?" he growled. "Did you really come in here all by yourself and put on that dress and try to fight it with no backup or—"

His words became a burble in my ear. Because all I could think of was the regret that had pierced my soul when I realized I'd never get to tell him how I felt—how I *really* felt—with no filter, no bullshit.

I wanted to tell him.

Hell, I wanted to *show* him. It suddenly seemed like the most necessary thing in the world.

"Annie." His voice pierced my thoughts. His hands tightened around my shoulders. "Dammit. Tell me you're okay. I can't fucking live with myself if you're not okay—"

I kissed him.

It was another kiss like the one we'd shared on the gym floor: raw, visceral. He responded, his hands sliding from my shoulders to my back to pull me against him, holding me like he never wanted to let me go. He gasped my name between each kiss, like he was trying to reassure himself that I was still there. Still alive.

I felt consumed by him, overwhelmed by his lips and his hands and the heat of his body against mine. And I still needed to feel *more*, so I wrapped my legs around his waist and pressed myself firmly against him, gasping when I realized he was already hard and hot and ready. He groaned, his lips moving to my neck, my collarbone, a trail of fire against my skin. One of his hands slid up my ribcage to cup my breast. The lace of the bridal bra had seemed flimsy and insufficient when I'd put it on, but when his thumb stroked over the material, it rasped against my nipple, and I shuddered.

I didn't think it was possible for my excitement to intensify any further, but then he lowered his head and slipped my nipple into his mouth. It was still covered by the lace of the bra and the combined sensations—the wet heat of his tongue, the material rubbing against me—nearly sent me over the edge. I moaned, my fingers tangling in his hair, and I wondered if he could keep doing that forever.

He moved back up and claimed my mouth with his and suddenly I couldn't go a moment longer without touching him. I slid my hand between us and stroked him through his pants, thrilling at how hard he was and how that was for me—for *us*. I moved my hands back to his chest and undid his tie, the buttons on his shirt. I needed to feel skin. He growled against my mouth as I raked my fingernails over that hard wall of chest I'd fantasized about so much over the years. I moved my hand back down and worked the button on his pants—I wanted to make him groan like I'd heard before, as if it was coming from somewhere deep inside of him.

"Annie," he gasped. He pulled away from our kiss and searched my face. He was breathing hard and his eyes were so intense and deadly serious, so different from his usual playful warmth. It made me feel again like I was seeing the deepest, truest version of him, the man who felt things more than he ever let on, who always seemed so mellow and easygoing but lit me up like a firecracker whenever he so much as touched me.

"Are you sure?" he managed. I could feel his heartbeat quickening, matching mine. "Are you sure you want to . . ."

I reached up and cupped his face—I wanted him to know that this was who *I* really was. That if you stripped all the layers away from me, I felt things as deeply as he did. And that I'd never wanted anything as badly as I wanted him right here, right now. I'd just narrowly escaped death and desperately needed to feel every inch of him against me, needed to show him that I didn't care about anything except his mouth, his hands, his skin, and how overtaken I was by all of it.

"Yes," I said. "I want to. I need to." I reached across the floor and scrabbled around in my previously humiliating bag of sex toys and pulled out a condom. It was neon pink and apparently fruit punch-flavored, according to the label, and I probably should have been embarrassed—but right now, I didn't care. I held it up to him. "Please."

His eyes widened and I knew he wasn't embarrassed, either.

Between the two of us, we managed to get his pants unbuttoned, my panties off, and the condom on—frantic, clumsy movements that only turned me on harder. And then he was sliding inside of me and I gave over to that pure, all-consuming pleasure: not thinking about whether I should be doing this, whether I should be feeling this. Just *feeling* it, reveling in the way he buried his face in my neck, the way he tasted my skin, the way our bodies joined completely. I was still wearing the lacy bra and garters, and his clothes were sort of haphazardly pushed to the side and that just made things even hotter, like we needed each other so badly, we hadn't been able to waste time getting completely naked.

We moved together, wild and desperate, and the room fell away and it was just the two of us, needing this. His mouth found my nipple again and I arched against him, succumbing to the feeling, the sensation. And just when I felt myself spiraling further and further into pleasure, just when I felt like I couldn't take it anymore, he slid a hand between us and touched me right where I needed it and everything exploded into white light.

CHAPTER NINETEEN

WHEN I WOKE up the next morning, I spent at least two full minutes being confused. I'd slept very deeply, and as my eyes fluttered open, I had to reorient myself to the basic concept of being alive.

But I was still alive, I was wrapped in a tangle of sheets, and my back was pressed against a hard wall of chest. I dislodged myself from that position slowly, sitting up in my bed, allowing all the images from the night before to pile up in my sleep-fogged brain.

After thoroughly desecrating Marcus's precious salon floor, Scott and I had managed to get ourselves mostly dressed, gathered the scanner, trap, and the bag o' dildos, and gotten the hell out of there, leaving through the back door (which was also unlocked—Marcus really needed to get a better security system). We hadn't said much on the short walk home, except for him periodically asking me if I was okay, if I was sure I was okay, if we needed to wake Nate up to examine me. I'd maintained I was perfectly fine, even though being around him right after doing what we'd done made me feel exposed, like the softest, most vulnerable parts of myself were on display for all the world to see. I was definitely in full Annie Chang mode, and once we weren't having incredibly hot sex, I didn't know what to do with that.

But I was too tired, too wrung out, to be anything else.

When we'd gotten back to HQ, sheer exhaustion had taken over and we hadn't wasted time with any more words or questions. We'd gone to my room, crawled into bed together, and passed out with what was left of our clothes on. I knew sleeping together—just sleeping—wasn't nearly as intimate as what we'd done in the bridal salon, but waking up like this, with his arm locked around my waist, *felt* more intimate.

His arm stayed in that position even as I sat up, and he stirred in his sleep and pulled me closer, burying his face against my hip. I reached down and tentatively stroked his irresistibly mussed hair. He stirred again, but didn't wake. I had no idea what was next for us, so for a moment, I allowed myself to enjoy the warmth of being snuggled together in bed.

But only for a moment, because there were things I needed to take care of.

I gently extricated myself from his arm and pulled the covers over his shoulders. He didn't move and I was reminded of the lazy summer day between seventh and eighth grade when Evie and I discovered what a deep sleeper he was. He'd passed out on my parents' couch while we were watching *The Heroic Trio* for the millionth time and Evie and I had taken the opportunity to draw all over his face in permanent marker, turning him into an alien cat with multi-colored flowers on one cheek. I remembered the two of us giggling and trying to shush each other so we wouldn't wake him. Things had seemed so easy then.

I got out of the rags that remained of my clothes from the previous night, pulled on a tank top and yoga pants, and slipped out of the room, taking care to close the door quietly behind me.

I found Evie in the kitchen. She was seated behind the dining table, clad in ratty sweats, and appeared to have dumped the entire contents of a jumbo-size box of Lucky Charms out in front of her. She was picking through them and discarding the purple ones. This was normally a task she relished, but right now her movements were listless, like she was engaged in the most tedious household chore possible. She didn't look up when I entered the room.

I sat down next to her and surveyed the scene. She hadn't bothered with a bowl, the Lucky Charms were just spread all over the tabletop. And I had a hard time believing she planned on eating an entire tableful of junk cereal in one sitting, so this was clearly some bizarre form of stress relief.

I decided not to comment on any of that.

"Want some help?" I gestured to the cereal.

She shrugged. It wasn't a no. I suppose she'd given up on getting Hurricane Annie to actually hear the word "no."

I started picking through alongside her, running my fingers through the cereal bits, getting crumbly detritus under my nails. Touching every piece of the stuff probably rendered it unsanitary/inedible, but I decided not to mention that either. We worked for a few moments without saying anything, the soft rustle of the cereal against the table the only sound punctuating the silence.

"I'm sorry," I finally said. I kept my eyes trained on the cereal, scanning for telltale flashes of purple. It was easier than meeting her gaze. "I know I ruined everything. Well, I haven't quite ruined the wedding yet, but there's still time." She gave a little snort and I wasn't sure if it was a sound of derision or a near laugh, so I pressed on. "I really thought I was doing what was best for you. Giving you a beautiful party and soothing your nerves and taking care of the puppy demon and protecting you. Like I'm always trying to do. And that *is* what I'm always trying to do, even if it doesn't always seem like it."

I took a deep breath and kept going. "I feel like lately, everything I've ever known has just . . . unraveled. I've worked so hard and for so long to be Aveda Jupiter. I don't know how to do anything else, how to *be* anything else. And suddenly, it seemed like Aveda Jupiter was, I don't know . . . irrelevant. Not needed. Useless." I made myself say each word, shoving down the tears that were gathering in my throat. "All those months with no demons, it seemed like San Francisco might not need me anymore. And hey, even if demons were to return? Maybe they don't even need me then, because now they have something way better." I gestured to her. "A bona fide firestarter of a superheroine — who, by the way, is much more down to earth and relatable and awesome than I could ever hope to be." I gave her a slight smile. She stared at me, blank, wordless. It was disconcerting, and I had no idea what she was thinking. So I kept talking.

"I thought I could fix things the way I usually do. By working hard and being relentless and *willing* things to go my way. I thought if I made myself the best Aveda Jupiter ever — more kickass, more heroic, a better friend — it would solve everything. But it hasn't. It's not working. *Nothing's* working. So I don't know what I'm doing or who I am or if I'll do anything useful or even borderline positive ever again." I let out a long *whoosh* of a breath. "I've been trying so hard to do what I do best. But what Aveda Jupiter does best these days seems to be: fucking up every single thing that dares cross her path."

"Why do you think it's not working?" Evie said.

"What?" I shook my head, confused. She was staring back at me, still unreadable. But I sensed genuine curiosity creeping in around the edges of her expression.

"Why is your plan to be the best Aveda Jupiter ever not working?" she said, toying with a marshmallow bit.

"It's *Annie Chang*," I blurted out, frustration swelling in my chest. "That scared, ordinary little girl. The one who cried herself to sleep on prom night. The one who feels insecure like ninety percent of the time. The one who's always having these inconvenient bursts of weak, mushy, incoherent, totally unheroic *feelings* and fucking up Aveda Jupiter's path to awesomeness. I guess my whole identity crisis thing — all these feelings of being useless — made her come out hardcore. I mean, I think she started to come back when you were posing as me, showing me just how unnecessary I actually was. And I can't . . ." My voice caught and I swallowed hard. "I can't get her to go away."

Evie cocked her head, studying me. I shifted uncomfortably.

"Good," she said.

I stiffened. "Excuse me?"

"*Good*," she repeated emphatically. "I don't want her to go away. I *like* Annie Chang."

I shook my head, as if to banish the very thought. Evie gave me an amused look.

"You may have been Aveda Jupiter for a good, long while, but Aveda Jupiter owes everything to Annie Chang," she said. "Annie Chang is the one who protected me from all those bullies in the first place. The one who threatened to beat someone up for daring to not ask me to the prom." She reached over and took my hand, her eyes softening. "The one who's always been there for me no matter what. And who, before she was anyone's hero, was my friend."

I stared at our intertwined fingers, trying to make sense of what she was saying.

"Aveda Jupiter is fabulous," she continued. "Dazzling. A larger-than-life superheroine. But without Annie Chang, she's not real. She's not an actual human who feels human things for the other humans in her life. She's a bulldozer who sees things in black and white and doesn't realize that 'just try harder' is not the solution to every problem."

I gave her a look. "If this is a pep talk, it's a bad one."

She laughed. "I'm saying, Aveda Jupiter *needs* Annie Chang. Annie Chang makes her *more* of a badass, not less. Look, it's like Superman and Clark Kent—"

"Clark Kent is boring," I sputtered. "Weak, mundane. Hiding all of his superheroic light. No one cares about Clark Kent!"

Evie's jaw dropped. "Oh my god. That is such a *terrible* misreading of the Superman mythos." She leaned in earnestly. "When you read a Superman story, part of it is always about Clark Kent. Yes, he's a massively superpowered alien who has fantastical adventures, but his connections to people—the Kent parents, Lois Lane—are what make us care. They make him *stronger*, not weaker. Clark Kent is what allows him to be the best Superman possible!"

"But . . . but . . . things get so confused when Clark is an equal part of the story. You always wonder, which one is real?"

"They both are. They can't exist without each other."

I couldn't help but flash back to my exchange with Scott the night before.

Even Annie Chang had her Aveda Jupiter moments back in the day.

Of course she did. They're the same person.

I lived my life by rules I'd made for myself, by denying myself things my Annie Chang side craved—love, pleasure, carbs—so Aveda Jupiter could be as kickass as possible. Except . . . that wasn't working, was it?

Maybe Evie was right. I just didn't know how to let both sides of my personality have free reign without clashing and turning everything into a total wreck . . .

"Oh, god," I said, pulling away from her and putting my head in my hands. "I thought I knew what I was supposed to be. *Who* I'm supposed to be. Even when I haven't been sure of anything else, I've been sure of that. And now I have no idea. I'm such a fucking mess."

Evie gave a gentle laugh. "Remember when I said that exact same thing to you, about *me* being a mess? I think part of being the best superheroines we can be involves embracing that messiness. Realizing there's nothing wrong with us if we don't have every single thing figured out. Letting our big, messy pile of emotions make us stronger. Celebrating when we do well and admitting when we fuck up. And on that note," she reached over and took my hand again, "I'm sorry, too."

My head jerked up. "For what?"

"What happened last night wasn't all your fault. And even if it was partially your fault, I totally overreacted."

"What do you mean?" I could not fathom how last night could be *more* my fault.

"I haven't always told you what I really wanted when it came to the wedding or everything related to it," she said. "And even when I have, I just sort of went with it when you bulldozed all over me. Instead of speaking up or confronting you, I was more comfortable avoiding the issue entirely. And other people contributed to the general fucking up, too. Luce brought the bag of sex toys, Scott went along with your pretend engagement and secret demon entrapment scheme, and Bea agreed to test her powers on me because she was excited to experiment." She gave me a sardonic half-smile. "But somehow, all my ragey feelings still got directed at you. And everyone was perfectly fine going along with that. Well, except Scott. He tried to defend you after you left, but I wasn't in the mood to listen. It was easier for me—for everyone—to go with the idea that you were being the diva you'd been in the past."

She took a deep breath and met my eyes. "I think when we had our big talk after beating Shasta, it fixed some things—but not everything. We acknowledged there were problems, but we didn't really deal with them in a deeper way. We just kind of slapped a Band-Aid on it and—"

"—and went back to inhabiting slightly different versions of the roles we'd gotten trapped in," I finished. I gave her a small smile and repeated something she'd said when I'd dragged her to the Indie Fashion Market. "So many of my problems come from barreling headfirst into things without listening or thinking about the consequences."

"And so many of mine come from various flavors of avoidance and denial," she said, smiling back. "We need to learn how to talk to each other with total honesty. Like, I should have told you outright that as pretty as that red flower dress was, it's way too fancy and tight and it makes me uncomfortable, and I kind of can't breathe while I'm wearing it. And also . . ." Her eyes shifted to the side. "I, uh, might have chosen that awful bridesmaid's dress for you because I was unconsciously trying to get back at you for pushing me into things I didn't want to do."

"What!" I gaped at her. "That is downright diabolical, Evie Tanaka!"

"I mean, I didn't do it totally on purpose!" she protested. "I talked myself into it because it was so outrageous, so showy, and those are generally things you like. But deep down, I knew it was pretty hideous. I should have talked to you. I should have told you I need a dress that allows me to *eat* during my wedding. I really fucking need that, Annie."

"And when you say that," I said, laughing, "I should actually listen and take that into consideration instead of deciding what's best without consulting you at all." I let out a long sigh and looked at her affectionately. "I guess sometimes I still see you as that girl in kindergarten. The one who couldn't stop crying. The one who needed me."

"I still need you," she said firmly.

"Are you sure?" I'd meant for that to sound light, but it came out choked, almost a sob. I felt tears gathering in my throat again. Well, what the hell? I was supposed to be letting Annie Chang have her say. "Because you're on the verge of this perfect life, and you deserve that so much, and I guess I'm afraid that you really, really won't need me. That maybe you never did and you're finally going to realize that. And the thing is . . ." I swallowed hard. "I still need you. I need you a lot."

She squeezed my hand and gave me a sweet, earnest Evie look.

"I do need you," she said. "But I don't need you to save me anymore. I need you to be my friend. My co-heroine." She smiled. "And we both need to start seeing each other as we are now rather than how we've been in the past. I'm not that scared little kid anymore. And you're not an out-of-control diva who throws tantrums all over her personal assistant when things don't go her way."

I cocked an eyebrow. "You sure about that?"

"Yes," she said, giggling. "You're a badass superheroine

who's embracing her human side and learning how to use her relentless determination and truly awesome assertiveness as a Forceful Bludgeon for Good."

"So I'm still a bludgeon?"

"A bludgeon for *good*, don't forget! And I wouldn't have it any other way. Bludgeons get shit done."

We both laughed and I felt that warmth rushing between us, the bond we kept holding on to even though it had nearly cracked in two so many times.

"So," Evie said, "after you left last night . . ."

"The party got like a trillion times better?"

"Not exactly." She released my hand as an amused smile played over her lips. "Even though Maisy didn't appear to have anything to do with the puppy demon, we had to be sure. She agreed to be scanned, tested, the whole nine yards."

"And?"

"She doesn't seem to be doing anything evil this time," Evie said with a shrug. "She reiterated over and over that any weirdness on her part was entirely due to nerves about showing off her designs. I believe her exact quote was, 'I may put on an endlessly fabulous front, but even Maisy Kane has her insecurities!'"

"I can relate to that a little too much," I admitted with an eye-roll. "Luckily, I have a new lead for us." I recapped my exploits at Marcus's the night before, ending with Scott stuffing the dress in the trap. And leaving out everything that had happened after that. "So hopefully we actually captured something," I said. "And we should pay Marcus a visit. Maybe he's the human helping this thing."

"Or at the very least, he can tell us why he decided to recreate that dress after claiming the first one was such an abomination," Evie said, wrinkling her nose. "Let's get the trap down to the lab. Bea and Nate can run tests on the dress while you and I track down Marcus."

"Perfect," I said. "The trap's in my room, so I can get it. Um, myself."

Her eyebrows quirked up, and I realized I'd phrased that as awkwardly as possible.

"I mean," I said hastily, "I'm sure you want to go change or something before we head out, so I can go get it and . . ."

Evie cocked an eyebrow at me. "I thought we just said we were going to be more honest with each other. What do you have hidden in your room? More antelope skewers?"

"N-no. But . . . uh, there's no reason for both of us to go."

"You are the worst liar ever, Annie Chang. And you're bright freaking red right now."

I shrugged, unable to think fast enough to come up with a rejoinder. Yes, I had taken a completely sincere vow of honesty with my best friend. But we'd covered quite a bit of deep, emotional ground and the idea of having to talk about whatever Scott and I were doing on top of that felt like way too much for me to handle right now. Both Aveda Jupiter's and Annie Chang's mental circuits were currently totally overloaded, thank you very much.

Evie shrugged and threw up her hands. "Fine. Keep your weird secret. I'll go change and then we'll head out."

I relaxed a little, stood, and started for the door . . . just as she leapt out of her seat, shrieked "just kidding!" and blazed past me.

"Evie, wait!" I yelped.

But she was already racing out of the kitchen, down the hall, toward my bedroom. Shit. How had she gotten so *fast*? I was the better athlete by a wide margin. But she had a head start, and I guess all the emotional talk had drained my resources and thrown me off my game. There was no way I was catching up to her.

She skidded to a stop in front of my bedroom door, threw it open, and there was Scott. In my bed. Half naked. Dead to the world.

Evie's jaw dropped just as I managed to catch up to her and shut the bedroom door again.

"Aren't you the one who's always going on about knocking?" I sputtered. "Isn't that part of the social code or something?"

"Annie!" she squealed, then clapped a hand over her mouth when I shushed her. "Annie," she repeated, lowering her voice to an excited whisper. She grasped my shoulders, a giant smile overtaking her face. "It finally happened!"

I twisted my hands together and stared at the floor. I was pretty sure my face was bright red again. Last night, everything had seemed so clear. I needed Scott to know how I felt, needed to feel him inside me, just in case any rogue puppy demons decided to come along and kill me before I got the chance. Now whatever was between us felt new and fragile, capable of being destroyed if I breathed so much as a word of it.

Evie shook me a little. "Tell me everything!" she demanded. "Is this a thing that's been happening? Or was this the first time? Were you guys overcome with passion when you got back to HQ or—"

"It was the first time," I said, my voice slightly robotic. I latched on to each question, trying to deliver honest answers and nothing more. "And it happened before we got back. I'd just realized I wasn't dead, and he was looking at me like he thought I might still die and I was wearing nothing but that bridal lingerie—"

"Wait a minute!" she hissed. She released my shoulders and gawked at me, her expression somewhere between awe and disbelief. "Are you telling me you guys did it on the floor of a possibly puppy demon–infested bridal salon?"

"Yes. Though we'd determined the puppy demon was no longer on the premises . . ."

"And . . . ?" she coaxed, her giant grin returning.

"And . . . it was fucking fantastic."

Her grin stretched even wider.

"I knew it!" she cried, her voice spiraling into shriek territory again. She enveloped me in a bear hug. "I knew you guys would figure it out. Finally." Her voice shook a little, like she was trying to hold back tears, and I realized my eyes were wet as well. I hugged her back and allowed myself to just revel in the moment, to live in the giddy possibility of Scott and I figuring out whatever "it" was, living happily ever after, and having more amazing sex on the floors of possibly demon-infested bridal salons. Or other locations would be fine, too, I guess.

"I don't know if we've figured anything out," I said. "I don't know what's happening. I'm not even sure what to say to him now that it's . . ." I trailed off, twisting my hands together.

"Now that it's the morning after?" Evie said, cocking a knowing eyebrow. "Remember what we just talked about. It's okay not to have everything figured out. It's okay if you don't know how you feel for all time going forward." Her eyes softened and I knew she was thinking all the mushy romantic thoughts I wasn't allowing myself to. "But think about what Annie Chang wants to tell him. You can be honest, like you were with me. You can tell him how you feel right now. And that you want to kiss him a bunch more."

"We've kind of been doing plenty of that already," I murmured, thinking back to the day in the gym.

Evie's eyes widened to the size of dinner plates. "Wait. There's *more* you haven't told me?" She gave me a light punch to the shoulder. "Really, Annie. That's taking the whole 'protecting me' thing way too far. Hide the details of your demon-fighting plan, fine. But keeping the suddenly juicy details of your sex life to yourself? Definitely not okay." She gave me a teasing look, and I felt something release inside of me. Aveda Jupiter would never deign to share all the tingly, unsure, not-exactly-fabulous feelings she was having about her potential love life. But Annie Chang was definitely up for sharing *all the things* with her best friend. And that felt pretty damn good.

"From now on, I'll tell you everything," I said. And I meant it.

🔥

Evie convinced me to give her the trap to shuttle down to Nate and Bea so I could take a moment to talk things out with Scott. I still wasn't entirely sure how to do that.

Aveda Jupiter really hates it when she doesn't have all the answers. But Evie advised me to screw up my courage and speak from the deepest part of my Annie Chang heart.

Scott was sitting up in bed when I came back into the room, rubbing sleep from his eyes. His hair was still appealingly mussed and his shirt was rumpled and halfway unbuttoned, exposing all that golden muscle I'd finally gotten to experience up close and personal. I averted my eyes so I wouldn't skip the talking part in favor of pouncing on him.

"Hey," he said.

"Hey," I said, my voice soft and unsure. Evie's words flashed through my head: *Tell him how you feel right now.*

I forced myself to look at him again. If that made me pounce, so be it. Somehow I managed to get a hold of myself, cross the room, and perch on the edge of the bed.

"So," I said, looking down at my hands. They twisted together in my lap. Great, yet another tic to replace nail-biting. "Last night. I guess you should know that right before you showed up, I thought I was going to die. I've had that feeling before, of course. When you're saving the city from packs of bloodthirsty demon creatures on a regular basis, it's bound to happen. But this time was different. This time, it didn't feel like it would be a noble fate. It felt stupid."

I forced myself to meet his eyes. He was looking at me in that earnest, unguarded way that made my heart clench.

"Why?" he asked.

"For one thing, I still haven't been able to figure out how to use telekinesis on something if I can't see it," I said, trying to make my tone light. "And you know how I strive for perfection in everything. But beyond that, no matter where we are or what we're doing, I always manage to avoid telling you how you make me feel. I pull away from you and I've gotten so good at that, I almost don't realize I'm doing it." My voice quavered. I swallowed hard, trying to maintain control. "And dying without telling you seemed like the dumbest thing on the planet."

"How do I make you feel?" His voice was soft and tentative and even a little scared.

"Like one big nerve ending who wants to be naked with you constantly." No filter. No worrying about how I sounded or the fact that I was making myself intensely vulnerable to him. "I pull away because I'm scared that if you know that . . . I mean, it gives you power over me. Over my feelings. It means I've told you that you have the ability to hurt me. It takes me to a place I'm deeply uncomfortable with." *The Annie Chang place.* "I live in fear that going to that place makes me weak." Even though Evie seemed to think it would actually make me stronger. I still wasn't totally convinced. "And if there's one thing I absolutely don't want to be, it's weak. I've never been good at showing someone I'm actually scared. Not even Evie. *Especially* not Evie."

"I understand that feeling," he said gently. "I know what it's like to work so hard on a façade that you don't know what's real anymore. And any time you are real, it feels like the most painful thing possible." He hesitated, his eyes searching my face. "When I was a kid, my mom was always so stressed out, and I felt like I had to be there for her, you know? Make her laugh, make her feel some kind of happiness. Even though I was scared, too. I felt like she could never know that. She could never see *all* of me. And now I naturally put up that wall with everyone."

I nodded, thinking of how he'd taken himself from junior high wimp to high school hottie. How he made jokes and kept the mood light whenever it seemed like things were veering into uncomfortable territory.

"I don't know if I even understand how to be completely real with someone," I said. "But I'm trying to be more honest. And to let people be honest with me. So how do *you* feel? About what happened between us?"

I held my breath. He hesitated for so long, I nearly

passed out. Then, finally, he said, "It's what I've wanted since we were fifteen."

His voice was so tender, it made tears spring to my eyes.

"Then . . ." I took a deep breath. And I blurted out the question that had been hanging over my head for so many years. "On prom night—why was it with Evie and not with me?"

Yes, it was petty. And yes, I'd devoted considerable time convincing myself I was over that shit by now. But Evie had told me to be honest, and if I was being honest, their mutual deflowering was a continuous thorn in my side, the reason I'd believed for so many years that he wanted her, not me. Never me.

He studied me, and I wondered if he was going to tease me for bringing up something that was so far in our angsty teenage past. But, no. He looked sober, thoughtful. Like he was really considering my incredibly petty question.

"Well, on the one hand, we were young and drunk and your basic teenage idiots with no impulse control," he said. "But on the other, I think she and I needed each other in that moment. She wanted to be with Jay. I wanted to be with you. We settled for each other." He ran a hand through his hair, mussing it further. It took every fiber of my being to continue sitting still instead of pouncing. But I really wanted to hear what he had to say. "I was always trying to get your attention. Every time I made you laugh or yell at me, it was a little victory. But you still seemed so far away, like I could never *really* get your attention. Just like Evie could never get Jay's." He smiled. "Anyway. She told you it was pretty bad, right? Two virgins with absolutely zero sexual chemistry, both hung up on other people? The earth did not exactly move."

"She told me," I said, my voice faint. "But I still made assumptions and I've held on to those assumptions for so many years and . . . I guess I've been carrying that around for a while now. As you may have noticed, I'm not great about letting things go."

He laughed softly, shifted forward on the bed, and reached over to entwine his fingers in mine. "Considering that I held a grudge against you after the First Kiss Incident, I would say I'm not, either."

He hesitated, his eyes searching my face. I was trying to stay focused on everything he was saying to me, all these words that had built up between us for years. But my concentration was disrupted by the warmth of his fingers pressing against mine. That simple, casual touch sent little frissons of pleasure skittering through my stomach, and I couldn't seem to get them to stop.

Wait. Was that normal? To want them to stop? Just for a moment, so you could hear all the important things the really hot guy holding your hand was trying to tell you?

You're killing this relationship thing, Annie Chang. And not the good kind of killing it.

Scott finally spoke, snapping me out of my thoughts.

"When Shasta took you, I could barely function." His voice had gone low and quiet. "I felt like I was being torn apart. I'd kept you at a distance for so long—but even when we weren't speaking, I knew you were out there. Saving the world." He gave me a slight smile. "It never occurred to me how it would feel to actually lose you."

I had a flash of memory: Scott bursting into Shasta's shop, hellbent on saving me. I'd been nearly unconscious at that point, but I'd seen his face so clearly, his eyes wild and terrified as he scanned the shop, trying to find me. It had struck me as weird, seeing him like that, when he was usually so calm and collected. I'd chalked it up to the danger of the situation, but maybe there had been more to it.

"When it was all over and everyone was okay, it seemed like you didn't feel the same way," he said.

Ah. So he had noticed me pulling away from him at Evie's bedside.

"And I couldn't stand feeling that way again, the way I had when I tried to kiss you and you pushed me away—hollowed out, rejected." His eyes shifted to the side and embarrassment crept into his expression. "So I sort of . . . put a spell on myself."

"You did *what?*"

"It's like an anti-love spell," he said sheepishly. "That's why I was indifferent-bordering-on-hostile toward you in those months after we'd defeated Shasta. It was the spell taking effect."

"And what made you reverse it?" I was still trying to process the idea of an anti-love spell existing. "Or at least, I assume you did. Otherwise I also assume last night wouldn't have happened?"

"You assume correctly." He finally flashed me that impish grin I was so accustomed to, his blue eyes dancing. "To be honest, it was that day you flicked me. I realized you really wanted to try to be friends, to work on building something resembling an adult relationship. If you were going to step up, it seemed pretty immature of me not to. Even if my feelings for you weren't returned."

"And then I proceeded to pull away from you every chance I got—like that day at the lab, when you told me about grad school and how you'd been feeling confused." I shook my head. "Even if I didn't feel . . . the way I feel about you, that's no way for someone trying to have a true and honest friendship to act. I'm sorry. The truth is, I related way too much to what you were saying. Ever since things changed with Evie, I feel like I'm stumbling around, lost, desperate for anything to get me back on the path of Aveda Jupiter Awesomeness. Like I don't have anything figured out. And like I really, really should. And that means . . ." I took a deep breath and let myself be honest again. ". . . I don't know what we're doing here, either. Do you?"

He squeezed my hand. "No. I'm stumbling around as much as you are. And for the record, you're always awesome."

"Great!" I laughed. "So we're both big, stumbly messes."

"*Awesome*, big, stumbly messes," he corrected, grinning

at me. "And maybe that's okay. Maybe it's okay not to know exactly what we're doing."

I gave him a look. "Have you met me?"

"Annie." He chuckled. "What do you want right now? Don't think too hard. Just say it."

"I want us to be honest with each other. I don't want to pull away from you anymore. I want to try with every fiber of my being *not* to do that." I hesitated, then said the thing that scared me most of all. "And I want to be with you. Like a big, naked nerve ending."

He pulled me closer, so I was basically sitting in his lap. Now I really couldn't concentrate on anything except all the spots where he was touching me, so I hoped he wasn't planning on telling me anything else terribly important.

"Why don't we try that?" he said softly, brushing my hair away from my face. "And see what happens?"

They were simultaneously the most wonderful and most terrifying words I'd ever heard.

🔥

"So did you guys have sex again?" Evie asked, as we marched down the street toward Marcus's shop. "I know we had to rush out to embark on our mission, but part of being a superhero is figuring out how to make the best use of those small pockets of time between evil-fighting—"

"Look at you." I laughed. "Superheroing tips and sex tips all in one!"

She stuck her tongue out at me. "I've learned some things over the last few months, okay?"

"Apparently." I arched a suggestive brow. "This is definitely going to make the bachelorette party way more interesting—oh." I gave her an anxious look. "Do you still want me to plan the bachelorette party? After last night's disaster?"

Evie gave an overly theatrical sigh. "Well," she said, pretending to think very seriously about it, "as long as you actually listen to me and keep any and all desires for ante-lope skewers in check."

"Got it," I said, matching her serious tone. "But you have to at least let me get you some fancy lingerie, since I kind of ruined Maisy's perfectly nice gift."

"Let's circle back to that. Where do you stand on Lucy's big bag of sex toys? I suppose those are off the table entirely?"

"Actually," I said, tapping a finger against my chin, "I've grown rather fond of the bag o' dildos. The fruit punch-flavored condoms came in really handy last night."

"Wow." Evie laughed. "So there's still much, much more you need to tell me. Which you can do at the bachelorette party. Which will be?"

"Just you, me, Lucy, and Bea at Curry On. Better?"

"Perfect."

I grinned at her and squared my shoulders as we marched onward.

"This feels good," she said.

"What, talking about dildos and curry?"

"No. I mean—yes, but I was talking about *this*." She gestured from me to herself. "Us. We're, like, marching into battle together as actual co-heroines." She paused and played with the ends of her curls. "I know before all this puppy demon business started up, I said I was ready to be a real superheroine, but once that shit got real . . ." She shook her head ruefully. "I started having some, I don't know—performance anxiety? During the bridal tent incident and the fashion show disaster at Maisy's shop, when the puppy affected me, it reminded me of how I used to feel about the fire, that sensation of being totally out of control. I've learned how to harness and control my power, but with this thing, I just couldn't. There was nothing I could do except stand there and be helpless. It was like none of the stuff I've worked on as far as being a true superhero mattered. It scared the hell out of me. Made me think maybe

I'm not cut out for this superhero thing. And I should have brought that up with you, talked it out, but I think I was even more scared to actually say those things out loud. Especially to you. As usual, it was easier for me to just avoid the conversation."

"Believe it or not, I've noticed some of that—your uncertainty, your trepidation," I said, smiling at her. "And I should have talked to *you* about it. But as usual, it was easier for *me* to 'protect' you by going ahead with things like getting Bea to try her power out on you. I think this partnership is something we're still figuring out as well, you know? For so many years, I've seen myself as a solo superhero, and I know a lot of people think it's because I didn't want to share the spotlight with anyone—and okay, maybe that's a little bit true—but it's more that I'm just *used* to being that way."

"Aveda Jupiter, Lone Wolf," Evie intoned, making her voice deep and overly serious. "No, I get it. You've always been the one shoving down fear, never letting me or anyone else know those kindergarten bullies and demons of the Otherworld scared you, too."

"Yes." I reached over and gave her hand a squeeze. "But you're right. This—" I gestured from me to her. "—feels right. Like I have someone to fully share all that with, finally. Like we're the partners we were always meant to be."

"Aw, and talking things out in such a healthy manner," Evie said, giggling. "Let's keep this open, honest co-heroine thing going strong."

We rounded the corner and came to an abrupt halt. Marcus's shop was surrounded. A small crowd of women had clustered around the storefront and were pushing and jostling each other, trying to see in the big window. I recognized some of them from my previous trip to the shop. And the bridal tent. Honestly, I was getting to know the brides of San Francisco way too well.

"Let's get a closer look," I muttered to Evie. "But stay stealth. We don't want to call attention to ourselves just yet."

We made our way up carefully, trying not to spook the crowd, and positioned ourselves off to the side.

"That's weird," Evie said, bouncing on her toes. "It looks like there's nothing in the window."

"I did kind of steal the dress that was in there. Maybe that's what everyone's gawking at, the naked mannequin?"

"No." Evie craned her neck, trying to see just a bit further. "There's literally nothing. As in, the window is empty and it looks like the store is too."

"What?" Forgetting my previous edict to approach carefully, I shoved my way through the crowd, determined to get to the front. I was acutely aware of some of the brides-to-be throwing me dirty looks, of the chatter as the crowd turned in my direction. At this point, being hated by the bridal population of San Francisco was old hat, so I brushed it off and hoped Evie was following me.

When I reached the window, I saw that Evie's assessment had been correct. The window was empty—as was the entire store. Even the plush red carpeting was gone, ripped up to reveal dusty plywood flooring. I let my eyes wander to just above the window and—yep. Marcus's vibrant sign was gone as well. It was like he'd never been here at all.

I turned and faced the bridal crowd. There were about fifteen of them assembled, but they seemed to glower back at me as one. I was vaguely aware of Evie positioning herself next to me.

"Excuse me, citizens," I said, putting on my best assertive superheroine voice. "Can anyone tell me what happened here?"

They stayed silent. Glowering.

"Evie," I muttered. "Can you . . ."

"Oh—yes!" She raised her voice to address the crowd. "Can anyone tell us what happened here?" she parroted.

"Why are you still hanging out with her, Evie?" someone shrieked from the middle of the crowd.

"Yeah!" a familiar voice chimed in. I scanned the crowd

and found the source: Gwen. "I mean, getting engaged and announcing it at your party? That's the lowest of the low."

"That's not what happened!" I protested. "I'm not really engaged—"

"So you're faking it?" Redhead Bride from the bridal tent let out an appalled gasp. "That's even worse."

"Listen," Evie said, irritation sparking in her eyes, "all that stuff has been blown out of proportion. Annie— Aveda's been nothing but a fantastic maid of honor and y'all need to simmer down and get off her back."

"My god," Redhead Bride said. "She's really manipulated you into thinking she's the bee's knees, hasn't she?"

"You need to break free from her," Gwen added. "I can recommend a good therapist who specializes in toxic friendships."

"Stop that!" Evie blurted out, her hands balling at her sides. "That's so unfair!" Her irritation was morphing into full-blown anger. Uh-oh. I put a hand on her arm. I appreciated her support, but there was no need to start setting people on fire on my behalf when all we needed was information. I cocked an eyebrow at her, trying to use our near-telepathy to convey that sentiment. She seemed to pick up on it, her shoulders relaxing, her hands unfisting, and she gave me a small nod.

"Um. Point taken. Aveda and I will definitely have a talk about that later," she said. "But for now, can one of you please tell me what happened to Marcus's shop?" She gestured to the abandoned space.

"He decided to relocate his store to LA," another bride-to-be piped up. "Put a notice on his website this morning."

"And all of you are here in protest?" I guessed. "Because he did so without fulfilling your gown orders?"

"Pfft, as if," Gwen said, letting loose with another massive eye-roll. "Get with the times, Aveda Jupiter, nobody wants a Marcus gown anymore. He probably had to move because his business was tanking. His designs are just so . . . modern."

"And that's bad?" I asked trying to keep up.

"Everyone who's anyone only wants true vintage now," Redhead Bride sniffed.

"So why are you here?" Evie said.

"We're celebrating, of course!" Gwen cried, brandishing a flask. The other brides cheered in near-unison. It was a little creepy. Wow. These ladies had gone to the trouble of gathering by Marcus's shop even though none of them wanted his dresses anymore? The intensity of wedding planning really did drive brides-to-be to irrational places and extreme behavior. Then again, I supposed the (mostly self-inflicted) intensity of planning *Evie's* wedding had kind of done the same thing to me. I remembered what Bea had said about the pressures of society and the "bridal complex" and tried to give the assembled women the benefit of the doubt.

"You should join us, Evie!" Redhead chirped.

"Maybe later," Evie said, giving her a game smile. "For now, my maid of honor and I have some important bridal appointments to get to." The mention of her disgraced maid of honor brought out the collective stink face again, but Evie ignored them and ushered me away, giving the crowd a little wave.

"What do you make of this?" she said as we shuffled away from the bridal mob.

"Awfully convenient for Marcus to pack up and leave the day after his store played host to a possessed wedding dress. Maybe we should get Mercedes to track him down in LA?"

Mercedes was an old classmate who had gained a "human GPS" type of superpower when the first Otherworld portal opened up. She'd tried to compete with me for the title of San Francisco's most beloved superheroine, but it hadn't worked out. She'd eventually relocated to Los Angeles, where there was far less superpowered competition.

Evie snorted. "You're actually suggesting we call Mercedes for something? Wow." She nudged me playfully. "You really are changing your tune when it comes to teamwork."

I rolled my eyes. "Aveda Jupiter believes in efficiency," I said crisply. "But while we're here . . ." I scanned the empty storefront. "There's a back entrance in the alley—and at least as of last night, it was unlocked. Why don't we try that, poke around the store? At least the parts that aren't visible to the mob." I nodded at the Bridezilla crowd that was still buzzing around the front window.

"So we'll try that stealth thing we failed at so miserably just now," Evie said, amused.

We stepped into the narrow alleyway, and I felt momentarily comforted by the relative quiet compared to the mob scene out front. I zeroed in on the back door to Marcus's shop, which was mid-way down the alley, and did a double-take when I spotted a lone figure slipping out.

"That's Marcus's assistant," I muttered to Evie. "What's he doing?" I raised my voice and called out to him. "Franz!"

Franz whipped around, his eyes widening when he saw me—then took off in the opposite direction.

"Wait, stop!" I cried. "We need to talk to you!"

Once again, so much for stealth.

I reached out with my mental feathers and wrapped them around him, gently pulling him back toward us and pinning him to the wall.

"Let. Me. Go!" he howled, writhing around ineffectually.

"Calm down!" Evie said, patting him on the shoulder. "Aveda won't hurt you. Much," she added as he raised a skeptical eyebrow.

"We did everything they asked," Franz spat out. "*Everything.* I was just picking up the last of Marcus's silk ribbon supply. Those ribbons were imported from Paris, they were very expensive, and they are a key component of Marcus's current inspiration board, so it was absolutely necessary—"

"Stop talking!" I snapped.

Franz glowered at us. But his eyes sparked with something more raw underneath all that ribbon-related bravado. He was afraid. And as irritated as I currently was, I didn't think he was reacting to me. I softened my telekinetic hold, but kept him pinned to the wall and gave Evie a subtle nod, trying to convey: *You are inherently more comforting than I am. So go for it.*

"Franz," Evie said, making her tone casual and conversational. "Aveda and I are looking into the shop closure. It happened abruptly and it might be connected to an important supernatural matter we're investigating. But we're totally lost here, so can you back it up for us? Who's the 'they' asking you to do things? And what were you asked to do?"

"I don't know who it was," he said, his eyes darting back and forth.

I snapped my fingers at him. "Focus, please," I said, making my voice as authoritative as possible. "Like Evie said, we're not here to hurt you. We're, like, the good guys."

Evie giggled.

"What?" I spat out. "We so are!"

"I know," she said, grinning at me. "But you saying 'we're, like, the good guys' in your most bossypants Aveda Jupiter voice is pretty funny."

"I can be funny," I said, making a face at her.

"Sure, just maybe not on *purpose*—"

"Uh . . ." Franz said.

"Sorry," I said, turning back to him. "We need to focus, too."

"Right," Evie said. "So again, who was asking you to do things?"

"We started getting these notes," Franz said, panic rising in his voice. "Demanding that Marcus recreate that infamous abomination gown—the one with the hideous red flowers. I guess a lot of people saw *you* wearing it." He cast a disdainful look at Evie. "But I don't know how they learned it was a Marcus dress. At first we ignored them. But then—" He shut his eyes, as if reliving the terror all over again. "The notes made mention of an, ah, unfortunate incident in Marcus's past."

"Which was?" Evie said.

Franz clamped his lips together and glared at us defiantly. Now Evie gave me a subtle nod, as if to say: *You are inherently more scary than I am. So now* you *go for it.*

I put on my best imperious face, matching his glare. He squirmed in my telekinetic hold, and I made it a fraction tighter. I didn't want to hurt him, but I also didn't want him wriggling free and making a break for it.

"You know," I said, injecting just the right amount of growl into my voice, "there's a whole posse of brides out front who would probably love to question you." Okay, maybe not exactly true, but he didn't need to know that. "They seem pretty mad," I continued. "Maybe you want to answer their questions instead of ours, but I can assure you that I am much, *much* more pleasant—"

"Okay, okay," Franz whined, giving me a peevish look. "So maybe, possibly, *perhaps* there was a moment a few years ago where Marcus was making some samples and ran out of the fabric he wanted and had to use . . ." He closed his eyes, his lower lip trembling, as if he was about to burst into tears. " . . . polyester."

"Uh. What?" Evie said.

"It was only one sample and it was destroyed immediately and he never did it again," Franz said, his words spilling out in a rush. "But Marcus takes pride in only using the finest of materials and his reputation has been built on that, and this person, this *blackmailer*, was threatening to go to all the news outlets."

"And if that got out, it would contradict everything Marcus stands for. It would be a disaster," I said. "I get it."

I actually sort of did. I had, after all, gone to great lengths to *not* admit I was injured when I'd hurt my ankle. The thought of people believing Aveda Jupiter was anything less than a total badass was displeasing.

"So Marcus caved and made the dress," Evie said.

"Yes. Luckily we still had some remnants of that awful scarlet frock we got from the vintage peddler," Franz said. "Although even that was one hundred percent silk, I assure you. The blackmailer sent further instructions: make not one, but two, of these dresses. Display one in the window and leave the other in the back."

"And I don't suppose it's still in the back?" I said.

"It's gone," Franz said. "I didn't see hide nor hair of it when I packed up the silk ribbons just now. Whoever wanted it must have taken it."

"Do you have any idea about the identity of the mysterious blackmailer?" Evie said.

"None," Franz said, drawing his lips into a thin line. "But even after we'd done everything they asked with the dresses, they sent one final order—close up shop and leave town. Or word of Marcus's polyester misstep would go out wide. The last note referred to Marcus as ..." He paused, his lower lip quivering again. "... 'a gentrifying scourge of New San Francisco' who had to go."

"Huh," I said, not even sure where to begin with that.

"So can I leave now?" Franz begged. "Marcus is in LA, scouting for space. We've already had numerous Hollywood brides express interest in his work."

"All right," I said, doing my best to sound stern. "But make sure we know how to find you if we have more questions. And definitely alert us if you hear from these blackmailers again."

I released Franz and he gave me a resentful nod, then pressed a tattered business card into Evie's hand.

"Contact number's on there," he said. "Farewell."

With that, he turned and flounced down the alleyway.

"Well," Evie said, toying with the business card, "that was weird."

"The puppy demon used that dress last night, no question," I said. "And this blackmail thing has to be connected."

"Maybe its human helper sent the notes," Evie said. "But why did it need that specific dress reconstructed?"

Before we could ponder this further, Evie's phone buzzed. "It's a text from Nate," she said, scanning the screen. "And ..." Her brow crinkled.

"And . . . what?" I said impatiently, peering over her shoulder.

"And . . . we got it!" she crowed, her face lighting up. She held the phone aloft, waving it back and forth in triumph. "It's there! There's something trapped in the dress." She grinned at me. "We're supposed to meet the team at Pussy Queen—time to nip this puppy drama in the goddamn bud."

CHAPTER TWENTY

"FINALLY, YOU'RE HERE!" I cried, bouncing to my feet as Scott, Bea, Nate, and Lucy marched into Pussy Queen. Evie and I had booked it over as soon as we'd gotten Nate's text. My excitement at the possibility of ending this puppy demon business had mounted while we waited for the rest of the crew to arrive. Shruti was absent from the shop again, but Maisy was flitting around, rearranging various displays, and Dave was parked behind his coffee counter. I'd spent fifteen minutes pacing the entire length of the store, only stopping when I realized the room was so warm, sweat was beading my brow. Dave must still be having temperature control issues.

By the time the team arrived, my blood was spiking with adrenaline and I felt about to burst with anticipation. Until I noticed who was with them, that is.

"M-mom?" I sputtered.

"She stopped by as we were on our way out the door," Scott said. "I tried to tell her to make herself comfortable while the rest of us ran our little, ah, errand, but—"

"But I explained that it made much more sense for me to come along," my mother interrupted.

"And on the way here, I told her about last night," Scott added. "How the whole fake engagement was part of a, uh, not-great party prank. That I came up with. All by myself. As my own idea."

"Oh, hush, Scott, no one is buying your very generous

attempts to save my daughter from herself," my mother sniffed.

"Actually, I think it's to save her from you," Bea muttered. Evie nudged her in the arm.

"Mrs. Chang—" Evie tried to cut in.

"Anne," my mother continued, fixing me with her piercing stare. "Really. I know you like attention, but last night's party was supposed to be about Evie—"

"And Evie totally enjoyed it once the whole prank thing was explained to her," Evie said, plastering a bright smile on her face.

My mother ignored her again and stepped toward me, placing a hand on my arm. Out of the corner of my eye, I saw Nate, Bea, and Lucy lugging the trap to the dark portal, talking amongst themselves. I was desperate to hear what they were saying, but my mother seemed determined to go into great detail about what a fuck-up I was. Evie and Scott stayed next to me, flanking me on either side. I felt a rush of warmth at their refusal to abandon me for what was surely more scintillating discussion of the newest wrinkle in the puppy demon predicament.

"Anne," my mother said very seriously. Her eyes searched my face. "I am concerned about you. Your behavior has always been erratic, but this is something else. On a whole other level."

Even though I was still fixated on whatever Bea and Co. were doing with the trap on the other side of the room, I felt a hot rush of frustration, my mother's words burrowing under my skin and making me prickly all over.

"Did you even think about how such an ill-conceived prank would look?" my mother continued. "How faking something as important as an engagement would make our family look? How—"

"No," I snapped, the prickly feeling getting the better of me. "No, I didn't think about that, Mom, because as far as most people are concerned—I don't *have* a family."

I pulled away from her and stomped off, the blood

roaring in my ears. I may be starting to accept Annie Chang into my mental fold, but my mother always made me feel like the most helpless, hapless version of myself, and I couldn't take her poking at me when we might, in fact, be on the verge of finally solving our puppy demon problem. I came to a halt next to Dave's coffee corner, resting a hand on the bar, trying to get a hold of myself and re-center my thoughts around the mission at hand. Dave looked up, his eyes sleepy.

I braced myself for the usual fortune cookie aphorisms. Something about seasons or small frogs.

"Where we come from is not the only thing that makes us who we are," he said solemnly. "But journeying to our true identity is often littered with . . ." He glanced over at my mother, who was talking to Scott and Evie. ". . . many stones along the path."

I goggled at him. Was that . . . had he just said something that sort of made sense and was actually relevant to my situation? Was he actually trying to help me? Huh. Well. Annie Chang kind of wanted to let him.

"That's very true," I said hesitantly, meeting his eyes. "The harder I try to figure out who I am, the more, er, stones I seem to encounter."

He nodded. "But in every stone there is a lesson." He looked down at the chipped Sunny Side mug in front of him, frowning into its depths. "Often a sad one."

"Well . . . sure." I looked back over at my mother, who was now being guided out—and apparently soothed—by Scott and Evie and felt another rush of warmth. "But I think those lessons are necessary to help us figure out who we are."

Dave met my eyes again and his face was so wrenchingly sad—as if he was experiencing a sudden moment of pure, unstoned clarity—I winced. "I am lost on the path. The stones are too great."

I found myself reaching over the coffee bar and giving him an awkward pat on the arm. I couldn't help but feel a sudden stab of sympathy for this poor, broken man. Oh, who was I kidding—I related way too much to every single thing that was coming out of his mouth.

"That's how I've felt recently, too," I said to him. "But you know what? Even the greatest stone can be overcome. It just might be a little harder than you imagined. And . . . I'm so sorry about your café closing."

He frowned again into his mug, his expression going stormy. "Someday I will take it back."

"That's the spirit," I said, trying to sound encouraging. "You know, Maisy—for all her faults—is actually a whiz at this small business thing. Maybe she could give you some tips, help you find a new space?"

He looked up and stared at me for a long moment. Then leaned forward, eyes darting back and forth like he was about to share some especially deep pearl of wisdom. I found myself leaning in as well, wondering what he was going to say.

"Running in circles gets your shoes worn down on one side."

So we were back to fortune cookies.

"Hey," Evie said, coming up behind me. Scott was with her. "We, ah, saw your mom out."

"Thank you," I said, turning away from Dave. "Thank you for helping me deal with her. I don't know why I let her get to me that way. And I know I shouldn't have snapped at her, but . . ." I let out a long gust of a breath.

"It's okay," Evie said, grinning. "Despite all your insistence to the contrary, you're human."

"And we're here for you," Scott added, taking my hand.

"Aw!" Evie exclaimed, clapping her hands together. "Look at that!"

"Look at what?" I said. "Scott touching my hand?"

"Scott *holding* your hand!" she said, getting a bit misty. "It's so cute and couple-y and . . . and . . ."

"And Scott is standing right here, yet getting talked about like he isn't," Scott said, quirking an eyebrow.

"And you need to stop," I said to Evie, laughing. I felt the tension from my mother's visit slowly easing away as I soaked in the warmth of them standing next to me, helping me deal with my mother, us teasing each other like we were back in junior high. And I realized I could see, at least a little bit, what Evie had been trying to tell me about Clark Kent. Knowing they were there for me actually did make me feel stronger.

I squeezed Scott's hand and released it. "Thank you for being here for me. Now let's please, *please* go deal with this puppy issue once and for all."

"So what've we got?" I said, nodding at the trap. We were all gathered around the portal. Even though the trap was nothing more than a plain, unassuming gray box, I felt like it was projecting an aura of muted indignation. Like it was somehow giving us the finger.

"Is it the puppy, trapped in that Marcus Wong original?" I continued. "Or I guess not so original, since it was the second version? Oh, and speaking of that, apparently there's a third version floating around out there."

Evie and I exchanged a glance, and I quickly filled the others in on our encounter with Franz.

"Fascinating," Nate said. "Blackmail would seem to add a new level of complexity to whatever plan the puppy and its human helper have been concocting."

"Why is it obsessed with that particular Marcus Wong?" Evie said.

"Everyone loves custom tailoring," Lucy quipped.

"We still don't know how that piece fits in and we're going to get Mercedes to follow up with Marcus—and we should probably scan his shop and the surrounding area," I said. "But back to what we have here . . ."

"It's the puppy," Bea said. "It's not just an echo, like the energy the scanner picked up in Pussy Queen before. But there's something off about it."

"Off?" I repeated.

"Our tests indicate it's in a weakened state," Bea said. "But we're not sure why or what that ultimately means."

"We've done every test we can," Nate said, running a hand through his unruly hair and making it stand on end. "The resulting data isn't giving us anything more to work with. But Scott managed to get some additional information." Nate motioned for Scott to pick up the thread.

"I was finally able to use my spell to forge a stable connection with the puppy," Scott said.

"He totes mind-melded!" Bea crowed.

"Well, sort of," Scott said, giving her an indulgent half-smile. "Like before, it was angry, frustrated—and at this point, I'd definitely characterize it as sentient. Its thought patterns seem to increase in complexity every time I connect with it. I couldn't pull it out of the dress; it's bonded too tightly. And when I tried to ask it questions, it shut down. Finally, it told me it would give me more answers if I brought it here."

"To Pussy Queen?" Evie said.

"To the portal," Bea clarified.

"And we're just doing what it says?" I said, raising a skeptical eyebrow.

"Yeah, what if that's part of its evil plan, and it's going to use the portal to really fuck our shit up?" Evie said.

"The trap has it well contained," Nate said. "That combined with its weakened state means it shouldn't be able to do much right now."

"So now that we're here, now that we've granted that request, I'm going to try the spell again and see if it will tell me anything," Scott said, kneeling next to the trap.

He placed his hand on it, his brow furrowing and his breathing deepening as he concentrated on putting the spell in motion. We all watched, the silence in the room turning thick and weighted with meaning. It felt like we were collectively holding our breath, hoping for answers. I reminded myself to exhale.

"All right," Scott finally said, his voice low and even. "I'm connected to it. It's calmer now. I'm not getting that pulse of constant rage, but . . ." He frowned. "It's still in distress. It's . . . scared."

"Because it's trapped?" Lucy asked.

"Not just that." Scott cocked his head to the side, like he was trying to make sense of what he was hearing. "Because it's lonely."

"Lonely?" I repeated, my voice incredulous.

"Yes, it's . . ." Scott's eyes widened, and he swallowed hard. "The feeling is overwhelming. It's so lost, so alone . . ." Tears welled in his eyes. He paused and gave the trap a gentle pat, like he was trying to console what was inside. I found myself misting up, touched by his unabashed empathy, how he always felt so deeply for those in need—how he had the ability to do that even when this particular thing-in-need had spent a good deal of time trying to kill us.

"I want to help you," Scott whispered, pressing his hand more firmly against the trap. "I promise, that's all I want, if you'll stop hurting people. Tell me how I can help you." He frowned and shook his head. "It's shutting down, trying to pull away from me again."

"Well, make it stop!" I blurted out, frustration getting the better of me. "Remind it that we did what it wanted, we brought it here, now it needs to fulfill its side of the bargain. Or else."

He shook his head again and gave me a soft, teasing smile. "I think this requires a more delicate approach, Aveda Jupiter."

I blew out an exasperated breath, even as warmth bloomed in my chest. Where did he get off being so cute and nice and well . . . *sexy* during such a tense moment in our investigation?

Scott turned back to the trap. "I don't want to harm you," he said, his voice earnest and laced with compassion. "Tell me . . . tell me about what's been happening. Please." He cocked his head again, listening, and sucked in a deep breath. "It's communicating with me again. And it's actually giving me a lot of information. But it's jumbled, incoherent, let me see if I can . . ." He fell silent, listening again.

"What, what?" Bea pestered.

"First of all," Scott said, staring intently at the trap. "Whatever we've captured—it's the puppy." He turned to look at us, his eyes incredulous. "But it's not . . . the whole thing."

"*What?*" Evie squeaked.

"It's basically a scrap of the puppy," Scott said, turning back to the trap. "A piece that was broken off and sent into the dress."

"So the majority of the puppy is still out there? Like, in the world?" I said, my heart sinking. I'd thought—hoped— maybe this would be the end of it.

"And is this little piece o' puppy what we've been chasing around the whole time?" Bea asked.

"Yes, I think so," Scott said. "To both of those things." He frowned again. "It's coming out garbled, but I think what it's trying to tell me is that it keeps breaking off this little piece of itself and sending it out into the world."

"To do eeeeevvvvillllll," Bea whispered theatrically.

"But every time this piece has been broken off and sent somewhere, it's made the whole thing—the puppy/human combo platter—weaker," Scott continued. "Before now, the puppy was able to pull itself out of places as soon as it sensed it was in danger."

"So that's why we didn't find it in my original dress after the fashion show debacle," Evie said.

"And why the way it affects people has been so erratic," Bea chimed in. "Remember how Evie and our OG Bridezilla were so frakballs pissed in the bridal tent and then all of a sudden just weren't?"

"Yes," I said. "Not to mention Cakezilla Carol's back-and-forth personality switcheroo at the bakery. It must have been jumping all over the place that day."

Scott nodded. "If I'm deciphering what it's telling me correctly, moving around like that used to be easy for it.

The fact that it's currently trapped in here"—he tapped the trap—"is adding to its confusion."

"Can you ask it to tell us more about its connection to the human?" Nate said.

"And most importantly, who is that frakkin' human?" Bea added.

Scott pressed a hand against the trap again. "Take me back to the beginning," he said softly, his voice taking on that earnest quality. Once again, I admired his ability to be so kind to something that had been causing us so much grief. He sounded like he truly wanted to understand it.

We all fell silent for another weighted moment and I focused on taking deep breaths, trying to release some of the tension from my body, so I could focus on whatever the puppy was going to tell us next.

"The puppy and the human," Scott finally said. "Are currently existing in a sort of symbiotic relationship. They're feeding off of each other, learning from each other."

"Oh em gee, they're like the Trill in *Star Trek*," Bea exclaimed. She waved a hand at Evie, Lucy, and I. "Just in case the jocks here need a simplified explanation of 'symbiotic.'"

"We got it, Bea," Evie said.

"The puppy's connection to the human is what's helped it gain the level of sentience it has," Scott said. "It keeps getting more and more aware the longer they're bonded. But its increased awareness also means it's feeling . . . conflicted. About what they've been doing."

"You mean the whole attacking brides-to-be to the point of nearly killing them thing?" Lucy snorted. "So it's developing a conscious?"

Scott nodded. "Of sorts. It's telling me . . ." He studied the trap hard, concentrating. "At first it liked being sent out into the world. It thought these adventures might help it find more of its kind. But as time has gone on and that hasn't happened . . ." He shook his head. "It doesn't like hurting people."

"So help us out with that," I said, unable to keep the impatience out of my voice. "Tell us who its human helper is, so we can take this whole symbiotic Trill mess down."

Scott pressed his hand against the trap again. "Its thoughts are becoming fragmented. Breaking up. I'm not getting any clear answers, except . . ." He cocked his head to the side. "Home. It wants to go home."

"It wants to go back to the Otherworld?" Lucy said. "Because that place sounds truly dreadful." She gave a delicate shudder.

"Maybe for you, but for the puppy it *is* home," Bea said.

I blew out a long, frustrated breath. "Say we figure out how to send it back. How do we know that's the end of it?"

"We don't," Scott said. "But maybe it could be the beginning of the end. Maybe it will somehow attract or pull the rest of the puppy with it."

"How do we send it home?" Nate asked.

"It's telling me . . ." Scott paused again. "It's telling me I can use our current connection to 'talk' to the portal. To get the portal to hear what it wants, open up, and welcome it back to the Otherworld."

"So you're like a conduit for puppy demon feelings," Lucy said, her voice wry. "How sweet."

"Because it's bonded to the dress so tightly, we're going to need to dump the whole dress in the portal, though," Scott said.

"Evie and Aveda," Bea said, "y'all need to be on high alert when we try this. Just in case one of those freaky bolts comes out and tries to eat Nate again."

"This is so exciting!" Maisy cooed, sidling up to Evie. I jumped. I'd forgotten she was there. Even though Maisy had been cleared of evil-doing, I wasn't feeling anything remotely warm or fuzzy toward her. She'd still thought the best course of action last night was humiliating me and ruining Evie's engagement party.

"Once again, my shop is home to a momentous event in San Francisco's supernatural history," Maisy continued. She shoved her phone in Evie's face. "Care to give your pal Maisy an exclusive interview?"

"You're not my pal right now," Evie said, brushing the phone aside and frowning at Maisy. "I know Annie got a little crazy at the engagement party, but you didn't have to do what you did."

"I was only doing what I thought was best for you, Evie," Maisy sniffed.

"Since when has that ever been true?" Evie said, rolling her eyes. "Your blog used to portray me as Aveda's slobby, mousy, hapless assistant who was then Aveda's reckless, out-of-control, power-hungry assistant. You called me 'Rude Girl,' remember? And lately, you and your commenters have been pushing the idea that Aveda is some kind of . . . of . . ."

"Attention-hog diva and raging bossypants bitch who can't stand to let anyone else have the spotlight," I supplied.

"Yes!" Evie cried at Maisy. "You set up this idea that we have to be perfect superheroines, but—"

"But your definition of 'perfect' changes constantly, is completely unrealistic, and is always the exact opposite of the way one of us is supposedly acting," I continued.

"Which conveniently pits us against each other, playing into the idea that there can never be more than one female superhero being awesome at a time, which is totally gross and sexist and mostly just gives you an excuse to pick other women apart," Evie added.

"And I think we've definitely had enough of that," I said, straightening my spine and giving Maisy my most imperious Aveda Jupiter look.

"My god, yes," Evie said. "We love each other, we're both awesome, and we both have various personality quirks that make us human."

"Which is what makes us really fucking good superheroines in the first place," I finished.

And then Evie and I just grinned at each other. Our best

friend near-telepathy was alive and well, and it felt so damn good.

"Nevertheless," Maisy said, clearly struggling to maintain her cool. "I thought you were trying to undermine Evie, Aveda. She is *the bride* and—"

"And that doesn't make me more important than anyone else," Evie sputtered, her shoulders tensing. "I really wish everyone would stop acting like it does."

"Hey," I said, resting a reassuring hand on her shoulder. "It'll be okay. The wedding's in a week and after that you can go back to being less and/or an equal amount of important in relation to everyone else. Buck up, little camper."

She met my overly serious eyes, and I cocked an eyebrow to let her know I was kidding. She giggled, her shoulders relaxing.

"So shall we . . . ?" I inclined my head at the trap and the portal.

She nodded. "Hell, yes."

As she turned to confer with Nate, Lucy put a hand on my arm and pulled me aside.

"Darling, I must commend you, that was some ace maid-of-honoring," she said with a wink.

"Yeah," Bea said, sidling up to us. "And you didn't even need my awesome mind control to do it."

"I . . . well . . ." I was so unused to getting compliments from either of them.

"You really comforted her," Lucy said, patting my arm.

Huh. I had done that, hadn't I? I'd reacted instinctively, been honest, and offered up the first comforting thing I could think of. Not bad, Annie Chang.

"Thank you," I said to them.

"We also wanted to offer a bit of an apology to you, Aveda," Lucy said, knotting her hands together. "We expressed some . . . concerns to Evie about making you maid of honor in the first place, and I know we've been the first to pounce whenever something's gone wrong."

"Well, I haven't exactly done everything *right*," I murmured. "To put it mildly."

"Maybe not," Bea said. "But we also kinda blamed you for stuff that wasn't your fault or where, like, your intent wasn't really bad."

"We were still viewing you through the diva lens," Lucy said. "And not acknowledging that you have truly made great strides in character."

"And even when you weren't making those strides," Bea chimed in, "you've always loved Evie. I know that for a fact. You're doing some amazeballs maid-of-honoring and we should step up and give you credit for that."

"Well, thank you," I said again. My voice was faint, but my lips tilted into a genuine smile.

"Annie!" Evie called out. "Bea, Lucy. Come on, let's do this."

I gave her a nod and we gathered around the portal.

"Okay," Bea said, settling in next to the trap. "I'm going to man—sorry, *woman*—the trap here. Scott will do his spell to try to connect the puppy with the portal and then hopefully we'll be all good. Evie and Aveda—"

"Keep watch for rogue energy bolts. We got it," I said.

Bea popped the trap open and nodded at Scott. He closed his eyes, concentrating. The dress slithered out of the trap like a wary snake.

"That's it, that's it," Bea murmured. "Go into the portal, little puppy dress."

The dress slithered over to the portal, a pool of ivory chiffon flowing over the floor. It stopped abruptly at the edge, then pulled back, as if it sensed evil.

"Come on," Bea muttered.

The dress hesitated, as if it didn't know where to go. The bottom of the skirt reached out, as if testing the waters, and tapped the edge of the portal—then abruptly recoiled as if it had been burnt.

Then—before any of us could quite process what was

happening—it flung itself into the air, speeding across the room in a haphazard arc, a blur of fabric cannon-balling over our heads.

"Shit!" Evie spat out, ducking before the thing smacked into her.

"What's it doing?" Lucy squawked.

"It seems *very much* like it's trying to avoid the portal," I growled.

"Scott, are you still connected to it?" Nate called out.

"No, it's broken its link with me," he said, his voice laced with frustration. "Hold on, I'm trying to get it back."

The dress landed in a pile of chiffon next to the dressing rooms. Evie and I were already on it, racing toward the thing. But just as we reached it, it swept itself off the floor again and danced out of our way: a macabre, disembodied ghost of a dress. It whizzed past Dave's bar, upending a box of panties, and finally dived behind a rack of clothes in Shruti's pop-up.

Evie and I were hot on its heels. "Is it hiding?" I hissed.

I scanned through the racks of Shruti's clothes, my eyes finally landing on a flash of white. That little bastard was hiding behind a crush of vintage petticoats. Evie saw it too and lunged, but I held up a hand. Trying to grab this thing only seemed to make it flit away from us.

I concentrated on the flash and reached out with my mental feathers, trying to clamp on. But just as my feathers closed in on it, it zipped out of sight. "Fuck," I muttered under my breath.

My innate stubbornness kicked in, and I reached out again anyway, trying to envision the flash of white I'd just seen, trying to find it with my mind. One of my mental feathers brushed up against something . . . something solid . . .

And just like that, it slipped away.

I concentrated harder, sweat beading my brow, the beginnings of a headache creeping around my temples. The shop was still way too warm. My mental feathers brushed up against something again, and this time I reached out wildly, trying to latch on to it, trying to grab hold of something I couldn't see ... but I *felt* it, dammit. I knew I did. I pulled hard and backed up from the rack, half expecting nothing to emerge.

But there it was: the possessed dress. Wriggling in the air as I towed it away from its hiding place. A surge of triumph welled in my chest.

I did it. I moved something I couldn't see!

I felt the dress resisting me with all its might, pushing against my mental feathers. I held on harder, my mental feathers clamping down with all their might.

"I've got it!" Scott bellowed. "I'm connected to the puppy again, but it won't talk to me, it won't ... and I still can't pull it out of the dress."

"Try the guiding spell on the whole shebang," Bea yelled out. "The dress, too!"

"Yes, excellent proposal, Beatrice," Nate added. "Perhaps the force of Scott and Aveda combined ..."

I glanced over at Scott. I was focusing so hard on towing the dress, I could barely see straight, but I saw that he was also concentrating on the dress, on working his spell, on pulling it toward the portal. The dress moved another fraction of an inch. I clamped on harder with my mental feathers, willing them not to give out.

"That's it!" Evie cried out. "You guys have it!"

I staggered backward, keeping a hold on the dress, Scott's spell towing it along with me. I felt the support of it in my mind, bolstering my feathers, giving us a stronger grasp on the whole thing. But holding on to it was still taking every ounce of energy I had.

Just a few more feet ... Just a few more ...

Blood roared in my ears, and my face was soaked with sweat. I could barely hear, could barely see, I was focusing on this one thing, on keeping hold, on not letting go ...

Then, just when I thought I couldn't take anymore, the

dress flung itself into the portal's waiting arms. The portal gurgled, sparked, and pulled it inside—then went still yet again.

I was breathing hard, sweat making my shirt stick to my back. My power ponytail had come partially undone, and I was sure I looked like a big mess. I met Scott's eyes. And we smiled at each other. It felt like we were existing in a small, private plane of the world, just us, closed off from everyone else and basking in the triumph of a mission accomplished.

"Wow!" Lucy exclaimed, breaking the moment. "That was *amazing*." She looked from me to Scott, a devilish grin spreading over her face. "Also, you two are so totally do-ing it."

DEMON ENCOUNTER REPORT

Submitted to: Sergeant Rose Rorick (Demon Unit, SFPD Emergency Service Division), Dr. Nathaniel Jones (Aveda Jupiter, Inc.)

Submitted by: Beatrice Constance Tanaka (Super Awesome Note-Taker/Researcher/Mentee who is gaining *so much* IRL experience, y'all, and really showing that she has what it takes to be promoted!)

Short Summary: We sent that bee-yotch back to the Otherworld! *(Note from NJ: "bee-yotch" is not an official classification.)*

Long Summary: Partial containment of Unidentified Demon Specimen #8765—Still At Large has been achieved, but there is not enough data to downgrade **at large** classification. Though we hypothesize that Specimen and Specimen's human counterpart currently exist in a weakened state and seem to have stopped causing trouble for the moment, Team Tanaka/Jupiter remains in active data-collecting mode. We must remain alert just in case it suddenly gains a bananas amount of power and takes over the city via evil wedding gown possession. *(Note from NJ: "bananas" is also not an official classification.)*

Report Writer has made attempts to follow up on several angles. First, RW tracked down the host of the estate sale where boutique owner Shruti Dhaliwal procured the shady red vintage dress that was later incorporated into the Marcus Wong "abomination" gown(s). *(Note from NJ: "shady" is not . . . do I really have to say it?)* Said host was very nice, but mostly seemed interested in showing RW about a thousand pictures of her cats rather than revealing anything in the way of true evilness.

RW then tried questioning S. Dhaliwal herself, since the shady dress was originally part of her pop-up's stock. But S. Dhaliwal mostly just revealed herself to be as awesome as Aveda Jupiter keeps saying she is, and RW ended up spending three hours debating the best *Star Trek* series with her over milkshakes. (It's *Deep Space Nine* and RW is not budging on that one.)

Finally, RW tried exploring the whole Marcus Wong blackmail angle but to no avail—the third "abomination" gown remains missing, and scanning M. Wong's empty storefront umpteen million times has produced zero results. Magnificent Mercedes, LA's superheroine of traffic jams, interviewed M. Wong and his assistant, Franz, but procured no new data. Report Writer suggested MM should, at the very least, procure some of those kimchi pulled pork chalupas from that hot new LA food truck and send them up to Aveda Jupiter, Inc. HQ, but she didn't seem terribly willing. :(

In any case, Team Tanaka/Jupiter is proceeding with the big Tanaka-Jones wedding as planned, even if Specimen #8765 is still at large. Because in our line of work, you can't stop living your life whenever there's metropolis-threatening danger going on—that just means you won't have a life at all. *(Note from NJ: This is editorializing. It is also true.)*

CHAPTER TWENTY-ONE

BACHELORETTE PARTIES HAVE a certain reputation. I wasn't sure ours was going to uphold it.

We didn't look like a particularly wild bunch. Evie, Lucy, Bea, and I were clustered around one of the rickety tables at a hole-in-the-wall Japantown eatery called Curry On, stuffing our faces with hearty Japanese curry over rice. As kids, Evie and I had ended up here after one of our many *Heroic Trio* viewings, making it a post-movie tradition. The place was hardly fancy—the tablecloths were bright yellow plastic, the chairs were mismatched and falling apart, and the décor was a collection of framed black-and-white photos of various Asian movie stars. (As far as I could tell, the only thing they all had in common was that they were Asian. None of the pictures were signed, so it was doubtful that they'd patronized the place. Also, some of them were dead.)

But the food was delicious—tender pork katsu cutlets drowned in spicy pools of curry—and our long-time connection to the place made it feel like home. And since I was kind of sort of banned from The Gutter "for the foreseeable future," according to Kevin, Curry On seemed like a good approximation of what Evie had wanted for her wedding-related parties in the first place: comfort venue, comfort food, comfort company. I'd lined up a few surprises for the night, but this time, I'd asked others for advice and considered each element carefully, thinking things through by asking myself a simple question: what would Evie's face look like when she saw it? It was amazing the insight this added to the party-planning process.

A week had passed since we'd dumped the puppy dress into the portal, and it was the night before the wedding. We'd all been on edge, waiting for the human/puppy combo platter to make itself known, but it was apparently still skulking in the shadows, weakened and waiting. And tonight, I was determined for us to relax and have as much fun as we possibly could.

"Oh, *yum*," Evie groaned, slurping a mouthful of curry and rice off her chopsticks. "You know, whenever I see one of those new so-called trend foods popping up, I always wonder why it isn't this. I mean, white hipsters have latched on to every other Asian food thing, and this is basically the Japanese equivalent of chicken nuggets drowned in gravy."

"Quite," Lucy agreed, taking a more delicate bite. "It deserves to be at least as big as poutine."

"Way better than antelope skewers," Bea said with her mouth full. She cocked an eyebrow at me.

"Yes, yes, I get it," I said, pointing my chopsticks at her. "Can we maybe start letting that one go?"

"We can," Lucy said, giving me a sly look. "On one condition."

I took a bite of curry, savoring the way it burned down my throat. I'd anticipated the bachelorette night might involve embarrassing conversation or even juvenile slumber party games like Truth or Dare. I'd told myself to suck it up and roll with it if that's what Evie wanted—but I wasn't sure I knew *how* to roll with such things. She and I might be working things out, but I still didn't feel like I was part of the familial unit. A lone wolf does not change its spots overnight. Or something like that.

Oh, well. Surely Aveda Jupiter could handle whatever potentially humiliating truth question or dare task Lucy might be about to lob my way? Maybe I could even figure out a way to make it extra fabulous?

"Shoot," I said, taking another bite of curry. "What condition?"

Lucy grinned at me. "You must tell us absolutely everything that's going on with you and Scott. I mean . . ." She glided a bright red fingernail over the plastic tablecloth in a manner that was somehow suggestive. ". . . *details*."

Oh, god. I had no idea how to make *that* extra fabulous. Or how to talk about it in a way that was even a little bit coherent. I flushed, set down my chopsticks, and patted my lips with a napkin. "It's really spicy tonight," I murmured.

"Not why you're blushing, though," Evie said, poking me in the arm. "Pretty sure of that."

"This is *your* bachelorette party," I said, poking her back. "Shouldn't we be talking about *you*?"

"Please." Evie rolled her eyes. "Everyone has already barged in on, interrupted, overheard, or teased me about my sex life. I think we're ready for a new topic."

"Evie's right," Lucy said. "We all know Nate's buttoned up in the streets, uncaged beast in the sheets. And in the closet, the car, the Pussy Queen dressing room—"

"That was *one* time," Evie protested.

"And I'm guessing Rose would be much the same," Lucy mused. "But Scott—"

"Wait, what *is* going on with Rose?" I said, hoping to deflect some of the attention from me. "How have you not sealed that deal yet?"

"I'm still doing a slow burn on that one," Lucy said, examining her nails. "When I'm in pursuit, I have a very meticulous strategy that involves specific steps pertaining to revealing every facet of my fabulousness. Now, about Scott—"

"Bull. Shit," I blurted out.

She arched an eyebrow. "Excuse me?"

"I . . ." I hesitated. Was I Hurricane Annie-ing all over Evie's bachelorette party? The words had spilled out before I could stop them, hastened by the cheap, BYOB champagne we'd brought with us. We hadn't even bothered

with glasses, just popped it open and were drinking directly
from the paper bag-encased bottle.

But Evie had encouraged me to embrace my Annie
Chang side, right? And Annie Chang definitely had some
feelings about Lucy's avoidance of this situation. I took a
swig of champagne and met Lucy's eyes.

"We've established that you like Rose," I said. "And
when you like someone, you usually don't hesitate to go
for it. What's the hold-up, here? She's great. You're great.
Why not make your move and become the ass-kicking,
justice-enforcing, attractive-to-the-point-of-over-the-top-
ridiculousness power couple you're so clearly meant to
be?"

Lucy goggled at me. "You're one to talk, Aveda Jupiter,"
she sputtered. "You waited *over a decade* to make your
move on the guy you've wanted to boink since you were a
teenager."

"Not true, they kissed once before all this," Evie said,
waving her chopsticks around.

"What?!" Lucy squeaked.

"Not important to the current situation," I said hastily.

"Except it sort of is," Bea said. "Because—"

"Not important to *Lucy's* current situation," I clarified. I
turned back to Lucy. "Also, Rose obviously likes you, too—
remember that night after Evie's big karaoke win? She was
all up in your business. And why shouldn't she be? You
have the athletic prowess to take down men three times
your size, you put together excellent outfits, and you kill at
karaoke. What are you afraid of?"

Lucy pressed her lips together and frowned at me. I
leaned back in my seat, took a smaller sip of champagne,
and tried to calm the nerves telling me that despite all good
intentions, my Hurricane nature had probably just ruined
Evie's party. Again.

Lucy blew out a long breath and reached for the champagne bottle. "Give me that, please."

I passed it to her. She took a long swig, then met my gaze

again. "You're right," she finally said. "I am extremely fabulous."

"Hear, hear," Evie said, squeezing her shoulder.

"And normally when I go after a crush, I turn that all the way up," Lucy continued. "Shine a freaking spotlight on it. Get them to see the most outrageous, utterly irresistible version of me. But . . ." She paused and took another swig. "Rose is different. I tend to get bored easily. But I never tire of talking to her, spending time with her. The moments we've engaged in thoroughly mundane activities—like walking around Pussy Queen, chatting about how the scanner technology works—make me feel all . . . glowy inside." She wrinkled her nose, as if this was a confusing, alien sensation. "We spend hours texting about nothing, absolutely nothing. And I can't get enough. I want her to see the me that's underneath all the fabulousness. The me that sits at home on Saturday night, watching Netflix and cleaning my knife collection."

"Still pretty fabulous," Evie said.

"You want someone who truly understands the intricacies involved in polishing a custom-made Damascus fighter blade," Bea said, swooning a little.

"Not someone," Lucy corrected. "I want Rose. And I want her to want me—the *real* me. Who is fabulous. But, like, in a different way. So I'm trying to take the time to show her that. While completely freaking out that she won't like this version of me as much."

"I get it," I said, taking the champagne bottle back from her. "I'm in the process of kind of . . . figuring out the real me. Who is hopefully fabulous." Under the table, Evie squeezed my hand. "Showing that to someone is probably the scariest thing I've ever done."

Lucy smiled, took the bottle from me, and raised it in a toast. "Amen, sister."

"Excuse me, would you ladies like anything else?"

We turned to see a tall, broad-shouldered teenager standing over us, smiling genially—Sam, nephew of Curry

On's kindly old owner, who we knew only as Mr. Fujikawa. Mr. Fujikawa had let us have Curry On to ourselves for this special night and was doing all the cooking while Sam handled waiter duties.

"More curry? More rice?" Sam said, cocking his head to the side. His jet-black hair, which had that artfully tousled look that appeared effortless but actually took a lot of work to achieve, fell over his forehead. "Dessert menu?"

"Pleeeeeaaaasse, Sam Fujikawa, we know the only dessert you have here is green tea mochi from Trader Joe's," Bea said, with an eye-roll. "Why do you need a whole menu for that?"

"It's more of a verbal menu," Sam said, grinning at her and brushing his hair back into place. "Recited by yours truly."

"Which makes it even less appealing," Bea said, waving a dismissive hand. "We're good, thanks."

Sam crossed his arms over his chest, his grin turning teasing. "Man, have I missed you shutting me down over the most minute minutiae, Beatrice."

"Text me," she said. "I'll shut you down any time. We don't even have to be in the same room."

Evie, Lucy, and I had been following this exchange like spectators at a particularly lively tennis match, our gazes whipping back and forth between Bea and Sam. Evie met my eyes and cocked an eyebrow, and I felt our near-telepathy click into place, both of us thinking the same thing: *What's going on* here?

Sam laughed and leaned against the table—he moved with the easy grace and confidence found in star quarterback homecoming king types. "You should come back to school," he said to Bea. "I'll let you copy off my homework."

"As if I would ever need such a thing," Bea said. "I'm pretty sure you want me to come back so *you* can copy off *my* homework."

"I enjoy healthy competition," he said. "And if you keep skipping out, I'll have *no* competition for valedictorian."

"I am completing all my coursework at home with permission from my teachers, per section nine, code twelve of the school district rules and regulations handbook," Bea said primly. "My valedictorian status is in the bag, and you should focus on Battle Royale-ing it out with everyone else for second best."

"Not a chance," Sam said. "But here's another enticement. I'm currently building possibly the most badass engine ever in auto shop, and I know that big, weird brain of yours would be all over checking it out. Can't do that while you're 'completing coursework' at home."

Bea looked up, clearly trying to hide the interest sparking in her eyes. "Text me when you get stuck on the build," she said with an elaborate shrug. "I'll be happy to offer my superior expertise."

"Excellent." He gave her a little nod, his dark eyes dancing with amusement, then turned to the rest of the table. "I'll bring more curry. And some green tea mochi, just in case you change your minds."

"I do want green tea mochi," Evie said, poking Bea in the arm as Sam sauntered off. "Also, what was that next level flirting all about?"

"Not flirting," Bea said. "Sam is my academic rival, we have a blood feud, and I intend to prevail. Bro-dude gearheads with more muscles than brains do *not* win valedictorian. Enterprising brainiacs who hold down scientific research-heavy real world jobs while also maintaining perfect GPAs on the other hand . . ." She gestured to herself with her chopsticks, then muttered, "Anyway, he's annoying."

Evie and I exchanged a glance. We both knew where "he's annoying" could lead.

"Back to you, Aveda Jupiter," Lucy sang out. "You successfully diverted the conversation to me and Rose, but I haven't forgotten where we started." She flashed a grin. "As I was saying before, we need to know *all* about Scott. He's still a mystery to us when it comes to intimate matters. Well,

maybe to just me and Bea, since Evie's also had the pleasure of—"

"That was hardly a pleasure." Evie snorted. "We were
teenagers, we were drunk, and we have no chemistry in that
regard. I'm just as in the dark as the rest of you."

"He's so mellow," Lucy said, steepling her fingers and
regarding me keenly. She looked like a Bond supervillain
preparing to divulge her master plan. I resisted the urge to
squirm. "So chilled out. What's it like when he gets . . ." She
trailed off and waggled her eyebrows for dramatic effect.

"Totes in the passion zone," Bea supplied.

My face felt like it was on fire. I took an extra-long swig
of champagne. I thought maybe if I drank for long enough,
they'd move on to another topic, but everyone was still
staring at me expectantly when I set the bottle down. And
since we were the only customers in the place, the silence
seemed extra thick.

The bubbles from the champagne swirled through my
head, making me feel lighter and loosening my tongue. My
face was even hotter now, my blush intensified by my alcohol-
induced Asian Flush.

"Well," I said slowly. "In the past, sex has been a very
distancing experience for me. Mechanical. And I know my
body very well, so I usually had to provide some instruction. Which tended not to go over very well."

The words tumbled out, unvarnished, and I hesitated, my
face still flaming.

"It's important to voice your needs in that department
when someone isn't getting the job done," Lucy sniffed. "I
practically had to draw a diagram for the last girl I was
with."

"Remember Richard?" Evie said, naming the preten-
tious professor she'd dated years ago. "He never gave me
an orgasm. Not one. And I never said anything because I
assumed there was something wrong with *me*."

"Maybe if you had said something, you wouldn't have
gotten so pissed and burned down the library when you

caught him cheating," Bea chimed in. "So much pent-up frustration."

Everyone murmured in agreement and turned back to me. I opened my mouth, closed it. They actually seemed . . . interested? Encouraging, even? I hadn't been expecting *that*. Feeling emboldened, I took another hefty swig of champagne.

"Well, you know how he usually has to make a joke out of everything," I said. "But when it comes to us being together, he's actually very serious. I would even say intense. Like what's happening between us is the most important thing in the world and *I'm* the most important thing in the world and he's letting me see this private side he never shows anyone else and . . ." I knew my face was beyond Asian Flush now. I probably looked like a tomato. " . . . in that moment, he really sees me. I mean, *all* of me. Not just the naked parts."

"The *real* you—like we were talking about earlier," Lucy said, giving me a warm smile. "And do you provide instruction?"

"No." The champagne fizzed through my bloodstream, and I found myself flashing my megawatt Aveda Jupiter grin and affecting a bravado-laced pose as I rakishly tipped the bottle toward my mouth again. I cocked an eyebrow and gave my words an overly satisfied edge. "I don't have to."

As they squealed with appreciative laughter, I realized the megawatt grin spread over my face was completely genuine. For this whole dinner, I'd done what Evie suggested I do with Scott—just be honest. Not worry how it might come off. My Aveda Jupiter attitude had laced itself through, coming naturally instead of being forced out because I thought that's what people wanted or because I was trying to get something *I* wanted. And I hadn't stopped to think about which persona I was inhabiting. I was Aveda Jupiter and Annie Chang all at once, and it wasn't confusing. It just felt right.

It also seemed like . . . they liked it. They liked *me*. It felt childish to take so much pleasure in that, but I did. And that mean little voice that usually piped up in the back of my head, the one that told me I wasn't good enough, that my presence wasn't wanted, that *no one* would ever like me, was totally silent.

Evie threw her arms around my shoulders and hugged me tight. "I'm so glad this happened. I totally 'shipped it."

"Me too," Bea said. "And Nate owes me ten dollars."

"You and Nate bet on whether our OG superheroine and our resident surfer mage would hook up or not?" Lucy said, looking vaguely scandalized.

"I know," Bea said. "I should have made it *twenty* dollars."

We all laughed again. I felt giddy and it wasn't just the bubbles; it was that fizz of companionship people were always talking about, that feeling of being in the moment with friends.

"Let's have a toast," I said impulsively, holding the champagne bottle aloft.

"Raise a glass to the four of us, tomorrow there'll be more of us . . . or something!" Bea sang.

"To Evie Tanaka—our bride-to-be—and a night out in her honor!" I said.

"A night of awesome friends!" Evie exclaimed.

"And no freaking puppy demons!" Lucy cried.

I grinned and passed her the bottle. "Amen, sister."

🔥

We lingered for a long time over the last vestiges of curry and mochi, talking and laughing and having a good time. Mr. Fujikawa had sent Sam home and was cleaning up in the back and I was taking a last slug of champagne when we heard a loud, disapproving voice behind us.

"Oh my god," the voice brayed. "What is she even *doing*?"

We all swiveled to find a group of four women glowering at us. Well, at me. I recognized all of them. Gwen, Cakezilla Carol, Redhead Bridezilla from the bridal tent, and Petite

Blonde Bride from Marcus's salon. They were all dressed in lacy white dresses with high necklines, giving them a weirdly Victorian vibe, and full skirts made even fuller by petticoats. The look was enhanced by their elaborate head-pieces, concoctions of feathers, netting, and in Carol's case, a tiny fake bird.

"Well, hello, don't you all look nice," Evie said, giving them an appeasing grin. "I love your hats." She gestured to their headpieces.

"They're fascinators," Gwen chirped. "Bridal fascinators. All true vintage, of course."

"Lovely," Lucy said, in a tone that indicated she thought they were anything but.

Silence fell and the women returned to glaring at me. I shifted uncomfortably.

"You know, darlings, it's so nice of you to stop by and say hi to Evie, but we're really having more of a private event, here," Lucy said. She met my eyes, and we shared a moment of connection: we needed to get these women out of here before Evie's inherent niceness took over and she invited them to join the party.

"Evie's bachelorette, you mean," Carol said. "So funny. We're actually having our bachelorettes tonight, too!"

"Hilarious," Lucy muttered.

"All at the same time?" Bea said, giving them a confused look.

"Of course," Gwen said. "We believe in bridal solidarity. Which is why we *had* to come by when we saw what was happening here." She turned her frown back to me and gestured to the bottle I was holding. "I mean, really. Who does Aveda Jupiter think she is, getting all tacky and wasted at her best friend's bachelorette? And off of some dirty-ass paper bag dollar store liquor."

"Hey, I was with her when she bought it and it was at least *five* dollars," Bea said indignantly.

"That's nice of you all to be so concerned," I said, putting a hand on Bea's arm and turning to address the assembled

brides. "But Evie's having a great time. Aren't you?" I shot
her an anxious look. Given how badly I'd predicted the last
party, maybe these brides had sensed something I hadn't.

"Fantastic," she said, giving me a reassuring pat on the
shoulder. "This is the best bachelorette I could have asked
for."

"But it looks like you're not even playing any of the traditional games," Carol said, making a little tsk-ing sound.
"And where are all the dildos?"

"Funny story about that," Lucy began.

I kicked her under the table.

"It's lucky we arrived when we did," Redhead said. "It's
great to have maids of honor to do your more menial tasks,
but only other brides-to-be can truly understand your
plight."

"My plight?" Evie said, her brow crinkling.

"We're here for you now," Blonde said, in what she probably liked to imagine was a soothing voice. "And we'll make
sure you experience *all* the things a bride should."

"Really," Lucy said, rising to her feet, her bodyguard in-
stincts kicking in. "I think maybe it's time for you to let
Evie enjoy her party in peace."

"We'll leave," Gwen said. "But not before Evie's had the
divine pleasure of experiencing . . ." She reached into her
large tote and pulled out a handful of white tissue. "The
toilet paper game!" she crowed.

"The whatsis, whosis, now?" Bea said.

"Wait," Evie said. "I've actually heard of this. You make
a dress for the bride out of toilet paper, right?"

The brides squealed and jumped up and down, making
near orgasmic faces of joy. "Yes!" they shrieked. "Yesyesyes!"

"Yikes," Lucy muttered, resting her head in her hands.

"Since we're all brides, we were going to play together,
craft our own creations!" Blonde said.

"Isn't that technically playing *against* each other?" Bea
said.

"And now San Francisco's most awesome bride-to-be

can join us!" cried Redhead. "Besides getting engaged, this is the best thing that's ever happened to me!"

"Dream big," I muttered before I could stop myself and heard Lucy snort-giggle.

"Will you please play with us?" Blonde wheedled, clasping her hands together. "Just do the toilet paper dress thing with us and we can get a picture and oh my gosh, my fiancée will freak. She is such a huge fan. It will be the perfect wedding day gift!"

"Well . . ." Evie scanned their pleading faces and I knew there was no way in hell she was turning them down. She may have abandoned most of her pushover ways, but her heart was still soft as butter. It was one of the things that made me love her.

"We can do it," I said softly, patting her on the arm. "We'll all help you to make it go by faster. I mean, uh, to make it more fun."

"Okay, then," she said, giving the brides-to-be a game smile. "As long as it's okay with Mr. Fujikawa?"

Mr. Fujikawa gave us a thumbs-up from behind the counter. And my eardrums were nearly shattered by the screams from the brides-to-be.

Before I could process what was happening, rolls of toilet paper were being thrust into my hands and Carol, Gwen, and their two friends were already hard at work on their creations, brows furrowed as they twisted and tied the toilet paper around themselves.

"Um," Lucy said, staring at the roll that had been handed to her, "aren't your bridesmaids supposed to make the dresses for you?"

"We're bending the rules since we're all brides," Redhead said, flashing us a manic grin.

"But you should go ahead and help Evie," Carol added, twisting a strip of toilet paper over her shoulder to form a strap. "She deserves extra support, of course."

"Right," I said, trying to go along with it. "Let's get to it, team."

I ripped off a long strip of toilet paper and started wrapping it around Evie's torso, gesturing for Lucy and Bea to follow suit. Evie held out her arms obligingly, like a snow angel suspended in mid-air.

"This'll be good," she said, giving us an amused wink. "The wedding's tomorrow, and I still don't have a dress thanks to all the hijinks that have been going on. I could rock a toilet paper creation down the aisle, right? Nate might be into it?"

"You could wear a garbage bag and Nate would think it was hot," I snorted, trying to fluff a piece of toilet paper into a flower accent. "But we actually have something better for you on that front."

"Shh!" Bea elbowed me. "It's supposed to be a surprise!"

"A surprise?" Evie said, her voice apprehensive. Given some of the other surprises I'd sprung on her throughout this whole wedding process, I guess I couldn't blame her.

"A good surprise," Lucy clarified, tying a toilet paper sash around her waist. "Which will be revealed once we get back to HQ. If we ever get out of here, that is." She cast a disapproving look at the bridal foursome who had disrupted our party. But they were too busy working on their creations to pay her any mind. All four of them were focused with laser-like intensity on the toilet paper—scraps flew everywhere as they ripped it apart and twisted it into new shapes, causing a mini-blizzard to swirl around them. There was an odd sense of quiet frenzy, as if they were performing some urgent, rapid-fire task like defusing a bomb. Perhaps this was the bachelorette equivalent.

"Time!" Carol crowed, even though there had been no mention of a time limit when we'd started. I gritted my teeth in frustration and eyed the dress we'd thrown together for Evie. It was passable—in that it had a skirt, a top, and a whimsical toilet paper veil stuck to her hair—but the others were clearly more refined. Carol's skirt had actual tiers and Gwen's sleeves were finished at the ends with tiny toilet paper ruffles.

Had these ladies *practiced* this game or something? I tried to shake off my irritation. No need to take it seriously, though in all honesty, I still wanted to win. Even the inherent dopiness of the toilet paper game couldn't dampen Aveda Jupiter's competitive spirit.

"How do we determine who the winner is, anyway?" Bea said, as if reading my thoughts. "Everyone here participated, so there aren't any impartial judges."

"Soooo glad you asked," Carol said, whipping out her phone. "There are actually extensive rules posted online, which—"

"Fantastic," I muttered, leaning back against the table. How much longer were we going to be subjected to Carol and her bridal crew? Hours? Months? At this rate, Evie would be MIA at her own wedding. Because we'd still be *here*.

"If this is gonna take a while, I'm gonna eat some more," Bea said.

As Carol droned on, Bea reached behind Evie to grab her plate and chopsticks. But as she inched the plate over, Lucy leaned against the table, jostling the entire setup. Bea's plate bounced. And the remains of the curry splattered all over Evie's toilet paper skirt.

"Oh, shit!" Evie exclaimed, jumping a little. She looked down at the damage then gave a sheepish chuckle. "Welp. I guess I lose, huh?"

But the bridal foursome wasn't laughing. Carol stopped reading her long, laborious list of rules. Gwen froze in place, her eyes widening. Blonde and Redhead looked similarly scandalized. An awkward silence descended.

"You know, I think that means the game is over," I said, making my tone firm. I was past the point of caring if these brides thought I was a diva. "Why don't we get those pictures you wanted and—"

"*No.*" Carol glowered at us and threw her phone to the ground. Gwen moved to flank her, her frown deepening.

"She has disrespected our bridal queen," Carol snarled, pointing at Bea. "And she will pay."

"Hey, hey." Evie held up her hands as I moved in front of Bea. "It's really okay. No harm done."

"But there is harm," Gwen growled. "And therefore, we must dole out harm in return. It is in keeping with the order of things. The old ways."

Her bridal cohorts echoed her, their voices rising up in an eerie chorus that seemed to bounce off the walls and surround us.

"The old ways ... old ways ... old ways ..."

"Ladies," Lucy hissed under her breath. "I don't want to jump the gun, here, but I think—"

"These motherfuckers have been *puppy demoned*," Evie blurted out, just as Carol lunged at Bea, snarling.

The strange glow in Carol's eyes seemed to intensify, giving her the appearance of a rabid dog. I wrapped my mental feathers around Bea and shoved her to the side. Then I stepped into Carol's path, blocking her.

"Get out of my way, Aveda Jupiter!" she snarled.

I stepped around her, grabbed her arm, and tried to twist it behind her back in a modified version of the move I'd used on her before. But this time, she darted out of my way, sending me a smug look. Was it my imagination or was she also moving faster than a normal human?

Shit. There were too many of them for me to effectively use my telekinesis—I wouldn't be able to hold them for long ...

"Annie!" screamed Evie, and all of a sudden, I saw plates of curry leftovers being thrown my way. I figured out what she wanted immediately, seizing the plates with my mental feathers and sending them soaring directly into Carol's face.

"Owwwwwwww!" she shrieked, clawing at her eyes as hot curry splashed all over her.

Before we had a chance to savor this minor victory, she was snapping her fingers at her Bridezilla squad.

"Take out the one who has sullied our queen!" she demanded, pointing to Bea. "But also, take out *that one* as well! Because she has sullied our queen from *the very be-ginning!*"

And of course, she was pointing at me.

I darted back over to Evie and Lucy, who were forming a protective wall around Bea. I scanned behind the counter for Mr. Fujikawa, but he seemed to have taken off. Smart man.

"Lucy," I said, my words spilling out as quickly as I could form them, "get out of here with Bea. Run as fast as you can back to HQ, get the others and whatever supplies we might need to corral them, the trap and all that stuff. Evie, you and I are going to make this Bridezilla squad follow *us*."

"How?" she said, her eyes wide with apprehension.

"Like this." I grabbed two plates of curry—one in each hand—and smashed them against her toilet paper dress. They left an impressive mess, the golden brown drippings smearing everywhere with the occasional rice clump giving it a 3D effect. "Now act like you're mad at me," I whispered. I jerked my head at Lucy and Bea and mouthed, *Go.*

Lucy grabbed Bea's hand and bolted out the front door. Gwen and Blonde Bridezilla turned, as if to follow them.

Luckily, Evie picked up on what I was doing.

"Um . . . holy shit. How dare you!" she screamed at me.

Gwen and Blonde Bridezilla turned back to us. Their eyes had the same weird glow as Carol's.

"You . . . you've ruined everything!" Evie continued, pulling an exaggerated rage face. "You are such a *ruiner!*" In spite of the clearly dangerous circumstances we were in, I had to smother the urge to laugh. She was an awesome superheroine, but her improv skills left something to be desired. Still, it worked. Carol, Gwen, and their cohorts were now regarding us with great interest, Bea's infraction forgotten.

"I mean, I'm the, uh, queen!" Evie bellowed.

That got the snarls going.

"Destroy the ruiner of our queen!" Carol commanded.

"Run," I said to Evie.

And we did, bolting out the front door and setting off through Japantown. It was late and the streets were mostly empty, save for a few clusters of tourists.

"Get off the streets!" I barked. "Move, move, move!"

The tourists obliged, fanning out to the sides and creating a clear path for us.

"So I guess the puppy got some of its strength back?" Evie said.

"Either that or they're *really* big fans of yours," I said.

"I think I only want moderate level fans from now on. But how is it affecting all of them at once? Is it back in the air rather than in a dress?" She stole a glance behind her shoulder and winced. "They're still chasing us. And they're not harming anyone else, they really only seem interested in getting to you. So what's the plan?"

My mind was working a mile a minute, keeping time with my sprinting feet, trying to figure that out.

"Let's get them to that deserted spot by the big fountain—the one where we had your last fire show," I said. "The space is pretty open. Maybe we can corral them with your fire until the others get to us with the scanner and the trap."

Evie nodded. "On it."

We increased our speed, and I could see her digging in mentally, finding the strength and emotion that was going to help her channel the flames and cage the Bridezilla squad. I, meanwhile, managed to get my phone out of my pocket and texted Scott our location.

We reached the spot by the fountain and stopped abruptly, whipping around to face Carol and Co. Evie balled her fists at her sides, her brow crinkling. She was concentrating, getting ready to unleash fiery hell.

"Get behind me," she growled.

"What?" I glared at her. "I will *not*."

"They're after you, they won't hurt me. So get behind me, dammit." An amused grin broke through her ferocious expression. "Just this once."

She had a point. I stepped behind her, but kept my fists up and my mind ready, determined to help her in any way I could.

"We're here to save you, bridal queen!" Carol shrieked. "We are sorry we allowed your deceitful maid of honor to kidnap you in this fashion!"

"We should have anticipated her treachery after all she has done!" Gwen chimed in. "Stealing the offering we left for you was the last straw!"

"I'm not kidnapping her, and I haven't stolen anything," I blurted out, exasperated.

"The offering!" Redhead squawked. "The gown in the window of the loathsome gentrifier was meant to attract our queen! Not *you*!"

"Enough!" Evie bellowed, raising her fists. "And you all need to calm the fuck down."

And with that, she opened her hands and released a stream of fireballs into the air. They whizzed by the Bride-zillas, plunking ineffectually into the fountain behind them. The Bridezillas snarled, their eyes glowing in that way that was definitely not natural. I shuddered.

"Shit," Evie muttered.

"Let me help," I said, stepping out from behind her. "Shoot your fireballs."

She opened her hands again and let them fly like tiny, flaming missiles: *whoosh, whoosh, whoosh.* I reached out with my mental feathers and caught them, carefully arranging them into a literal ring of fire. The Bridezillas stopped glaring and hissing at us and stared at the circle of flames in the sky. It hung above them for a moment: a fierce, glorious creation, as if a dragon had let out the full force of its monstrous breath over the city. Then I pulled on my mental feathers and slammed the ring of fire down with all my might. And they were trapped.

"Gaaaaaaah!" I heard Gwen scream. The ring of fire was so high, we couldn't see any of them. "We have been tricked by the enemy of our bridal queen!"

"Do not fear, Evelyn Tanaka!" Carol howled. "We will take down your enemy and we *will* save you!"

"Yeesh." Evie shuddered. "I think I'm good." She squeezed my shoulder. "A-plus team work. That was fucking badass."

"Indeed." I was focusing hard, keeping my mental feathers wrapped around the ring of fire. I had to hold it in place until the cavalry arrived. I felt sweat pool at the small of my back and my head was starting to hurt.

Just as I was certain I was about to collapse from telekinetic exertion, I saw Nate, Bea, Lucy, and Scott, charging over the hill. Bea was toting the trap, Scott had the scanner, and Lucy and Nate had fire extinguishers. They were a glorious sight—I could practically hear the action movie score swelling behind them.

"We're here, we're here," Lucy said, waving to us. She arched an eyebrow at the ring of fire. "Well. This is quite showy." She grinned at me. "I mean that as a compliment."

"Thank you," I said. My voice was faint, and my arms were shaking. "We think the puppy might be in the air rather than the dresses since it seems to be affecting all of these ladies, but . . ."

Scott held out the scanner, his brow furrowing. Bea started setting up the trap. Lucy and Nate lifted the fire extinguishers, at the ready. Through my shaking and fuzzy vision, I felt myself let out a long sigh of relief. Yes, I was hovering on the edge of passing out—but it felt so good to have the team united like this, working like a well-oiled machine. Or I guess it was an extremely weird, occasionally argumentative machine wherein several of the members were currently engaged in illicit after-hours activity. But hey, wasn't that what being a team was all about? Evie gave me an encouraging smile. I knew she felt it too, this sense of unity. I also knew she'd call it by a different name: *family*.

And suddenly, finally . . . I felt it, too.

It was strange to feel the truth of that rushing through my veins in that moment, facing down a bunch of angry

Bridezillas surrounded by fire, right on the heels of an epic curry battle. But there it was. I had a family beyond the one I'd been born into, and they were pretty damn awesome.

I heard the scanner *BEEP* one long, shrill note, and was vaguely aware of Scott yelling into the air.

"No, wait, I can help you! Please! Come back!" he bellowed.

I shook my head, trying to get rid of the fuzziness that seemed to be overtaking my vision. Spots appeared in front of my eyes.

"Annie?" Evie said uncertainly. "You're shaking. Are you . . . ?"

"Shit!" I growled. One section of my fire ring vanished for a moment, and I pulled the two ends together, closing the circle once more.

"It's gone," Scott choked out, his voice tight with frustration. "The puppy. It was here, and I was able to connect with it, but now . . ."

A sickly feeling slid through my gut.

"Lucy, Nate: can you . . . ?"

Without further prompting, they lifted the extinguishers and sprayed the blaze. Once the white smoke cleared, it became apparent that my sickly feeling had been correct. There was no one there.

The Bridezilla squad had disappeared into thin air.

CHAPTER TWENTY-TWO

"THEY MUST HAVE slipped out when I lost control and allowed that space to appear in the ring of fire." I shook my head, frustrated.

We were back at HQ, gathered in Nate's lab, trying to figure out what the hell had just happened. I couldn't believe Evie and I had done all that awesome teamwork for nothing. That I'd let the Bridezilla squad escape.

"I know you're already caught in an Aveda Jupiter 'always in a fight, I do my best' shame spiral, but you did everything you could," Evie said firmly. "We all did."

"So was that the puppy?" Bea said. "Or something else entirely? Scott, you connected with it, right? That's what you were yelling about?"

"Yes, it was the puppy and yes, I managed to connect to it," Scott said, frowning contemplatively. "Its thoughts were a big, chaotic mess this time. I think it's still in conflict with its human helper. And I tried to reach out and let it know I could help it, but . . ." He shook his head. "I at least got some information I think we can use. So first of all, Annie's right, the brides escaped when that space opened up in the fire."

"When I let it happen, you mean," I grumbled.

Evie poked me in the arm. "No shame spiral. That ring of fire was still fucking badass."

"I could feel the puppy's relief in that moment," Scott said. "It's still in its weakened state, and it was happy to have the opportunity to escape."

"How was the puppy affecting so many Bridezillas at once?" Nate asked. "Was it in the air again, like we hypothesized it was in the bridal tent and Cake My Day?"

"No. It was definitely in a dress," Scott said. He paused, looking grim. "Actually, here's the really freaky part: I'm pretty sure it was in *all* of them."

My stomach dropped. "So now it can possess multiple dresses at a time?" I said. "How is that . . . how is *it* . . . ?"

"Wait a minute." Bea held up a hand, her brow furrowing in concentration as she tried to work it out. "When we captured that piece of it in the Marcus Wong gown, we thought the puppy could only send out one little piece of itself at a time — and that little piece was the only thing we'd been chasing around." She smacked the countertop and shook her head at Nate. "We totes made an assumption based on limited data."

"We, ah, 'totes' made a *logical* assumption based on existing data," Nate said. "Aside from the bridal tent — when we thought it was in the air — we've only witnessed it possessing or trying to possess one person at a time."

"Until tonight," I said, gnawing on my lower lip.

"Maybe not — maybe we just didn't realize . . ." Bea began. "What if . . ." She hesitated, her eyes narrowing. "What if it's been using dresses since the very beginning? If it can possess more than one dress at a time, it could've been in both Evie's dress and the dress of the redhead bride she was fighting with in the tent. And hey, if it's not limiting itself to wedding gowns — 'cause what the Bridezillas were wearing tonight was bridal adjacent at best — maybe it was in Cakezilla Carol's dress during her bakery meltdown?"

"Are we thinking it has the ability to split off a *bunch* of little pieces of itself all at once and send them into multiple dresses?" Lucy said. "And that it's had that ability for a while now?"

"That means we have who knows how many Bridezillas to worry about," Evie said, looking grim.

"Hold on," Nate said. "As Scott said, it's still weakened.

And as the puppy conveyed to him back at Pussy Queen, splitting itself off is the *cause* of it being weakened. So in theory, the more Bridezillas there are, the easier it should be to contain this thing."

"In theory, yes," Scott said. "But there's another piece of information I picked up. Or that I think I picked up. The puppy was reluctant to share this with me, but—"

"But your mind-meld game is *strong*," Bea said, giving him a solemn nod.

"Something like that," Scott said, giving her a half-smile. "From what I was able to piece together, the puppy/human combo is looking for a way to restrengthen itself. And somehow, it's decided it needs ..." He hesitated, swallowing hard.

"Spit it out, Cameron," I said.

"It thinks what it needs," he said slowly, "is another human."

"What?" Lucy gasped.

"How would the other human fit into the current puppy/human configuration?" Nate asked.

"And once it gets that human, once it restrengthens itself?" Evie said. "What Bridezilla-related horrors are we in for?"

"I don't know," Scott said ruefully. "It escaped before I could get anything else out of it."

"So we still don't know what its ultimate plan is," Bea said. "Looking at it from another angle, what kind of human does it need for this restrengthening? I'm assuming the other Bridezillas aren't worthy, since the puppy/human combo doesn't seem to be taking advantage of them in that way. It's mostly using them as its own personal zombie horde—using them to attack."

"Really just to attack me, in this case," I muttered.

"Although you mentioned, Aveda, that the brides seemed to be displaying enhanced abilities?" Nate continued.

"Yes," I said, calling up the memory. "They were moving faster, and their eyes had a weird glow. I mean, maybe they're all trained sprinters who've discovered some innovative new cosmetic technique, but I kind of don't think so."

"Could that be a result of the cumulative time they've been affected by the puppy?" Bea mused. "Maybe the more it gets into your clothes, the more demon-y you get?"

"That makes me wonder how long some of these ladies have been affected," I said. I thought back to the bridal chaos at Marcus's shop the day Shruti and I had visited, and the crowd outside after the shop had closed. "Because we've definitely been seeing some truly bizarre bridal behavior these past weeks. And tonight, it escalated. I blamed it on the pressures of wedding planning and the so-called bridal complex, but ..." I trailed off, frowning.

"Back to my question," Bea said. "Who's the puppy's—and its human's—ultimate match?"

Silence fell as we all considered this. What did this bizarre, mashed-up entity want? Who was it looking for?

I found my gaze wandering to the white board, which still contained Bea's drawings. The smiley-faced Shruti. The angry Evie, veil jutting out of her head like a crown ...

"Evie!" I gasped.

She turned to me. "What?"

"No, I mean ..." I strode over to the white board and pointed to Bea's drawing. "It wants—they want—Evie. Remember, the Bridezillas kept saying she was their queen? I thought it was hyperbole, an exaggerated version of all the adoration the brides of San Francisco seem to have for you, but ..." I turned back to the group. "Maybe she's it. She's the human they need to gain full strength."

"That's a bit of a data deficient leap," Bea said.

"Wait a minute," Evie said, "there's actually at least one other, er, data point that backs this up. Remember at the fountain, when one of the brides mentioned the 'offering' they made to me, the gown in the window? They must have been referring to—"

"The Marcus Wong dress!" I crowed. "That could be why he was blackmailed into re-making it. Why it was displayed so prominently in the window. They were trying to tempt Evie with it. Little did they know how much you actually dislike that dress," I added, arching a brow at Evie.

"So I have to draw this thing out," Evie said, taking a deep breath and straightening her spine. "One last time."

"No," I said. I planted my hands on my hips and turned to face her, giving her my best Aveda Jupiter steel. "No more 'Evie as bait' plans. I forbid it."

"That's not how a partnership works," Evie said, giving me her own steel. "You don't get to forbid anything. We're in this together, remember?"

"Okay, I . . . strongly advise against it," I amended, frowning at her.

"And what's your alternative: Aveda Jupiter as bait with no backup? Because *I* forbid *that*," Evie said.

"We just said no forbidding!" I protested. "I propose something all-new and all-different. Both of us as bait."

She gawked at me, her annoyance dissolving into genuine surprise. "Wh-what?"

"They want you for their queen, whatever that means," I said. "But they also seem drawn to anyone who tries to attack, hurt, or even slightly disagree with you."

"So you're going to do one of those?" she said. Despite the urgency and potential danger of the situation we were discussing, her lips start to twitch.

"I'm going to *pretend* to do all of those," I said. "We're going to leak the details of our feud to the media—meaning Maisy—"

"We're having a feud?" Evie interrupted. Now she wasn't even trying to hide the amusement overtaking her face.

"We are now," I said, making my tone as imperious as possible. "Because I, supreme diva that I am, have not listened to any of your wishes for your wedding and am intent on making it the biggest spectacle possible and also all about me. I cancelled your adorable garden venue reservation, rented out the Palace of Fine Arts, invited the whole city—"

"You did?" Evie said, suddenly looking far less amused.

"Well. I will," I amended. "Once we're done talking here. Also." I paused for maximum dramatic effect. "I'm totally wearing white."

"You are *not*!" shrieked Bea.

"It's a ruse, Bea," I said. "To make the puppy and the Bridezillas think we're fighting."

"Oh, right," she said. "Sorry, I got caught up in the moment."

"Hold on," Nate said. "Before we *all* get caught up in the moment, what's the plan after you draw the Bridezilla squad out? We don't know how many of them there are or if they have some kind of enhanced abilities."

I nodded. "As kickass as Evie and I are together, we need help." I faced the team and planted my hands on my hips. "We need the whole team. Bea, you and Shruti can help us contain the bridal mob. Lucy, you and Rose can work civilian crowd control. Nate, you'll man the traps—we'll need to set up more than one. Scott, do you think you can get that piece of your spell working that will pull the puppy out of the dresses, even if they're bonded tightly?"

"I can try," he said. "And if that doesn't work, you and I can use the guiding spell/telekinesis combo to get the dresses off of them and into the traps."

"Shruti can probably help us with that too," I said, my brain whirring. "I had a tough time getting Evie's dress off of her back at Pussy Queen using just telekinesis, but if we combine our skills, I think we can handle it."

He nodded. "I can also try communicating with the puppy again, see if I can try to appeal to it or at least get more information."

"And if we can contain the puppy—the whole thing this time—maybe we can finally flush out its human counterpart and stop them both for good," I said.

I took a deep breath and looked at every person in the room in turn. Every member of the team. Every piece of my weird little family.

"We got this," I said. "Those Bridezillas better check themselves: the dynamic duo has morphed into a full-on fucking *super-team*."

Once we had a plan, things moved fast.

In order to preserve the illusion that Evie and I were really fighting, I was going to storm dramatically out of HQ at a certain time (which had been "leaked" to Maisy by Bea) and spend the night elsewhere (at my parents' house in Pleasanton—maybe not my first choice, but it was far enough out in the middle of nowhere that there was less of a chance of Maisy or some other paparazzi tracking me down than if I went for a standard hotel). I had Shruti send over the whitest, puffiest, most ostentatious monstrosity she could find for me to wear tomorrow. Everything was ready.

And yet, as I attempted to stuff my poufy dress into my overnight bag, I felt a twinge of uncertainty. Our pursuit of the stray puppy demon had proved to be unpredictable at best. Who was to say it—and its human counterpart—didn't have yet another set of tricks up its sleeve? What if the things we were preparing for didn't even occur and instead something *way worse* happened—

No. Nope.

I took a few deep, calming breaths and attempted to brush the feeling aside. I didn't know why I was even allowing myself to think that way. When there's superheroing to be done, Aveda Jupiter always rises to the occasion. I had a duty, a plan, a mission—and that was that.

Identify the Bridezilla problem—*check!*

Come up with a totally awesome plan that utilizes everyone on your super-team to their full potential—*check!*

Execute said plan and save the day so your best friend can finally have the wedding of her dreams—*check, check, check!*

Okay, okay—check pending.

To calm my nerves, I engaged in an exercise I'd once recommended to Evie as a way of keeping your cool right before a big battle. I thought of all the things I'd miss if the world suddenly weren't there.

Evie and I, hunched over the iPad, watching The Heroic Trio *for the kazillionth time.*

Scott's easy smiles—and that hidden intensity he seemed to save just for me.

That warmth that had welled in my chest when the team assembled around my ring of fire, that familial connection I'd had looking at each of them in turn—

Shit. Now there were tears welling in my eyes. Yes, I was embracing my Annie Chang-ness, but even Annie Chang knew I needed to concentrate on the battle ahead.

I shook my head, straightened my spine, and scraped a hand over my eyes. I wondered briefly if I should go say good-bye to Scott before I left. But, no. He was down in the lab with Nate and Bea, working tirelessly on perfecting his spell. That spell was crucial to our plan the next day and he needed to concentrate, just like I did—no disruptions. Anyway, we'd see each other tomorrow. We'd have plenty of time for whatever emotional moments we wanted to have *after* the assembled Lady Avengers took down the Bridezillas.

Right now, the battle ahead was all that mattered.

I nodded to myself again, re-focusing on our plan; that was what I needed to be thinking about. Oh, and I had to get back to the seemingly insurmountable task of shoving my stupid fucking dress into my bag. I tried pressing down on it with my telekinesis, but even that didn't quite work.

I had just managed to flatten the rhinestone-encrusted bodice enough to get it mostly in there when I heard a knock at the door. I cleared my throat, making sure there were no lingering tears.

"Come in," I called out.

Evie stepped through the door, giving me a tired half-smile.

"You ready?" she said, sidling up to me. She brushed her

fingertips against the massive white thing I was trying to cram into my bag. "Wow. That's ... well, that's a *dress*."

"Isn't it, though?" I said, pushing at the stiff material of the skirt. It folded slightly, then popped back out, as if mocking me. "Oh, for fuck's sake!" I spat out, letting my temper get the better of me. Before I knew what I was doing, I balled my hand into a fist, wound up, and punched the stupid thing as hard as I could.

"Annie!" Evie gasped. She couldn't help but giggle. "Did you just *punch* your dress?"

"It worked, didn't it?" I said, gesturing to my bag. The dress had finally relented, my punch sending the remaining material all the way inside. I zipped up my bag with gusto, feeling triumphant. "So," I said, turning to her, "you ready for me to totally diva up your wedding?"

She gave me a slight smile, then reached over to take my hand. "I know you're joking. But before we get into our big fake fight, before we possibly say horrible things to each other that we don't mean, I need you to know: You're a good friend. And you always have been, going back to The Spam Musubi Incident of kindergarten. I know we've had problems, but I'm so glad we're working through them. Being honest with each other. And I'm stoked that we'll be fighting alongside each other tomorrow—even if it looks like we're fighting *against* each other."

"D-dammit," I sputtered, the tears I'd successfully banished only moments earlier rising in my throat again. "Why did you have to go and do that just when I'd pep-talked myself into being all stoic and heroic and dedicated to this mission? Especially since I'm supposed to make *you* cry with my amazing maid-of-honor toast."

She pulled me into a hug, and as we stood there, I thought of something I'd completely forgotten about in the heat of battle planning.

"I just remembered!" I exclaimed, pulling away from Evie. "I have something for you."

I strode into the depths of my closet, found the big white box, and carried it over to her.

"This is the present I was going to give you when we came back here after your bachelorette," I said. "It was supposed to be the grand finale of your party."

She took the package from me, eyeing it curiously, and we both sat down on the bed as she unwrapped it.

"Bea and Lucy helped me with it," I said. "Bea especially. I mean, you'll see. There's kind of no way I could've done it without her help." I was yammering now, waiting as she pawed her way through the layers and layers of tissue paper. What if she didn't like it? What if I had, once again, calculated wrong?

"Oh," she said, her eyes widening as she pulled her gift free from the wrapping. She smoothed the layers of white silk, touching it carefully, as if she was afraid it would break. It was a very simple gown—no decoration, no scarlet flowers. Just a graceful whisper of silk topped off with a sweetheart neckline and thin straps. It would flow over her body beautifully. It wouldn't cut off her breathing. It wasn't as flashy as the Marcus Wong original we'd found in the bridal tent, but it looked like *her*.

"Is this—" Her eyes welled up and she swallowed hard.

"Yes," I said gently. "It's your mom's dress. Shruti fitted it for your measurements. And I just realized you should probably wrap it up again and pretend to open it for the first time in front of Bea and Lucy, because like I said, they helped with it so much, and I'm really not trying to hog the moment, it just came to me right now, and we're sort of pressed for time."

She cut off my second bout of yammering with a bear hug, throwing her arms around me.

"Watch out for the dress!" I shrieked, trying to pull away as the silk got caught between us.

"Thank you," she said, holding me tight. "It's perfect."

"We're going to beat this damn puppy demon thing once

and for all," I said, injecting that Aveda Jupiter imperious-ness into my tone. "And then you're going to get married and everything is going to be awesome."

She didn't respond, just released me from the hug and took my hand. I felt the strength of our friendship between us, everything we'd been, everything we'd fought for, every-thing we were now. I felt words bubbling up in my throat, what she meant to me, that I wouldn't change our fierce, messy, occasionally fractious friendship for anything in the world. But somehow, nothing seemed adequate.

So I let the silence stretch between us, silence that said more than words ever could. I reveled in my soft, mushy Annie Chang side and felt myself drawing strength from that, from this bond I wanted to protect, this bond that was going to be key in tomorrow's battle.

We sat there in silence, hands clasped, until it was time to go.

CHAPTER TWENTY-THREE

I KNEW WHAT we were doing was for the good of the city—and any person living in it who didn't like the idea of being terrorized by zombie Bridezillas. But after an hour with my parents, I was kind of ready to throw all that out the window and let the Bridezillas have San Francisco.

"Sophie's wedding plans are coming along very nicely," my mother said, giving the fried rice a final stir, then motioning for my dad to serve.

"They should be coming along very nicely," I muttered under my breath. "Considering that she's been engaged for like six years."

"It is a good thing you are getting a lot of bridesmaid experience from this wedding," my mother continued. "Although you may want to leave out these recent ... difficulties when Sophie speaks to you about your role in her ceremony."

I gritted my teeth and focused on my dad, who was silently spooning fried rice into bowls for us. Quiet as always, but I could feel the disapproval wafting off of him.

We'd decided to keep up the charade of my and Evie's brewing tension with my parents. The fewer people who knew, the less likely the Bridezillas—and the puppy/human affecting them—would catch wind of it. We needed for it to look as real as possible. I was trying with all my might not to betray any of the tension I was feeling about the impending battle, and it was sitting there in my stomach, coiled tight—a snake that desperately wants to strike, but has to wait until the time is right.

I *hate* waiting until the time is right.

"For the ceremony tomorrow, I am planning on wearing my lavender dress with the lilies on it," my mom continued. "Will that be acceptable?"

"What?" I said, snapping out of my reverie. "Oh. Of course, Mom. Wear whatever you like."

My mother snorted. "So it would be all right if I showed up in that pink sweatsuit with the 'fun' saying inscribed on the rear end? I do not believe that is appropriate."

"I don't know, I think Evie would find 'Be Fierce' a perfect slogan for her wedding." The sweatsuit had been a Secret Santa gift from one of my mom's well-meaning colleagues at the pharmacy. She claimed to find it more distasteful than fun, but refused to get rid of it because she didn't like to "waste" things. I was also convinced, however, that she secretly kind of liked the idea of being fierce.

"Anne." Mom let out a long-suffering sigh. "I can never tell if you are joking or not. And it wouldn't hurt to vet your own outfit for appropriateness. I know this is sometimes a challenge. For you."

My father grunted and shoveled more fried rice in his mouth. I couldn't tell if he was agreeing with her or just really enjoying his food. I took a deep breath, trying to ease the tension in my stomach. Every muscle in my body felt tight, on edge. Wanting to *do* something.

Tomorrow, I reminded myself. *Tomorrow, we're going to beat this thing once and for all.*

"Anne," my mother said, snapping me out of my thoughts once again. "Eat. You are too thin."

I was in the process of crafting, starting to say, and ultimately biting back a retort about how criticizing my body was a job better suited to internet trolls than the person who had given me life, when there was a knock at the door. My parents paused their eating and exchanged a quizzical glance. Mealtime at the Chang household was sacred, and all of their close friends knew that. It was too late for any kind of solicitor or kid peddling candy bars. Who could it possibly be?

Maybe someone had gotten wind of where I'd run off to after Evie's and my fake fight? Was I about to find Maisy or some other gossip outlet on my doorstep? The thought of Maisy colliding with my parents made me cringe.

But, no. The location of my parents' house was a closely guarded secret—hell, the fact that my parents were *alive* was a closely guarded secret.

Still, better to be sure.

Plus, answering the door would actually give me something to do that didn't involve heading off my mother's attempts to get me to do the exact opposite of whatever I was trying to do in the first place.

"I'll get it," I said, hopping up from my seat and bounding toward the door.

I opened the door, still half expecting to see Maisy standing on the stoop. Instead I found myself swept into a deep kiss that made my knees buckle.

"Scott!" I gasped when he released me. "What are you doing here? You have to leave. Now."

I started shoving him out the door. He resisted me, planting and not moving.

"Annie." His face was thunderous, that intensity I usually loved seeing rise to the surface on full display. Only right now, I wasn't loving it. Right now, we both had missions to concentrate on and didn't have time to be doing . . . whatever he thought we were doing.

"I had to see you," he continued. "You left without saying goodbye, without—"

"There's no goodbye," I shot back. "We'll see each other tomorrow."

"And what if something happens to you tomorrow?" he snapped.

"Nothing will." I crossed my arms over my chest and glowered at him. "Evie and I are going to take care of this thing, full stop."

He frowned at me. "You said you were done pulling away—"

"That's not what I'm doing—"

"That we were going to be honest with each other—"

"I am being honest! I need to focus. Really concentrate. And that means you need to *go*—"

"Scott!"

We both whipped around to see my mother entering the room, a rare smile crossing her face.

"You're just in time for dinner," she said. "Anne's not eating much, so there's plenty."

"He's not staying," I said, gritting my teeth and attempting to shove Scott toward the door. He gave me a challenging look, refusing to budge.

"I'd love to stay," he said, but his tone was grim, indicating that staying was more an act of defiance than enjoyment.

"How nice," my mother said, oblivious to the fact that nothing in his voice matched the sentiment of what he'd just said.

"We are going to talk after this," Scott murmured in my ear as we dutifully followed my mother back to the dining room.

"We are *not*," I countered. "We are going to eat and then you are going to leave so I can prepare for the battle tomorrow."

We settled in at the table and my father wordlessly handed Scott his own bowl of rice.

"Thank you," Scott said. "And thanks for inviting me in to dinner."

"You mean letting you crash dinner," I said.

"Give Scott extra rice," my mother ordered, waving a hand at my father. "He is always such a good eater." She scrutinized the fried rice, her brow furrowing. "Perhaps I should cook up another egg to fill it out."

"It looks great, Mrs. C," Scott said, giving my mom one of his winning smiles. "Just like always."

"Kiss-ass," I muttered under my breath.

"I'm not kissing ass, I'm being courteous," he muttered back. "Which some people here are apparently incapable of."

"Anne!" my mother admonished. "Why are you whispering? It's rude. Especially since we have a guest."

"He's . . . he's doing it, too!" I sputtered. "In fact, he's doing it *more*. He—"

"—is just really enjoying this delicious fried rice," Scott said, giving me a gigantic, shit-eating grin as he shoveled food into his mouth with chopsticks.

"And with perfect chopsticks technique," my mother said, smiling at him again.

"*I* have perfect chopsticks technique!" I snapped. "I have practically since *birth*, but suddenly, Big Charming White Dude waltzes in here and uses chopsticks—and not nearly as well as me, I might add—and it's worthy of comment—"

"Anne," my mother said, sending me yet another a disapproving look. "You shouldn't speak of your friends this way. Is this how you alienated Evie as well?"

"I didn't *alienate* her," I said peevishly, the irrational need to defend my side of our fake argument swelling in my chest. "We had a disagreement. We'll work it out. Like we always do."

"Or you could be the bigger person," my mother pressed. "Tell her you know you were wrong—"

"Why do you assume I was wrong?" I shot back. "You don't even know what the fight was about."

"Mmm," my mother said, poking at her rice with her chopsticks. And as usual, her "mmm" said everything.

Because you're wrong about everything.

Because you do everything wrong.

Because you refuse to be like Sophie, demure and studious and dull as watching fucking paint dry.

And suddenly, I'd just had it. I couldn't take any more of her disapproving stares, I couldn't take her pointed "mmm"s, and I *really* couldn't take Scott showing up and taking all available scraps of parental approval and getting upset at me for something I didn't fully understand.

Here I was, trying to prepare for a big battle, focused on

saving the city, and having finally mended my relationship with my best friend ... and still, I couldn't do anything right.

I set down my chopsticks and fixed my mother with a hard stare: the kind she usually gave me.

"Actually, Mom," I said, "Evie and I aren't fighting. Evie and I are finally handling our friendship like adults and working through our issues. We're *pretending* we're in a fight as part of an elaborate ruse to take down an evil demon that's been wreaking havoc around the city. Which, despite what you seem to think, is really important work — just as important as being a doctor."

"There's no need to be so dramatic," my mother said.

"Yes, there is a need!" I exclaimed. "There is!"

I could feel my face getting red as my voice rose, my blood pounding in my ears as my temper kicked up a level, the words shotgunning out of my mouth before I could stop them. I was vaguely aware of Scott's hand brushing my shoulder. I shook him off.

"That's who I am, Mom!" I continued. "I'm dramatic. And loud. And *aggressive.* And I don't fit your idea of what a good daughter should be, but that doesn't mean I'm not a good person! I work hard, I try to stand up for what's right, and I'm not too thin — I just happen to have really excellent muscle definition!"

And with that, I jumped up from the table (knocking my bowl to the ground in the process, of course) and stormed off. Hurricane Annie was blowing *out of here.*

I whirled into my parents' spare room and paced back and forth, my hands clenching and unclenching, my face hot. Moments like these, I couldn't help but marvel at Evie's control. She'd spent all those years tamping down on her anger, refusing to let it out. Holding it in never seemed to be an option for me. It pushed against my skin until it came gushing out like lava.

My parents' spare room was basically a catch-all for books, old papers, and unused sports equipment. And endless bits of detritus—sewing kits, ticket stubs, knick-knacks—stored in a collection of Danish butter cookie tins. I felt the sudden desire to go full hurricane, to pull all the books off the shelves and smash the windows with my dad's old tennis racket. I yanked a book from the shelf in front of me, thinking about how good it would feel to slam it to the floor, the satisfying *thwack* it would make, the—

Oh my god.

I was acting like a child.

I was thinking like a child.

I hadn't even been home for a full day and I was turning into *an actual child.*

I slumped to the floor, clutching the book to my chest. I had to get my head back in the game. I had to stay focused on tomorrow and the battle. I leaned back against the bookshelf, trying to breathe evenly, to calm myself. I forced my arms to relax at my sides. The book I'd been holding fell open in my lap. I stared down at the pages, wondering if I could use the lines of black and white text to lull me into a place of zen . . . when I realized it was actually a photo album.

I leafed through it, my brow furrowing. Various newspaper clippings and photos were pressed to the pages with those little triangular photo corners. And I recognized all of them.

They were all of me or about me—Aveda Jupiter, superheroine. Saving the city, attending galas. There was even a print-out of one of Maisy's blog posts critiquing some of my more unfortunate fashion missteps. But how could this be? My parents had no interest in my superheroing career. In fact, they were openly disdainful of it. Or at least that's what I'd always thought.

I was so engrossed in flipping through the pages, I didn't hear my mother come in until she was settling in next to me on the floor.

"Anne," she murmured. "Why can't you sit in a chair, like a normal person? The floor is so bad for your back."

"I like the floor," I said absently, still studying the album.

"Scott said I should come in and talk to you," Mom said. "He thinks I am too hard on you. He . . ." She regarded me keenly. "He speaks of you in a very complimentary fashion. Are you sure the two of you are only fake engaged?"

"Yes, Mom, I'm sure of my own fake engagement status." I gestured to the pages of the album. "Why do you have all of this? Why did you save it?"

"You are my daughter," she said simply.

"But . . . but . . ." I sputtered, flipping back and forth through the album, not sure of what to make of it all. "You always seem so uninterested. In my superheroing."

"I did not think you wanted me to be interested."

I frowned. "Why?"

"You told everyone we were dead." Once again, her tone had that simple, matter-of-fact cadence.

"I just thought . . ." I trailed off, staring into space. What had I thought? "I thought you disapproved of this like you disapprove of everything I do. Of everything I am. I made up that story so you'd never have to be associated with your embarrassing daughter."

"What do you mean?" My mother stared at me, looking perplexed. But underneath it, I saw a flicker of something else—something I hadn't really seen before. She looked like she was actually attempting to understand. I tried to think of how I could put twenty-seven years of parental frustration into words.

"You've never made me feel good enough," I said. "Or Chinese enough. Or something. You always compared me to Sophie. And when I first started superheroing, you seemed embarrassed. And disappointed that I wasn't going to be a doctor. Though, honestly, Mom, that was never going to happen anyway. I barely got a B in Biology I."

"Anne," my mother said slowly. But her voice didn't have its usual disapproving cast. It was almost gentle. "When you were younger, we were only trying to encourage you. To do better. The things you were good at—they didn't seem to have a clear path to success. Success leads to happiness, and we want you to be happy." She hesitated, searching my face. It was as if her usual Disapproving Asian Mom cloaking device had come down and I was seeing the layer underneath. It was disconcerting, to say the least. "When you started fighting the problems that always seem to be plaguing the city, well . . ." She paused again. "We honestly weren't sure what to make of it. Your father and I are more familiar with traditional career paths. And this was far from traditional. We weren't sure if it would make you happy. Sometimes with you, it's hard to tell when you *are* happy." She held up a hand. "Yes, I know. Pot and kettle. And I am the pot." She gave me a small smile.

I nibbled my lip, stuck on the unspoken question she had just posed. Was I happy? Sometimes it was hard for me to tell, too.

"We needed some time to process it," she continued. "But then you—"

"I told everyone you were dead," I said, the realization of how I'd reacted—how I'd presumed to know what they were thinking, what they would do—sinking in. "Pushed you away before you could reject me and as loudly and flamboyantly as possible." It had never occurred to me that my parents would be hurt by my doing that. Honestly, it had never occurred to me that my parents *could* be hurt, period.

"I'm sorry, Mom." I reached over the album to take her hand. "It means a lot that you've kept all of this."

"Of course I have." She gave my hand a small squeeze. Which, for my mother, was like a monster bear hug. "And, you know, I am always trying to check up on you. In my own way." I thought of her showing up at HQ, at Pussy Queen. How it had seemed like she just wanted to pick at me, tell me what I was doing wrong. But maybe she'd been trying to tell me she cared. "About what you said before," she continued. "You are a good person. And I'm proud of you. But what I think of you shouldn't matter as much as what *you* think of you."

Tears filled my eyes. It was all I'd ever wanted to hear and all I needed to hear wrapped up in one. And she was right. I spent so much time worrying about what other people thought of me — my parents, my fans, Evie, Scott — that I never stopped to think about what *I* thought of me. Of Aveda Jupiter. Of Annie Chang. Of the mixed-up person who was somehow both of those things, but had never managed to get completely comfortable being either of them. But now I was trying to let both parts of me exist, to just be. I was trying to be at peace with my weird angles and rough edges and little broken bits — to appreciate them, even.

The more I thought about it, I realized that everything I'd said to my mother in the heat of our fight was true. I did work hard to save the city and stand up for what's right. Evie and I were working out our relationship like mature adults. And I did have really excellent muscle definition.

Also? Evie was right. Bludgeons totally get shit done.

"I think I'm pretty awesome," I said.

My mother laughed, a harsh, brittle sound that was unexpected, but not unwelcome. "On this, we can agree." She glanced over at the page I had the photo album open to. It was the print-out of Maisy's post critiquing my outfits, featuring a particularly unflattering shot of me in a bright purple spandex jumpsuit with a weird crisscrossing neckline that had seemed like a good idea at the time. I looked like a grape trying to disguise itself as a dominatrix.

"This look, though," Mom said, tapping the page. "Not so awesome."

I smiled at her. "We can agree on that, too."

❧

After dinner, I told my parents Scott and I needed some private time to talk. Surprisingly, Mom didn't take this as absolute proof that our fake engagement was real after all.

The moment of clarity with my mother had put some things into perspective for me. And as I followed Scott up the stairs and into my old childhood bedroom, as I watched the stiff set of his shoulders and the uncharacteristic tension in his movements, things got even more clear.

I ushered him into the bedroom and closed the door behind us. My childhood bedroom was pretty basic: white walls, twin bed, kind of terrible shag carpet that had grown patchy and faded over the years. Stack of *Battle Angel Alita* manga crammed into the lone bookshelf. My one bit of decoration was a *Heroic Trio* poster, crumbling around the edges and somehow still affixed to the wall above my bed with thumbtacks. Evie and I had hunted the poster down on the internet and purchased it from an eBay seller of questionable repute. It was still hard to find, especially in the States, and I couldn't bring myself to get rid of it.

I took a deep breath and turned to face Scott. "I'm sorry," I said.

He studied me. His eyes were tired and his face had a sickly gray pallor to it. I suddenly remembered what he'd said about the day Shasta had taken me—about how devastated he'd felt.

It never occurred to me how it would feel to actually lose you.

My heart twisted.

"I should have said goodbye to you," I said. "You're right. I pulled away again—and I didn't even realize I was doing it. I was gearing up for battle, in full Aveda Jupiter mode. You always bring out the Annie Chang side of me, and I'm trying to let both sides just exist, just be. But I'm still not very good at it. I'm not good at . . ." I hesitated. "At letting someone have all of me. Showing someone all of me. I think I'm still convinced they won't like what they see." I took a step closer to him. "But I do want to try to do that with you. I want to be my whole self with you. I don't want to pull away."

He met my eyes, and the chaotic mix of emotions in his gaze nearly made me lose my breath—intensity and tenderness and fierce wanting.

"It's hard for me too," he said, his voice hoarse. "To let

someone see all of me. When you push me away, it feels like . . ."

"I'm leaving you out there by yourself: naked, exposed," I finished. "Abandoned. Going back on our promise to be honest with each other." I studied his face. "I *like* all of you. So much. I like it when you make me laugh and I like it when you don't feel you *have* to make me laugh. When you can relax and let the wall down. When I left the way I did, I didn't mean to say you're not important to me. You are. And the only way I can think of to explain it is . . ." I paused. How could I tell him? "Evie asked me once how I keep from feeling scared when I'm going up against bloodthirsty demons and other monsters that could kill me," I said, trying to put the words together. "I told her I think of all the things I'd miss if the world suddenly weren't there. French fries. My vintage Lanvin dress. Evie. And the last thing I think of . . ." Tears welled in my eyes and my throat felt like it was closing. "The last thing I think of is always you."

His eyes roamed my face, but I didn't squirm or look away. I held his gaze. "I'm sorry, too," he finally said. "I overreacted. I didn't mean to get so upset, I just . . . I came here because I wanted to tell you something. And it couldn't wait until tomorrow." He reached up to cup my face, and I had that feeling of losing myself in him, of suddenly being aware of nothing but his warm hands, the summer scent of his skin, and those gentle blue eyes that only seemed to heat up for me. The moment felt like it lasted forever, the air in my little childhood bedroom becoming charged, making me forget all about the battle tomorrow. About everything, really.

Finally, he spoke. "I couldn't let you go into a big, terrifying, possibly life-threatening situation without telling you I love you."

If he hadn't kissed me right then, my jaw would have been on the floor. As it was, my eyes went wide for the first few moments of the kiss, not unlike Han Solo's when Leia lays one on him right after revealing that Luke Skywalker—

you know, the *other* guy she kissed—is her brother. I was still processing everything when he finally pulled away and looked into my eyes, his thumb stroking my cheek.

"Me?" I squeaked out. "I mean . . . are you sure? You love me?"

He smiled—a sweet, earnest, slightly amused Scott smile—and my heart skipped at least three beats.

"I've loved you for over a decade," he said. "I've loved you since you yelled at me for getting chewed-up grapes all over your sixth grade presidential campaign posters—and probably even before that. I loved you even when I was convinced you would never love me back. And I'm not telling you now to pressure you into anything—it's okay if you don't feel the same way or you're not ready or if you never will be. I'm glad we're finally being honest with each other and I want us to keep being honest with each other. But I *needed* to tell you." His mouth turned up again in a soft smile. "I love you," he repeated. "I always have."

I blinked hard—and realized that at some point during this beautiful speech, my eyes had filled with tears again. My blood felt like it was racing through my veins, like I was feeling every word he was saying in every single cell of my body.

"Annie." Scott's gentle voice pierced my emotional rollercoaster. His thumb stroked my cheek one last time, and then he lowered his hands and took a step toward the door. "I should go. Let you get back to preparing for battle."

"Wait . . . no!" I cried, my brain finally catching up with everything. I realized I hadn't actually needed all of those words to tell him what he meant to me.

I'd only needed three.

"I love you, too! I mean . . . of course I do! I . . . oh, god. Please don't go."

I flung myself at him—Hurricane Annie in action—throwing my arms around him and burying my face against his chest. His arms came around me and he held on tight.

"You don't have to—" he began.

"Shut it, Cameron," I growled. "I love you. And Aveda Jupiter does not say things she does not mean."

I tilted my face toward his and then we were kissing and kissing and kissing and it was the best thing I'd ever felt. My hands migrated to the front of his shirt and I dragged him toward my little twin bed and we collapsed in a tangle on top of it. I shivered as his warm hands slid beneath my shirt, his fingertips dancing over my bare skin.

The twin bed was a challenge, but we made it work.

Afterward, I stayed wrapped up in him, unwilling to disentangle myself even a little bit. If anything did go wrong tomorrow, I wanted to be fully here with him.

"I thought you said you had to focus," he murmured against my hair. "Really concentrate. This doesn't seem like—"

"Fuck it." I kissed him. "You know what? As confident as I am that Evie and I are going to kick major ass tomorrow, it would be a real shame if something happened and we didn't get to have 'I love you' sex. Evie told me that is, without a doubt, the *best* sex."

"Hmm." He was trying to affect a stern, serious expression, but I saw the mischievous spark in his eyes. "Did it live up to your expectations? Because I kind of can't believe we had 'I love you' sex while your parents were in the house. Not to mention the fact that we totally desecrated your childhood bed and your personal goddesses were there every step of the way, judging my, ah, performance." He nodded at the Trio staring down from their poster.

I arched an eyebrow. "I *know* you must have fantasized about some version of what you just described as a teenager."

"I did," he said, giving me a sly grin. "Only I think you were wearing page seventeen of the Victoria's Secret catalog." He twined his fingers through mine and raised my hand to his lips, pressing a kiss against my palm. Then he touched the plastic ruby ring that was still on my hand, his expression turning amused. "You're still wearing this?"

"Yeah, I . . ." I just hadn't taken it off. I'd started fidgeting with it whenever I was thinking particularly hard on something. Another tic to add to my repertoire.

"Hmm." He slipped it off my finger and studied it. "I think I should hold on to this tomorrow. As a token."

"A favor?" I snort-giggled. "Like I'm the brave knight and you're my lady in waiting?"

"Why not? I've been waiting for you for a long time."

He caught my mouth in a kiss: long, slow, full of promise. And then we didn't talk for a while.

I fell asleep in a state of bliss, the worries about the next day's battle slipping from my body. I was so sure Evie and I would be able to take care of it, no problem.

I should have known better.

CHAPTER TWENTY-FOUR

IT WAS A beautiful San Francisco morning. Crisp and cool, the sun just beginning to filter through the hazy gray cloud cover. The perfect day for a wedding.

Or for a puppy-possessed Bridezilla zombie squad to terrorize the city. Things could still go either way.

I had positioned myself next to the rotunda at the Palace of Fine Arts, where Evie was supposed to meet me at exactly nine a.m. We'd stage our fake fight, the Bridezillas would come after us, and we'd take 'em down in time for Evie to get good and married by noon. Then we'd have a simple lunchtime reception (I'd convinced Kevin to cater with a mix of cheese-covered snacks, spam musubi, and Japanese curry from Curry On), I'd give a rousing toast—and finally, I'd have accomplished my mission to defeat the puppy demon *and* be the best maid of honor ever.

I should have been nervous, but I was so freaking excited I could barely contain myself.

This was the point before a big battle when my adrenaline kicked up a notch, when my pure joy at getting to *do things* (and most importantly *punch things*) took over, my vision narrowed, and it was just me and the upcoming fight.

Only this time, I realized, it wasn't just me. I had bona fide allies in the fight. Worthy teammates I could stand shoulder-to-shoulder with, secure in the knowledge that we were in this together.

Aveda Jupiter liked that feeling. She liked it quite a lot.

A sudden chill swept through the air as the sun disappeared behind the clouds again, and I shivered through the thick, satiny material of my gargantuan dress. I hopped from foot to foot, trying to keep warm. Though it was attention getting, the dress didn't provide for super great range of movement, so I'd have to rip parts of it off once the battle got going. Luckily I had a real bridesmaid outfit ready to go for the actual ceremony, a red silk dress that mimicked the simple cut of Evie's gown. And my hair was pulled into an extra sleek version of my power ponytail.

Scott had kissed me goodbye moments earlier and headed to the pre-wedding groom's waiting area to get his spell ready and help Nate and Bea prepare the trap situation. We were setting up multiple traps, just in case Scott couldn't pull the puppy out of the dresses and we needed to contain a bunch of them. Bea had used her tech know-how to devise a remote control system that would open and close multiple traps all at once. (And Evie had texted me the night before letting me know Bea might have consulted with a certain Sam Fujikawa about getting the mechanism just right. Not that she would ever admit that.)

I straightened my spine and told myself to stop shivering. I was ready for the puppy, the Bridezilla posse, all of it. And I was sure Evie was, too. But where was Evie? I glanced at my watch. 9:02. She was never late. Maybe she had wedding day jitters? Or Bridezilla zombie horde jitters?

I danced around, going automatically into my kickboxing footwork warm-ups, trying to keep loose and limber. The rotunda and surrounding area were eerily silent. Normally, the rotunda had a majestic quality, its sculpted pillars and beautiful arches and impossibly high, domed ceiling giving it a stately air. The lagoon that surrounded it on three sides was clear and blue and usually populated by a smattering of ducks. But today the stillness of the air and the lack of people milling about made it seem more ominous than awe inducing. It was almost like the whole place was holding its breath, waiting for the shit to go down. I scanned the whole area. Danced around some more. Still no Evie.

After fifteen minutes of dance-hopping, shivering, waiting, and giving myself a rousing pep talk, I was ready to abandon my post and go look for my missing best friend, when Nate lumbered up, his expression stormy. He looked handsome in his dark suit and crisp white shirt, but his hair was sticking out in several different directions and his features were tight with tension.

"Evie's missing," he said without preamble. He ran a hand through his unruly hair, mussing it further.

"Missing?" My heart sank.

"She was supposed to check in with me and the rest of the team before coming out here to meet you. But she never showed up. Bea's been texting her, and Lucy and Rose are canvassing the area around here and by HQ, but no one can find her." His hands balled into fists, his knuckles going white.

I gnawed at my lower lip, ignoring the chill in the air that seemed to be intensifying with every second, and shoved my jitters to the side. "I thought you guys planned to leave HQ together."

"We did," Nate said. "But she decided at the last minute she didn't want me to see her in her dress before we got to the venue. Even if she checked in with me before coming out here, I would still be . . ."

"You would still be seeing her for the first time in her dress at the location where you're getting married." The idea was so sentimental, so Evie.

"She said she would find someone else to leave HQ with so she wouldn't be traveling here alone, but I guess by the time she was ready to leave, everyone else had already gone," Nate continued. "And now we can't find her."

"Shit." The dread worming its way through my stomach intensified. Evie missing under normal circumstances would be cause enough for worry, but Evie missing during a supernatural crisis involving a bunch of Bridezillas that wanted to claim her for their own? That was disastrous.

"What do we do?" Nate said, shoving a hand through his hair again.

I exhaled slowly, surveying the scene. That eerie quiet still blanketed the space, but the air suddenly seemed thick with tension, with a sense that whatever was about to happen had just gotten a whole hell of a lot worse.

"If the Bridezillas and the puppy have taken her, I don't think they'll hurt her," I said slowly, trying to imbue my words with more conviction than I actually felt. I gave Nate's arm a reassuring squeeze. "She's their queen, their prize. Last night they were trying to attack anyone they saw as a threat to her. It's me they see as their enemy."

"So they might still show up to confront you?" Nate asked. "And bring Evie with them?"

"Yes." I shoved aside the knot of dread coiled in my stomach and tried to replace it with that trademark Aveda Jupiter steel. "And you know what? I'm gonna give them some extra incentive."

It seemed liked the Bridezillas were big on keeping up with the internet even when they weren't zombified, so I instructed Bea to send out a series of increasingly inflammatory tweets from the official Aveda Jupiter account, detailing my disenchantment with "my former best friend Evie Tanaka, who seems to have let all this bridal BS go to her increasingly swelled head." And yes, I included plenty of photos of me in my white dress.

Then I stood in my original spot by the rotunda, flanked by Bea and Shruti. Waiting for the attack. We'd decided to have Bea try some of her reverse empathy on the mob, see if she could soothe them. Then Shruti and I would use our combined telekinesis/hair trap/ass-kicking powers to subdue the Bridezillas while Scott used his spell to pull the puppy out of the dresses and guide it into the traps, which Bea and Nate had set up around the rotunda. If the spell didn't work—if the puppy was too bonded to the dresses— Scott, Shruti, and I would use our combined powers to rip the dresses off the brides and pull them into the traps. And Scott was still going to try to communicate with the puppy as best he could.

Rose and Lucy were acting as security, guiding early bird guests to a roped-off area to the side of the rotunda and keeping a watchful eye on them. Since Evie's kidnapping had thrown off the timing of our plan, the hour of the actual wedding was fast approaching, and people had started to show up. All the usual Jupiter/Tanaka fans were on hand, and I'd seen Maisy and other local luminaries in the mix as well. I also thought I'd caught a glimpse of my parents arriving. We'd discussed evacuating everyone, but the crowd was just too unwieldy to do that safely, especially since we didn't know where the Bridezillas would be approaching from. It would be way too easy for innocent wedding guests to get entangled with the horde. And anyway, their first goal, before they tried to attack anyone, would likely be to take me out. So I was hoping they'd basically ignore everyone else.

Everything was ready.

I was *so* ready.

But as the minutes continued to tick by, I couldn't help but get restless. Where was the mob? What were they waiting for? And as I stared at my watch for the umpteenmillionth time, as the numbers switched from 11:58 to 11:59 . . . I got it.

They were going to arrive just in time for the wedding.

Sure enough, as the clock finally ticked over to noon on the dot, we heard it.

Snarling.

Groaning.

Growling.

Sounds wafting in from a distance.

Every muscle in my body tightened, every nerve in my being perked up. Shruti and Bea tensed up next to me, and I felt a pang. *I wish Evie was here.*

The snarling and growling intensified and then finally, they came into sight, a parade of rage forming on the other side of the lagoon. Carol, Gwen, Blonde, and Redhead marched shoulder to shoulder. They were outfitted in various vintage wedding dresses and their fascinators from the night at Curry On. They had attached veils to their fascinators, and the long trails of white gauze and netting whipped in the wind, making it appear as if they were marching under a beautiful, impressionistic cloud.

They waded into the lagoon, snarling all the way, splashing toward the rotunda. But where was Evie? I craned my neck, trying to get a glimpse of her. Then I froze. Because what came next was way more horrifying.

It started with the sound. The growling, the snarling, increased in volume, until it was as if a swarm of angry bees had descended on the rotunda. I resisted the urge to cover my ears.

The next wave of Bridezillas emerged, gathering on the grassy section, then wading into the lagoon.

And the next.

And the next.

There were easily fifty ... seventy-five ... maybe a hundred of them. And they just kept coming. It wasn't a squad. It wasn't a posse. It was an actual Bridezilla *army*. And they were all headed for us.

The four Bridezillas from Evie's bachelorette party had only been the beginning. In reality, every freaking engaged woman in the city was part of the horde. The puppy demon had gotten its hooks into *tons* of dresses.

"Lucy!" I bellowed. "Move the civilians as far away as you can!"

"Already on it," Lucy called back.

Out of the corner of my eye, I saw Lucy, Rose, and Rose's team herding the crowd away from the rotunda.

"Get ready, girls," I muttered to Bea and Shruti. "We got this. I know we do."

In truth, I didn't *quite* know that. There were more Bride-zillas than I'd imagined and if the puppy/human combo had been able to glom on to Evie and bring her into its bizarre symbiotic ménage a trois ... well, I didn't know exactly what we were up against. But Aveda Jupiter could not crumple just as a battle was about to begin. Aveda Jupiter had to set a good example for her fellow kickass superheroines.

"Bea, start projecting that happy, soothing feeling now," I said. "Shruti, do you think you can separate your hair into different sections—like, different ropes? Restrain as many of these ladies as possible?"

"I can try," she said, giving me a grim nod.

"Let's get eyes on Evie ASAP. Maybe I can use my tele-kinesis to sweep her to safety before the battle gets going."

I took a deep breath and warmed up my mental feathers. We could do this. We *had* to do this.

"Well, well, well," Carol screeched, as the bridal mob finally reached the rotunda, "if it isn't everyone's least favor-ite diva, Aveda Jupiter. Trying to make Evie's wedding all about you again!"

"Or possibly even trying to flat-out *steal* Evie's wed-ding," Gwen chimed in. "Look how she's positioned herself right in front of the rotunda."

"And wearing *white*," Redhead gasped.

They were moving in on all sides, surrounding us. I stole a glance at Scott. His face was twisted in concentration as he prepared his spell. He gave me a little nod. I searched the crowd of Bridezillas, trying to find Evie.

Where was she? What had they done with her? I'd been so sure they would never hurt her, but what if I'd been wrong? What if—

"Now, now, calm down, everyone. Annie would *never* try to steal my wedding."

The voice pierced the air, sharp and clear. The words were pure Evie—generous and kind—but the tone was arch, sarcastic, mocking. Like her voice had been run through a blender.

The Bridezilla mob parted in the middle to allow her through. Their queen, Evie Tanaka, striding toward us with her head held high. Everything about her was regal, stately, and overdone to the point of being artificial. Her wild, curly locks were piled on top of her head in an architectural updo, hairsprayed into submission. Her makeup was a thick layer of bright colors. And of course, she was wearing the dress—the missing third version of the Marcus Wong—that extreme mermaid shape and bright scarlet trail of flowers curving over her body.

"Evie?" Bea squeaked out.

Evie flashed Bea a look like she was a bug, barely worth an iota of attention, then turned back to me. Bea seemed to freeze in place, her eyes filling with tears.

"Bea," I murmured. "Go help Nate with the traps."

She fled, casting one final terrified look at her sister.

"Really, Aveda Jupiter," Evie said, enunciating every word. "I know you're *sickeningly* jealous of me, but this . . ." She gave my white dress a disdainful once-over. "This is too much."

"You're possessed," I said, the words clunking out of my mouth like anvils. "The puppy's got its hooks into you. You don't know what you're saying—"

"Oh, I do," she cut in, her eyes flashing. "And I'm relishing every word. I wouldn't call it possessed. I would call it liberated."

My fists balled at my sides, clenching and unclenching. We hadn't prepared for the possibility that the puppy and its Bridezilla posse would actually capture her. Now we had to improvise. One of the Bridezillas to my left snarled and I jumped. Better get to it before Queen Evie ordered them to attack.

"Go for it, Shruti," I murmured under my breath. "But isolate Evie in her own separate hair trap, okay?"

"You got it," she said, her tone grim.

Her hair shot outward: long, powerful tendrils unfurling and wrapping themselves around the Bridezillas in groups of five to ten at a time. They hissed and snarled, struggling against the iron grip of Shruti's hair.

I concentrated hard, sending my mental feathers spinning outward to reinforce the restraints around each group of Bridezillas. I could feel them fighting me, pushing back, trying to get free. I could feel Evie fighting hardest of all.

"I can't believe you, Annie Chang!" Evie shrieked, training her gaze on me. Her eyes were unnerving, intense yet strangely blank. She wriggled against her hair bonds, struggling to get free. I saw her trying to raise her hand, the hint of a flame forming.

"Shruti!" I gasped.

"On it," she said, curling her hair tightly around Evie's fists, encasing them so she couldn't get the fire going.

Evie glowered at me. "I've kissed your ass for *years*, but you can't even let me have one freaking day that's about *me*."

"It's still about you," I insisted, not sure why I was trying to placate a possessed version of my best friend. I couldn't help but think the real her was in there somewhere, that this was the unfiltered version of how she really felt, deep down inside. "I tried to give you everything—"

"Ha!" She spat out a harsh sounding laugh. "You've never given me anything. You just *take*. You've taken everything from me since we were kids and then the moment I tried to take a little bit of it back, you couldn't stand it. You really can't take not being the *star*."

"That's not true." And despite my efforts to keep my voice level and my focus on helping Shruti hold the Bridezilla army in place, I felt my cheeks get hot, heard my words shake, felt my telekinetic hold wobble. "I want you to have everything good in life, I want us to be true co-heroines, I've told you that, and any recent weirdness is me trying to figure things out. Trying to figure myself out."

"Seriously, Aveda," shrieked Carol. She was struggling

hard against Shruti's hair bonds, her face pink with exertion. "Just shut up and let Evie talk for once! She's the one we want to hear. She's our classic bride, the one who's going to take us back to the old ways—"

The other Bridezillas echoed her, chanting "*the old ways, the old ways*," a cacophony of creepy, too-loud voices echoing off the walls of the rotunda. Evie didn't join, just looked around at them regally, like ... well. Like a queen. Surveying her subjects. As they chanted, their struggles against Shruti's hair bonds and my telekinetic hold seemed to surge, grow more frantic. They were fighting us off in earnest now. I tightened the grip of my mental feathers. Sweat beaded my brow and pain danced around my temples. I'd never tried to maintain a hold for this long, on this many things. And I was betting Shruti wasn't accustomed to holding an entire freaking bridal army in place with her hair. I cast a sidelong glance at her and saw that she was also starting to sweat.

"Scott ..." I called out.

"I know," he said, his voice strained. "I'm working on it, just give me a minute."

"We got this," I murmured to Shruti. "Just a little longer."

"Ohhhhh, I'm sorry," the possessed Evie shrieked, letting loose with a cackle. "Is the great *Aveda Jupiter* actually not perfect at something? Despite spending a million hours in the gym and another million doing her hair? Despite working her whole life toward one pathetic goal, only to see her mousy best friend come in and take everything from her just like that?" Her eyes glittered as a malicious smile spread across her face. "Of course, I already took the most important thing, didn't I? Way back on prom night. I don't know why you were so surprised. Of course Scott chose me over some ice queen bossy-ass *bitch* whose own parents can barely stand her—"

"I know that's not you," I said, through gritted teeth. "I know it's the puppy controlling you." It was getting hard to do anything—even speak—beyond concentrating on maintaining my hold. It was taking every bit of energy I had, draining all my resources, turning me into a sweaty, aching mess, a mass of cells and nerves and blood that was barely human anymore.

"Or maybe it's *more* me," she taunted. "Maybe it's the me that was always meant to be, the me that's been dying to come out for years, the me that was *always* too good to be your best friend."

Her eyes flashed as I winced. She knew she'd gotten to me. I blinked hard against the tears that were, despite my best efforts, gathering in my eyes and focused on holding the Bridezillas in place. But possessed Evie was relentless and I felt my hold wobbling further.

Shit. Fuck. I couldn't maintain this much longer.

"You were right, Annie, I don't need you. I never did. *Nobody* does. All your whining about not knowing who you are: Aveda Jupiter, Annie Chang . . . who cares? Nobody can stand either one of them. Nobody *needs* either one of them. I'm the one who took down Shasta, I'm the one everyone loves, and I'm the only reason anyone tolerates you in the *first place*—"

"Annie!" Scott yelled. "The spell . . . it isn't working!"

"Dammit," I growled. "You mean you can't get it out of the dresses? Then move to Plan B, let's get those dresses *off of them.*"

"No!" he said. "That won't do any good. What I'm saying is, the puppy isn't in the dresses."

"What?" I sputtered. "Then where the fuck is it?"

A smile spread over Evie's face. It crept across her features, then oozed past the point of being a normal smile, morphing into a creepy rictus grin. The effect was so unsettling, I took an inadvertent step back.

"Haven't you figured it out yet, Annie Chang?" she said.

"It's . . ." Scott hesitated. "It's in *them*. Somehow it's moved from the dresses. Into their *bodies*. And I can't pull it out."

What. The. Fuck.

"I'm trying to connect with the puppy, to communicate with it," he continued. "But it's . . . it's so *entrenched*. In this new configuration with Evie and our mystery human. It's blocking me."

"Keep holding them," I said to Shruti. "We'll . . . we'll figure something out."

But what? How could we pull this puppy demon bullshit out of *actual humans*?

The Evie thing opened her mouth and a ghoulish voice emerged. It was lower than Evie's natural cadence, and strangely monotone.

"The old ways," it said. "The old ways . . ."

This triggered something in the mass of Bridezillas, and suddenly their faces were arranging themselves into similar rictus grins.

"The old ways," they echoed, and the Evie thing's grin seemed to stretch even wider.

I heard Shruti next to me, breathing hard, and pain danced around my temples once more. I wasn't sure how long we could hold on.

"The old ways," the Evie thing said.

"Wisdom can only be attained when the glass is full," Carol said.

"There are no shortcuts to any place worth going," Gwen said.

"A small frog knows when to leap," Redhead said.

Why did all of that sound so familiar . . . and why was the temperature in the air suddenly all over the place, warm, then cold, then *freezing cold* . . .

My stomach twisted and bile rose in my throat.

"Shruti," I breathed.

"Fuck," she spat out. "Fuck, fuck, fuck."

"My sentiments exactly," I said, scanning the crowd wildly and trying to think of how I could tell Lucy to go find the person we needed without letting it be known that we were onto him.

As it turned out, I didn't need to worry too much about that. Because he came straight to us.

"Fortune favors the bold," Dave said, emerging from the crowd. He gave me a ghoulish grin that matched Evie's and took his place next to her. "And today, fortune especially favors *me*."

CHAPTER TWENTY-FIVE

BEFORE I HAD a chance to process a fraction of the what-the-fuckery going down, Dave turned to Evie and uttered a simple command. "Make them push back."

She smiled, nodded, and the Bridezillas stood to attention as one, trained their ghoulish grins on me and Shruti, and I felt a hefty shove against my telekinetic hold. I winced and redoubled my efforts.

"Shruti . . ." I said.

"Oh, yeah," she said, her voice strained. "I feel it too. I . . . frak. It hurts."

I tried to gather my wits about me as I struggled to maintain my hold. Tried to divert brain power to actual thinking beyond *just keep going, just for a little longer.*

But how much longer? Because we'd already ascertained that Plan B was useless. And we didn't have a Plan C. We were stuck in these positions indefinitely with no way out, no way to save the day, no . . . no . . .

Focus, Annie Chang. This is just like fifth grade, when you decided you were going to become the only person in your entire class—not the only girl, the only person—to do three whole pull-ups. You had to work up the mental stamina—because at least half of it was mental, not physical—to hold position for those few seconds. It hurt like hell and once you finally accomplished it, you had to ice your limp noodle arms for hours before they stopped hurting. But you still fucking did it.

I tried to remember that feeling of being poised on the pull-up bar, of yanking myself upward, through the pain.

So Dave was the human connected to the puppy and now the Bridezilla army. But why? How had he even gotten there? Maybe if we got him talking, it would give us more time to figure out Plan C.

"Wow, Dave," I said, struggling to make my tone neutral, even as the Bridezillas shoved back against my mental feathers. "I never pegged you as a Bridezilla whisperer."

His ghoulish grin turned into a frown. "Solitude is life's worst punishment," he said.

"Uh, what?" I knew most of my concentration was wrapped up in trying to maintain my telekinetic hold, but I was pretty sure that didn't make any sense.

"Wait," Shruti said. "I think I know what he's saying."

"Because you're around him so much and you know how to interpret his stoned fortune cookie language?"

"That and I've seen that 'Darmok' episode of *Star Trek: The Next Generation* about a kazillion times," she said. "The Tamarian captain speaks only in metaphors and Captain Picard has to figure out how to talk to him and—"

"And please get to how this relates to Dave." The sweat was pouring down my face and neck, pooling uncomfortably in the small of my back. I cursed the fact that I hadn't had a chance to rip off any part of my poufy white dress.

"He's doing the same thing. In his own way. I think what he just said translates roughly to 'I was lonely.'"

"Lonely?" I repeated. That was how the puppy demon had felt, according to Scott.

"The Sunny Side was his home," the Evie thing interjected, her voice still flat and strange. "His community. And then it was ripped from him by interlopers. Gentrifiers. By *new San Francisco*."

I flashed to Dave talking to me at Pussy Queen on the day he'd seemed semi-coherent. How he'd talked about taking his café back.

"So he wanted to go back to the pre-gentrified 'old ways'?" I guessed. "But how did that turn into drafting a puppy demon and a Bridezilla army into doing his bidding?"

I was nearly lightheaded from holding the Bridezillas in place and I was sure Shruti wasn't feeling much better. But we had to keep going. I didn't know what would happen if I let go, but I was pretty sure it wouldn't be good.

"The spirit emerged," Dave intoned. "From the dark place. And we were one."

"The dark place . . ." I murmured, trying to work through the pain stabbing my temples. To drag myself through it, like I had with the pull-up bar.

"From the portal—the Pussy Queen portal!" Shruti exclaimed. "The puppy demon emerged from there—"

"Back when it first opened," Evie finished, giving us another malicious smile. "Back when *I* saved the day with no help whatsoever—"

"This egocentric version of you is extremely unappealing," I retorted.

"So it emerged when Evie and Aveda defeated Shasta," Shruti said, trying to get us back on track. "And became one with you, Dave?"

"It was from the dark place," he said insistently. "It could not imprint—as some of its forebears could not."

"So it was like the previous incorporeal puppies, the ones from those reports Bea was organizing," I said, putting some of the pieces together. I paused for a minute as a wave of pain shot through me—the Bridezillas pushing back again. "But before, these incorporeal puppies just made people ragey and then went away. How did it merge so fully with you, Dave?"

"It was lost and alone," he said. "As was I. So we became one."

"That's the only reason?" Shruti said skeptically. "You were both lonely?"

"The puppy was super drawn to him," Evie said, giving Dave an adoring grin. "Love at first sight. Well, not exactly 'sight' since the puppy was invisible and all."

Dave shrugged modestly. "I sent it on missions. An emissary through time and space. And into the precious babies."

"The ... what, now?" I was totally lost again.

"Babies!" Shruti exclaimed. "That's what I call my frock finds. So he somehow sent the puppy into the dresses in my pop-up ..."

"I ascended to a higher plane," Dave said, looking smug.

"Duh, people, it was his power level-up," Evie interjected, her voice dripping with disdain. "It finally took hold. He figured out he could send certain supernatural elements through the air while changing the temperature of said air. So he sent little pieces of the puppy out and proceeded to really fuck shit up." She gave me a ghoulish grin, as if this was a good thing.

"He sent it into some of Shruti's dresses," I said, forcing my brain to work through it. "Definitely that dress Marcus Wong repurposed for the red flower gowns. But ..." I took in a long breath, trying like mad to focus. "Redhead Bride and Carol ... they weren't wearing dresses they bought from Shruti when they experienced those first possessions in the bridal tent and Cake My Day. I remember, the dress Carol was wearing was totally different, and Redhead was wearing something more modern."

Dave gave me a benevolent smile. "The truth you seek will be found in the underneath."

"Please don't try to rhyme," I moaned. "I can't take it."

"Wait!" Shruti gasped. "He's talking about ... oh my goodness. It was in the *petticoats*. From my pop-up. I sold Redhead hers a couple weeks before the tent incident. And Carol ... she must've gotten hers when she bought a dress. Remember how I thought Maisy had charged too much? It's 'cause Carol wasn't buying *just* a dress, she was buying a petticoat, too! And we couldn't see it in that Polaroid, because she was wearing it underneath!"

"God." I gritted my teeth and tried to restrengthen my mental walls. "That's right, Carol and Gwen were both wearing ridiculously gigantic petticoats at Cake My Day. And I vaguely remember Redhead's, because it contrasted so much with her modern dress. And I can't believe *petticoats* were a major fucking clue here."

"My emissary did not find its bearings immediately," Dave said, suddenly looking perturbed. "It was chaotic. Unpredictable."

"Right, the initial possessions were erratic," I said, remembering. "You and the puppy were still figuring it out. I mean, in some cases it seemed more like it wanted to straight up murder brides—like me and Evie in those Marcus Wongs—than possess them."

"Our method had not yet attained perfection," Dave sniffed.

"And the puppy was able to escape the dresses whenever it thought it was in danger," I said. "What we didn't realize was that it put itself right back into all these Bridezillas' dresses once it thought the coast was clear. And then—"

"—it was spread too far, too wide," Dave said, looking sorrowful.

"You split it up too much and it was weakened—*you* were weakened," I said and was hit by a fresh wave of pain. I redoubled my concentration, trying to stay focused. And upright. Upright would be good. "Which is why you need Evie, but . . ." The pain surged through me again and I gasped.

"Why did you target brides in the first place?" Shruti said, picking up the thread.

"The power," Dave exclaimed, his eyes glowing with excitement. "I witnessed the power of the betrothed!"

"He saw the video of *me* at the bridal tent," Evie said, preening. "You know, the one that went viral? It really conveyed the focus, determination, and zeal of brides-to-be. He knew if he could build a full bridal army, it would be the most powerful force ever!"

"But the handful of existing engaged women in the city wasn't enough," I guessed, thinking back to running into Gwen at Marcus Wong's shop, how she'd been suddenly and unexpectedly engaged. "So wearing the possessed dresses also made people want to *be* brides."

"Very good," possessed Evie said, giving me a mocking smile. "See, Aveda Jupiter, you can be borderline smart, when you really put your mind to it. Even if those instances are extremely few and far between."

"And wearing any possessed clothing longer—particularly once the puppy lost the ability to escape from the dresses, once it was just stuck in them all the time—meant the brides were more and more affected," I said, doing my best to ignore her. Between that and trying to keep myself upright and projecting my telekinesis, I was multitasking like crazy. "That they even developed supernatural powers, like we theorized last night?" I thought maybe reminding Evie of this—of our time making battle plans less than twenty-four hours ago—would speak to whatever part of the real her was still in there.

"*Minor* powers," Evie said, with a massive eye-roll. "Like, sometimes they could pass the possession on to other pieces of their clothing or the clothing of good friends and such, meaning brides were added to the posse here and there. But they needed *me* to co-host the primary puppy power with Dave in order to get that possession passed into their bodies, locked in nice and good, and truly reach top bridal status. Now we're strong enough to send the possession into so many people."

I swallowed hard, feeling numb. I could barely move my head. I knew there were still missing pieces, but I couldn't think straight enough to put them together. Every ounce of strength I had was going into keeping my hold on the Bridezillas.

"This brings us back to why, though," Shruti said. "Why build the bridal army in the first place, Dave? What were you hoping to accomplish?"

"Solitude is *life's worst punishment*," Dave repeated peevishly, his brow wrinkling again.

"So all this is because you wanted friends?" I spat out. I

was too exhausted to even try to placate him anymore. "*Everyone* wants friends. I want friends and I want to *be* a good friend, and you know what? I'm kind of bad at it. I nearly ruined my best friend's wedding—"

"Nearly?" mocked Evie.

"—by not listening to her and bulldozing ahead and thinking I could just will people to do whatever I wanted them to," I continued. "But at least I know now that's wrong. And I know that forcing people to be your friends by turning them into zombie bride minions is *especially* wrong."

Dave was shaking his head back and forth like a recalcitrant child. "No," he said. "No, no, no. I am a lost warrior, wandering the land, encountering so many stones on my path—"

"So you're having an identity crisis," I snapped. "So am I! That doesn't give you the right to destroy the whole city."

"I have my queen now," he insisted. "I can do anything. She can do anything. She is the *key*."

Evie turned her ghoulish grin on him, beaming. The other Bridezillas mimicked her. I would have shuddered if I wasn't about ready to collapse from telekinetic exertion. I could really feel the Bridezillas pressing against me now. Spots danced in front of my vision, pain stabbed at my temples, and I struggled to stay upright. Dave's words pulsed through my brain, an eerie echo: *She is the key . . . the key . . . the key . . .*

Evie cocked her head to the side. The Bridezillas mimicked her again. They mimicked her *exactly*.

Wait . . .

"Scott," I managed to call out, a hunch forming in the back of my stressed-out mind. "If I can get the puppy into the air, do you think you can grab hold and guide it?"

"I think so," he said, his voice laced with frustration. "But I can't get a handle on it while it's still inside of them, it's too merged."

"That's all right. Just get ready to find it in the air," I said.

My vision swam, and I swallowed hard, trying to regain my concentration. "I have an idea."

This time, I thought firmly, *Evie will be grateful for my Idea Face.*

The Evie thing threw her head back and cackled, a bone-chilling sound.

"You can't beat me, Aveda Jupiter!" she cried. "I am so much stronger than you."

"You're right," I said. "You are. Despite what you've thought about yourself in the past—despite what *I* might have thought about you in the past—you are the strongest person I know. And that means I know you can fight this thing."

She shook her head at me, rictus grin still firmly in place. My vision swam again.

"Shruti," I murmured. "I need you to hold the brides in place by yourself for just a minute."

"You got it," she said, her voice grim.

I released my telekinetic hold on the Bridezillas. And then I gathered up my mental feathers and flung them at Evie with all my might. I flung them hard, visualizing them plunging into her chest, into her body. Finding her heart. Finding all the important pieces of her that I loved so dearly. I poked around, feeling my way, and then I felt the thing that didn't belong, the foreign bit of energy. It was sad and scared and practically wailing with hurt, with loneliness. I knew that had to be it. The puppy.

I didn't think about how I wasn't merely grabbing on to something I couldn't see—I was grabbing on to something *inside my friend's body*. I couldn't think about the fact that I had no idea what the effects of moving it would be. I just tightened my grip, prayed I had it right, and pulled as hard as I could.

"Get out of my friend, you asshole!" I screamed.

The effect was immediate and disconcerting. Evie shrieked so loud, I thought the entire rotunda might collapse. Then she and the rest of the Bridezillas fell to their knees in unison, like puppets whose strings had been cut. Dave clamped his hands over his ears and wailed.

"Scott!" I yelled. "The puppy! It's outside of them, it's in the air, it's—"

"I got it!" he yelled back.

I heard the click of the trap, finally imprisoning the puppy for good.

I sagged to the side: drained, hollowed out.

The brides woke up slowly, blinking, looking dazed. Evie met my eyes, her expression a mix of confusion, terror, guilt. Dave, for his part, collapsed in a heap. Which was probably good, because as the brides took stock of their surroundings, their expressions quickly morphed into full-on glares. All directed at him.

I stumbled toward Evie, wobbly on my feet, finally slumping to the ground and throwing my arms around her.

"And people say *I* can't do anything halfway," I sputtered. "But you weren't content to just be Bridezilla—you had to be Queen Bridezilla. The Bridezilla-est ever." My words were light, but my voice was shaking, my eyes full of tears.

"Thank god you were right there being the Aveda Jupiter-est ever," she said, hugging me back hard. Her voice was shaking too. "You saved me yet again."

I pulled back, met her eyes, and felt warmth surge through me as I saw that tangled mess of love and friend-ship and all the joys and sorrows of our complicated past reflected back at me. I smiled at her, happy that we'd both survived an attempted Bridezilla takeover—and that we'd be by each other's sides to survive whatever the future held.

"I think we saved each other," I said. "Just like always."

DEMON ENCOUNTER REPORT

Submitted to: Sergeant Rose Rorick (Demon Unit, SFPD Emergency Service Division), Dr. Nathaniel Jones (Aveda Jupiter, Inc.)

Submitted by: Beatrice Constance Tanaka (Super Awesome Note Taker/Researcher/Mentee who would just like to say that she is open to being promoted to a non-Mentee position at *either* AJI or SFPD! Not picky!!)

Short Summary: We defeated the bad guys again! Yay!

Long Summary: Analysis of all collected data indicates Puppy Demon Specimen #8765, referred to in previous reports as Unidentified Demon Specimen #8765—Still At Large, can now be classified as **contained**. A timeline of events has been pieced together using data collected from various Specimen analyses and interviews with Aveda Jupiter, Shruti Dhaliwal, Maisy Kane, Scott Cameron (who initiated one last connecting spell with Specimen post-battle), and Evelyn Tanaka. E. Tanaka indicated that thanks to her time as a possessed puppy demon co-host, she retained memories/thoughts from Specimen and Specimen's Co-Conspirator, simply known as "Dave," and was therefore able to fill in many blanks in the timeline. Dave/SCC fell into a major coma post-containment and shows no signs of regaining consciousness anytime soon. Physicians speculate this has to do with the length of time he was connected to Specimen—the two were so merged, he may be unable to function without it. Report Writer is most relieved about this since Dave/SCC seemed intent on taking over San Francisco via the use of a massive bridal army! *(Note from NJ: reactions from "Report Writer" may be editorializing; also, please quantify "major coma" using more specific language.)*

Dave/SCC targeted E. Tanaka as the "co-host" he needed to strengthen his and Specimen's power after seeing how popular she was among the city's brides—both possessed and not possessed—and sought to make her the Queen of the Bridezilla

Army. Dave/SCC told E. Tanaka he tried to make various existing members of the bridal army the co-host, but none were deemed worthy or powerful enough. He needed someone the army was pre-disposed to following blindly, possession or no.

Dave/SCC tried to tempt E. Tanaka via various methods, like possessed custom bridal lingerie and resurrected versions of Marcus Wong's "abomination" dress. While demon hybrid lingerie vendor Maisy Kane designed and sewed the lingerie, it was Dave/SCC who encouraged her to incorporate materials from S. Dhaliwal's possessed dresses. (M. Kane would like to state again for the record that she is "completely innocent" of all wrongdoing.) But once A. Jupiter became suspicious of the lingerie, Dave/SCC pulled the possession (A. Jupiter would like it noted here that she was "actually right about the lingerie and only wrong about the ultimate culprit"), instead blackmailing M. Wong into making two new versions of the "abomination" gown. Bridezilla army finally managed to capture E. Tanaka on her wedding day with the third gown. Dave/SCC made her co-host of the puppy and a Bridal Queen was born!

But not for long. Thanks to the quick thinking and actions of A. Jupiter, S. Dhaliwal, and Co., San Francisco's bravest team of superheroes was able to capture and contain Specimen. A. Jupiter noted that she put two crucial pieces of information together: E. Tanaka's possessed self referencing co-hosting a "primary puppy power" and the fact that the rest of the Bridezilla army mimicked E. Tanaka's motions in a way that went way beyond Single Hapa Female or whatever. A. Jupiter deduced co-hosting the "primary puppy power" meant that as Bridal Queen, E. Tanaka was able to control the whole army—and pulling it out of her would shut the whole shebang down! Luckily she was right. The captured Specimen is expected to be dumped back into the Pussy Queen Portal once analysis is complete and further testing and analysis of PQP is recommended as well.

The wedding afterward was beautiful and Report Writer totally caught the bouquet!

(Note from NJ: Beatrice, this is a good start. But please watch for editorializing language, generalities, and casual use of exclamation points. Also, I removed all of the emojis originally contained in this report.)

(Note from RR: I like the emojis. I put them back in.)

CHAPTER TWENTY-SIX

EVIE DID END up getting married that day. It wasn't the dream wedding I had pictured, and it probably wasn't what she was expecting, either. But it was still perfect.

The Bridezillas all seemed to be fine (if understandably pissed off) and Dave had been rushed to the hospital, comatose. His body didn't appear to contain any remaining trace of the puppy demon, but he was being scrupulously observed. And he'd have a lot to answer for whenever he woke up.

After that was taken care of, I stood by Evie's side, bursting with pride as she and Nate exchanged vows. Lucy, Bea, and I managed to get her out of the latest possessed dress and into her mom's gown, and even though her hair was a tangled mess and she had lost her shoes at some point during all the Bridezilla-ing, she looked more beautiful than I'd ever seen her.

As the ceremony wrapped up and everyone milled around taking pictures and doling out congratulations, my parents rushed up to me. And for once, my mother didn't look disapproving or put out. Her face was flushed, her eyes were bright, and she actually appeared to be kind of excited.

"Anne!" she said, squeezing my arm. "We couldn't see everything from our vantage point—and the security people told us we weren't allowed to get any closer—but what we did see was remarkable." She smiled. "Watching you was like watching one of those movies with all the men in tight outfits saving the world from explosions."

"Superhero movies? Wow, thank you, Mom." It was about all I could manage to say through my complete and total shock.

"Hello, hello," Maisy said, bustling up to us. She brandished her phone. "I'm taking some exclusive snaps for my blog, and I want to get some of the maid of honor."

I saw my parents out of the corner of my eye, inching away from me. Preparing to disappear into the background, where they usually existed whenever my Aveda Jupiter public persona came out.

I grabbed my mother's arm.

"Of course, Maisy," I said. "Why don't you get one of me and my parents? Yes, they're totally alive. And I'm not explaining that any further."

Maisy's jaw dropped, but she still managed to take our photo.

"Well," my mother said, her less-than-impressed exterior returning as Maisy toddled off. "That was a bit showy, wasn't it? No need to call extra attention to yourself by calling attention to us, Anne."

I just smiled and gave her a hug. But when I looked at the photo of the three of us on Maisy's blog later, I saw my mother beaming at me with unabashed pride.

I sent my parents over to the newlyweds to deliver their congratulations and then set off on my own mission—to find Scott. He had moved away from the crowd to one of the grassy areas near the rotunda and was crouched next to the trap that now held the infamous puppy demon. The puppy had apparently reassembled all the little pieces of itself once it was in the air, so we'd only needed one trap to contain it.

"Communing with your puppy pal one last time?" I said lightly, settling myself next to him.

"I do feel an odd sort of affection for it," he said, patting the box. "Is that weird?"

"No," I said, smiling. "To be honest, I can't help but sympathize with Dave. In a way, he was going through the same kind of identity crisis I've been dealing with these past few months, feeling like I was useless, like I just needed a plan and a mission to solve everything."

"Maybe so," Scott said, reaching over to take my hand and giving me a lopsided grin. "But you didn't feel the need to zombify a bunch of people into being your friends and then use them to take over the city."

"Was that his ultimate plan?" I said. "I'm still not entirely clear on what he was trying to accomplish in the end."

"I was able to get some last details from the puppy just now," Scott said, nodding at the trap. "And yes, sort of? Dave was hoping to squeeze everyone who wasn't part of his possessed posse from the city, just as he believed his café was squeezed out of the Mission. And then I guess he and his new 'friends' could just hang out all day, doing whatever they wanted."

"Was he the driving force behind all of this?" I asked. "I know you mentioned that at times, the puppy felt conflicted about what they were doing."

"As with most things in life, it's complicated," Scott said. "When Dave and the puppy merged together, they influenced each other. The puppy gained more awareness, sentience, and Dave gained supernatural know-how. That's how he knew they needed Evie for the whole 're-strengthening' deal."

"About that." I frowned, then voiced something that had been picking at me. "I know they were using her as the co-host for the primary puppy power, but I was wondering . . . I mean, Dave and the Bridezillas all seemed to retain elements of their natural personalities. But Evie—"

"None of that was her," Scott said softly, squeezing my hand. "The co-host gig totally overwhelmed her—it was a very full, very strong possession. She didn't believe any of what she was saying."

I nodded quickly, a mixture of relief and affection for him blooming in my chest—he'd known exactly what I was worried about without me having to say it.

"The Dave-puppy merger was unlike anything we've seen before," Scott continued. "They really did imprint on each other, in a way. And the longer they were merged, the harder it was to tell where one started and the other began. But at its core, the puppy didn't like hurting people. It actually tried to escape. The day the Pussy Queen portal opened and nearly killed Nate—that was the puppy desperately calling out to it, getting it to open up so it could go home."

"What about the day we dumped the dress into the portal?" I said. "It seemed very much like it was trying to *avoid* going home."

"Dave was trying to pull the piece we'd captured back to him," Scott said. "It was running away from him, not us."

"And what's its deal now?" I said. "It still wants to go home?"

"It does," Scott said, smiling and patting the trap again. "It's been wishing for others of its kind to hang out with for a long time now. I asked it—just to make sure we don't need to be looking for any other incorporeal puppy pests— if it was the only puppy who's managed to come through the Pussy Queen Portal. It said it was—and it doesn't plan on making that mistake again anytime soon."

"Wow, that actually sounds kind of snarky," I said with a laugh. "The puppy developed a whole personality."

"It did—but its thought patterns are becoming less complex the longer it's separated from Dave. I'd guess it will eventually revert to its mindless state." His face turned contemplative. "Which seems like kind of a shame, honestly— it was gaining so much awareness, intelligence, and yeah, personality. Now I guess it'll go back to just wanting to eat everything."

I gave him a look. "Only you would find that to be a 'shame.' Must I remind you that the Otherworld seems to be populated by evil-leaning things that mostly want to kill us? How do you manage to have so much freakin' empathy for every single being out there? How are you so damn *good*?"

He laughed. "Trust me, I can be bad. Very bad." He waggled his eyebrows at me and pulled his mouth into an exaggerated sneer.

"Mmm." I shook my head at him. "Not convinced."

His dorky expression morphed into a sly smile and he pulled me close, lips brushing my ear and making me blush. And then, in a husky voice that made me blush even more, he said:

"I'll convince you later."

We adjourned to The Gutter for the after-party, where everyone sang bad karaoke and ate worse food. Although after Scott coaxed me into trying the nachos, even I had to admit the fake cheese substance Kevin slopped on top did appear to contain some kind of crack-like component. And Letta's cake made an excellent dessert. Meanwhile, my parents drank enough to be coaxed into serenading all of us with a duet version of "I Will Always Love You," Lucy stayed locked in what looked like intense conversation with Rose all night, and Evie and Nate disappeared for about an hour in the middle of things and returned looking rumpled and flushed.

Everyone had a fabulous time.

As we all rolled back to HQ around three in the morning and split off to our respective rooms, joy bubbled through me. But just as Scott and I had managed to stagger into my room, I had a sudden realization: "I think I'm hungry."

"You want me to go get you something?" Scott asked, flicking open the buttons of his shirt to reveal an expanse of tan ab muscles. I nearly drooled. But I was still hungry for actual food.

"I'll go," I said. "You keep getting undressed."

"Bossy," he said, cocking an eyebrow and giving me a slow smile. But he said it like, you know . . . he *liked* that.

I bounded downstairs, flouncing into the kitchen to find Evie sprawled behind the table in front of a massive bowl of ice cream. Her dress was all bunched around her and her hair was still a mess.

"Oh!" she exclaimed, then giggled. "I guess maybe you had the same idea?"

"Those nachos were consumed hours ago." I grabbed a spoon and slid into the chair next to her. "I'm starving."

I took a bite of ice cream, savoring the cold and sweet, then pointed my spoon at her. "What are you doing down here? Shouldn't you be upstairs with your sex machine husband, consummating the marriage?"

"My sex machine husband passed out before he got his shoes all the way off," she said, grinning. "It's been a long day. Anyway, we already sort of ... consummated. In the Gutter closet."

"The *closet*?"

She flushed and gave a not-so-innocent shrug. "That's where we first kissed. And did some other stuff. Well, I guess technically we first kissed in the hall, and then he carried me into the closet, but you get the idea."

"Evie!" I laughed. "So that's why The Gutter holds 'special meaning' for you guys. Here I thought that was a deep statement on the true nature of your love. When actually, it's just a deep statement on boning."

"Boning has special meaning!" she protested, poking me in the arm with her sticky spoon. "As you should know by now."

We both laughed and she leaned against my shoulder and suddenly we were twelve again, and I knew deep in my heart that everything would be okay.

"You'll have to tell me this story about your first kiss at The Gutter," I said. "In detail, please."

"Annie?" Scott strolled in then, looking confused. He was still wearing his unbuttoned shirt, and his hair was mussed, and he somehow looked way more delicious than the ice cream I was currently licking off my spoon.

"Sorry!" Evie jumped up and tossed the now empty

bowl in the sink. "I totally waylaid her, Scott. You can't really blame her: I had ice cream."

"I see that," he said, smiling faintly.

"Take my seat," she said, gesturing expansively. "I need to go wake my new husband up. He still hasn't seen my bridal lingerie. It's extra sexy because it's totally, one hundred percent *not* possessed."

Scott crossed to the fridge as she left, opened it, and pulled out a plate of something covered in foil. Then he walked over and took Evie's seat, setting the plate in front of us.

"Dark chocolate cake," he said, pulling off the foil. He grinned at me, his eyes dancing. "Your favorite from Letta's bakery."

"Mmm." I studied the luscious dessert in front of me. The scent of chocolate wafted through the air, rich and sinful. "I don't know. I don't think I can be trusted around dark chocolate cake."

"You?" he said, his grin turning teasing. "What about me? I don't think getting an erection in a bakery is appropriate behavior."

"You did *not*."

"Trust me. There was some . . . adjusting going on."

I laughed and leaned in close, my lips inches from his. "Why didn't we do this earlier? We wasted so much time. Not kissing. Not having sex. Not eating cake. Not doing anything fun together."

"I know. We should have gotten married with that plastic engagement ring back in seventh grade."

"Speaking of that, you should return the ring to me now that my battle's over. The knight is triumphant and requires her favor back."

He hesitated, his fingertips drifting over my cheek. "I think I'm going to keep it."

"What? Why?" I said, mock indignant.

"Because someday I want to give it back to you—for real."

My breath caught in my throat, and I knew I was blushing madly, but I didn't care if he noticed. In fact, I *wanted* him to notice. "I'm always in favor of making a long-term plan. Any other plans in the works? What about grad school?"

"I'm sending in my application tomorrow," he said. "You inspired me."

"I did?" I cocked an eyebrow at him.

"They have a part-time option," he said. "It will take me a little longer to finish, but that means I can keep helping out around here. You know, doing superhero magic stuff. When you talked about trying to show me all of you, trying to be your whole self, it made me really think about things. It made me think, maybe I don't have to pick and choose pieces of myself. I can go to school, I can keep using magic to help people—maybe I'll be able to figure out how to combine both into a whole new path. And I don't have to have every single thing figured out right now. I can still be happy."

He smiled at me and I knew I was truly seeing all of him. The Scott who was good-natured and goofy and cracked teasing grins and made dumb jokes. The Scott who had conflicting, messy, imperfect emotions under all of that. The Scott who desperately wanted to protect people, even when he couldn't protect himself.

The Scott who was finally letting me see all the deep-rooted passion that had always been there, just underneath the surface.

"I love you," I said. "I love *all* of you."

Then we were kissing again, and I found that I actually didn't regret all the time we'd spent not kissing—because we'd needed that to get us here, to this moment, to right now.

He pulled back and cupped my face, giving me that fierce, sweet smile I'd come to know so well.

"I love all of you too," he said.

I rested my head on his shoulder as he pulled me close.

All of those pieces that made up my hurricane identity felt like they were finally at peace with one another, like I had accepted my weird angles and rough edges and little broken bits that made me who I was.

I remembered my mother telling me she wanted to me to be happy. That sometimes with me, it was hard to tell. That I hadn't even been one hundred percent sure in that moment.

But now I knew. Now I could answer with absolute certainty.

Yes, I was happy. Aveda Jupiter was happy—and so was Annie Chang.

After all, they're the same person.

ACKNOWLEDGMENTS

As always, thanks are due to my many badass superhero teams: the Girl Gang, the Shamers, the Ripped Bodice writing crew, NOFXGVN, Heroine Club, the Cluster, and the incredible Asian American arts community of LA.

Thank you to my agent, Diana Fox, and my editor, Betsy Wollheim—mighty superheroines, excellent vintage shoppers, and tireless champions of Aveda and Co.

Thank you to Katie Hoffman for your thoughtful Aveda insights and your appreciation of sexy oranges—two key things that made this book the best it could be. Thank you to Alexis Nixon for all your awesome PR-ing and the slightly delirious convention funtimes. And thank you to Sheila Gilbert, Josh Starr, Kayleigh Webb, Brynn Arenz, Isabel Kaufman, and everyone at DAW and Fox Literary for all the love and care you put into bringing this book to life.

Thank you to Jenny Yang for crying in coffeeshops with me—and for your extra special read of this book. Thank you to Sandy Johal and Diya Mishra for being reading superstars and giving me insights that made everything better.

Thank you to Amber Benson and Seanan McGuire for a magical (girls) first book tour that was everything I could have asked for, to Jenn Fujikawa for always being my best twin, and to Tom Wong for bringing me sugar at a crucial deadline moment.

Thank you to Sarah Guan for encouraging my Japanese gummy candy addiction, to Jason Chan for once again taking care of my girls and bringing them to glorious life on the cover, and to Javier Grillo-Marxuach for continuing to be a superheroic mentor who always believes in me.

Thank you to the proprietors of The Ripped Bodice— Bea Koch, Leah Koch, and the always hungry Fitzwilliam Waffles—for fostering a wonderful safe space that champions love, female empowerment, and happily ever afters. And thank you to the writers—Rebekah Weatherspoon, Jenn LeBlanc, C.B. Lee, Janet Eckford—who make it a community where I always feel at home.

Thank you to the many folks who shared an important meal, Family Reunion show, and/or Asian Dessert Club with me this past year—Keiko Agena, Marc Bernardin, Christy Black, Mel Caylo, Julia Cho, Will Choi, Christine Dinh, Sina Grace, Naomi Hirahara, Traci Kato-Kiriyama, Naomi Ko, Paul Krueger, Andrea Letamendi, Scott Okamoto, Atsuko Okatsuka, Liza Palmer, Erik Patterson, Amy Ratcliffe, Thomas Reyes, Jenelle Riley, Trinity Shi, Kelly Marie Tran, Michi Trota, Wendy Xu, Phil Yu, and Maryelizabeth Yturralde. You fed this book in so many ways, great and small.

Thank you to all the booksellers and readers who embraced *Heroine Complex* so enthusiastically. I am so grateful for you.

Thank you to my family for being my family: Dad, Steve, Marjorie, Alice, Philip, and all the other Kuhns, Yoneyamas, Chens, and Coffeys.

Thank you to Jeff Chen, who I can never seem to find the exact right words to thank enough—you're my hero.